Riches & Rags

Things are seldom as they seem.

A novel

By Camille Nagasaki

Riches & Rags
By Camille Nagasaki
Published by
CAMELOT BOOKS

Riches & Rags © 2016 Camille Nagasaki

ISBN: 978-0-9950080-0-7

1st Edition

All rights reserved. No part of this publication may be reproduced, distributed, or transmitted in any form or by any means, including photocopying, recording, or other electronic or mechanical methods, without the prior written permission of the publisher, except in the case of brief quotations embodied in critical reviews and certain other non-commercial uses permitted by copyright law.

This is a work of fiction. Names, characters, businesses, places, events and incidents are either the products of the author's imagination or used in a fictitious manner. Any resemblance to actual persons, living or dead, or actual events is purely coincidental.

Cover design by Camille Nagasaki
www.CamilleNagasaki.com

This book is dedicated to my late mommy, Carol Nagasaki, a queen of a woman, who encouraged me and believed in and cheered for me in everything I did. I hold you in my heart.

xo

Only when we venture past the surface do we truly appreciate the truth and meaning beyond what we perceive.

1

I give an effort. Really, I do. I make a valiant attempt to focus on the latest issue of *Veranda*. As I slide the pages along, I try my utmost to become engrossed in the stunning designs and to *not* obsess over the precious time slipping away with every painstaking minute that drags by. I strive to remain calm and to overlook my frustration that is reaching a near-boiling point. Honestly, if only—

Oooh.

"Look at this Michael Amini table; it's exquisite." I lift my tablet for a closer look. "This piece would definitely be gorgeous in our dining room—that is, if I decide to go über modern!"

I glance up, hoping he's listening or showing any sign of interest, and am offended to see he isn't. I narrow my eyes and heave an incredibly loud and obvious sigh, hoping to force his attention.

Nothing.

I've been hunkered down in Micky's study for what feels like forever—though his office aboard *Victory,* our yacht, is impeccable. Gleaming, floor-to-ceiling polished mahogany; illuminated turquoise glass panels for a contemporary touch; plush, ivory Italian leather sofas; linear gas fireplaces; and, of course, views of the glistening Pacific Ocean from every porthole are enough for anyone who craves luxury, comfort, and excess. Micky is beautiful to watch; his baby face is divine, even when deep in concentration. His smooth, tanned skin exudes a healthy glow and his eyes appear to dance as they move across the screen.

But even *my* patience has a limit. I drum my nails on my tablet in a deliberate and irritating pattern while piercing him with my eyes—just waiting for a reaction. He continues typing away on his laptop with a laser-like intensity, seemingly oblivious to my presence.

I sigh again and, as I can't stand it anymore, I fling my tablet to the side like a Frisbee and shoot Micky the look of death.

He—*finally!*—raises bemused eyes to mine for a brief moment as he stretches his arms above his head. "What's the matter, baby?" His voice is soft and tender. But now I'm too agitated to be warmed by his charm.

"What do *you* think? It's our anniversary get-away, and I'm bored as hell!" I can't help letting the hurt creep into my voice. Why does he always have to work like a fiend, and on our anniversary of all times?

Micky's attention wanes and is sucked back to the computer vortex and his beloved business.

"Honey," he says in a distracted voice as he reads something on his screen, "go enjoy the sun. I'll wrap this up soon."

Riches & Rags

Soon. Could he be vaguer?

I now realize my efforts have been futile; there isn't a glimmer of hope in gaining his undivided attention. I might as well go outside and take advantage of the last few hours of sunshine; there sure as hell isn't anything else to do.

Defeated, I inhale a deep, quivering breath and rise from my seat. Shaking my head in dismay, I shoot one last, pitiful glance in his direction before I leave the study. Then I pull the door behind me with a bang and plod my way to the outer sun deck upstairs.

Outside, the air is pungent with sea and salt. The wind whips at my hair as I lean against the freshly polished rail and inhale deeply. Our yacht slices through the water in all its 110 feet of majesty and grace. The hull's rise and fall is hypnotic and soothing. For a moment, I take in the beauty of my surroundings. The landscape of British Columbia's Sunshine Coast is truly breathtaking—rolling green hills, snow-capped mountains, and majestic forests are displayed in perfect harmony as far as the eye can see. The ocean is particularly striking today, turquoise and glistening. It's slightly windy, but the sun is shining, so I can't complain—although, this would be a hell of a lot more enjoyable if Micky would ditch his miserable work shit and get this anniversary started! I sink into a leather chaise and pull on a pair of Versace sunglasses.

Hmm. Still bored.

Well, I'll just have to make my own fun.

I sit upright looking alert, and—sure enough!—a crew member, dressed impeccably in navy and crisp white, stands at a discreet distance, though he appears ready and eager to serve. I don't believe I've seen him before; but that doesn't matter.

"Would you like something, Mrs. Capello?"

"It's Carson," I snap, irritated by his slip-up.

"Sorry?"

"Ms. Carson. I don't go by my husband's last name. *God*, weren't you briefed?"

"I'm very sorry, Ms. Carson. I wasn't. How may I be of service?"

I groan inwardly and say nothing, waiting for the momentum to build. It's nice to have *someone's* attention, and I'm not going to squander it. "Tell the chef I feel like something." I sink back into the chaise and stretch, trying to relax my nerves and play the part like I don't have a care in the world.

"Of course. Would you like something savory or sweet?"

Sigh. Who the hell *cares*? I'm not even hungry, but there's nothing else to do. "Well, I'm not sure." I pretend to consider his question. "I want…seafood. Shellfish. And maybe some Nicola gnocchi served with a glass of Quails' Gate Pinot Blanc. And don't bother with truffle oil; it's overrated." I glance at Server Boy to find he's smiling at me with a ridiculous grin. "Aren't you going to write this down?" I scoff. I can't help it, this kid infuriates me.

"No need, Ms. Carson, it's all right here." He taps at his temple and gives me a *wink* of all things.

I frown in return and fix him with a menacing stare. "I also want fresh key lime pie." I raise my eyebrow, challenging him.

"Oh, actually, I'm not sure if we have—"

"That'll be all. Now, pass this on to the chef and hurry back." I turn away, and after a brief hesitation, he retreats to the galley. I'm not done with him yet. Speaking of finishing, where's Micky? I feel my blood start to boil but concentrate on control and deep breathing. Ok, just chill. *Don't* stress, he'll be here soon.

Someone clears their throat, and I lift my eyes to find Server Boy has returned. "Good, you're back." I flop onto my side and sigh.

Riches & Rags

"Would you like something else, Ms. Carson?"

"This chaise is on the hard side. But I don't want to move, the sun is ideal where I am. I need you to fetch some cushions, pillows, and a cashmere blanket. Make me a nice nest, will you?" I admire my french manicure, and he retreats once more.

Moments later, he emerges with two other crew members, their arms laden with soft, lovely pillows and blankets. Perfect. "Put some cushions behind my back—but I don't want to sit erect," I instruct a female crew member. "Support my arms, and put one under my legs." I move about to allow the crew to place the pillows, enjoying their fawning and feeling almost like royalty. Damn right!

"I'm really getting hungry." I direct my pointed gaze to Server Boy, and he scurries away to the galley.

"I need my iPod from my cabin," I say, turning to the girl. She nods and dashes off in the direction of my room, followed closely by the third attendant.

"And *you* can fetch my sunblock and some gum," I call after him. "Also, get my sunhat. Can't anyone around here anticipate?" And where the hell is Micky? I grab my phone and compose a quick text.

This anniversary blows. I should have just married myself.

Micky replies almost instantly.

Don't worry baby. Relax. Done soon...

I won't hold my breath.

The crew return with my things. And a while later, the server approaches with a tray. The first thing I notice, with displeasure, is the pecan pie. I like pecan pie, but I asked for key lime.

"Where's my pie?" I demand. Server Boy mumbles something about not having the right ingredients on board. I dismiss this with an exasperated wave, and move on to inspect the main dish. The gnocchi is topped with fresh prawns, mussels, and scallops. I reach for the glass of wine and take a swig. The wine is perfect, but that was to be expected. Next I raise a mouthful of prawn and gnocchi to my lips. It's steaming hot but tastes bland. The gnocchi is slightly gummy and the prawn could be a hell of a lot fresher—considering we're on the bloody ocean! I let my fork fall to the plate with a clatter and sink back into the pillows in dismay.

"Is there a problem, Mrs....uh...Ms. Carson?"

"I've lost my appetite." I pout.

"Ohhh. Well, what's wrong?" he asks, appearing concerned.

"You take this back and tell the chef I'm unimpressed. Better yet, tell her to start looking for a new job when we get back to port."

Server Boy's placid features betray an array of emotions, from shock to outrage. His civil charm has evaporated, and now he's gawking at me like *I'm* nuts. Nobody looks at me like that. Not on my boat. "What the hell are you looking at?" I bolt forward, ready for a fight.

"I can't believe you would do that. She's an amazing chef, and you're just going to fire her based on one meal?"

"Listen, you little shit! Don't tell me what I can and cannot do! I'm incredulous at your nerve, so guess what? *You* can join her in the job search." I sink back into the chaise with satisfaction. Ha! Two crew fired, but well worth the entertainment value. Plus, how can Micky expect to wow clients aboard *Victory* when the food is mediocre? And who needs staff with attitude? I'm pleased with myself for making such well-executed decisions.

I relax against the down pillows and close my eyes, enjoying both the rhythm of riding the waves and the cool breeze on my face. After a moment, I hear the subdued server turn on his heel and plod away.

Riches & Rags

I'm startled awake to find the weather has cooled and the sun is low in the sky; I can't believe I drifted off to sleep. I shiver and wrap my bare arms around myself. Scanning the horizon, I realize with a start we're back near Bowen Island.

What?

I toss the blankets and pillows aside and scramble to my feet, growing more bewildered by the second. I race to Micky's study, sprinting down the deck toward his quarters, heels clipping and hair flying. Why are we going back? We're supposed to be heading out to Savary Island.

I fling open his door and barge inside, hands on hips. Micky is on the phone, looking tense, and I notice his left hand is clenched into a tight fist. He seems annoyed by my intrusion but continues his conversation. "I don't give a damn if the legal team is against this. Bloody well remind them they work for *me*. The entire acquisition depends on this, and we can't afford delays. Don't call me until it's rectified, goddammit!"

He chucks his phone to the side and whirls around to face me with obvious exasperation. "I thought you were tanning, Lane. Why are you barging in on me like this?"

"Why are we going back?" I demand, squaring my shoulders.

Micky clenches his jaw and sits back down at his computer and begins scrolling through a document. "We're picking up a potential client. I need to nail this guy before Forester seals the deal."

"A *client?* You've invited a client? To our anniversary?"

Micky glances up and his features soften. "I'm sorry, baby. Really I am. Don't worry; I'll make it up to you. We'll do a shopping trip to Milan or something soon. And please, be on your best behavior. I *need* you with me on this. Understand?" He doesn't bother waiting for my reply.

The way he says things is so final—conversation over. There's no way I can convince him to cancel the meeting. I already know what the answer will be. And now Micky has become engrossed in whatever he's reading.

"I DON'T BELIEVE THIS!" I scream. I'm seething with rage. It's *un*fathomable how many times his business takes precedence over our marriage. Now, our romantic getaway for *two* has become a fucking party, and I have to spend the night as arm candy—the trophy wife. And make idle chat with some wretched client. And not even a client, a *potential* client. Fuck me!

I *cannot* believe this.

I leave the workhorse to his bloody business and flounce off to my own stateroom on the lower deck. I slam the door, flop onto the king-size bed, and yank out my phone to call Billy.

"Billy Jean Florist," Billy answers, in his singsong way. I feel instant relief just hearing my cousin and best friend's voice. Billy's full name is Willame Jean, pronounced the French way, as his birth father is Haitian. Billy happens to be a dedicated Michael Jackson fan, and he's incredibly proud of his name.

"Billy my anniversary getaway is horrible!" I wail. I know I'm whining, but I can't help it. I relish the chance to have someone to vent to and feel myself growing more dramatic. "In fact, we're on our way back to Coal Harbour to pick up some *asshole* client, and now I have to entertain the fuckhead! Can you believe it? And now our plans—"

"Lane, I'm with a customer here. Talk later, okay, bye."

I stare at my phone, gobsmacked. He did not just...

I drop my phone with a huff. So much for that! And, hey—Micky hasn't even presented me with an anniversary gift. I can always expect some jewelry—purchased by one of

Riches & Rags

his assistants, no doubt—waiting for me in my stateroom. Even last year's Harry Winston diamond tennis bracelet, virtually identical to 2007's birthday gift, was better than nothing. My anger and frustration toward Micky builds. I really have no way out of this predicament. Unless…

Inspired, I pick up my phone again and text the crew to pack my room. Next, I text Denise, my maid, to schedule a town car to Coal Harbour, my Shiatsu masseuse for this evening at home, and a meeting with Billy in my home spa for tomorrow at 9:00 a.m. sharp. If Billy's too busy to speak with me, we'll schedule it in.

Feeling satisfied, I roll over on my bed and wait for the staff to pack my things.

As *Victory* makes her way through English Bay, I emerge from my cabin and saunter up to the main deck. Micky is standing at the rail near the stern of the ship, drink in hand and looking his usual impressive self—muscular build, tall frame, slim hips, thick dark hair blowing in the wind. He's all tanned, thanks to his Italian heritage, and dressed impeccably in a Hermes polo shirt and Armani khakis.

The Vancouver city skyline is aglow from the sinking sun when we enter Coal Harbour Marina. We approach our dock, and the crew time their leaps from the ship and expertly tie *Victory* into place.

I narrow my eyes at a couple approaching our berth. The woman is on the shorter side, mousy and plain, with short brown hair and a pixie-like face. As she comes closer, I realize she has attractive features and a nice body—though nothing like mine, of course. I lift my chin in superiority and at once feel powerful aboard my glorious yacht. I pose nonchalantly on the rail and look down on the woman. The man she's with, her husband *and* the potential client, I'm presuming, is flamboyant to say the least. The guy has better hair than I do—well, not really—all thick, blond waves and perfected highlights, and his walk can actually be classified as a prance. I eye his Louis Vuitton bag and Italian shoes. They definitely make a contradictive duo.

"Welcome!" Micky booms as he descends the vessel, and then proceeds to dazzle the guests with his charm and grace.

Opportunist! Well, good thing I'm not sticking around for the show. If he thinks he can conduct business on *my* anniversary, he's got another thing coming. I turn around and nod to the crew waiting with my luggage. They nod back, appearing capable and ready.

"May I present my lovely wife, Lane? Laney, this is Mr. Fenwig and his wife, Faye." Micky motions for me to join them. I take a deep breath, raise my chin, and sashay my way off the boat and *right* past the trio. I shoot Micky a triumphant look, pleased he's gawking, open mouthed, at me and at the crew carrying my belongings. Ha! Micky, at a loss for words. Mousy Woman and her husband exchange uncomfortable glances. I can hear the crew following closely behind and the wheels humming from my Prada suitcases as we make our way up the ramp to the awaiting town car.

"LANE! Where are you going?" Micky calls from behind; but I don't bother turning around.

The driver welcomes me with a courteous smile and opens my door. In a moment, we're whisked away from the joke of an anniversary celebration.

I glance in the review mirror to find Micky has turned back to his guests and is escorting them toward the yacht. My heart sinks in despair. He never bothered to follow me.

2

The traffic on the Lions Gate Bridge heading into West Vancouver is surprisingly mild, and we approach our gated drive in no time. Impressive, black iron gates open to welcome us, and we pull into the driveway, which sweeps past numerous species of palm trees and impeccable landscaping that features banana trees, giant Gunneras, Tasmanian tree ferns, an abundance of flowers, and cascading ponds. I love our house so! I never tire from feasting my eyes on the exquisite twelve-thousand-square-foot, three-story, Mediterranean-style home, complete with a terraced entrance and multiple waterfalls.

The driver stops the car and helps me with my things. After he leaves, I swing open the door to the lavish foyer and survey my surroundings. I can hear the children squealing and giggling from a faraway room, no doubt receiving adequate attention from whichever nanny is on duty. Laura? Or maybe Alison? Not wanting to waste time before my massage, I tiptoe upstairs to the East Wing.

Ahh, the East Wing; my haven in a dark world. We built our home to include two massive master suites—East and West—as Micky covets his privacy, and I've learned to love mine. I push open the heavy crown-molded door and enter my beautiful world of pale, buttercream-colored walls with white accents, crystal chandeliers, Renaissance paintings (mostly Botticelli and Bellini), ornate window dressings, silver vases filled with creamy roses, and my absolute favorite—my peach, satin-canopied four-poster bed. My bed is luxury, indulgence, and tranquility in the most lovely of ways.

In addition to my grand bedroom, I have a series of adjacent rooms, including a study, a sitting room, a dressing room that would rival any upscale clothing boutique, and my newest project—I'm converting my bathroom and a spare room into a home spa, complete with a wood burning fireplace, sauna, outdoor terrace, rain shower, massage table, and waterfall whirlpool. When the spa is complete, I don't think I'll have either want or need to leave the East Wing ever again.

I wander into my dressing room and peel off my Prada skinny jeans and cashmere top in favor of a snuggly terrycloth bathrobe, in preparation for my Shiatsu massage. My masseuse will be here in about fifteen minutes, just enough time to order a tea from our maid, Denise, and unwind.

I awake with a start, feeling unnaturally alert. Judging by the soft light coming through my canopy, I'm guessing it's just about dawn. Maybe 4:00 a.m. I reposition myself and close my eyes.

I hear a creak, and my eyes fly open. It sounded like the door. Or maybe it was the wood floor. Someone is here in my room! I lay absolutely still, straining to listen. Nothing more.

Riches & Rags

Maybe it was a dream. It must have been. Still, I can't help feeling the hairs on my arms prickling and my heart racing. Go back to sleep, Lane, nobody is here. Breathe. Okay.

The floor board creaks. All right, who is it? I push myself up onto my elbows and strain to listen. This is ridiculous!

"Who's there?" I demand. More floor boards creak. Tired of these charades, I whip back the satin canopy and can make out a tall figure swaying a few feet away. I grab my cell phone and shine its light at the figure.

It's *Micky*! Micky, of all people. He's *home*? But what happened with his clients and the trip? "Micky, what are you doing here?" I rarely get visits from Micky, especially in the middle of the night.

"Baaaby."

My God, he's drunk. I can now smell the heavy stench of scotch. But Micky barely drinks. Not enough to be drunk and slurring at least. He's always in control; it's part of his makeup.

"Micky, what's going on?" I flick the lamp switch beside me, illuminating the room in a warm glow. Micky is gazing at me with an absent expression, eyes unfocused.

"You left *me*," he whines. He stumbles over and collapses onto the bed. His breath is hot on my face, the alcohol putrid, I turn away, repulsed.

"You were gonna help me, Laneeey. With Fenwig. You embarrassed me." His voice sounds lost, like a needy child.

I roll my eyes and inch away from him. Men! They can be so emotional. What about my anniversary? He had it coming.

"And you fired Faye's nephew. She's really mad!"

"Who the fuck is Faye?" I ask. The name is familiar, though I don't know why.

"Faye Fenwig!" Micky's voice sounds shrill and high pitched with emotion.

Oh, shit! Well, how was I supposed to know that was her nephew? The kid had it coming, and I don't need Micky's attitude. Not at this hour.

"Micky, get out of my room! I have an early meeting. We can talk about this tomorrow. You *ruined* my anniversary, and for once I didn't play the role of the doting wife. Suck it up!"

Micky doesn't reply, and after a few seconds starts snoring softly. Well, so much for that!

"Micky, get up!" I kick him in the shin to rouse him, but he doesn't so much as flinch. Damn. I'm so used to sleeping alone; I'll never catch my beauty rest with this freight train/barn animal sharing my bed. I jerk away from him, irritated, and struggle to clamber out of bed. When I peer out the windows, I can see dawn is progressing, and I'm guessing it's more like five o'clock. Still time to sleep two more hours before my meeting. Why did I book it so early?

In my sitting room, I lower myself onto a sofa and curl my long legs into a fetal position. Sleep does not come. I toss and turn, eventually drifting into a conscious doze. But after about an hour of this, I sit up with a huff, afraid to sleep past my meeting. Why didn't I schedule it later? What could be so important first thing in the morning anyway?

When I drift downstairs an hour later, freshly showered and dressed impeccably, I'm greeted by a screech of excitement from our eldest daughter, Margo.

"Mommeee." Margo grins at me with exhilaration only a four-year-old could muster, and jumps off the breakfast bar stool at breakneck pace. She races over and skids to a stop right in front of me, and I can't help flinching and stepping back. She's dressed smartly in a navy tartan jumper and proper tie over a white short-sleeved blouse. Her hazel eyes shine, and she has the most enormous grin, as though I've done something magnificent for her.

Her look is unnerving.

"Mommy, you remembered!" she says, with such joy and awe.

"Um..." I shoot the nanny a look for help, but the stupid cow plays oblivious, smiling back in amusement.

"Sorry? I...remembered?" Frantically, I search my brain for some clue but come up empty.

"My first day of kindergarten. This morning!" Margo is literally jumping up and down, and her baby sister, Rory, is bouncing along in her high chair, smiling a gummy grin full of adoration for Margo.

"Oh, right. Already? Well, have fun!"

"Mommy, I want you to take me."

"Margo, I can't take you to school today. I have a meeting, so Alison will take you."

Margo's excitement appears to falter briefly, but then she resumes bouncing, unfazed.

"Yes you *can*, Mommy. Today's the first day! All the mommies come on the first day. They do. Please, Mommy!" Margo is starting to get a hint of hysteria in her voice, which is my cue to leave.

"Sorry, Margo, I can't. As mentioned, I have a very important meeting." Again, I shoot her nanny a look of desperation as I continue to shake my head and back away.

"Noooooooo, mommmmmeeeeee, pleeeeeeeease! I want you to. You have to. I don't want to go to school without my mommmmeeee!" Now Margo is wailing and red faced, tears streaming down. Her sister mirrors her, her little features set into a deep frown, her concerned eyes locked on Margo's face. Both girls break into a wail, and I make a run for it.

"Sorry. Can't!" I stride away, firm and determined in hopes that Margo will understand my answer is final. From the upstairs landing, I can still hear her wailing hysterically; but mercifully, when the door to the East Wing closes behind me, peace is restored and the irritant silenced.

At 9:00 a.m. sharp, I'm standing in my suite, looking over English Bay through the floor-to-ceiling windows. The weather is mild and beautiful again, another gorgeous September morning. Tiny waves dance, and sailboats are so numerous I can't even count them. Across the channel is Kitsilano, the coveted and charming neighborhood where I grew up. I stare with longing, for though West Vancouver is great, Kitsilano will always feel like home. Maybe I should speak with Micky again about moving there.

My phone pings, and I see a text from Billy saying he's on his way up. I stride over to the small foyer of my suite to welcome him.

Billy greets me with shining eyes and a big grin. "Miss Laney!" He waltzes into the suite and surveys it with apparent approval. "Looking nice, as always."

"Who? Me or my house?" I tease.

He eyes me critically for a second and saunters casually to the window. "Since you asked, you look tired today." He turns to face me, tilting his head to the side. "Still upset about the anniversary?"

"Well, wouldn't you be?"

He shrugs, and then seems to remember why he's here. "Soooo, what's so important you needed to drag me away from my store for a scheduled meeting?"

He's a bit impatient, I can see, but he's hiding it well. I become animated as we make our way over to my spa. "Well, I needed you to come today for something *very* important."

"Well, I'm glad it's important, because I have five weddings this weekend and I'm running off my feet."

"You're looking at what will become my very own SPA!"

Riches & Rags

I announce triumphantly, as I lead him into the space and make a sweeping gesture with my hands. "*So*," I say, grabbing him by the arm and pulling him to the vast corner of the room, "I need you here because I'm installing a waterfall with a whirlpool beneath. The rock-wall waterfall will be twelve feet high and will reach the ceiling, and I want it to be a living wall." I glance over at Billy's face, and my smile falters. He doesn't look impressed. Why the hell not? This is monumental, and *I'm* designing it! "Um, so anyway, I need your expertise," I continue. "Can you suggest which plants I should incorporate into the living wall? Keep in mind the waterfall will probably have a lot of spray, even on the area that doesn't have cascading water and..." I trail off when Billy turns to me, a shadow of disbelief clouding his face.

"This is why you brought me here?" His voice is almost a whisper, and I'm taken aback by his exasperated demeanor.

"But—" I close my mouth, then open it again, not sure what to say.

"You had your maid schedule a meeting with me. She insisted it was important. She said it needed to be at nine. I had to move my *entire* schedule for the day, not to mention there's no one manning the shop right now!" Billy's voice rises and he eyes me with disgust, his green eyes flashing. I can't believe his overreaction.

"You haven't even started this renovation; but I needed to come today, huh? Well, some of us need to work for a living, Lane. We don't all live in fairyland. Get real!" And with that, he whirls around and stalks out of the spa, out of the East Wing, and maybe out of my life.

I press my lips together and swallow the lump that's burning in my throat. What's wrong with everyone? My husband is a workaholic freak, and my own best friend just abandoned me.

Trying to steady my breath, I retrieve my phone, and with shaky hands, text Denise to schedule another massage —this time with hot stones. Hot stones cure all.

3

Hot stones didn't cure all. It's been a few days, and I've moped around the house, staying mostly in my quarters. Micky hasn't been around, which I guess is a relief in a way. I sure as hell don't need some lecture about my behavior for firing the deckhand and ditching Micky's little work party. Micky leaves before I wake up and works late into the evening, as per usual. Billy hasn't bothered being in touch, despite the Cartier watch and Papyrus card I sent in apology. I can't exactly send flowers to a florist. To top it off, even the weather is gloomy, the ocean mirroring the gray sky. I don't mind weather, be it sun or rain or wind; but to have gray skies drag on for days feels like purgatory.

Thankfully, today I have plans—a luncheon with the other wives at Victoria Hughes' home in Shaughnessy, which is probably Vancouver's most prestigious neighborhood, with sprawling streets and canopied old-growth trees. I peel my eyes away from the gloomy ocean view and wander over to my dressing room. What to wear? I finger the fabrics from my afternoon attire collection, which includes Chanel dress suits, Miu Miu knits, Burberry plaids, and Alexander McQueen couture. Oooh, I forgot about *this* piece.

I select a Stella McCartney tunic dress, and with some satisfaction, I head over to accessories. Once I've chosen six-karat diamond earrings and Christian Louboutin heels, I strip naked and apply a spritz of glorious Joy by Jean Patou.

As I'm reaching for my satin thong, I catch a small movement in the mirror and nearly jump out of my skin. A pair of large hazel eyes watches me intently.

"Margo!" I gasp, trying to catch my breath. "You scared me half to death. What the hell are you doing in here? You know I don't like you in the East Wing. The *last* thing I need is kiddy fingerprints all over the place and broken crystal ornaments!" I can't believe she just barged in on me like this. I have to lock my door from now on. Not to mention, I'm *naked*!

"Mommy, I'm sorry, but I had to come. We're home alone!" Margo looks bewildered and desperate.

"What do you mean? Where's your nanny?" I scramble to pull on my bra, panties, and stockings.

"Alison left." Margo regards me apprehensively and waits for my reaction. I cannot conceive how Alison could just leave the kids alone.

Shit—*Rory*!

"Where's Rory?" I ask in a bit of a panic, until I remember she's only a baby and can't get into anything yet. Margo grabs my hand, and before I know what's happening, the tunic falls to a crumpled heap on the floor, and I'm dashing off on a babysitter quest.

"Don't worry, Mommy. Rory is in her crib. Alison put her there when she left."

I snatch my cell phone as we leave the East Wing. I need to call Alison and fire that airhead for leaving me in this predicament.

"Hi, you've reached Alison. I'm either working, sleeping,

or in the shower. Leave a message." And the voicemail beeps.

"Alison, Lane Carson. You're sure as hell not at work! I'd like to know why my kids are wandering around aimlessly and where your hopeless ass is at this minute. Call me ASAP or you can forget about your job!" I smash my perfectly french-manicured finger on the end button, wishing for days long gone when I could slam the receiver into the phone base with satisfaction and triumph. I can already hear Rory screaming and wailing up a storm as I follow Margo down the grand, winding staircase and into the main-floor nursery. Rory is in her crib, her face red and puffy, eyes squeezed tight as she screams and screams.

"All right, enough already!" I pull her out of the crib and hold her in my arms. Her eyes are dry, so she must have just been yelling her face off but not actually crying, which is somewhat amusing.

Then I smell the wretched stench emitting from her diaper. "Oh, gross!" My hand is covered in kid shit. I pull Rory away from me to examine my poo-smeared lace bra and bare stomach. "Margo, get Denise!" I wail, as I plunk Rory down on the change table. Margo stares at me, transfixed. "Hurry up! Denise needs to change Rory, and I have to shower again. I have an important luncheon."

Margo sighs and rolls her eyes, muttering quietly to herself, something about all luncheons being important.

Whatever.

"Mommy, Denise isn't home." Margo stands, little hands on hips and all matter-of-fact, as though *she* is the adult in control.

"What? What do you mean she's not here?" What's going on with everyone? I feel like I've been transported to some funny farm dimension.

Rory begins to squirm and fuss, no doubt wanting to be changed and to be picked up again.

"Grocery shopping. Today's Thursday, remember?"

How am I supposed to know what day grocery shopping is done? I can picture Denise right now, enjoying a Starbucks coffee outside of Whole Foods, or even worse, ditching my shopping for dumplings and tripe at Osaka, that Asian food market. Honestly, what's the sense in having hired hands if they all disappear? I hit redial on my phone and toss it into speaker mode, then try to tackle the poo explosion from hell, armed with a full pack of wipes and impatience to get this over with so I can go shower. The phone rings a couple of times, and I'm surprised but relieved when Alison answers.

"What the hell is going on?" I yell into the phone. Rory is startled by my voice and breaks out into a loud and tortured cry.

"Ms. Carson, I'm not coming back."

Not coming back? I don't understand. "What the fuck does that mean?"

Now Margo looks horrified, hand clapped over her mouth and eyes wide.

"Well, hmm, let's see..." Alison's annoying little smarty voice chirps away in my ear. "First, I'm treated like crap. Not a thanks or a kind word, ever. Second, I hate the way you treat your own flesh and blood. You don't care about them at all, and nor does your husband. You don't ever bother to question how they are or spend time with them, like this morning. And third, I haven't been paid in over three weeks. So I quit! Send me my money and we're done!" Alison hangs up.

The little, ungrateful bitch actually had the audacity to quit and hang up on *me*! And why hasn't she been paid? Micky deals with that. He must be so busy he forgot. The doorbell sounds off in the distance, and Margo instantly perks up.

"Mommy, can we get it? Can we? Who's here?" She

tears out of the nursery, and I follow behind wearily, carrying the heavy lump of a freshly changed Rory. Margo swings the door open, and there's *Billy*! Billy sweeps us with his eyes and his mouth drops open. Then I remember I'm half naked and poo smeared. Nice.

Margo flings herself into his arms with the zest of long-lost love. "Uncle Billy!" she squeals, and he envelopes her into a bear hug, then puts his arm out for Rory, who immediately lunges for him.

Am I *that* bad?

"Well, well. What have we here?" Billy bounces Rory in one arm and raises his eyebrow in question, a hint of a smile tugging on his full lips. I feel immense relief just seeing his kind face.

"Oh, God, Margo scared me half to death when I was changing, and the nanny walked out on me. You should have heard the cruel things she said. And Rory had this monster diarrhea all over me. And Denise is probably at the spa getting a massage for all I know, because she's not fucking here where she needs to be. Shit! And I have to go to—"

"A portant luncheon," Margo finishes with satisfaction.

Billy's lip twitches. His eyes are smiling, but he's a good actor—or at least a good friend—because I think he's trying to be understanding. But what does *he* know? He's a bachelor.

"So, I got the Cartier," he sings, as he does a dramatic sweep of his sleeve to reveal the steel Tank Française model. Margo and I ooh and ahh, while Billy basks in the glory.

"Nice touch there, Laney, but for the record, I'm not mad anymore—just really busy. I have to head back now actually. Glad things are going so smoothly here. Love you!" Billy plants a quick kiss on Rory's forehead, then hands her back to me, does a little wave, and waltzes out the door.

"WAIT!" I run after him remembering my luncheon.

"What are the chances you'd like to have your nieces for the day?" Oh, fingers crossed. Billy barely glances back, and I can hear him laughing. *Laughing!* Margo seems to think this is funny too. She's staring after her uncle longingly and chuckling softly. How nice to be four!

A thought hits me.

"Hey! Why aren't you in school today?"

Margo shrugs as though that answers my question.

"Don't you know?" I ask, hand on my hip.

Another shrug. "I don't know why. Alison just didn't take me."

Oh great, the imbecile of a nanny couldn't even remember to bring her to school. Well, good thing she's gone. I try calling Laura, the other nanny, but all I get is voicemail. I don't even know where the list is, or if there *is* a list with babysitter names. I text Micky.

You forgot to pay Alison! My afternoon is bloody ruined as now I have to be with the kids. What's the point of having staff if they're not available? We need more help ASAP!!!

Rory is getting heavy. We head back to the nursery and I plunk her into an ExerSaucer. Margo grabs her bin of Barbies and sets up shop beside Rory. Having run out of all options, I text Victoria Hughes.

Apologies Victoria. Something came up and I'm unable to make it. Look forward to seeing you soon.

I stare back at my phone and wait for a reply. No reply comes so, feeling pathetic, I put the phone aside and sink into a chair. I'd love a cup of tea, but there isn't even anyone to make it. Honestly!

Ooh, a ping.

Sorry to hear you can't make it. Trina Rogers was just talking about you! All the ladies are disappointed to miss you. We

Riches & Rags

were so looking forward to hearing about your romantic getaway. Hope it was a great anniversary!

Trina Rogers! Ugh, I can't stand that gossip-obsessed hag. Maybe it's a good thing I didn't go. I mean, *obviously* I would have lied. I would have told them some magnificent story; and it would have been so much fun to tell and so good to have the envy from the wives—for that moment it would have been real to me too. I hear a car door and jump up to see who it is. Margo races ahead to the foyer, blonde hair flying. She peers through the bay window and slumps her shoulders.

"Oh, it's only Denise."

Oh perfect, Denise is home. Now I can go wash off this baby poo.

Margo wanders back to her Barbies, while I grab my Burberry trench coat from the foyer and step outside to greet Denise. The trunk to her red Corolla is open, revealing dozens of shopping bags and a massive pile of plastic-coated dry-cleaning. I don't see any Osaka bags, but I'm not taking any chances.

"Took you long enough. What did you do? Take a few hours off for yourself and go to the spa?" I holler from the door. Denise, wide eyed, swings around, almost dropping a paper bag full of groceries. She straightens up and wipes her short, black hair away from her tired face, then fishes something out of her jacket pocket. She makes her way over to me, climbs the stairs and hands me a folded piece of paper. She then turns back without a word and trudges back to the car, still holding the groceries. I frown at her back and unfold the paper. It's the grocery list, and it's massive. All organized into stores and compartments of meats, dairy, grains, and produce. In addition, there are the to-do's, which include picking up the dry cleaning at two separate locations, going to the specialty wine shop, shopping for birthday presents, and buying school supplies for Margo, new organic sheets for the spare bedrooms, and contact lenses for Micky, and on and on. Okay, so she wasn't at the spa, but she still could have come home to at least check on things. Maybe break up the shopping to two trips or something.

"Well, anyway," I call, "I'm going to the East Wing now. The girls are in the nursery, and you'll have to watch them because the nanny is incompetent." I quickly turn around and race inside. Obviously, I just gave orders and she has to abide; but I feel a tinge of guilt because the poor woman looks so bloody haggard and worn. But I'm sure she'll be fine.

I mount the spiral staircase, and my spirits seem to lift with each step. Looking after the kids is hard bloody work —thank God for nannies. Ooh, I should order a cup of tea.

Almost as soon as I've closed the door behind me and drifted back into my blissful world of the East Wing, there's a soft knock. *Now* what? Still wearing the Burberry trench over the poo-stained bra, I fling the door open. It's Margo.

"Daddy is home."

"Really?" That's strange. Why would Micky be home in the early afternoon? "Did he say what he was doing?"

Margo hesitates, appearing to consider this. "No, but he went into his office."

Oh. Right. I don't know why I get my hopes up. Of course he's not coming home in the middle of the day to spend time with me. I shake my head, almost laughing at myself. Margo observes me with a perplexed look. Well, enough conversation.

"All right, go back to Rory for me okay?"

Margo nods solemnly, and I close my door once again.

Riches & Rags

A while later, arms laden with toiletries, I pause at the bay window on my way for my bath. Outside, the ocean is still and peaceful as the evening sun sinks into a glorious display of color. I pad over to the existing Jacuzzi, let my robe fall to the floor, and slide into the steaming, rose-scented bubble-bath water. Breathing deeply, I inhale the glorious scent of roses, close my eyes, and feel my tension melt away. I smile as I imagine I had gone to Victoria Hughes' luncheon today, all the wives eager to hear every detail. I would tell them about the quaint islands we visited, the romantic way we clung to each other like newlyweds, the glorious emerald-and-diamond drop earrings he gave me, the inside jokes, the couples massages... It wouldn't have taken much imagination to deliver a truly believable and enviable account. If only they knew.

I sigh with bitterness, open my eyes and almost leap *right* out of my skin. Micky is here, sitting on the edge of the bath, looking bewildered and anguished. I suck in huge gulps of air trying to regain my composure.

"What the—" I'm at a loss for words. I've never seen him look so utterly broken and consumed. I lean forward in the water, desperate for Micky to speak. Instead all I hear are bubbles popping softly all around me.

"What's *happened*?" I try again. Did someone die? Did he lose his job? Well, obviously not. I relax somewhat at knowing this can't be the case. Micky is the master of his own universe, of his own enterprises. Someone must have died. But...who? Micky's hazel eyes are wild, and he leans forward, pressing his face into his palms and clawing at his hair like a madman.

"I lost it, Lane. All of it."

"Lost *what*? What are you talking about?"

Micky moans into his hands. "All the goddamn money. It's gone."

I feel the breath seep out of me. *Oh God, no. No!* I'm dizzy with desperation and panic. This can't be happening.

"I...I don't understand. What do you mean?" My heart is hammering away in my ears. The water is too hot. The room spins.

Micky still clutches at his head in devastation. "I don't know," he whispers. "I've been trying to save things, trying to make it work. I put all my money into this one venture. But it tanked. It tanked and we did too." His face crumples as tears pour down his cheeks. *Tears!* I've been married to him for twelve years, and I've never seen him cry.

As I try to resume control, my mind races over possible scenarios to rectify this. "Well, I'm sure you can work your way out. I mean, come on, you have how many companies? I mean, this can't be the *end*, right?" My skin is turning prune-y, and I'd give anything to get out of this water. Micky is shaking his head with obvious shame. Well, he should feel shame! I'm outraged but still confused. Where does this leave us? What's going to happen next? And...telling me in the bath...God!

"What's going to happen?" I can't believe this is real. This can't be real.

Micky gazes at me with swollen, red-rimmed eyes, and shrugs. *Shrugs!*

"I need to get away, Lane. I need...some time to clear my head, to find myself again. Maybe I can come back with a new perspective." He looks so deflated; his usual strong and proud posture is gone—this man before me is a shadow of his former self.

"What are you talking about? You can't go away! *Where*?!" My voice rises, all shrilly and desperate. It sounds foreign to my ears. Micky stands, shoulders slumped. His eyes have a detached look that I don't recognize.

"I need space to get back to where we need to be. To where we were. I'm taking my bike on the road for a while."

His motorcycle? He hasn't ridden in years, what is he even talking about?

"But what about *me*? What should I do? Are you leaving me money?" I don't understand. "My *Visa* works still, right?"

"THERE'S NO MONEY LEFT, LANE!" Micky seethes. His face is now scarlet and his eyes are cold and wild. I recoil, at a loss for words. He takes a few deep breaths and lifts his eyes to mine. "Lane," he continues in a horrible patronizing tone, "there is no money. A grand at best in the checking account. You can have it; God knows you and the kids will need it."

The kids! Shit. I can't look after kids. I don't know how. They don't even *like* me. "What do you mean? I'll have the kids *alone*?" I can't even fathom this.

"Lane, you're their Mom. Like it or not."

"AND YOU'RE THEIR GODDAMN DAD!" I scream with all the rage and all the fear I can muster.

Micky ignores this and walks to the door. "Oh," he turns around, "you should know the bank is foreclosing the house in two days. You need to be out by then, and you can't take anything of value. The bank is going to auction everything off, and if we come up short, I could face jail time!"

Jail? Shit.

Well, who cares? He deserves it! Deserting his family like this.

The door closes and Micky is gone. This feels like a nightmare. To be in such a luxurious environment, only to know that in two days' time it will all be gone, and I will have two kids and no money and—

Oh God! I slide under the water, this time to escape the sickening smell of roses.

I stagger frantically out of the steamy bathroom, hair dripping, and wearing a satin robe I don't bother to fasten. I'm overwhelmed with panic and grief, but since I'm not the type to cry, I don't. Instead, I do what any rational person would. I drink. I reach for a bottle of Grey Goose tucked in the back of my wardrobe, spin the cap off, and take a long swig. The liquor burns my throat, but I feel its warmth and comfort instantly.

I survey my lovely bedroom in my grand East Wing. The cream walls, elaborate window treatments, a mix of fine antique and contemporary furniture, and all the lovely pieces I have collected over the years. I pick up a piece, and another, then grab anything and everything in sight, and carry armloads of fine pieces to my canopied sanctuary and pile them onto my bed—crystal vases I'll take, and porcelain ornaments, sterling silver vanity sets, silver flower bowls, Swarovski crystal beveled mirrors, mahogany chests of fine jewelry. I continue my rampage, pausing every so often to suck at the bottle, until I'm bleary-eyed and swaying.

I reach for another armload of crystal and silver and, making my way to my bed, I trip on the robe's sash and crash to the floor, causing a thunderous clamor of breaking glass and clanging silver.

Damn! My hand is covered in blood and I'm too dizzy to stand up. Before I can do much to help myself, Denise is at my side, cooing softly. She is efficient and discreet as she goes about cleaning and bandaging my hand and sweeping up pieces of broken crystal. She clears all my treasures from the bed, while I begin to shiver violently. Denise helps me up off the floor and into bed, covering me like a child with blankets and quilts.

"I'll just go fill a hot-water bottle and I'll be right back." She disappears into the bathroom and I lie still, feeling pathetic but grateful to Denise as I nurse my injured hand. She returns with a hot-water bottle, and tucks it in by my side. The contrast of the ice pack on my hand and the heat at my side are momentarily distracting. Denise turns off the lights on her way out of my room. I let out a long and quivering sigh as I stare up at the ceiling, unable to think rationally about any of this—what has happened or what will be. Mercifully, I black out.

4

Soft sunlight streams through my windows, gently waking me with the promise of a beautiful day. I lie still for a brief moment, relishing the indulgence of relaxing in bed. Then, I attempt to roll over. *Ouch!* My hand. *Oh God!* It all comes back to me. Micky's lost the money, and in two days I'm out. "Ohhhhh," I groan and will myself to disappear, to sink into the mattress and just *poof*—gone. Where do I start? How am I supposed to find a place to live in *two* days? And with just one lousy grand.

Wait! I bolt upright, and... *Ouch!* Again. My head is starting to pound. Why did I have to hammer back vodka, of all things? Like today won't be bad enough without a hangover. I yank my satin robe on and stumble over to the dressing room. God, I hope it's still there. Well, why wouldn't it be? It's not like anyone would know in a million years.

In the boudoir, I approach a mirrored dresser and pull the bottom drawer all the way out. I crouch down on my knees and stretch my hand into the very back of the dresser. There's a little wooden panel, and I feel around behind it. Is it there? *Yes!* Relief and jubilation are a welcome respite from my pounding head and growing anxiety. It's all here.

Five thousand dollars in cold, hard cash. Hardly a windfall, but this is going to give us a couple of months of breathing room if I spend it very carefully. I only wish I had put aside more money. Why I had the insight to stash some cash, I'm not sure. There's something about having money close at hand—not in a bank or via a plastic card—that offers a tangible feeling of security.

I shove the velvet bag of cash into my pocket and glance in the mirror. Already I look down-and-out, haggard and *old*. Hallow eyes stare back at me. My face is pale and dark circles have formed under my eyes. Nice. Okay, *think*! I need a place to live.

I retreat to my bedroom and power up my tablet to review the rental listings. I don't even know where to begin. It dawns on me that I've never had to look for a rental before. Feeling overwhelmed, I flop back onto the bed, and regret it instantly as my headache worsens tenfold. I need backup. I reach for my phone and am about to call Billy when my bedroom door flies open and Margo is here—once again!

"Mommy! I woke up and nobody is here! Not Denise or Laura or Alison or anyone!" Her eyes flicker with worry and confusion. The realization hits me that it's just us now. Until Micky comes back and saves us from this misery, there will be no staff and no support.

I raise a finger to shush Margo and fidget with my iPad, buying time while I try to decide what to say.

"Why don't we check on Rory?" is all I can muster. I lead Margo out of the East Wing and down the hall to Rory's bedroom. I burst into the room and wake a sleeping Rory, who is lying on her back in her pale yellow sleeper. She sees my face and, I guess from surprise or maybe distaste, breaks out into monstrous wails. Her little body shudders as she screams.

Margo gives me a wry grin and shrugs. "Can we get some cereal, I'm soooo hungry!"

Ugh, food. Without knowing what else to do, I pull Rory out of her crib, and we make our way downstairs. The kitchen is unusually still, with no welcoming smile from Denise, no glorious aromas of freshly baked pastries, no coffee percolating on the stove, and no platters of perfectly ripened fruit, sliced and artistically arranged. Nothing. Just bare granite counters and a lonely light above the gas stove. Well then, cold cereal it is. Where *is* the cereal?

"Margo, you choose your cereal and I'll get the milk." I swing Rory onto my hip and shuffle over to the fridge. Margo and I meet back at the breakfast bar, and I pour a bowl of Nature's Path cereal. Margo seems pleased to have her breakfast, and for a moment she's absorbed with eating. Her spoon clangs the bowl and milk drips back into the cereal, and the rhythmic crunching fills our ears. At least it does mine. Margo keeps slurping, and it's annoying. I glance at Rory, who is watching Margo's food with intensity. What does Rory eat? Am I that bad of a mother that I don't know what my own baby eats for breakfast?

"I think Rory's hungry."

Margo stops mid bite and observes Rory. "She likes Pablum or mashed banana." She continues to crunch.

All right, mashed banana; I can do that. I sit Rory in her high chair and set off for the fruit bowl. The kitchen door swings open and we all turn in surprise. It's Denise!

"Denise, what are you doing here?" I ask breathlessly. I just figured she'd been let go.

She holds up some empty boxes. "You'll need boxes, so I picked up some at Osaka."

Ha! The irony. I almost want to laugh—or cry. Yesterday I was furious because I had to miss an inconsequential luncheon and blamed Denise for going to her own grocery store, and today I'm packing my things in the boxes from that very store. I wonder if I'll ever even see Victoria Hughes or any of the wives again. Well, why would I? I no longer have envious jet-setting stories to share, or anything of interest. It's all gone.

Denise surveys us briefly, marches into the kitchen, washes her hands, and prepares mashed banana for Rory. "You go find a place to live, and I'll watch the girls while I pack some things for you."

I nod, grateful for her control of the situation and for the chance to escape and call Billy. As I make my way up the stairs, I hear Margo ask Denise if we're going on a trip. My stomach drops at the thought of the kids having to leave the only home they've ever known. I wonder how Denise even learned the news. Obviously Micky must have told her, though—what an awkward conversation. I'm furious at Micky for what has happened; but at least he kept Denise on for a couple of extra days. How I could manage the kids, the packing, and the move without her, I'll—thankfully—never know.

I speed-dial Billy and fill him in on what's happened. He sounds more shocked than even I am. "Just a minute, let me toss you on speaker phone. I need both hands for these corsages here. Okay, you're on speaker, Lane. God, I don't even know what to say."

"Yeah, I know. Listen, we can talk about all this later. For now, I just need a place, and fast."

"Well, have you looked online yet?"

I glance over at my tablet and heave a big sigh. "No, I don't even know what to search for."

I survey my beautiful room. I created this space, from helping design the plans before the house was built, to hand-picking each and every showcased piece. The thought of having to leave it all behind makes me sick.

"Well, go ahead! Get on your computer and read me some listings."

"Really? But you're busy."

"Don't worry. I'm working as we speak. Go on."

"All right, all right." I jump online and pull up Craigslist.

"Where are you going to look?"

"I have no idea. I mean it's temporary, so it doesn't really matter."

"Yeeeeah, but you don't know how long it could be for. You might as well like where you are."

True. "Okay then, I want to go back to Kitsilano." There! It's decided.

"Good, now search Kits. Just a minute, I'll be back."

I search Kitsilano rentals and leave all options open for prices and bedrooms. Shit, it's expensive. Nineteen hundred and fifty dollars for a one-bedroom *basement* suite. Ugh. The thought of living in a basement is pure misery.

"Okay, I'm back. Find anything?"

"No. There's nothing! It's all super expensi— Oh wait! Here, there's a two-bedroom for eleven hundred, and the pictures are beautiful. Hardwood floors, balcony, *fireplace*..."

"Really?" Billy sounds skeptical. "Read me the ad."

"Okay, 'well-appointed two bedroom suite in the heart of Kitsilano, only two blocks to the beach.'"—Yes!—"'Suite has dishwasher, granite countertops, fir floors, outdoor terrace, and many other perks.' Oh doesn't it sound fantastic?"

"Yeah. Too fantastic to be true. Keep reading."

"'I am a doctor working in Africa in orphanages. This is my condo, please send a deposit and I will send you the keys.' Ha! You're right!"

"Scam. Well, this might be harder than we thought." Billy sounds dejected.

I sigh with bitter disappointment. I'm wasting my time. I need a place TODAY. "I'm going to go there myself."

"Where, Africa?"

Billy is laughing at his stupid joke. Who can laugh at a time like this?

"Noooo. Kitsilano, dumb-ass! Wish me luck."

Billy laughs harder. "What are you going to do, bang on people's doors begging them to take you in?"

Well, it's not a bad idea.

"I don't know, but maybe I'll see some For Rent signs, and maybe I could view places today?"

"Maybe. Okay, bye!"

"Ciao."

I get dressed, then grab my purse. To Kitsilano I go, and I'm not coming home until I find something!

Outside, the weather is beautiful. The sun is bright, which aggravates my headache, and I pull on a pair of Donna Karan sunglasses. I turn the corner and stop in my tracks. A tow truck is hitching itself to *my* Range Rover. What the hell? "What do you think you're doing?" I scream.

A skinny man with shaggy hair continues his work, only much faster. "Hey! Don't ignore me. This is private property, I'll call the cops."

"Save your breath, lady!" he snarls, as he cranks the hitch and locks it into place. "It's called pay your bills or the repo man comes."

He jumps into the cab of his truck and turns to me. "And *I*"—he tilts his ball cap—"am the repo man. Good day!" And with that, my baby of a white luxury SUV, complete with customized just-about- everything, rolls its way down the driveway and through the gates.

I'm left motionless and shocked. Although shouldn't I have known this was coming after last night's news? Now I am left homeless *and* car-less. Maybe screw going to Kits. No, I *can't*. I *have* to go. But how?

For a second, I entertain the idea of catching a cab, but the round trip will probably run me over sixty bucks. I briefly imagine I'm one of those cycling people who can leave vehicle traffic in their dust. But looking at my five-inch heels, I see that's not going to happen. I press the automatic garage opener for the other garages, and am dismayed to find them all empty. How is it that we lived in such excess but still had a mortgage and car payments? I'd take Denise's car, but she must have been dropped off today. Well, only one option left. The loser-cruiser.

5

When's the last time I was even on a bus? I don't remember, but I know it was before I met Micky. Micky would have had a conniption had his precious Lane rode around on public transit. "WELL, LOOK AT ME NOW!" I want to scream.

I teeter in the direction of Marine Drive to catch the bus. I wish I had a disguise or something. What would the society people say about seeing the wife of venture capitalist tycoon Micky Capello at a *bus stop*? I'm convinced more than ever that I need to move to Kits and away from people who know me. I don't need the sneers, or worse—the pity.

Riding on the bus is even worse than waiting for the fucking thing. I'm crammed between some drug addict chick, who must be on quite the trip as she keeps flailing forward and swinging back up, chanting, "I like, I like…I love, I love," over and over again. At least she isn't yelling or doing anything violent.

The dork on the other side is talking my ear off. The guy has zero social skills and should keep his trap shut. "So, I'm on my way to this job. Yeah, I'm kinda nervous. Hey! I can show you how to make a footprint on the window with your hand. Well, I could if the window was fogged. Yeah, so I'll be working at Safeway…"

Oh, just shut the hell up already! Why didn't I think of bringing earbuds so I too could be blissfully out to lunch like every other passenger who happens to *not* be sitting on either side of me? Misery!

And then to add the bloody icing on the bloody cake, a street bum with three overflowing garbage bags of aluminum cans just clambered aboard and is bumping his dirty wet bags into me. The scabs on his skin are revolting. And the stench—I don't even want to go there! I stuff my face into my sleeve in despair and suck air through the fabric until we reach downtown.

The liberation I feel once I step off the bus is short-lived, for now I have to catch *another* one.

The ride on bus number two is marginally smoother. I get off at Fourth and Vine. Ahh, Kits. How do I love thee? There is the usual hustle as beautiful people go about their shopping and errands. The storefronts are pleasing to the eye, displaying all the tantalizing goods available inside.

Okay, where to begin? I head in the direction of Whole Foods. Coffee first, apartment hunting second.

With my drink and chocolate croissant in hand, I begin pounding the pavement.

Why I had to wear these shoes, I'll never know. My toes are murderous after just two blocks. I tread toward the ocean, away from buildings and onto the streets boasting beautiful detached character homes. These houses are exquisite, but they have nothing on mine. "MY HOUSE IS BETTER!" I want to yell. Why do these people get to stay in *their* houses but I have to leave mine? Why can't I live in one of these homes? What do these people have that I don't? Oh right—money. I sigh.

My feet are *killing* me. They feel like they're going to fall off any second. I collapse onto my butt right on the side-

Riches & Rags

walk. I don't even care. Hell, I should just lie down and die, or at least wait for someone to rescue me. I yank my phone out of my bag and pull up the Craigslist listings. I might as well try to set up some viewings.

I discover an ad for a place that is expensive but still doable. It's twelve blocks from the ocean, but still in Kits. Twelve hundred square feet will be tight, but anyway.

"Hi, my name is Lane Carson and I'm interested in your suite," I say when the woman answers. I tell her I'm a quiet, non-smoking professional—professional what?—and I ask questions about the suite. She sounds very friendly, and everything we discuss sounds positive.

"Are there any other people who will live in the suite?" she asks.

"Yes, I have two small children. Very quiet and well behaved."

A pause.

"Oh, I'm sorry, the suite isn't suitable. It's too small."

Seriously? "But the ad says it's twelve hundred square feet. That's fine for us."

"Yes, but some of the space is unfinished, so it's not suitable," she says. And then she hangs up. Just like that!

Half a dozen more phone conversations follow along the same lines. I mention kids and the person I'm speaking with backs away. Well, *excuse* me. Why are there so many anti-discriminatory laws when hiring someone, but when renting, you can't find a place that allows kids? That's bull-shit!

A lawn mower revs up right behind me, and I'm startled for a second. I toss my phone back into the bag and stand to stretch my legs. The man mowing the expansive lawn looks incredibly worn and old. Man, he needs to just sit in the sun and hire someone to do this. I take in the house. It's beautiful—or at least it once was. It could use some TLC. And some fresh paint. I notice there isn't a feminine touch to be found. No lacy curtains, hanging baskets, or cutesy welcome mats in sight.

Well, well, well.

My pulse quickens and I feel my lips curl into the closest thing to a smile since the devastating news. I cock my head and check the driveway. No cars. I'm going to take a second wild guess and say this isn't a multi-unit home. Glancing up, I see there are three sprawling floors. Plenty of room.

Honey, I am *so* home.

I stand tall and proud, lift my chin, and stride purposely up the cobblestone walkway.

The man continues cutting grass, until *finally* he spots me and kills the engine. His eyes narrow and he starts making shooing motions at me, yelling, "No solicitors, no solicitors!"

Whoa, *calm down*, old man. I'm not *selling* anything. I put my hands up to surrender and shake my head. I plant a fake smile on my face and take a deep breath. "Hello sir, I am not selling anything."

"Then what do you want? Everyone wants something." His voice is crotchety and full of bitterness.

Wow! I wasn't expecting this reaction but, okay… "I like your house," I say.

"Are you one of those sneaky realtors? Get off my property! No solicitation!"

"Hey! Just *calm down*. I'm not *selling* anything. I like your house and I want to know if you would be interested in renting out the top floor?"

"Huh?" The old man seems lost for words. He glances up at his sprawling third-story windows and appears momentarily contemplative, when he abruptly blurts, "No way! I've lived on my own for thirty-seven years. The last thing I need is to have noise from some pesky tenant."

"Oh, I'm not loud. I'm actually looking for a quiet place

myself. You wouldn't even know I'm here. Promise!" My smiling is starting to hurt my face.

"No. Not interested. Now get off my property!" He shoos me away like I'm some kind of bad dog.

"Listen, old man!" Before I can stop myself the words tumble out. "You see West Van?" I jab my finger in the direction of the West Vancouver hills visible across the bay.

"What about it?"

"That's where I live. Until tomorrow when the bank repossesses my house, that is. And I only found this out last night. My husband never even warned me! I need a place to live and fast. I like your house, and the location is perfect." There!

"What's with you? Are you a gold digger?"

I'm momentarily offended, but rebound quickly, narrowing my eyes at his faded gray ones. "No I am not! And if I were, I would have someone *much* younger *and* richer than your sorry ass!"

"For someone who wants to live here so bad, you have quite the mouth."

"I just don't sugar-coat things!"

"Well, neither do I."

"Good. Finally something we can agree on. Lane Carson, pleased to meet you." I extend my hand, and the old man throws his hands up as if to say he gives up, and places one wrinkly, soft hand into mine. I smile at him, this time genuinely.

"How can you say you want to live here? You haven't even seen upstairs."

"Like I said—location, location." With the ocean views and Kits Beach less than a block east, well, I couldn't imagine a sweeter spot.

The old man sighs. "The name is George, George Harris. I'm a retired admiral. Follow me." He swings the front door open, and in we step to my new home.

"Take your shoes off!" he orders.

I feel like telling him he's not an admiral anymore and should drop the sergeant voice. I pull my heels off and feel instant relief. Ahh, *much* better.

The foyer to the home is bare. Pretty tidy for an old bachelor, but lacking any warmth or décor. The house is old, most of the walls are fir paneled and the windows are a mix of lead pane and stained glass.

"This is *my* washroom, and it's not to be used by you or your guests." George motions to a bathroom door beside the main staircase.

"Done," I say.

Together, we climb the stairs, each step creaking. The walls along the stairs are also wood paneled and lack picture frames or paintings. We make it to the second landing, which boasts a long corridor and numerous rooms. This house is pretty massive. We continue the climb to the third floor. I feel weary just imagining lugging Rory and a bunch of groceries, but remind myself it's short term.

"George, how long have you lived here?"

"Sixty-three years. I moved in as a newlywed."

Wow! I can't imagine living in the same house for *sixty-three* years. "So, that makes you pretty old."

"Well, I stopped counting at eighty," he says.

"And I stopped counting at twenty." I laugh at my own joke—mostly because it's true—and to my amusement, George gives a small chuckle. We come to the third floor, which has a small landing and a single door. George turns the amethyst-tinted glass knob and swings the door open.

My first thought is, *Wow it's bright!* Then—I see the carpet. Oh. My God. It looks like someone cloned Oscar the Grouch a thousand times to make this rug. The slime-green shag carpet is at least two inches long; and it's *everywhere!*

The attic is so dusty, I start sneezing. Trying to look past the carpet, I take in the rest of the space. The entire space is open-concept, except for the washroom—if there is one.

"Where's the washroom?"

"There's two. One has a toilet, and the other has the sink and tub."

No shower? I follow George across the room to a set of doors. He swings one open, and there it is—the toilet. The room is decorated with floral wallpaper; but that's the extent of it. The second washroom has an enormous claw-foot tub, which I like—until I peer inside and see yellow stains from what looks like years of water residue. I'll have to Google how to get rid of those stains. And yes, no shower. Sigh. The sink is a pedestal sink, and there's a wooden medicine cabinet to the side. This larger bathroom has a window that would look out to the ocean if the view wasn't obstructed by the massive elm tree. Maybe there are views in the winter—not that we'll be here then.

We leave the washrooms and return to the main space. I notice some sparse furniture. A small dining room table is situated by a single french door leading to a balcony. I attempt to open the door but, fortunately, glance outside first, and halt to a stop. That is NOT a balcony. It's an accident waiting to happen. It's a decrepit, shaky sort of ledge at best. There's no way in *hell* I'm going out there.

"Fire escape," George says, coming up behind me.

"Yeah, you know, I think I'd rather stay inside with the fire than try to escape on that thing."

"Oh, it's fine. Stable enough. This house is solid; I've been here for sixty—"

"Three years, yes you've said." I move away from the deathtrap and try to imagine where the furniture would go. My bed can go near the door, and— Ooooh, a fireplace! "You have a fireplace here," I say, drifting over to admire it.

The fireplace is tiny and adorable. It has a mosaic of turquoise tiles and a handsome wooden ledge. I run my hand along the dusty but smooth surface of wood and imagine a lovely fire crackling away. Now I need to learn how to build a fire—a proper fire that won't die out once the newspaper has burned away.

"George, where's the kitchen?" I ask, glancing around.

"Well, this isn't a proper suite. My grandson sometimes stayed here while in University. We made a makeshift kitchen area, and he used this hot plate." George leads me to a two-burner apparatus lying abandoned on the Oscar carpet.

Okay, breathe Lane. What the fuck?! "You expect me to cook? On *this*?" I turn to George in shock, mouth agape.

"I could probably get a microwave up here."

Microwave? *Microwave*? Is this what my life has become? I'm going to start eating like a frat boy? Really?

"Anyway," George continues, "you just put the hot plate on the counter and it's fine. Worked well for my grandson."

My headache that had miraculously disappeared is now back with a vengeance. How am I going to feed my family on that? "And…what about a kitchen sink…and a bloody fridge?"

"I have a bloody fridge in the basement. It's a bar fridge mind you, but suitable for one person. And as for a kitchen sink, come here." He brings me over to a small three-by-five nook. It has ugly laminate flooring, a short countertop, and a tiny sink.

This is the kitchen? Oh my God.

"Beggars can't be choosers," George says.

"I am not a beggar. Never have been, never will be. But I need this apartment, so I'll take it! I'll be back tomorrow to move in."

I turn to leave, but George shakes his head and puts his hands up. "Now wait a minute, not so fast. I haven't decided yet on this. I can't just say yes right *now*. In fact…I don't think this will work."

Riches & Rags

What?

"No, George, what do you mean?"

He's turned around and is now slowly making his way down the stairs. *Creak, creak, creak.* I follow right on his heels. "George, please, I thought we already decided. I need a place by tomorrow."

"So you said. But what does that have to do with me? I'm just an old man going about my business. I don't need a tenant and I don't need the money."

"George, please. I'm desperate. You won't regret this. Please, there must be some way I can convince you?"

George stops on the second-floor landing, turns around, and peers at me. "Well," he hesitates and rubs the back of his neck, "there is something you can do."

Oh. *Oh* no.

Please don't ask for a blow-job. If he asks for a blow-job, I'm going to smack him. "Oh?" I ask, my voice barely a tentative whisper.

"Yeah. There's something I haven't had done for me in a long, long time."

Oh God.

I flex my right hand and gear up to drive him one.

"I'd like you to go down—"

That's it! I swing my arm and my hand flies toward his face. He catches it mid swing, with the precision and coordination of an athlete.

"What the hell are you doing?" he growls.

"I was about to ask the same thing."

"What did you think I was going to say?"

"Something sexual, you *nasty* old man."

"Sexual?" George chuckles at this. "I'm years passed being interested in anything sexual, believe me. And if I were, well, you're not my type."

Not *his* type. Well, now I'm offended. "Not your type? I happen to be everyone's type! And anyway, if you weren't

47

going to say something dirty, what *were* you going to say?" Now my curiosity is piqued.

George shakes his head. "It doesn't matter anyway. Like I said, I don't need a tenant or the money."

This man is infuriating. I want to shake him, and yell at him, and tell him it's not all about *him*. Hey, that might be the answer. "Well, just tell me what you were going to say."

"You're one determined woman, you know that?" We've reached the foyer and George turns to me. "I hate grocery shopping."

Wait. *What?* "That's what you were going to say? You hate grocery— Oh! That's what you wanted me to do for you."

"That's right. My wife used to grocery shop, and I just hate it. I get overwhelmed, and it's hard to shop for one person. I usually come home with half the things I should have picked up." He gives me a sad smile.

"Well, how often would you want me to shop? Hypothetically, I mean." Reel him back in…

"Oh, I don't know. Once a week?"

"I could do that." Not a big deal, really. I could do both grocery shops at once. "Also," I continue, "you said you're a retired admiral and that you don't need the money. What about donating the rent money to a worthwhile cause that benefits the Navy, or the ocean, or a charity along those lines?"

I've slipped my shoes on and we're now back outside and are making our way up the path. When we reach the sidewalk, I know my shot at this will be over. George is silent. Oh, *please*.

"All right."

Really? I turn to him in surprise.

"Thirteen hundred a month, utilities included."

I cannot believe my luck. I want to hug this man, and I'm definitely not the huggy type. "Deal," I say. It's hard to contain my relief and excitement. I want to jump around like Margo does, but I settle on grinning like an idiot. I've got to get home and finish packing; there are a million things to do. "Thank you, George. Thank you!"

I wave goodbye and practically dance my way back to the bus stop. Who would have ever thought I would be thrilled to live in a dusty, shag-carpeted attic? But—oh, Kitsilano, it's good to be back!

6

Today is moving day. I awoke with a heavy heart and sick stomach that hasn't let up. I can't eat or drink, or care about eating or drinking, or anything at all really. The victory I felt yesterday for scoring a place to live has dissipated and now feels like a childish feat. Who the hell cares?

Boxes are everywhere, and what's even more rampant is the baby gear. With the playpen, high chair, booster seat, car seat, and kids' toys, books, and clothes, there will be limited room for my bed and *my* belongings.

Once he's finished delivering flowers for weddings and other events, Billy will be over to move our things in his florist cube van.

Upstairs, I sit on my bed, all dressed and ready to go. Go where? How can I even manage with kids on my own? It's incredibly daunting and overwhelming. The scariest thing is I can't picture my future. It's one big, gray question mark. The only thing I *can* picture is us hanging out in that shagged attic, which is hardly thrilling. I feel like I can't catch my breath. My room is silent. The silence is deafening, pounding in my ears and reverberating off the walls. I lift my face and, for the last time, take in the surroundings of

Riches & Rags

my heavenly East Wing. It feels surreal that I'll be leaving this all behind.

My eyes settle on a framed picture of my mom and me when I was a child. I cross the room and peer at the photo to get a closer look. Mom and I are swimming side by side at Spanish Banks, a beach near Kits. Our faces mirror each other's happiness and simple joy of a beautiful afternoon swim together. I can't help but smile at the picture. How I long for those days that still seem so real I can practically feel the cool water and floating sensation. Even more vivid is the feeling I knew so well of being in the safety and love of mom's presence. What I would give to feel that sense of security and well-being right now.

"Lane."

"Huh?"

"We're ready to load the van, okay?"

"Uh-huh."

"Lane, you okay?"

I turn to Billy in a daze. Nothing seems real. Billy gives me a sympathetic smile. Or is it pity? I'm not sure.

"Aren't you going to take your canopy?" he asks, heading over to the bed and fingering the delicate peach fabric.

"I can't take the four-poster bed, so what's the point" I mumble in reply.

"*Oh*, come on, Lane. It's all good. You have a nice place to go, and everything is going to work out. Plus, as you said, Micky will be back and..."

I tune out as Billy rambles on in an apparent effort to soothe my spirits. He's slipped off his shoes and has jumped onto my bed to untie the canopy fabric from the wooden bed frame. I watch in silence, feeling a glimmer of gratitude for this small comfort in the new place. It's going to look ridiculous against that carpet.

Billy finishes untying the last ribbon and leaps to the

floor, looking pleased with himself. "Ready?" he asks, coming to stand at my side. I inhale a meager breath, and surveying my beautiful retreat one last time, I nod and turn quickly, clutching the picture of Mom and me.

Downstairs, Denise is piling the final boxes at the door, and Rory is seated in her car seat, gnawing on a teething ring with exuberance.

"Where's Margo?" I ask.

"I'm not sure, Ms. Carson. Try her bedroom."

I turn around to head back upstairs. The door to Margo's room is ajar, and I push it open. Margo is sitting on her bed and appears to be lost in thought. We're two of a kind. "Margo, we need to leave," I say.

Margo scrambles to her feet. Her eyes seem larger than usual, and today she carries a solemn demeanor well beyond her years. I know how she feels, but I can't seem to find the right words to say so. We stand before each other in silence. Finally I extend my hand to her. She hesitates only briefly before coming to my side and placing her small hand in mine. We descend the grand staircase together for the last time.

A Chinese man I've never seen is helping carry boxes to the van. Denise introduces us. "Ms. Carson, this is my husband Alec."

Husband? I didn't know Denise was married. Good, Micky thought to hire additional help for moving day. I nod to the man and then move on to see what Billy's up to.

Alec and Billy make trips back and forth to the van. I pretend to be engrossed in my phone so I don't need to help, but I see Margo is carrying some small boxes.

"Should we bring my mattress down now before the truck is too full?" I ask.

"Good idea," Billy says, and he and Alec abandon the boxes and follow me upstairs. My mattress is king sized and pillow topped. Between us—Alec, a small Chinese man,

Billy, a waif of a man himself, and me, a lightweight—we are barely able to get the mattress off the frame.

Once we've heaved it onto the floor, we hold it upright and pause for a break, panting like ragged dogs.

"Lane, did you say your suite is on the third floor?" Billy asks, his voice thick with dread.

"Uh, yep."

Billy lets go of his corner of the mattress, and it topples to the floor with an alarming thud. "Any other *smaller* mattresses?" he asks, raising one perfectly arched eyebrow. Alec looks relieved this beast is staying behind.

They follow me to our third spare bedroom, the lowliest of all our spares. There's a simple double mattress and box frame, without pillow top layers and added weight. We easily slide them down the stairs and into the waiting van. In no time, the van is loaded and bursting at the seams, and a cab is en route to pick us up. There's no way in hell I'm busing to our new place—I'll ride in semi comfort by splurging on a taxi.

While Billy secures the van doors, I wander over to Denise. "Good thing Micky kept you on for the last two days and hired Alec to help out. I can't imagine having to do this all on my own." I turn to her for acknowledgment, but she remains silent. "Denise?"

"Mr. Capello gave me notice of termination that was effective immediately."

"What do you mean?"

"Well…I wanted to stay and help." She gives me a shy smile. "It would have been too much to do on your own with the kids."

My mouth hangs agape. "Micky never asked you to stay on?"

"No, ma'am."

"And your husband? Is he here because he was hired?"

"No. Again, you needed help."

I gaze at Denise in amazement. For the first time, I see her. I mean *really* see her for who she is—a caring human being—and not simply the "hired help." I mean, I didn't even know she had a husband. I never bothered to ask anything of her personal life; never even asked how she was doing—yet she is here for me anyway.

"Denise, I don't know what to say." I stand before her at a loss for words.

"Don't mention it. You would have done the same."

I would have? Somehow I doubt that. "Denise, if I can make this up to you, one day I will…"

"It's all right, Ms. Carson."

"Lane, please."

Denise nods, her eyes full of warmth. "Be well, Lane." She says her goodbyes to Margo and Rory and tears up as she hugs them. It dawns on me that Denise has been with us since the girls' births and has watched them grow up.

A yellow cab pulls into the drive. Billy helps me fasten Rory into her car seat and Margo into her booster. I take a seat beside the driver and press my face as close to the smudged window as I can without actually touching it. Goodbye home!

Memories flood back—from the first time Micky and I came to view this magnificent land, to the excitement we felt with each building phase completed, to the tranquility I was able to experience in my East Wing.

I notice with puzzlement the fountains are not operating but standing still and lifeless, already abandoned and forgotten. We circle the drive slowly so I can get a last look. I drink in the details and confirm it to memory for keeps. Maybe we can get it back someday, when Micky is able to sort out this mess.

What if he *can't?* I push the thought away.

We pass the elaborate, perfectly manicured and professionally detailed gardens. And then, we exit the massive gates and turn onto the road, and the house is gone.

Across the bay, George Harris is having his afternoon tea in the company of his Siamese cat, Piper. He takes in mouthfuls of steaming tea, almost scalding his tongue. His mind is on other things. How could he have had such a terrible lapse in judgment and have agreed to the harebrained idea of having a tenant? Of course he doesn't want a tenant after living alone for over thirty years. *And a single woman? That single woman? No way! Women like that are trouble, with their sharp heels and sharper tongue.* The last thing he needs in his predictable old age is a young hen squawking about the place and making demands. And noise! *Never mind she would be on the third floor. Young people these days like loud music—rap music.*

He lets out a low groan, and Piper leaps into this lap, purring as if in an effort to appease his mood. George pats the cat's soft head; and with that, she jumps to the coffee table, almost knocking over his hot tea.

"Damn cat! I've told you not to go on the table," he yells and swats at Piper, who swats back, leaving a light scratch on George's forearm.

"Damn cat!" He shakes his fist at her. She hops to the floor, bellowing a loud, screeching meow. "No, you can't share my biscuit!" George pops the last of his biscuit into his mouth. "I've told you before. No tabletops or counters for you." Piper gives him a long look and saunters off to lie in the patch of sun, and George goes back to his tea and musings.

No, it wasn't a good idea at all, and it won't work. That's

it. He'll just have to tell her when she comes that there's been a change of plans. She won't be moving in.

"She can't move in. I've been on my own for over thirty years. What was I thinking?" Piper's ear twitches ever so slightly and she flicks her tail, but otherwise she seems to play oblivious to the old man. His question hangs in the air unanswered, like all his other ramblings.

"Well, it'll just have to be."

Feeling satisfied with having rectified the situation, he heaves his tired body from the tattered armchair and trudges over to kitchen to wash his cup.

"Okay, we're officially in Kitsilano," I say, turning in my seat to face Margo. She cranes her neck to get a better view as we make our way along Cornwall. In a few minutes, we'll be driving right by Kits Beach, and judging by the warm September day, it should be absolutely packed. Margo's face is peeled to the window, but she is unusually quiet. As for me, I try to not think about the monumental change this will be, and instead, break it all into manageable bits. Like, right now, we are driving down Cornwall. That's all.

"Rory is sleeping," Margo whispers.

Oh good! At least that makes things easy for unpacking.

"Look, Kits Beach!" I say, as we make our way past. The beach is dotted with hundreds of people tanning, swimming, and playing volleyball, and I notice a trio practicing circus moves on a tightrope tied between two trees. There are always eccentric people practicing their craft on the beach.

"Turn right on Point Grey Road," I tell the driver as we come to the end of Kits Beach. The driver hangs a right, and I lean forward as we curve around a bend and head for the end of the block to George's home.

I pay the driver and unload Rory, who's sleeping. Margo clambers out of the car, dragging her booster behind her. The moving van isn't here yet, but that's fine. I carry Rory's car seat, which must weigh eighty pounds, I swear.

"Well, here we are," I announce to Margo, as we stand staring at the house. I'm careful not to say the word "home," or even anything along the lines to "this is where we'll be living."

We've just made our way up the cobblestone walkway, when the heavy front door bursts open and George bustles his way toward us. I can't help but notice from his expression that he's agitated, to say the least. Here we go!

"Who the hell are these kids?" he demands, coming over to me and getting all up in my face.

"Well, hello to *you* too," I retort, not bothering to answer his question. I heave the massive car seat to the ground. The seat shakes and Rory stirs. Oh, *please* don't wake up. Rory's eyes pop open and focus on me; and with that, the wailing starts.

"Who the hell are these kids?" George yells over her cries.

"They're *my* kids," I yell back, shrugging as though it's no big deal.

But George only gets more irate. "Kids? You have kids and you didn't even bother telling me. Wait, do they not live with you?"

"Of course they live with me," I snap. Stupid old man! What's it to him?

"This isn't going to work." George wags his gnarly finger in my face. I'm about to argue back, when I see Billy pulling up in the van.

Oh, thank God! Billy leaps out and saunters up the path like it's his own personal catwalk. I smile in appreciation and admire his graceful moves and golden brown curls. Margo runs to meet him, screeching, and Rory stops crying momentarily to see what drama has possibly overshadowed hers. I glance at George and feel instant distaste; I don't like the way he's looking at Billy.

"George, this is my cousin and best friend, Billy." I stand aside to let them greet each other.

Billy gives George a warm smile and offers his outstretched hand. To my horror, George doesn't return the handshake.

Awkward!

I glance back at Billy as he lowers his hand to his side. I'm trying to gauge his reaction but his features remain stoic.

"I was just telling Lane, here, that this arrangement won't work. I actually decided this morning I don't want a tenant."

Billy shoots me a horrified look and turns back to George. "What do you mean you don't want a tenant? You mean Lane can't live here?"

George shakes his head, and I'm about to interject, when I notice Margo is at George's side, tugging on his pant leg. "Margo, leave the man alone," I say. She ignores me and continues to tug at his pant insistently. The old man fixes her with a grumpy, even stare, but Margo gazes back, unfazed. She motions for George to come down to her level.

"I can't bend that far," George says. "Here, I'll have a seat on the stair. Now, what is so important young lady?" Margo climbs a stair and leans over and starts whispering to him.

What is going on?

Billy and I watch intently. I also notice with relief that Rory has cried herself back to sleep. Margo is whispering on and on, and George's face is deadpan. What is she saying?

Finally, George turns to her and nods a single, decisive

nod. Margo rewards him with her mega-watt smile and he smiles back, flashing his dentured teeth. Margo stands up, grinning, and announces with pride that we can start moving our things in.

And just like that, we're good to go.

7

Upstairs, I swing the door open and step aside for Billy. He enters the attic, eyes bulging in horror.

"Oh. My. God."

"My sentiments exactly."

"This carpet..." Billy seems at a loss for words.

We stand motionless as I take in the hideous, hairy, green nastiness—I swear it's grown an inch since yesterday. I shoot Billy a woeful look, but he's regarding me with a mischievous gleam in his eye.

"Are you thinking what I'm thinking?"

"Run like hell?"

"No, better. Let's rip it out. Right now!"

"Right now?" I glance at Margo, who is hovering near the door, Rory sleeping at her side.

"Come on," Billy insists, "before all your things are moved in. Go borrow a couple of screwdrivers and box cutters from the old man." He starts wandering around, exploring the attic, with Margo following closely behind him. Judging by her expression, she's hardly impressed; but why would she be?

With one more glance at Rory, who's still sleeping peacefully in her seat, I grab my chance and race downstairs at breakneck speed. We're getting rid of the Oscar carpet. YAY!

After settling Rory and Margo on the bathroom floor with some Barbies and cookies for entertainment, we get to work. The dust is going to be insane, but Billy says we're lucky the place doesn't have baseboards because we'd have to rip those out too.

"No *way*!" Billy yells, as he pulls up one corner of the hideous carpet.

"What?" Margo and I cry in unison and rush over to Billy's side. Did he find money or hidden jewelry?

"Laney, today's your lucky day. Because, my friend, hiding under this carpet is none other than hardwood floors! *Oh* yeah."

"Let me see." I peer at the floor. Sure enough, they *are* hardwood. Margo doesn't seem to share our enthusiasm and makes a beeline back to the bathroom. "They need work though," I say.

"Lane! Would you try to be positive for once in your life? We're getting rid of the carpet, and you have *hardwood*. Come on!"

I open my mouth to retort but decide against it, and together we start ripping out the carpet and padding. The carpet has the nastiest stains, and I swear my sinuses all but collapse from the barrage of dust. We fold Oscar into the middle of the space and then pull out the tack strips and staples. Rory starts crying, but her timing is impeccable as we're just about done.

By the time we have the carpet out of the house, sweep, and move things in, it's nine o'clock. Billy was sweet to order Chinese, as I wouldn't know where to begin with fixing dinner. And that hotplate, ugh! I don't *ever* want to go there. George just about had a hernia when we came downstairs lugging manageable bits of Oscar. He stamped and shook his fist, yelling something about having to hear my rap music now that the insulation is gone. He's delusional, obviously.

I clear the final take-out container into the garbage and survey the attic. The floor has been swept but is in bad need of refinishing. Boxes litter the space and, as I didn't pack, I have no idea what was packed or which box contains what. I feel incredibly overwhelmed, and my heart sinks every time I think of Micky. I cannot believe I'm going to be cooped up in this random attic with the kids and no husband in sight, and no idea of what is going to be.

"You look like crap, Lane." Billy is peering at me closely, one hand propping up his chin.

"I'm overwhelmed. And this place, I mean, come on, what a demotion. I mean, I don't even have a real kitchen. And George says I can start cooking by *microwave!* What would the society wives say if they could see me? God..."

"Lane, listen to you. Come on! I'm so bloody sick of having to deal with 'Lane on a pedestal, all high and mighty.'" Billy's going to fall out of his seat if he leans any closer to me. "Ever since you met Micky you've been a downright *bitch*; but that's not who you really are. Drop the veneer, Lane. It's over. You don't have to be the bitch anymore."

I roll my eyes at him, but I can't help feeling stung. Certainly, I'm not *that* bad.

"You used to be real. I mean, you've always been a bit stand-offish, but you were at least lighthearted until your Mom—"

"Yeah. You know, I think you need to get going." Margo is entertaining Rory with some baby toys, but I've noticed she keeps rubbing her eyes. "You know, we don't all live in fairyland. Some of us have kids to put to bed." I give Billy a wry smile, and to my relief he grins back.

"Oh, I almost forgot." He jumps up and dashes out the door, and I bring the girls into the bathroom to wash up.

Billy returns a few minutes later carrying a monstrosity of a flower arrangement featuring lilies, gladiolas and roses. In the other hand, he holds a self-burning fire log.

"These flowers are a housewarming gift and the log is a literal house warming." He laughs at his joke and continues. "You said you couldn't build a fire, but with this you just have to light it—and voila!—a roaring fire for three hours."

"Very nice, Billy. Thanks for all your help today. Really, thank you." When I accompany him to the door, the feeling of terror that's gripped me for two days starts to build. "Billy...," I whisper frantically.

"What?" he asks, narrowing his eyes.

"I'm...I'm scared." The words sound foreign to my ears. When do I ever admit fear?

"Of what?"

"Uh..." I shift my gaze to the girls playing on the floor, then back to Billy's face.

"Oh, I see." Billy seems to consider this, and then he gives a little shrug. "You'll be fine, Lane."

"But I don't know how to be a parent. I have nothing to go by!" The panic rises in my voice, and I feel hysteria start to build. How can I do this?

"You had a really great mom, Lane. If you're half as good as she was, you'll be just fine. Just do as she would have done." Billy leans over and brushes a light kiss on my cheek, then slips out the door.

And then there were three.

I manage to make my bed after locating the box of linens. Both girls are in their pajamas and ready for sleep. I feel a bit embarrassed not knowing the bedtime routine, but I guess I can make a new one.

"All right!" I command. "Into bed." Margo hops on the bed and then, enjoying the bouncing sensation, continues hopping and giggling and mangling the nicely laid blankets. "Calm down, you're going to get yourself hyper and you'll never sleep," I scold. Rory kicks and squeals in my arms, enjoying the entertainment.

"Will you read to me?" Margo asks when she finally calms down.

"No. I don't know where the books are. We haven't got to that box yet."

"Well, can't you tell me a story, then?"

Tell a story? Ugh. The last thing I feel like doing is telling a story; but then, my mom would have. Okay, all I can think of is Goldilocks, so it'll have to do. I place Rory beside her sister on the bed and sit down on the mattress as I begin telling the story.

"Goldilocks was a little girl who went for a walk," I begin. I hand Rory her bottle and hold it in place as I try to recall the story details. "There were also three bears that went for a walk because their porridge was—"

"Where's Dad?"

"Sorry?"

"Where's Dad? And when is he coming back?"

Ohhh. "Daddy is on a motorcycle trip to work some stuff out."

"What stuff?"

"Grown-up stuff. But listen I'm trying to tell you about the bears."

"What bears?"

This is exasperating. "The *three* bears. And Goldilocks." I go on recounting the story as Margo listens, her expression placid. She's staring at me with an intense focus, and I can't tell if she's actually listening to the story or thinking about other things. It's unnerving, and I find myself speeding along to wrap up the story-line. "And Goldilocks ran away, never to return. The End!" I pronounce. Good, done.

Rory's eyes are growing heavy, and her pudgy little fingers are wrapped around mine, holding the bottle. Even Margo is looking less alert, which is a relief.

"Hey!" I suddenly remember. "What did you say to George?"

"Who's George?"

"The old man downstairs."

"Oh. I said he looked like a grandpa and that grandpas shouldn't be grouchy, they should be nice."

"That's all?" I ask, unconvinced.

"Yep. And I said me and my baby sister want to stay at his house so he can be our grandpa."

"*What?*" I practically shriek, and Rory's eyes fly open in alarm. "Why would you say something like that? He's a stranger, and you already have two grandpas."

"He's not a stranger. He's George. And I don't see my Grandpas."

Right. Micky's dad lives on the East Coast, and my dad…my dad is another story altogether. "I'll call my dad soon and you can see him."

"Okay!" Margo is obviously pleased and she snuggles under the covers.

Rory's eyes are heavy again, and her drinking has slowed down to the point where it's hard to tell if she's actually getting anything.

"Goodnight, Margo. Go to sleep," I say.

"I miss Laura." Margo's eyes well up with tears, and her face looks so lost and broken. Our nanny, Laura, has been with the girls since they were born—I feared Margo would have difficulty with this.

Rory's eyes have closed completely, so I pull the bottle away and begin setting up her playpen. How does this bloody thing even go? And, seriously? The so-called mattress is made of fiberboard and feels about as comfortable as a rock. I wouldn't sleep on this if my life depended on it. I toss the useless mat back into the playpen. Well, we'll just all have to sleep in my bed.

It's unbelievable how I go from having my own suite to having to now share my *bed*.

There's a rustling sound, and I look over to find Margo rocking her entire torso back and forth, arms stretched out to the ceiling.

"What on earth are you doing?" I ask in wonder.

"Rocking," Margo answers as she continues the back and forth motion.

I'm at a loss. "W-why?"

"It's how I fall asleep."

Oh my.

While Margo rocks herself to sleep, I start opening some boxes to familiarize myself with everything. So far I haven't found any of *my* things, but Denise did pack away some food, including dry goods, spices, and even some wine. *Yes!* I grab the bottle of Wolf Blass and—thank God for screw tops—take a long swig from the bottle. Forget finding stemware, if there is any.

The floral arrangement from Billy looks more suited to a funeral home than this depressing attic. I mean, a housewarming gift in here? What a joke. Well, time to light the log and see what a homey, crackling fire will do to the joint. I toss the log in the fireplace and— Ooh!

I find a pack of matches on the mantle. I light the fire and flop down onto a chair, heaving a massive sigh. Being a poor, single parent is incredibly rough. This is crazy. I guzzle more wine, and then some. The log is burning, but it's hardly a roaring or even a crackling fire. Just one small, pitiful log with a meager flame.

The more I drink, the more upset I become. And

looking over at the girls, sleeping nestled up to each other, I decide I can't do this. I can't be a dedicated parent, let alone a single parent. I'm just not meant for this. To have kids cared for by nannies is one thing, but to care for them myself? I don't know what to do. And where's Micky? *Where* is he? Riding his motorcycle, sure. But where? Is he on his way back? I drop my face into my hands, but I don't cry. I can never bloody cry, even when I want to. And right now, I just want to curl up and cry and have someone care for *me*, goddammit. I can't care for anyone when I'm in this state.

And then I think of Micky's mom. Elsa. Yes! Elsa can take the kids. She is, after all, their flesh and blood. Perfect. I grab my phone and dial her number. After four rings, the voicemail clicks on.

"Elsa, it's Lane. Micky left and I have the kids, but I can't do this. I need you to come get them ASAP. " I hang up, feeling better. Maybe she can even come tomorrow. I finish the last of the wine and let the bottle fall to the floor.

Oops, it's not carpet anymore. Shit. Broken glass.

Tomorrow.

I nod at the fire, its warmth finally taking the last of the stress away.

Why was I upset? I don't remember anymore.

We're on the beach, Micky and I. His hazel eyes sparkle with laughter, and he looks deep into mine. We hold each other, laughing, foamy waves crashing all around. A loud, high-pitched noise is there too. We continue holding each other and laughing, but the sound keeps blaring. I'm frowning. What's that noise? Something's wrong.

Huh? I shake myself from my dream, and the alarm is

ever present. Oh my God, a fire alarm. It sounds like it's coming from downstairs. I scramble to my feet and sway from the effects of the wine.

Shit. The kids!

The fire alarm continues blaring. I fumble for my phone and dial 9-1-1. I can absolutely smell smoke. OH MY GOD!

"Wake up," I scream, and I dash over to Rory and Margo.

"Nine one one. Police, Fire, or Ambulance?" asks the dispatcher.

"Fire!" I yell and give the address. How I managed to remember it, I'll never know. Both girls are startled awake and break into wails, no doubt bewildered at the unfamiliar surroundings and my hysteria. Grabbing Rory in one arm and pulling Margo with the other, I dash over to the fire escape, fling the french door open, and stick my head outside. The bloody thing is as horrific as I remember. If we stay and wait for help, we may not die; but if we try to chance that rickety thing, we *will* die.

"OH MY GOD!"

"Mommy!" Margo screams, and Rory screams right along with her.

The stairs! Yes. I run over to the door and feel the knob, which isn't hot. I remember hearing if the knob is hot in a fire, don't open the door. I fling it open and some smoke drifts in.

We stumble-sprint our way down the stairwell as I scream for George. Where is he? On the second landing, I sway, still incredibly drunk. I pause, calling his name, as smoke billows from under one of the doors. Do I run downstairs with the girls to get them to safety, or try for the old man? Screw the old man, he's in his eighties anyway and my girls are just little, with their whole lives ahead of them. I abandon George and stagger down the stairs, two screaming, crying children in tow.

8

Outside, the air is cool. Having escaped the burning house, I feel tremendous relief and want to laugh and cry at the same time. The fire engine sirens are blaring; they must be right around the corner. Margo and Rory are still hysterical, so I bring them down the stairs and up the cobblestone path to the sidewalk.

I check them over, and they appear to be shaken but otherwise fine. I look back at the house and the bright light from the fire is illuminating one of the rooms on the second floor, and black smoke is billowing out the open window.

The first fire engine arrives and a fireman rushes over to us with blankets, while the others go about unraveling hoses and unloading equipment.

"Ma'am, are you all right?"

"Yes, but there's an eighty-year-old man still inside." My voice is high pitched and breathless. With that, the fireman takes off to join his team.

"Mommy, will George be all right?" Margo shivers with hysteria and huddles close.

"I don't know," I answer truthfully. How can the bloody old man be so deaf—he didn't hear the alarm or me calling for him? Rory is whimpering but has calmed down, and we all collapse together and watch the firefighters battle the angry flames. I hear yelling from down the street and recognize that crispy old voice at once—it's George! Margo leaps to her feet and runs to greet her new "grandpa."

"OH MY GOD, MY HOUSE. WHAT ON EARTH?!" George is absolutely freaking out.

Where did he even come from?

"How did this happen?" he demands, eyes blazing into mine.

Is he *accusing* me?

"How should *I* know? We're here for only a few hours and already you're trying to kill us!"

"Kill you? More like kill me. In all my years, I've never had a *fire*. And now! Well, you must be some psycho pyromaniac."

"Oh please! I have better things to do with my time than get my kicks at watching things burn."

"Are you intoxicated?"

"Of course not."

The fireman who spoke with us before races over.

"Is this the man you had previously thought to be inside?" he asks.

"Yes, I am the owner of this home. Retired Admiral George Harris."

Well, whoopty doo.

"Sir, may I ask where you've been?"

"Piper and I went for our nightly walk."

"Who's Piper?" I chime in. George gives me a nasty look, then lifts his black shoulder bag to the fireman, revealing a mesh window. We peer through the window, and two yellow eyes peer back.

"It's a cat!" Margo squeals. The fireman asks a few more questions and retreats back inside. By now the flames we had seen before are gone, and things appear to be under control.

Riches & Rags

After nodding off on the boulevard with both girls curled up against me, I'm gently awoken. I open my eyes to find one of the other firemen at my side. His face is stained with black soot and he looks like he's been to hell and back, but his brown eyes are warm and his approach is gentle. I notice too, it's already dawn. We've spent the entire night outside. I shiver, damp to the core from the dew, and I draw the blanket closer.

"Ma'am, how are you feeling?"

It takes me a moment to find my bearings, and the memories of the fire come rushing back. "I'm all right, thanks."

"Ma'am, under normal circumstances, an extensive evaluation occurs before residents are allowed to return to the premises. Evaluations would cover everything from testing for asbestos, to analyzing if structural damage occurred to the integrity of the house."

"Well, how long is that going to take?" I ask, panic rising.

"It could be anywhere from three days to two weeks, or longer."

"Are you kidding me? Two *weeks*. Where the hell are we supposed to go?"

"Well, ma'am. Here's the unbelievably good part. It appears as though the fire was entirely contained within the bathroom parameters and damage is nothing more than superficial. Aside from some minimal damage to the tiles and drywall, and some sacrificial linens, you've been given the OK to return immediately. Though, of course, in the case of any fire, you are all very lucky to have escaped unscathed."

I shudder at the thought of what could have been, but am equally baffled by our good fortune to not have to couch surf at Billy's for two weeks.

"Additionally," the firefighter continues, "we've identified the source of the fire."

This piques my interest, and I momentarily forget about being homeless with two kids.

Did crazy old George leave the stove on? Maybe he lit his dentures on fire, mistaking them for his pipe.

"And?" I ask, waiting for more.

"A fire log was burning in the attic hearth and some of the embers fell through the floor of the fireplace. It appears as though there were some floor tiles missing."

Holy shit, Billy's literal housewarming present almost burned down the *entire* house. But how was he to know? If anything, it's George's fault for not ensuring the fireplace's safety in the first place, just like that bloody fire escape. Ohhh!

"I have something I need to show you," I inform the fireman. I shake Margo awake and hoist Rory onto my shoulder. With that, I march around to the back of the house, leading the curious firefighter. Take that George!

"TEN THOUSAND DOLLARS!"

Ugh, George is so close I can feel the spit flying from his wrinkled old mouth. It's midday, and we've all napped the morning away. Unfortunately, our peaceful breakfast was rudely disturbed by George, as, for some reason, he's decided *I'm* the person to blame for letting his house disintegrate. I tilt my head to the side and stare at him. His face is so red I think a heart attack is just about a given. He continues screaming as he paces back and forth on my newly exposed hardwood.

Please—old men can be so dramatic.

Riches & Rags

"It's not like you don't have the money, *Admiral*."

George continues ranting; he doesn't even see me. He wants only to hear his own crotchety voice. He stamps his foot and seems to hold his breath. He's getting redder by the second.

"You all right, there?" I feel mildly concerned, until I see his hairy eyebrows furrow. He continues spouting on about how I am the worst possible person to ever come into his life, blah blah blah.

"Tell you what," I say, "you hurry downstairs and make a grocery list because I need to run some errands." I hop up from my chair and grab a cloth from the counter to wash the girls' breakfast off them. Both girls seem relieved we're heading out. And anyway it's been a long night. The chance to wander beautiful Kitsilano and escape this geriatric hellhole is an opportunity I just can't pass up. Plus, soon I'll have to start the job search. Sigh!

Today is fantastic. At least it has been since we left the house. We ran the errands, and now we're buying groceries from George's very sad grocery list. It reads:

Milk 1 lt.

Can of Spam x 2 (Nasty! I didn't think anyone actually ate that stuff.)

Bananas x 2

Whiskas cat food - senior (Even his cat is old!)

Mr. Noodles x 7 (Seriously?)

Can of sardines x 1

White bread x ½ loaf

Brussels sprouts x 14 (Again, nobody likes brussels

sprouts. Old man George's taste buds are totally screwed up!)

At first I thought this was some kind of joke. But this is his actual list. Margo has fun counting out the brussels sprouts. One goes in the bag, one rolls on the floor. Giggle, giggle. I don't think the produce guys like us. Also, Safeway is very drab. Having Whole Foods on the next block is an unfair tease. But, for now, my budget is Safeway. So sad. I try to piece together George's menu for the week. I'm thinking his dinners must be Mr. Noodles with two floating brussels sprouts—every night! No wonder he thought microwave cooking was acceptable. I haven't been a fan of the man since he was such a bigot toward Billy; but *nobody* should have to eat like this.

Anyway, enough about George!

We drop off the groceries and survive the chaos of packing for the beach, then make our way down to Kits Pool—the longest saltwater pool on the continent, boasting extraordinarily beautiful views of English Bay. I'm not certain, but I think I can actually pinpoint our very house across the channel in West Van, which leaves me feeling melancholy and agitated, until I hear Billy's sing-song voice calling me. I turn around with a grin as Billy strides over, wearing aviators and a Gucci swimsuit. I notice a couple of brown paper bags poking out of his beach tote, which can only mean one thing—pastries! Margo is a few feet away splashing around in the pool. I lower Rory's feet into the glistening water. She starts kicking wildly, mesmerized by the sensation and the splashing.

"Here, pass me the baba so you can take a little dip," Billy says.

I hand over Rory and plunge under the cool water, opening my eyes to the exquisite turquoise underworld. Peace. I feel a lightness I haven't felt since the East Wing. And the silence is incredibly precious. Underwater, I feel at

Riches & Rags

home—safe, hopeful, and serene. I come up for a big gulp of sea air and plunge back under. I flip onto my back, still submerged a couple of feet, and watch the water ripple above me. This is one of my favorite things to do underwater. I smile at the thought of knowing I live less than a block away from this pool now and can experience this whenever desired. *If* I find a babysitter first that is. Speaking of which, time to find Billy.

Billy is lounging on a towel with the girls, and he and Margo are filling their faces with croissants. Margo hops up as I approach, flashes me a huge grin, and splashes back into the shallow water to play. I flop down onto the towel beside Rory.

"Fear not, dear cousin, there's some for you too," Billy says, handing me a bag.

"Perfect, thanks," I say, pulling a chocolate croissant from the bag and biting into the buttery flakes.

"So, tell me. How was your first night at Casa George?"

Ha! Wait till he hears.

"Well, interesting you should ask. Turns out we had a house fire, and yours truly, along with your beloved nieces, were lucky to have escaped alive!"

Billy's eyes widen and he sucks in his breath. I fill him in on all the details, ending with George's ten-thousand-dollar fine.

"TEN THOUSAND DOLLARS?!" Billy has stopped mid chew and is gaping at me with those enormous, green eyes.

"That's right!" I confirm, lounging back on my towel and taking another bite of my heavenly chocolate croissant. I glance over at Margo to see her playing with two little boys and their water toys. Rory has fallen asleep. I reach out to touch her delicate, golden tresses. My lips curl into a slow smile as I think about George's reaction to the fine.

"I can't believe this. I can't believe you! You're a downright, first-class bitch, Lane." Billy shakes his head, smiling.

"The fireman was astounded at George's lack of responsibility to have such a decrepit fire escape for a woman and her two young children. It was a *major* offense according to the city," I say, eyes large for maximum drama. "The City of Vancouver Standards of Maintenance bylaw constitutes a maximum fine of ten thousand dollars for an unsafe fire escape. And George was struck with the maximum." I pause for effect. "And," I continue, "serves him right for calling me a pyromaniac—I mean, *please*." I throw my head back and laugh just thinking of George's angry, red face and crotchety yelling in protest to the fine.

"Oh! So *that's* why you did that; to get back at him for calling you a pyro?" Billy raises an eyebrow.

"*No*. I wouldn't risk taking my kids out on that deathtrap fire escape for anything. So he has to pay a little fine and have it fixed. Well, it should have been fixed a long time ago, and *THAT* is not my fault." I shrug my shoulder and take another greedy bite. Yum!

"Unbelievable." Billy is still shaking his head. "Since when have you gone all Mother Hen on me?"

"I haven't gone all 'Mother Hen'; I just don't want to endanger my kids. Do you realize I could sue him? I mean, we almost *died*!"

"Lane, you're wild. You're the one who begged him to live there; he never asked you to. And *you* started the fire!"

I raise my hand in protest and wag my finger back and forth. "It was a broken-down fireplace. I could sue for that too!"

Billy rolls his eyes and crumples his paper bag from his croissant and chucks it at me. We both dissolve into peals of giggles when it misses me by about three feet and hits a nearby sunbather on the bum. Billy always was hopeless at sports.

Riches & Rags

Back in the attic, Billy and I are seated at the awkward little table, after having fed the girls and finally put them to bed. They were both out of their minds with tiredness, but, thankfully, after a large outpouring of tears, a bottle of milk each, and a quick story from Uncle Billy, they both conked out.

"So, what's the plan?" Billy asks.

I take a slow sip of wine to buy time, as I consider my options. "Well, Margo is registered at General Gordon School, so tomorrow is her first day."

"Oh good. Now what about you? Are you okay for money?"

"Oh yeah, I'm fine, really."

Billy narrows his eyes, saying nothing, so I do a quick calculation. "Let's see, I have about four grand left after rent and the deposit."

"You need a job, Lane."

I roll my eyes and collapse back in my chair, gripping my wine close to me for comfort.

"What do you want to do?"

Ha, like I have any choices. "Billy, get real! I'm in my thirties and I've never had an actual job. It's not like the world is my oyster anymore." The reality that I have to put myself out there and actually try to find employment is incredibly daunting and depressing all at once.

"Come on, just throw around some ideas. What do you *want* to do? If you could, you know, do anything?"

Hmm, I probably haven't given this much thought since I was a naïve teenager thinking I'd one day move to Hollywood and become famous.

"All right, I want to be an actress," I say, raising my eyebrow to challenge him.

Billy actually chokes on his wine; he sputters and coughs and his face goes all red. I remain stoic, waiting for him to get a grip. Surely he couldn't be *laughing* at me.

Though he is.

"Lane, I'm sorry." Tears are now running down his face.

Who's the actor now?

"Lane, you're probably the most emotionally detached person I know. How can you possibly break through those layers to reach your authentic emotional self to properly portray a character?"

I tilt my head to the side and narrow my eyes. "Since the fuck when do you know anything about acting?"

Billy gives a small, shy smile, which is unlike him. "Um...well. Since I started dating an acting coach."

"WHAT? You have a boyfriend? Since *when*? How come I'm only hearing about it now?"

"Well, you're a bit fragile, hon, and I didn't want to upset you. It's all very new."

"What's his name?" I demand.

"John Childs. And, oh, he's beautiful." Billy actually blushes, and I giggle in response.

"Oh yeah?" I smile. "I love beautiful men." This reminds me of Micky, and I stop smiling.

"Stop that thought!" Billy says sharply.

Shit, now he's reading my mind.

"Anyway, this isn't about me, this is about you. You want to act? Like, seriously?" Hmm, seriously? I don't know. But why not?

"Absolutely," I confirm.

"Okay, well I'll speak with John, but in the meantime you need something like NOW."

Right. "I can be a personal trainer," I offer, since the world is my oyster and all ideas are free flowing.

"Lane, you cannot be serious. You don't even exercise!"

"Neither do you!"

"Yes. But I'm not the one wanting to be a personal trainer."

"Oh, come on. How hard can it be? Plus, I happen to know how much money the society wives paid their trainers, and I want a piece of that."

Billy shakes his head, laughing, and pulls out his iPad. He taps away. "Which Wi-Fi connection is yours? There's B-V-N-J, Harris twenty-seven, Johnson…"

"Harris. That's George."

"Damn. It's password protected."

Hmm, what would George's password be? Some good bets could be Admiral, SPAM, Piper—oooh! "Try Piper," I suggest.

"Okay. P-I-P-E-R… and we're in! How'd you know?

"Lucky guess."

"No fire today?" Billy motions to the fireplace.

"No," I pout. "George won't let me use it anymore. He threatened to put danger tape around it as a reminder. Can you believe it? Not everyone is eighty and senile!"

Billy and I giggle. Then he gets all serious on me. "Okay, so jobs. Do you want to place an ad as a personal trainer for the Kitsilano area?

"Go for it!"

Billy starts typing away, and I stiff a yawn. See, I haven't even started working yet and already it's tiring. Billy uploads my ad and then starts browsing the job postings. He seems focused on the task at hand so I sneak away unnoticed and slip into the bathroom where I browse my nail polishes. I select OPI Bubble Bath and start painting away. Bubble Bath reminds me of the last bubble bath I had when Micky kiboshed my fairy-tale life.

"Lane, get back in here," Billy calls, and I stick my head out of the bathroom, shushing him to be quiet. The last thing I need is a crying baby when my nails are wet. I saunter back to the table and professionally lower myself into the chair as though at a job interview.

"So, there's a job fair. And guess what? It's tomorrow."

"*What?* Tomorrow? No way."

"Well, why not. It's downtown at Library Square, and it's not until noon, so you can do the school drop off and pick up."

"Yeah? And what do you suggest I do with Rory?"

Billy shrugs. This is going to be impossible. Why even bother?

"Now, what about a resume?"

I groan and drop my head into my hands. After a beat, I whip my head back up and grin. "Tomorrow, I'll take Rory to the library and 'stumble' upon the job fair, which will explain why I have my kid and no resume!" Oh, I'm so genius. Billy claps his hands with glee. "Now, please can we change the subject? No more talk about the J-O-B."

Billy nods, looking relieved, and pours another round of wine. "Have you heard from Micky?" he asks casually.

I gulp a huge mouthful of liquid inspiration, hoping to numb the dull, ever-present pain that keeps hammering away at my heart and my soul. I can't even think of him. Every time I do, my stomach bottoms out. "No."

"All righty then, switching topics again. So, I've made a decision."

"Oh yeah?" My interest is piqued, and I lean forward.

"It's kind of a monumental decision, actually."

"Don't tell me Lover Boy is moving in. It's too soon."

"No, no, nothing like that."

"Waiting…" I'm losing interest at an alarming rate.

"I…I want to find my birth father."

"What? *Seriously?* But you don't even talk about him."

"That doesn't mean I don't think of him." This baffles me. Billy must be feeling a complexity of emotions and thoughts—worries, fears, and dreams—but his face doesn't give it away. Though our mothers were identical twins and I've known him my whole life, I realize there will always be more to discover.

His mom traveled to Haiti in the '70s with some girlfriends for a vacation. Apparently, she fell hard for a Haitian hottie and had a romantic fling. When she returned home and realized she was pregnant, she wasn't ever able to track down Billy's dad.

"Well, what are you going to do? Are you just going to go to Haiti and search for him yourself?"

"No, God no. I've actually hired someone to do it. A private investigator, actually."

"While he's at it, he can look for Micky too." I laugh, which sounds more pitiful than jovial.

"Have you tried getting in touch?" Billy's face is full of concern.

"Yeah, but it always just goes to voicemail. He must be having a very difficult time."

"He'll be okay, *really*. Listen, it's getting late, and you, my friend, need your beauty rest for tomorrow. Good luck!" And with that, Billy does a little wave and sashays out the door.

I down the rest of my wine and examine my nails. Tomorrow I'll look trés professional for sure!

9

Margo is at my side, her little face white and solemn and her eyes wide with obvious trepidation. We're standing outside the school, waiting for the first bell to ring. I've tried to coax her into playing at the playground or at least strolling around the school grounds, but she outright refuses.

When the bell rings, we find her kindergarten class, and her bubbly, frizzy-haired teacher introduces herself. Margo is still exceptionally rigid, and I feel a momentary pang for not being with her on her first day at Collingwood School in West Van. She obviously could have used my support.

"Okay Margo, why don't you give your mommy a hug and come join the class?" her teacher says with a warm smile. Margo appears quite shocked at the suggestion to hug me, and I find myself shrinking away.

"Goodbye, Margo." I give a little nod. "You'll do great," I add. Margo just stares at me and pops her thumb into her mouth. Oh boy. I turn quickly and make a mad dash away from the school.

Later, when we've caught our bus downtown, I realize we have almost half an hour to kill, so I really do take Rory to the library. Library Square is a coliseum-style building

Riches & Rags

with a massive, airy interior promenade featuring cafes and shops, and six stories of books. The dress code among the stay-at-home moms seems to be more Lululemon and less couture. I toss my head, feeling superior, until I remember, with horror, that I have nothing to feel superior about anymore. Well, anyway. I show Rory some books and am encouraged when she takes a great interest. She grips the board books with intensity and seems eager to look at all the pictures. To appease her, I grab a stack of books to borrow, and some for Margo too.

By the time I've returned to the atrium, the job fair is just getting under way. I feel a woman from the registration table eyeing me as I push the stroller forward. At the last second, I "happen" to casually glance in her direction and read the notice for the job fair.

"Oh," I say in mock surprise, "a job fair. I might be interested."

"Great." She beams, obviously impressed with such a high-quality candidate. "Why don't you register and collect a name badge?"

I start filling out the form.
Name: Lane Carson
Date:

What's today's date? September 16? I think? OH MY GOD! No, it can't be the sixteenth.

"What's the date?" I demand from the woman, who looks taken aback at my urgency.

"Why, today is September sixteenth."

Oh my God. Margo.

Margo's birthday is September 13, and with the move and the drama and the fire...I forgot. I am officially the worst mother to walk the face of this earth. Her fifth birthday, and I didn't even remember. My guilt morphs into exasperation as I think of Billy. Billy should have remembered. I'm going through so much, how can I possibly manage everything? Billy is going to get an earful.

I fill out the rest of the form and scroll my name on a badge.

"Do you have a resume with you?"

"Hmm? No, I was at the library with my *niece*. I didn't realize there was a job fair today."

The woman looks relieved to know the baby isn't mine and ushers me along to meet some prospective employers and headhunters. All is well, aside from Rory babbling, squealing, and wailing in her stroller. I shove one of the library books onto her lap, and that seems to do the trick.

I've embellished quite the extensive career in administration, marketing, and PR, and am almost starting to enjoy myself, when I hear someone behind me taunt, "Well, well, well. If it isn't little Miss Pillows and Blankets? And at a job fair, no less."

It's a disturbingly familiar voice. I spin around to see the server from *Victory* glaring at me with a loathing so intense I'm at a loss for words. I recover quickly. "Watch your mouth, you little dick," I hiss in a low voice. "It just so happens, I'm looking to hire some personnel." I raise my eyebrow and almost consider sticking out my tongue. Now *that* would be juvenile.

"Oh yeah? Then why are you wearing a name tag labeled *Seeking* Employment?"

What? I glance down in horror to check my name tag:

SEEKING EMPLOYMENT
Hello My Name is:
Lane Carson

I rip the bloody sticker off my Chanel suit like a waxing strip and crumple it into a ball. "They gave me the wrong name tag, *obviously*. Good luck with your job search; you'll need it, as you *certainly* won't be getting a reference from me." And with that, I swivel on my Miu Miu stiletto and saunter away, head held high.

Outside, the sunshine is blinding. I pause to collect myself. How humiliating and ironic. I pull my phone out from my bag and quickly check email. What's this? Who the hell is Jennifer Fairweather? I pull up the message and—I don't believe it—an actual personal training client wanting to work with me TODAY at 2:00 p.m. She only lives four blocks away, how ideal. Woohoo! The thrill I feel is so exhilarating, I actually go around the stroller and celebrate with Rory, grinning, squealing in delight, and squishing her baby cheeks. Rory regards me as though I've gone officially insane and makes it known—to everyone within earshot—she is less than thrilled at my sudden outburst of affection. And so she begins her own high-pitched wails.

When we arrive home, I mount the stairs two at a time, gripping Rory under one arm like a football. I swiftly feed and change her, then tear through the boxes, trying to find suitable workout attire. Denise seems to have packed a wide range of outfits, including formal and casual, but there isn't anything that screams personal trainer. Crap! What am I going to do? I have a coral halter top and black booty shorts that could *possibly* pass. I pull the halter top over my padded bra and admire my cleavage in the mirror. The shorts slide over my lean legs and look great. Now, on to shoes… After locating the box of shoes, I'm freaked to see nothing that even resembles running shoes. The closest thing is a pair of Tod's ballet flats. What am I going to do? I check the time and realize I should have been out the door five minutes ago. I slip on the ballet flats, grab a thick pair of socks, and scoop Rory into my arms.

Downstairs, I holler for George, and within a few seconds he emerges from his kitchen, looking somewhat bewildered.

"George! I need to borrow running shoes ASAP."

"My shoes? You want to borrow my sh—"

"Yes, your shoes. Hurry up! Please!"

"Well, what in devils name has got into..."

"GEORGE! I have a *job*. I need to leave, please."

He mumbles under his breath but disappears, thankfully, and materializes a moment later holding a hideous pair of worn, blue-and-white, no-name sneakers. I recoil at the thought of putting those even *near* my feet.

"Remember, beggars can't be—"

"Yeah, yeah," I snap, grabbing the ugly shoes and dashing outside to strap Rory into her stroller.

We arrive at Trafalgar and Second, and I park the stroller in front of a large colonial home. I slip the flats off, pull my socks on, and shove my feet into George's shoes, which happen to be about four sizes too big. I pull the laces as tight as possible and hope to God my client won't notice them. Ooh, I have a client; I like the sounds of that.

Mounting the stairs in the massive shoes is a struggle, so I gingerly side step up. I ring the doorbell and await Jennifer Fairweather. With a name like that, I'm guessing, she's middle-aged, maybe pudgy, and wanting to start a walking routine. I hear footsteps approaching, and the door swings open.

Oh God. The woman before me is perhaps middle aged, but she has got to have the most toned, athletic body I've ever seen.

"Can I help you?" she asks, giving me the once-over with a critical eye.

Riches & Rags

Shit, she definitely saw the shoes. I take a breath and assert myself. "I'm Lane Carson, your new *personal trainer*."

Jennifer Fairweather frowns and then gives a little smirk. "Um, actually, you're not my new personal trainer. I happen to already have one. But he's out of town for three weeks, and your ad said you specialize in long distance running and triathlon, and I'm training for both."

Shiiiiiit. I'm going to absolutely *kill* Billy.

"Great!" I squeak. I don't even know how much I'm getting paid for this, but it better be fucking amazing.

After a slight hesitation, Jennifer sighs. "All right. Let me grab my water bottle and I'll be right out." She closes the door in my face, so I side step my way down the stairs and assume my position behind Rory's stroller. Why didn't I think to bring water and *why* did I have to drink that Venti Caramel Macchiato at Starbucks less than an hour ago to celebrate my first client? I need to pee.

Jennifer comes bounding down the front stairs, looking incredibly impressive in her sleek running gear. "Ready!" she says.

"Okay, let's go," I say, and I start running as fast as my oversized runners can carry me, all the while flexing my feet with each step so the shoes don't fall off. Jennifer calls me and I turn around.

"Hey, slow down! What about stretching, I'm going to tear a ligament!" she calls after me.

Right, stretching, shit. How could I have forgotten? I turn Rory around and continue my awkward run back. It feels about as natural as running in flippers or clown shoes. Damn Denise for not packing proper shoes.

"Apologies, I'm eager to run. I love running," I gush. I put my hands on my hips and start rotating them like my P.E. teachers used to do. Then I try to touch my toes. Crap, almost. I pull my knee up to my chest, and finally Jennifer stops gawking and starts stretching. My heart is pounding in my chest at this mess I've gotten myself into. Rory starts squawking from her stroller. Her squealing soon escalates to an angry little cry.

"Who's the baby?"

"My niece," I mumble. Yep.

"I'm done stretching," Jennifer says after a good eight minutes or so. And this time, she takes off down the street, and I am left scrambling to reposition the stroller and race to catch up. The coffee in my stomach is swishing. I can feel it, but worse—I can hear it. It sounds like bloody Niagara Falls. What was I thinking? I catch up with Jennifer—miraculously—and struggle with all my might to keep up. She doesn't speak but seems to slip into her own rhythm, which I sure as hell wish I could slip into too. My face feels hot, my eyes are watering, and the damn coffee in my stomach sloshes away. I know she must hear it too, and I would give anything for Rory to start crying right now to mask it. My legs are burning, my arms are burning, I feel like I can't get enough air, and to make matters worse, I'm losing ground. Jennifer, in her comfortable jog, is four, then six, then ten feet in front of me. I have to stop, oh my God.

And this is when my shoe flies off, landing with a pitiful thud on the road.

"Sto-op," I yell hysterically. Jennifer spins around and runs back. She jogs on the spot, eyeing me with a menacing glare and looking pissed to say the least.

"You're wasting my time. What kind of bullshit ad was that anyway?"

I'm panting and gasping for air, ripping the other shoe off and reaching for my ballet flats from the stroller undercarriage. But I still have the fight in me. "Well, there are different levels of exercise, how the *hell* could I have known you'd turn out to be an iron woman?"

"Because, you airhead"—Did she really just say that?—"you posted a specialization in long-distance *running*!"

I feel mortified. I don't know what to do, so I turn the stroller in the direction for home and start back.

"You're a fraud, Lane Carson! Get a real job," Jennifer yells after me. "Oh, and Jerry Seinfeld called. He wants his sneakers back!"

I mentally close my ears to that wretched woman and continue striding away, chin held high.

Except, I don't feel proud. I feel pathetic, and there's nothing more I'd like to do than wallow in a little self-pity; but I realize with a start, it's already time to pick up Margo, and I *really* have to pee.

10

After making a quick pit-stop home to pee and ditch the booty shorts, I'm a total of nine minutes late to pick up Margo on her first day, which makes for an anxious kindergartner and a pissed off teacher—I'm not sure which is worse.

"Margo, I'm so sorry," I gush. Margo virtually ignores me but showers Rory with a special "hello" and kiss. My mind races thinking of a way to win her back, and then I've got it!

"Margo, guess what?" I ask, summoning as much excitement as possible. Margo hides her curiosity well and fixes me with a blank stare. "It's your birthday soon," I say, eager for her response. We stroll side by side toward the playground. It seems every kid at school has opted to stay and play to enjoy the glorious weather while it lasts.

"I already know that," Margo answers, clearly unimpressed.

My pulse quickens. Could she possibly know it's already gone by? "How do you know?" I ask, dreading the answer.

"Laura told me before. Is it soon?" Now I have her attention.

Riches & Rags

"It is! We're going to celebrate on Sunday," I say, relieved my cover's not blown.

"Can we have cake?"

"Of course." I laugh. Kids are so simple. Hopefully, last year's Cirque du Soleil-themed party Denise hired a planner for won't perpetuate unrealistic expectations for this year. Margo dashes off to join the other kids on the monkey bars.

Rory is fussing, so I collect her from the confines of the stroller and hold her in my arms, giving her a little bounce on my hip like I've seen other parents do.

A nearby mother is engaged with her young son, and just by sizing her up I can tell she has it all. Her auburn hair is in a perfect chignon, and she's dressed in a fitted blouse, a gray, knee-length fishtail skirt, and Betsey Johnson pumps. This woman couldn't possibly have had a frazzled day, judging by her calm, in-control, and sunny disposition. She reaches into her bag and puts her phone to her ear. From the sounds of it, she's conducting business. Perfect and successful in her own right, must be nice. As I keep one eye on the woman and the other eye on Margo, my own phone rings. I don't recognize the number; it must be a job offer! My heart hammers in my chest, but I assume a dignified, professional air.

"Lane Carson," I answer in a loud voice for all to hear, and wait with eager anticipation.

"Hello, this is an automatic message. Did you know—"

"Oh, shut up," I yell and throw my phone back into my bag with utter disappointment. I seem to have Perfect Mother's attention, because she's gazing at me, a slight frown on her face. I ignore her and instead turn my attention to Rory, making cooing faces at her in an attempt to one-up Perfect Mom. Rory rewards my effort with a deep frown and explodes into a fit of wails. I roll my eyes and plop her back into the stroller, and her cries cease immediately. Thanks kid.

Margo keeps attempting the monkey bars, but she doesn't have the upper body strength. She's determined, though. Another woman has joined Perfect Mother, and the young boy runs to *her*.

"Hi Mommy," he greets her with a hug.

Mommy?

"Bye, Auntie Robin," he calls to Perfect Mother—who I guess is not a mother after all—as she waves and leaves the playground. Right. Maybe there's no such thing as a perfect mother, well aside from my own. Maybe we're all in this together. Maybe—

My phone's ringing! Another number I don't recognize. Bloody telemarketers. "What?" I bark.

"Oh! Hello? I'm looking for Lane Carson, please," says a pleasant male voice.

"Speaking," I say, switching to a friendly, professional tone.

"Hello, Miss Carson, my name is Aaron from BNE Home Securities. You met with our human resources personnel this morning at the job fair."

I want to giggle. B&E Home Securities; he's got to be joking. "Of course," I confirm.

"We were very impressed with you, and though it's a bit outside your realm of PR, well we'd like to offer you a job."

Wow! A Job. Me! My first real job. And how timely; we *so* need the money.

"Thank you for the offer," I purr. "What did you have in mind?"

"It's an assistant managerial role in our collections department."

Say what? Collections? How bloody drab and depressing. "Ohhh" is all I can muster.

Margo waves at me and motions for me to watch her. I flash a fake smile and continue to listen in horror. The

Riches & Rags

thought of having to hound people all day to pay their home security bills is dreadfully dull.

"Unfortunately," he continues—could it possibly get any worse?—"we are only able to pay a starting salary of twenty-six thousand; however, on your annual review, we could *possibly* discuss a marginal increase."

I feel sick, literally like puking—which might be over dramatizing things—but to go from the East Wing to Collections Bitch is more than I can handle.

"The position starts tomorrow. Nine a.m. sharp. See you then." The guy rings off before I've said yes. *Did* I say yes in a roundabout way? Did I just commit to this? No I couldn't have. How can I even be considering this? I drop my phone into my bag, at a loss. I frantically motion to Margo it's time to leave, and I think I know just where I need to go.

We grab a bus on Fourth and head east. Margo is thrilled at the chance to ride a bus, and even Rory seems content to take in all the action.

"*So*, you haven't seen Pops in a long time." I start, unsure how to word things.

"Is Pops your dad or Daddy's dad again?" Margo asks, tapping her chin with one finger.

"My dad."

"Oh."

"Anyway, Pops is a bit…*eccentric*, shall we say?"

"What's centric?"

"He's just different." I picture my dad, shuffling about, with his unkempt hair and the lost look in his eyes. To say he's a shadow of his former self is an understatement.

Margo starts babbling on about how everyone is

different, and apparently to confirm this notion, she starts singing people on the bus, pointing out anything from skin color to body shape to weird clothes. I would be mortified, but most riders have ear buds in and seem blissfully oblivious.

We hop off at our stop, and within a couple minutes' walk, we arrive at Dad's building. To think my dad used to be well respected—he had a gorgeous house in Kits and a good life. Then he lost his wife, and consequently his mind; and this spiraled to the loss of his job as an electrical engineer, and finally, to the loss of the house. Now, he rents a modest one-bedroom in a subsidized building. I was always disheartened that Micky refused to support him. Micky dismissed him as a nut job. And maybe he is—but he's still my dad. The last time I visited, Dad seemed to have trouble managing his daily life—like forgetting to eat, not grocery shopping, and not bothering with house work. I sigh at the sad thought of what he's become.

Here we go! I press the buzzer code and wait. No answer. Margo and I turn to each other and shrug. Then we're buzzed in, just like that, without having to say who it is. How odd. We ride the elevator up and approach his door. I give Margo a firm reminder to keep her hands to herself and behave nicely. I knock and wait. How long has it even been since I've seen him? It's been a couple years at least. We hear footsteps, and then the door opens, and there's Dad!

Only he's not what I had expected. I stagger back in disbelief. The man greeting us is the man my Dad once was, only older.

"Laney! *Unbelievable!* I thought it was someone else. How wonderful." He comes forward and envelopes me with a warm, tender hug. I'm so taken aback, I barely return his embrace.

"Dad?" I croak in disbelief.

Riches & Rags

He appears to not hear me and turns his full attention to the girls. "Margo! My, how big you are. And this must be my precious grand-baby, Rory." He swings Margo into one of his arms, and I quickly release Rory from her stroller and hand her over. Both girls grin and squeal with delight, and Dad disappears inside with them, leaving me out on the stoop.

Thanks.

I come in, close the door behind me, and begin to take inventory. The home looks impeccably clean... I can't believe this. Countertops are clear, cushions are arranged, and an open window is letting in a soft, fresh breeze. Dad has sunk onto an area rug I don't recognize, and is tickling the girls and chuckling and playing with them. His color is just right, his hair is clean and styled, and his clothes look pressed. What the hell is going on?

Don't get me wrong; I'm overjoyed. Or at least I will be when I have time to properly digest all this. But, I can't help thinking these changes have come as a result of *something*. Has he joined a cult? Has he finally mourned my mom all he could and has just naturally moved on?

"Laney?"

"Huh?"

"I said, would you like a drink?" he asks, standing and catching his breath.

"Oh, uh sure. Whatever you have," I say and follow Dad into the galley kitchen.

Margo wanders around contentedly, inspecting everything, and Rory practices some rocking on her hands and knees; it won't be long before she's crawling.

"Tea?"

"Okay."

Dad opens the cupboard and proceeds to set up tea cups with saucers, milk and cream, and even a tray of what looks like freshly baked cookies. What the fuck? This is like a surreal twilight zone.

"*Dad*," I start, wanting to get to the bottom of this.

"How's life, Laney?" he asks, turning to me, his face attentive and familiar.

Oh boy, where do I begin? "Fine, nothing new," I say, avoiding his eyes. He hesitates, and then nods slowly, as though not totally convinced. "But more importantly," I say, raising my eyebrow, "*you* seem to have a lot going on. Dad, I can't believe how good you look."

Margo comes around the corner holding a '65 Mustang model car. "Pops, this is so cool."

Dad abandons the tea and slides into a chair, pulling Margo onto his lap and showing her the car and explaining all the parts and functions. She shrieks with delight as he shows her the doors, trunk, and hood can open. I shake my head in confusion. His behavior with Margo is exactly the same as how it was with me when I was little—I can't understand where this is coming from. I carry Rory over to see the car, and while the girls are distracted, I go for in for the kill.

"Dad, what's going on? You seem so different from the last time I saw you."

"That was a *long* time ago Laney," he says, but doesn't look up from the car.

"Yes. I realize that. Is there…is there someone new in your life?" I ask, dreading the answer. Oh God, why did I even ask that? I don't want to know the answer.

Dad's eyes lock with mine, and a slow smile spreads across his face.

Holy Shit!

"As a matter of fact, Laney, I *do* have someone new in my life."

"Oh?" I ask, my voice barely a whisper.

"Yes, I'll introduce you when he wakes up."

Riches & Rags

Did Dad just say *he*? *HE*? Dad's *GAY*? No *way*! I feel faint. Did Mom know? Did Dad always know? Wait...does that mean he's *here*? After all these years, I can't believe it. Maybe that's why he was so depressed, because he couldn't be his authentic self. Maybe...

"Don't look so concerned, Lane. I'm sure he'll be happy to meet you."

I gape at him, not having any clue of what to say or what to do next. "Dad...," I squeak, "Dad, I didn't realize..."

"Realize what, honey?"

Okay, now he's playing dumb.

"That you're *gay*." Duh!

Dad frowns, and then laughs a whole-hearted chuckle.

"Honey, I'm not gay." He rolls his eyes and smiles.

What? *Not* gay? "I don't understand. Why, then, do you have a *man* sleeping in your bedroom?" I have a feeling we're heading into uncharted territory.

"He's not a man. Lane, I adopted a son. I have a boy!" Dad announces, his voice overflowing with pride.

I'm gobsmacked and stunned and—Oh My God!—I'm frozen in my seat. I dare not breathe, nor move, nor think.

"He's awake!" Dad says with a grin, and hops out of his chair and disappears down the hall at breakneck speed. My heart stops and I hold my breath in anticipation.

"Who's Pops' boy?" Margo asks, coming over to me, wide eyed. I shoo her away; like I need to discuss this with a four—five-year-old!

Dad rounds the corner, cradling someone covered by a thick blanket in his arms. Dad's face is like a child's bursting with some fantastic secret about to be revealed.

I feel sick.

"Laney," Dad booms, "meet your new *brother*!"

And with that, Dad pulls the blanket away, revealing...

Oh. My God...revealing, a cheeky-looking VENTRILO-QUIST *PUPPET*! My mouth drops open.

"Yeah!" the dummy yells and does a fist pump in the air.

"Is...is this some kind of sick joke?" I blurt out. Instantly I regret opening my big, fat mouth. Dad's face has crumpled. I need to remember how fragile he is.

"I...I'm sorry, Dad," I stammer. I turn my attention to the emerald-eyed, wild-haired dummy, just as Margo comes forward with large eyes. She approaches the dummy with such care, and touches its hand ever so lightly.

"How's it going, toots?" the puppet asks, boasting a New York accent of all things.

I don't believe this.

"Wow, he speaks!" Margo says, her voice rising in awe.

"Of course I speak; do I not have a mouth?" the puppet taunts. Dad kneels down beside Margo so she can get a better look. As for me, I don't know where to look, so I scoop Rory up and trudge over to the window to take in the dismal view.

"What's its name?"

"I'm not an 'its,' toots!" the puppet says. "The name's Riley—Uncle Riley to you."

Now I've heard it all.

"Hi, Uncle Riley," Margo says, settling herself on the floor.

"You look a little young to have a baby, toots." Riley says, pointing to Rory.

"That's my sister, Rory," Margo says.

"I thought it was a boy," Riley says, smacking his forehead. Margo shrieks with giggles.

"And meet your beautiful sister, Lane," Dad says, beaming as he motions to me.

"What's up, Elaine," Riley calls over.

"It's Lane, dumb-ass."

"Lame Dumb-ass, pleasure to make your siblinghood!"

I cringe and shake my head.

"She don't like me so much," Riley says, throwing his head down in a huff.

"Just give her time, son," Dad says, patting Riley's head.

This wouldn't be the most bizarre thing in the world if my dad didn't have to insist the bloody puppet is his *son*. Goes to show, things may look normal again on the outside, but Dad is still a nut job through and through.

"Where's the tea, Pops?" Riley demands. "I wanna cookie too. Chocolate."

"Mind your manners, son. Lane, do you mind?"

Uh, it's not like I'm holding a baby or anything.

"Me too, can I have a cookie?" Margo chimes.

I've lost my appetite. I plunk Rory beside Margo and carry the tea to the table. As I'm pouring the cups of steaming, red tea, the buzzer goes and Dad jumps up to answer it. He beeps the visitor in and hurries over to me, looking a bit anxious. I stop mid pour when I see his face.

"What is it, Dad?"

"Well…um…listen, Laney, I know this might be hard for you. I mean, you haven't seen each other in a very long time."

"Dad! What's up?"

Even Riley has fallen silent at his side.

"Aunt Louisa…" Dad's concerned eyes meet my own. Oh my God, just when I thought the day couldn't get worse.

"Why the *fuck* is she here?" I yelp.

"Lane, *language*!" Dad speaks sternly, which he doesn't do often. Margo is watching us, wide eyed.

"Dad! How could you invite her over when you knew I was here?" I cannot believe this. My late mother's identical twin! I purposely haven't seen her since the funeral. How could I? And now, here she is! There's no escape.

"Lane, with all due respect, Louisa looks after me and

she was invited today, whereas I didn't know you would be here. She'll be just as shocked to see you."

Bullshit!

Riley swings into his upright position and throws his arms around Dad. "Suck it up, Princess. Louisa don't bite."

"Shut up before I break your plastic face."

"You talkin' to me?"

"Do I hear my favorite nephew?"

I stop in my tracks. Her voice! It's just like Mom's voice. I haven't heard her voice in so many years—my mom's voice that is. But I can't even process this, because she's coming in...and three, two, one...

"Oh *my*, Lane!"

There she is. Blonde, soft waves frame her face, so lovely and bright. She's staring at me open mouthed, like a scared animal. Her face! Her eyes! This is so cruel. I want to run to her like a child, but she's just a mirage. With wild eyes, I turn to Margo, scoop up Rory, and make a beeline to the door.

"Mom, what's happening? Why are we leaving? We haven't had cookies!" Margo calls hysterically behind me.

"Take this for the road, toots," I hear Riley say.

Dad can choose to speak as himself or Riley, and he chose Riley. It's like one colossal joke, and the jokes on me. I jab my finger on the elevator button. Margo is at my heel, still whining about leaving. Tears have welled up in my eyes, where they sit blinding me, refusing to spill over. Why can't I cry, *dammit?*

"Oh, Mommy." Margo sees my face, and without respecting the barriers I've always had in place, she hurls herself into my arms, and suddenly I'm holding my girls, holding on to them for dear life. And nothing else matters.

11

On autopilot, I bus home, then feed and bathe the girls, and put them to bed. I'm getting used to using the hot plate, but my cooking is crap at best, and I know it.

Tonight was gummy mac n' cheese with over-steamed broccoli that sagged into a putrid mush when I tried lifting it with a fork.

I can't get my Mom's face out of my mind—well Louisa's face that is. I've texted Billy an SOS, to no avail. I also emailed Micky because his phone still goes to voicemail. I gave him our address at George's, for when he gets back to town. I told him everything is great, which is a massive lie, but I don't want to scare him away further. Why doesn't he call? What if something happened to him?

I pour a tumbler of wine and perch myself on the newly built fire escape. There's enough space for two adults now to sit quite comfortably—and safely.

My phone rings and I grab it, hoping against hopes it's Micky.

Oh—Juliet! "Wow, you're back!" I say, unable to contain my excitement.

"Lane! God, it's good to be home. I missed you so

much. Why don't we meet for a drink tonight? We have so much to catch-up on."

Don't we ever. "Uh, yeah, I can't."

"Why? Do you have plans?"

"Not exactly."

"Great, meet me downtown then!"

"I can't, I can't leave the kids."

"What do you mean?"

Oh this is painful. "Juliet, it's a long story."

I give Juliet a quick rundown of my last month—Micky losing his money, moving into George's attic, the great quest for a job, and my new puppet brother. I leave out the part about Louisa. Better to discuss that in person. Juliet's voice is thick with concern, and she promises to come over right away. I don't even have a buzzer, so I tell her to text when she arrives.

In the meantime, I nurse my drink, and it nurses me.

After a short wait my phone pings, and I scramble back inside and down the two flights of stairs. I swing the door open, and there she is—my best childhood girlfriend. Juliet looks just the same as ever—bright auburn hair, shining blue eyes, and a smile that could end a war. Before I can brace myself, she flings herself at me, squeezing me into a massive bear hug and planting a loud smooch on my cheek. This is my third hug of the day, probably a record.

"Laney! So good to see you! You're looking...um..."

Hmm, well at least you're honest, Juliet. We turn to go inside and almost smack into George. Oh bloody hell, now what?

"Lane!" he barks in his crispy voice, "where are my shoes?"

"How the hell should I know?" I ask, rolling my eyes and pushing past him to the stairs.

"*Because,*" he yells, throwing his hands up, "you needed them this morning. I've been shoe-less all day as a result."

Riches & Rags

I'm about to tell him off, when Juliet pipes up. "Oh no, shoe-less? We have to find your shoes." She turns to me for help. I shrug. I honestly don't remember. Unless they're still in the bottom of the stroller. Or maybe somebody jacked them on the bus. For all I know, Riley took them, the little shit. But anyway I have more to be concerned about than geriatric Seinfeld shoes.

I try to pull Juliet away, but she's now engrossed in conversation with George about his stupid cat and the plight of no shoes, yada yada yada. As I jog upstairs to the attic, I hear her offering to take Piper on this nightly walk since George has no shoes. Juliet was always too kindhearted for her own good. Well anyway I have work to prepare for.

After choosing an outfit for work tomorrow, all black, appropriate for a funeral—after all, my life as I knew it is officially over—I wash up, change into pajamas, and crawl under the covers between the girls. Margo and Rory both snuggle closer. Their child-like scents are sweet and delicate and surprisingly comforting. It's been a hell of a day from the job fair, to the Jennifer Fairweather fiasco, to meeting Riley, to seeing Aunt Louisa. And of course, to top it off, I have the new job. It dawns on me that I never had a chance to ask Dad to babysit tomorrow, which defeats the whole purpose of going to see him. I'll have to call him in the morning. He better be available to watch Rory, because you can take a baby to a job fair, and you can take a baby on a run, but you certainly can't bring a baby to work in an office. Sigh.

There's a faint knock on the door, and Juliet pops her head in.

"Sorry to take so long, Laney. It was really important to George that his cat be taken out. Anyway, I know you're really tired, but know I'm here for you. If there's anything I can do just—"

"Actually, there is something," I say, propping myself up on my elbows. "Any chance you can take Margo to school and watch Rory tomorrow?" Please say yes.

"Of course! I'll be back at eight'ish, does that work?"

"Perfect, you're a lifesaver," I say, and mean it.

"Nighty, night." Juliet retreats, and the door closes softly.

Well, that's taken care of. I flop back on the down pillow, thinking of tomorrow. It's surreal, I have a job!

As I'm drifting off to sleep, I hear the pitter-patter of tiny feet running behind the walls. Mice!

Why am I not surprised?

It's 8:46, and the office is a block away. I'm standing in front of Starbucks, contemplating getting a coffee. I see through the window the lineup is long—but will it take fifteen minutes? Oh screw it; everyone's entitled to coffee, especially those who have to bust their ass in collections for a living.

I assume my place in line and tap my foot in irritation, checking the wall clock every ten seconds. How can it take so long just to get coffee? Come on, people!

8:51: I'm now the third person in line. More foot taping and loud sighing.

8:59: Drink in hand; I begin a great balancing act, trying not to slosh Caramel Macchiato on my black suit, as I refuse to drink out of a plastic lid. Burning, sticky coffee is splashing all over my hand, shit!

9:14: In lobby waiting for the archaic elevator that never bothers to show—I don't blame it.

9:17: Taking the *bloody* stairs up six *bloody* flights.

9:21: Arriving at the BNE office, red faced, panting, and covered in sticky caramel, with clothes blotched in wet coffee. I enter the office, which is shabby and disorganized. Boxes, files, and stacks of loose papers everywhere. The fluorescent lights burn my eyes, and I'm about to turn around, thinking I might be at the wrong suite, when one of the clerks glances up and acknowledges me.

"Can I help you?"

"Yes, my name is Lane Carson and today is my first day," I say. The gal asks me to wait a moment, and I suck back my coffee, trying to absorb as much pleasure as I can because the day's going downhill from here. A red-headed man comes around the corner dressed in a cheap, gray polyester suit and scuffed brown shoes.

"You must be Lane." I recognize his voice from the phone call yesterday. "I'm Aaron Patterson, the director of BNE."

I nod and arrange my features into the closest thing I can muster to a smile.

Aaron's smile falters and he leans closer. "Lane, it's in poor taste to show up late on your first day."

"Yes, well, your elevator operates on sloth mode."

Aaron sighs, but invites me to meet my direct boss. He leads me to a dumpy office, where I'm greeted by Magda, the collections manager.

Magda, a robust woman in her fifties, stands and offers me a warm smile and firm handshake. "Pleasure to meet you, Lane. Aaron tells me you have quite the impressive PR background. I do hope you'll find collections equally satisfying."

Don't hold your breath. "Nice to meet you, Magda."

"Welcome to the family," Aaron says over his shoulder as he leaves us.

Magda smiles again and motions for me to sit. I pull up an ugly tweed chair and wait as she fumbles around on her computer. "So, Lane, we don't have a desk set up for you just yet, and unfortunately I'm stepping into a meeting shortly; but you can review our company portfolio and website. Also, I'd like you to review these two collection folders and tour the call center down the hall. Any questions?"

Yeah, when can I go *home*? "I think that about covers it," I say with false enthusiasm.

"Great. Oh, and you can take your lunch hour at one o'clock. Our office hours are nine to six, in case you didn't already know."

Six? Nobody bothered to bloody mention that tidbit of information, shit. Twenty-six thousand dollars a year for nine-hour days. Is that even legal?

Magda leaves me alone. I sit back with a huff and grip my coffee close for comfort as I regard her office. The poor woman isn't even granted a window, and the walls are so drab it's a wonder she can stay awake. I pull the portfolio closer and flip open the cover, to find some stats on residential break-ins and how BNE's service offers a necessary peace of mind, blah blah. I can't bring myself to waste another second on this shit. I flip it closed.

I wonder what time it is. I pop my phone out to see it's 9:43. That's it? Oooh, I also see I have a missed text from Billy.

> *Lane sorry to miss you last night but I'm making it up to you. Guess who has an audition today? It's at noon downtown for a Budweiser commercial. You're going to rock it!*

What? Is he talking about *me*? I have an audition, just like that?

WTF? Where? How? WTF?

My phone pings with the reply from Billy.

I asked John's assistant to let me know about open auditions for you! You don't even need an agent...though you can send ME the 15%!!

I can't believe I have an audition! My heart starts hammering in my chest, and I dial Billy for the details.

Billy says I have to wear clubbing clothes. The sticky, black suit will never do; which means I'll have to bus home for a change of clothes and then bus back downtown. Billy also says commercials can pay upwards of five thousand dollars!

I shove the BNE folder away in disgust and go off in search of Magda. I finally spot her through a glass door at a conference table with some talking suits. She's facing me, so I figure I'll just stare her down until we make eye contact. I stand at a discreet distance from the door, trying to get her attention, which doesn't work as she's presenting to the group and seems oblivious to anything else. Shit, it's 10:02. I need to leave. Oh, what the hell! I march up to the glass conference door and tap on it hard with my nail. All heads shoot toward the door, and Magda stops mid-sentence. She frowns at me and excuses herself from the group.

"Lane, is there something urgent? I'm making an important presentation."

"It is urgent. I actually need to leave for a few hours, but I should be back by one or so," I say, hoping she'll understand.

She doesn't appear to. She actually looks pissed. "I'm sorry; did you say you need to *leave*? As in, leave work? For three *hours*?"

"That's right. I have a very important audition, and I just can't turn down this opportunity."

"An audition?" Magda echoes.

"That's right. For Budweiser. Listen, I know it sounds far-fetched, but I have two small children and I'm supporting them on my own. I *need* to take every opportunity I can get."

"Lane, this is absurd. I cannot possibly allow you to leave work for an *audition*. Ever!" Before I can protest, Magda retreats into the conference room, closing the glass door in my face.

Now what? I can't *not* go to the audition; we absolutely need the money. It would take me months to make that in collections.

I find Aaron, who's on a phone call that seems to drag on. I realize he's speaking with a customer who keeps tripping their alarm. After listening to this nonsense for what feels like an eternity, I march back to Magda's office, scroll a note about needing to leave with or without her approval, and promise to return by 1:30.

It's 10:43. Just enough time to zip home, change, and bus back to the audition. The excitement and adrenaline of a real audition kick in, and I happily forget all thoughts BNE.

Nobody is home. Juliet must have taken Rory out somewhere, so I quickly change into a skintight, white mini and halter top. I volume-ize my hair and apply a layer of hot pink lipstick, and voila! I look the part.

Once downtown, I feel kind of silly in this barely there skirt and stripper heels, but I stride purposefully to the warehouse where the audition is taking place. Inside, there's a cattle call, and I'm irritated to see I'm probably the oldest one auditioning. By ten years! Nonetheless, I decide the others have nothing on me, and I toss my hair over my shoulder and raise my chin.

Finally, just after 1:15 my name is called, and I enter a room the size of a gymnasium. The warehouse is virtually empty, aside from the two black women seated at a table in the open space. They glare me down and don't even bother with a welcome or introduction. This is so intimidating.

"All right, we're gonna play some music and we want you to dance for us like you're in a nightclub," one girl barks. The music starts blaring from this weak, little ghetto blaster, and I have no choice but to dance. I hesitate for a beat, then begin shaking my hips, all the while feeling ridiculous. Are all auditions like this? Here I am in this vast warehouse, and my audience—from the looks of it—is not appreciating my moves. And I *can* dance. They don't motion to end the music though, so I close my eyes to separate myself from their menacing stares and imagine a packed club, cute guys, friends…

Oh no! My little skirt is wiggling its way up my torso. How embarrassing. Almost baring my butt, I struggle to shimmy the skirt back into place, all the while trying to keep my dancing rhythm. And so it continues; I shake my butt and move my arms to the music while being acutely aware of my rising skirt and tugging it back down in time with the beat.

After what seems like forever, the music abruptly shuts off. The dead air hangs.

"What would you do if you were at a club and a girl came over and splashed her drink in your face?"

What? "Well, I'd ask her why she did that," I say with hesitation, not knowing what the judges want from me.

The girl with the cornrows leans forward accusingly.

"Then you'd be starting something," she says, raising her eyebrow.

I frown again. "Um, *no*. She already started it by splashing her drink in my face!"

"All right then," says the other gal, "what would you do if you were at a club and you were dancing and some guy was grabbing your butt, and you told him to leave you alone, and he didn't?"

"I'd hit him!" I say with absolution. Damn right!

"*What?!*" Both women look horrified, as though I've assaulted *them*. Abruptly they tell me to leave the audition, and I turn away, stupefied.

After changing, I head outside and text Billy, letting him know the audition was so crazy and that they kept quizzing me with these nightclub scenarios. Before putting my phone away, I check the time and am shocked it's already quarter to two.

Back at the office, the elevator comes almost immediately, to my relief, and I ride the car up, dreading a sure-to-be dull afternoon of getting to know the property security industry. Ugh!

Inside the office, I'm making my way back to Magda when I hear Aaron calling my name. "Lane?" He ushers over with an urgency that halts me in my tracks. What's up? "Lane, I'm sorry, but after the stunt you pulled today, I have no choice but to terminate you effective immediately."

"*What?*" He's firing me? "I explained I was leaving. I couldn't turn down that opportunity."

Aaron shakes his head firmly, and I realize he's escorting me back to the elevators.

"Yeah?" I call, my voice rising. I feel the stares from the other colleagues, but I don't care. "Only this morning, you welcomed me to the family. Some family!" I yell. And with a final glare at Aaron, I add, "This is bullshit!"

And the door closes behind me.

My phone pings as if on command, but I ride the elevator down in numbed shock.

Only once I'm outside do I bother reading the text from Billy. And when I read it, it all makes sense. I am officially the world's biggest idiot.

Turns out John's assistant got the information wrong. It wasn't a Budweiser commercial, but a Budweiser promotional for which they wanted girls to hand out free beer in local clubs for $10/hour. Oops.

You've *got* to be kidding.

12

"Margo, just put some damn pants on and let's go!" I holler from the attic door as I struggle to fit Rory into her Baby Bjorn carrier. I've used this once with Margo, I think, and no matter how I fiddle with the straps, Rory is sitting too high, obstructing my view. This is ridiculous. I feel hot and bothered, and sweaty, and bloody short fused.

Margo is sulking in a heap by the dresser, refusing to wear anything aside from her bathing suit. "I'm not wearing them!" she snarls in my direction, and I roll my eyes.

Total drama queen. I adopt a fake, patronizing voice and try again. "Margo, it is freezing. You want to go to the beach for your birthday, but you need to wear some pants, otherwise we *can't go*."

"I'M GOING SWIMMING!" She screams with such intensity, even I'm taken aback.

"Margo! You were with me when they closed the pool. It's almost October, the pool is closed!" I let out a frustrated groan and grab my phone to check the time.

"NO!" Margo screams.

"We're supposed to be there right now, come *on*." I set Rory down, and she starts practicing her backwards shimmy crawl. I stalk over to Margo and grab her by the arms so we're face to face. "Margo," I yell, "get some bloody pants on. Or a dress and tights, *I don't care*."

Margo starts thrashing around, red faced, and I let her go in a huff and yank the dresser drawer open. I grab a pair of pink pants. Surely she can't protest—they're *pink*! I try unsuccessfully to wrestle them onto her, which only escalates things until she's screaming and grabbing at my hair. She's baring her teeth like a wild animal, like something possessed. I have absolutely never seen her like this. She starts sobbing uncontrollably, and I can't decide if I feel angry because she's being a spoiled little brat, or sorry for this whole fight. It is her birthday after all, or at least she thinks it is.

I stride across the attic back to Rory and hunker down beside her, then pull out my phone and text Billy, instructing him not to meet us at the beach anymore, but to come over ASAP. Margo continues to sob and hiccup and kick. Rory watches me with concerned blue eyes and points to her sister. I give her a small smile and shrug my shoulders. Rory seems to accept this and reverts back to crawling practice, and I try to remain calm while waiting for Billy. Finally, he texts, and I carry Rory downstairs to let him in.

"She's possessed," I announce, as I swing open the door.

Billy's eyes sparkle in apparent amusement, and he waves me away as though it's nothing. "She's going through so much; this is totally normal." Billy turns his attention to Rory and mushes his face against hers, and she coos and squeals as she reaches out for his hair.

"What do you mean she's going through so much? She's five, what could be so difficult?"

"Come on, Lane. Her father is gone and the only home she's ever known is gone, not to mention the staff she knew. That was her world."

I consider this as we mount the stairs. Margo doesn't talk about that life much anymore, and she seems settled in her new school. Upstairs Margo's quivering and hugging her knees to her chest.

"Hey love," Billy calls, as he passes Rory to me and takes a seat beside Margo. She ignores him, but after a few minutes of gentle consoling, she nods at something he says and rises slowly to her feet. She pulls open a dresser drawer and pokes around, finally pulling out a pair of faded, pink tights. Billy helps her pull them on, and she pussyfoots over to the door, eyeing me like a timid animal, then swiftly grabs for her running shoes. I guess now wouldn't be the time to fuss about wearing tights with no skirt or dress, and instead, mouth "thank you" to Billy. After successfully strapping Rory into the carrier, we're all set to go to Margo's beach birthday party—providing the drama stays at bay.

Outside, it's absolutely freezing! The cold air whips at my face, and I shudder to think we'll be spending the next couple of hours beach side for Margo's party. This is when I wish I had money for Chuck E. Cheese—well...on second thought...

Storm clouds hover above, blanketing the morning with a doomed probability of rain. Margo dashes ahead, as Billy and I walk in stride down Point Grey Road toward Kits Beach, with Rory taking in the sights from her carrier.

Billy gives me a once-over and breaks into a mischievous grin. "I take it you won't be up for beer commercial auditions anymore?"

I smile wryly and shake my head. "Just not the Budweiser ones."

"Well, I hope you'll consider pursuing the acting thing anyway."

"Sure. Why not? It was mortifying but definitely an unexpected experience, and I have to admit the whole thing intrigues me."

"If you're interested, John—"

"Who's John?"

"Oh my God, Lane, my *boyfriend*!"

"Keep your pants on, it's not like it's a unique name, okay?"

"Whatever. Anyway, John Childs, aka my *boyfriend*—"

"Of like, three weeks."

"Longer than that. Anyway, let me finish. John was telling me about an acting class he'll be teaching next week that sounds pretty…unorthodox. It might be good for you."

"I don't have time."

"You also don't work. Of course you have time. Plus, it's just a one-day workshop. And between your dad, Juliet, and I—babysitting should be covered."

"Fine, I'm in." This should be interesting.

We've entered Kits Beach Park, and Margo turns around and waves back to us with great enthusiasm. From her wide smile and jovial step, you'd never know she just had a mass meltdown. But I guess that's kids for you. We pass Kits Pool where the seagulls have reclaimed their winter oasis and float around the once clear waters in peace. Up ahead, I spot a group at a picnic bench decked in a pink table cloth and balloons, which must be Dad and Juliet. For Margo's sake, I even invited Laura, and was disappointed—but not really surprised—when she didn't bother replying.

Margo races up to the picnic table, squealing and grabbing at the balloons. Juliet helps her untie a couple, and Margo gallops back to us and hands a balloon to Rory. "I'll have pink, and you can have purple."

"Thanks, Margo, that's sweet," I manage to say before

she dashes back to the table. Rory grips the string and gazes up, mesmerized. Dad and Juliet are unloading salads, sandwich toppings, and treats from their picnic baskets.

George's crotchety voice calls out to Margo, "Happy Birthday, kiddo," and I realize with a start I totally forgot I'd invited him. I guess we all could have come over together—oops.

"George, this is my dad, Roger, and of course you've met Billy and Juliet."

George nods at Dad and turns with fondness to Juliet. "*You*, my dear, are an angel."

Juliet beams as she shifts over to make room for George.

Dad says, "Margo, my dear, somebody special wants to say happy birthday." Then he leans over to retrieve something from under the picnic table. My heart sinks, as I know very well who that something is.

Dad pulls out a baby carrier, and for a second I think it's Rory's, until I realize with horror the carrier belongs to none other than my new brother. Sure enough, Riley appears looking just as wild and freaky as the last time I saw him; only this time he's nestled into his carrier like a smug-faced infant. Actually, he looks even wilder with his out-of-control, electrocuted-looking yellow hair sticking out from the top of the carrier.

Riley does his now-familiar fist pump, yelling "Yeah!" and I tear my eyes away to gauge the others' reactions. Juliet looks politely amused. George looks like he swallowed a lemon—but then that isn't the first time—and Billy remains expressionless, which to me is most amusing of all. I dissolve into giggles, and Billy turns to me, his eyes widening ever so slightly.

"You got a problem, Elaine?" the Muppet taunts, turning to me. I roll my eyes and decide to ignore him, and instead, concentrate on undoing my own carrier for Rory.

Riches & Rags

Billy comes over to help me, relieved for the distraction, I'm sure, and conversation resumes, with Dad asking George about his life in the navy.

"So, who's your dad's new friend?" Billy asks, eyes twinkling with delight.

"Why don't you ask your Mom?" I mutter, pain etched in my voice.

"I don't know what that's supposed to mean, but speaking of parents, you won't *believe* what happened."

I pull Rory's bottle out of the diaper bag, and she grabs for it eagerly. I swing her around so she's lying on my lap and I can watch her little cherub face as she suckles the bottle. Her blue eyes lock into mine, and I stare, mesmerized.

"Lane?"

Hmm? "Oh, what happened?"

"The investigator! He tracked down my birth father!"

I snap my head up. "Really?"

"Yes, he's still in Haiti, of course, on Gonave Island, and he's a single father with six grown kids and *eleven* grandchildren."

"Wow, you won't be short family any time soon," I say, feeling stung.

"Can you believe this? I have his contact info, so now all I have to do is get in touch."

"That's fantastic, Billy!"

"Come on everyone, let's eat," Dad says, so we take our places at the table.

I'm biting into a piece of cantaloupe, when Billy jabs me in the ribs, causing me to almost inhale the melon.

"What the fu—"

"John's coming," Billy cries, his voice thick with anticipation. I turn to where Billy has directed his gaze and catch my breath. I'd recognize those gorgeous golden waves anywhere, and that prance and theatrical flair is unmistakable.

It's Micky's client, Mr. Fenwig. But why...? I check to see if someone else is behind him—Billy can't possibly be referring to *Fenwig*. But their eyes are locked and both are grinning. Holy fuck.

Beside me, Billy stands to greet him and announces with pride, "Everyone, this is my boyfriend, John Childs."

I'm motionless, eyes transfixed on John's face.

Fenwig charms us with a gorgeous smile and a little wave. He greets each of us individually, exchanging hellos, until finally it's my turn, and the recognition flickers in his eyes. "Oh!" is all he can say.

I pass Rory to Dad and stand to eye him head on. "Why don't you tell Billy your real name," I say, a tame but growing rage building in my core. Billy watches us, eyes darting back and forth. "Why don't you go ahead and tell Billy," I continue, raising my voice, "that you're *married*?" The audacity of this slime-ball playing sweet and generous Billy is more than I can take.

Fenwig's eyes dart back to Billy, then to the group, and back to me.

"Can I have a word in private?" he asks me in a calm and soothing voice.

Unbelievable. "Uh, don't you think it's Billy who you should be having a word with?" I cross my arms in front of my chest. Fenwig sighs and shakes his head. My eyes narrow at him and after a beat I throw my hands in the air. "Fine," I say, as I stalk away in a huff, Fenwig and Billy at my heels.

"What's going on?" I hear Billy asking Fenwig in a loud whisper. I can't mistake the panic in his voice.

"Please—slow down," Fenwig calls, and I spin around on my heel to face him.

"All right. Go ahead. You have thirty seconds."

"My real name is John Childs."

Riches & Rags

"Bullshit!"

"It is. I'm an acting instructor...and an actor. I was hired to play the character of Mr. Fenwig."

WHAT? My head is spinning, I just don't understand. I'm standing before John/Fenwig, slack mouthed, trying to place the pieces of what he's telling me—but they just don't add up.

"Fenwig was my husband's *client,* not a character." Unless there is a real Fenwig that couldn't make the meeting, so an actor was hired. This is nuts. "Who hired you?" I ask. John/Fenwig gives Billy a pained look and turns back to me.

"Your husband, Mr. Carson, hired me."

I suck in my breath trying to digest this. "What were your instructions? W-what was the plan?"

"Well, if I remember correctly, you left in a rather dramatic fashion, and I was immediately dismissed as my talent was no longer needed."

"Were you paid?"

"Yes, handsomely."

I shake my head and raise my eyes to Billy, who looks utterly shattered for me.

"So if I hadn't left, what was your role as Fenwig?"

"I was to accompany my 'wife,' Mrs. Fenwig—"

"Was she an actor too?"

"No."

I sigh in disbelief and motion for him to continue.

"I was to play the role of this big shot billionaire and was told half an hour into the voyage I was supposed to excuse myself with a bad case of sea-sickness and retreat to a private cabin."

"And what were you to do in the cabin?" I ask with a frown.

"They didn't care. They said I would have a room attendant for any culinary requests or special needs, but I was to pretty much stay in the cabin unless I was summoned—in their words."

"I don't believe this," I say, knowing full well I do. But why did Micky hire an actor, and what was his ultimate plan had I not left the ship? I prompt John for more info, but he doesn't know anything more. This just doesn't make sense. We've talked in circles and there's nothing more to discuss, so we turn around and head back to the party.

"You okay?" Billy asks, his eyes pained. I feel dizzyingly confused and suddenly freezing. I shudder and John places a warm hand on my back. For once I don't flinch.

"I brought a thermos of steaming rooibos tea," he offers, and I nod, feeling momentarily comforted. As for the Fenwig plan that never went down, I'll have to brood over it later. But for better or worse, this is Margo's birthday, and Micky's not going to ruin it, dammit.

I raise my chin and give a cheerful wave as we approach the picnic table. Billy leans in and whispers, "Atta girl!"

13

"Happy birthday, dear Margo," we all sing. Margo is seated at the head of the picnic table, beaming.

Though this was such a simple party, it's all she really needs. I guess *we're* all she really needs. I smile privately, thinking about this special, unique little girl who, up until recently, I didn't know all that well. I feel an unexpected warm glow resonating through my body, and my smile widens into a full-fledged grin. Margo leans over to blow out her candles.

"Wait! Don't forget to make a wish," I call out. She pauses and her eyes meet mine for a brief moment before she leans in and blows out all five candles in one shot. We all clap, and I can't help but wonder if her wish has to do with Micky coming home.

The thought of Micky makes me queasy; I think about skipping the cake. Then again, for good luck, I should probably have some. Especially since Juliet is the most incredible baker. Dad hands me a plate of cake, and I dive my fork into the decadent Belgian chocolate and pop it into my mouth. It's absolutely divine—the richness is out of this world, but it's balanced by not being overly sweet. We're absorbed in our dessert, and conversation has all but died.

"Can we eat this on the sand?" Margo pipes up.

"No, don't be silly, we're already at the table," I say, rolling my eyes.

"I don't mind," George offers. I shoot him an inquisitive look. Someone took their happy pills today. Everyone echoes George's sentiments, so I shrug and stand with Rory in one arm and my cake in the other.

We clamber over the logs and onto the beach, and collapse into the soft, cool sand. Rory's eyes widen as she makes for a grab at the sand, which falls through her chubby fingers like an hourglass. She babbles and claps, while Margo regards her with a smile. I lean in to Billy and whisper, "Micky shouldn't be missing this. He shouldn't miss his daughter's first encounter with sand, and he definitely shouldn't miss his daughter's birthday. My patience with him is wearing thin." Billy stares ahead but nods, apparently lost in thought. I sigh and turn my attention back to my chocolate cake, which I should be enjoying right now. I should be enjoying my daughter's birthday and the company of family and friends, but to be honest I feel weary and tired.

I guess Dad overheard what I said because he leans in with an eager face. "Laney, why don't I take the girls back to my place for the afternoon? You can pick them up after supper; but in the meantime, take a bit of a break…I think you could use one."

My first reaction is to say "no, don't worry about it," but Juliet and Billy are nodding their heads in tandem. Margo's eyes are bright and pleading at the prospect of another visit to Pops' house. Not to mention quality time with Uncle Riley.

But Riley shrieks in his crazy Brooklyn accent. "Not happening!"

"Now son," Dad says in a mock stern voice, "that's no

way to treat your own flesh and blood. We'll have a great time."

I shake my head and stretch out onto my stomach, absently stirring the sand with a twig as Dad and Riley duke it out. When's this party over?

Juliet leans in, giving me another affectionate squeeze. "You so deserve some quiet time for yourself. Why don't you take your dad up on his offer?"

I glance at her caring face and warm blue eyes and then I smile, mirroring her.

"Okay."

And so it's settled.

"I can't believe I'll have time to myself. Do you want to hang out? You can tell me all about your trip, and I can actually give you my undivided attention."

"No," Juliet says, pulling her auburn hair into a ponytail. "Another time, for sure. But you need to be on your own. Crap, I think I felt a raindrop."

I wait a couple of seconds, and sure enough, I feel not one but two drops, and then too many to count. Rain starts pelting down around us in a deluge that appears almost artificial, like on a movie set. We all scream as we snatch up our belongings and run for cover.

We huddle under the large overhang from the Boathouse Restaurant until the pouring rain subsides. Margo uses the opportunity to treat the showers like one big lawn sprinkler, and dashes out from the shelter to twirl and laugh and literally sing in the rain. We look on, shaking our heads and smiling.

To her surprise, and our relief, the rain dissipates. Dad walks us back to George's house, chattering the whole way with George, who seems genuinely receptive. They're talking fishing—I'm just thankful Riley, who's in his baby carrier, is keeping his trap shut.

At home I pack the girls' belongings, lead them outside,

and fasten Rory in her stroller. I feel the unfamiliar pull at my heartstrings as I say goodbye to the girls and watch Dad, Margo, and Rory disappear down the street.

Upstairs, the attic is silent. Aside from the occasional car driving by or the faint sound of birds rejoicing in their post-rain glory, it's going to be one hell of a quiet afternoon. I need to make the most of it, though; because before I know it, I'm going to be running off my feet again. Especially when I start working…if I ever get a job, that is.

I wander into the bathroom and draw steaming water into the claw-foot tub. Denise had packed a small bottle of gardenia essential oil, and I pour in a generous portion and lower myself into the decadent oasis. The waters smell heavenly, and I'm instantly brought back to my East Wing. How I took it all for granted—the leisure time, the affluent lifestyle, even Micky. To this day, after years of marriage and supposedly knowing him so well, some things remain a mystery, like Micky hiring an actor to ambush our anniversary of all things.

What would my life be like if we hadn't met at all? My stomach churns at the thought of that fateful night Micky swept in like a shining knight to save me. It was so long ago, over a decade, and yet in a way it feels like it was just yesterday.

We lived in a shabby apartment on the east side, Dad and I. It hadn't even been a year since we buried Mom, and Dad was in a bad place, to say the least. He was deeply depressed and on long-term leave from work; and the money from his disability barely covered the necessities. Dad was unpredictable with any money he did have. It

Riches & Rags

wasn't unusual for him to cash his disability check and come home with most of it missing. His glazed eyes and delayed reactions were part of the depression—he seemed a million miles away, and I couldn't for the life of me understand his logic.

Sometimes, on impulse, he would give away his money; other times, he would carry the wad of money, set it down somewhere, and forget it. Or he would blow it on the most absurd purchases. Like the time he brought home an inflatable lounge pad for a pool, though we didn't have a pool. Or when he went AWOL in the hair care aisle of a drugstore, bringing home everything from curling irons (yes, more than one), tubs of hair gel, hair accessories, and synthetic extensions.

Why? That was always my question. Why couldn't the money go to the things we desperately needed, like food, clothing, and rent for our decrepit apartment.

So I got a job. I wanted to model, but my size 7 was considered far too curvy. At 18, I had the looks and the youth, and the naivety to go along with them. No, I didn't become a prostitute or a stripper. But I felt degraded nonetheless.

I was a brand promotions model, and I didn't mind the car shows and corporate launches, and such. Though one night, my usual agent couldn't accompany the models to the launch of a new casino in Surrey, so she sent this slime-ball, Rick.

I was naked and painted to reflect the casino's raunchy theme. Instead of doing something artistic, the artist played up the "sex sells" notion and accentuated my already full chest with metallic swirls of paint on my boobs and gold sequins on my nipples. Usually the art was tasteful and gave the appearance that I was clothed, but this was worse than being naked.

"I need your heels on, babe, it's ShowTime!" Rick called,

waltzing into the dressing room, reeking of cigarettes and booze. He took his sweet time looking me over, while licking his lips and rubbing his hands together. My heart quickened as I twisted back, wide eyed, to the body paint artist.

"You look amazing!" she breathed, admiring her work.

In the mirror, I saw my hair was teased and volume-ized and my eyes were heavy with make-up and false lashes. I had metallic bull's-eyes for boobs too. To my horror, when I turned around, I also saw that my ass had been painted to mirror two ripe cherries.

"Hurry the fuck up," Rick snarled. I scrambled for those ruby-red patent leather shoes with the six-inch platform stripper heels and struggled with the straps, while he circled me like a ravenous lion set to devour its prey. I stood wobbling, and he grabbed my arm, yanking me all the way to the main games floor.

"All right, you're on blackjack. Literally," Rick said, hacking a wicked, raspy smokers' cough. He led me to the table, which was draped with some felt material. "Help me with this, will you?" We spread the protective felt onto the blackjack table. The felt was identical to the game board.

Rick turned to me with a demonic gleam in his eye. "Climb aboard."

Wait. *What?* I glanced in confusion from the table to Rick and back to the table.

After a beat, he rolled his eyes and hoisted me up, as I let out a shriek of disbelief. "Doors open in a few minutes. Your job is to be provocative on this table. The casino isn't holding back. This is an adult entertainment facility and, well, the adults want to be entertained." He gave a meaningful look and sauntered off in the direction of the dressing rooms, no doubt to prep the other models.

Meanwhile, I perched awkwardly on the table, with my legs to the side and my hand covering myself. I was terrified of what would happen next. How far did they expect me to go with the "entertainment"? I considered bolting, but dressed like I was (or wasn't), not to mention being all the way out in Surrey, I stayed as if Velcroed to the felt. Plus, we needed the money; and for this, I would get two hundred dollars plus tips. *Tips for what?* a small voice said in the back of my mind. But the question was momentarily forgotten when loud music starting pumping and a throng of people, mostly men, poured onto the casino floor.

My heart raced, pounding in my chest, and my breath was shallow. I tried to control my breathing and sit perky on the table like I was enjoying this. The first cluster of men rounded the corner and goggled at me, naked and posing. There were five guys in their twenties and thirties with drinks in hand, obviously ready for a good time. I was slightly amused at their expressions, watching them exchange looks with their dropped jaws, unable to hide their surprise and excitement. I felt less awkward and smiled under the thick false lashes. I even managed to toss my hair and give a little wave. The guys swarmed around me like bees.

"What the fuck are you doing?"

Huh? My smile faltered as I reluctantly turned my attention to Rick, who had appeared out of nowhere.

"What are you talking about?" I hissed through my frozen smile.

"Bottoms up! I told you, they want nasty, and perched here like a little fucking priss with your legs glued together isn't going to leave a memorable casino launch with the guests. You hear me?"

"Well, what do you expect me to do?" I asked, immediately dreading the answer and fearing whatever sick vision he wanted played out.

Rick leaned in, his disgusting face so close, his sick breath rank and hot. "I want you to gyrate! Dance, move, get on all fours like a dog, show that cherry ass and shake it like a white flag in their goddamn faces." He straightened and took a step back, but remained firmly planted, his shark-like eyes boring into mine.

I shuddered and tried to move my hips to the music. I felt light-headed, and the room took on a contorted sort of view. Things started spinning. The men who'd seemed so fascinated with me moments before appeared hungry and cruel, their eyes begging for more. I could feel my face was hot and probably red. My throat was tight. The room spun. I swayed. Rick was back in my face, this time yelling. One guy leaned in and flicked my nipple. I jerked away, shocked. His friends laughed. Then another came forward to grope my other boob, his ugly fat thumb circling my nipple. All the while, Rick was spitting in my face to give more. A choke welled up in my throat and tears pooled in my eyes. I covered my face with my hands, until I realized there was a commotion.

I took a peek through my fingers and saw some guy pushing the men that grabbed me. He was beautiful, in control and protective, and I knew then I'd be okay. The perverts cowered and slunk away, leaving Rick and the beautiful mystery man face to face.

"Back off, these are guests. They're welcome to visit with the lady," Rick barked, waving around his nicotine-stained finger.

The beautiful man turned his attention to me, and his back on Rick, to my relief. "Miss?" he said, extending a powerful hand, which I accepted with gratitude. He helped me off the blackjack table and draped my shoulders with his

Riches & Rags

suit jacket. I shivered and took a step closer to him, while Rick went on a tangent, yelling his ugly little man-face off. "Come on," said my rescuer, as he lead me away.

"Now just wait. She's employed by Dynasty Promotions. This is her job," Rick complained, panic rising in his voice.

The beautiful man stopped and turned to me. "How old are you?" he asked, loud enough for Rick to hear.

For once I felt I could look Rick in the eye without terror. "Seventeen," I answered, loud and clear.

"*Seventeen?*" Rick squeaked.

"Apparently, you were just caught sexually exploiting a minor, *a child*. If I were you, dirt-bag, I'd start running."

Rick gazed in apparent horror from the guy to me and back again. Then he turned on his heel and actually started running.

The small crowd that had gathered seemed to enjoy the drama and whooped. I let the mystery man accompany me to the change-room so I could retrieve my purse and put some clothes on.

After I'd changed, he walked me outside into the rainy night. "I should properly introduce myself. Michael Capello," he said, extending a formal hand. I laughed and shook it. Micky's vivid, hazel eyes twinkled as he gazed into mine.

"Lane Carson. I...I can't thank you enough."

Micky waved a hand like it was no big deal. "Where do you live, Lane?"

"East Van."

"Can I give you a lift?"

I nodded with relief. The reality of what could have happened started to set in as we stood together and waited for the valet to bring his car. I started shaking from nerves, and Micky put a consoling arm around my shoulder.

"So what are you doing out here? How did you get mixed up in all this?"

I stared at my feet, not knowing where to start. "It wasn't like this before," is all I could say.

"Well, I should hope not," he said with a good natured laugh.

A gorgeous, black Maserati rolled up and the valet hopped out and gave Micky a discreet bow. Micky slipped a bill in his hand, and the valet attendant dashed to open the passenger door for me. I lowered myself into the impressive machine, noting the delicious smell of expensive leather.

Micky and I took off with a slight screech that sent shivers of excitement down my spine. Then we drove a few minutes in companionable silence.

Finally, to break the ice, I gave him a sideways glance and said, "You're not going to try any moves on me tonight? You know, rescue me from one sexually charged environment, only to replace it with another?" I laughed, trying to make light of it.

Micky's eyes remained glued to the road, his expression stoic. "You're just a child."

Ouch. The rejection burned. I lifted my chin. *Little does he know.* "I'm eighteen," I said.

"You said you were seventeen."

"I said that to scare Rick."

Micky gave me a look of disbelief, but started laughing after realizing I was telling the truth. "You think quickly on your feet, Lane. I like that. But seriously, how did you get started in this, uh, line of work?"

I sighed and sat in silence for a minute as we sped along the Pattullo Bridge, a light rain misting the windows.

"My Mom died. My dad is depressed and unable to work. Money is tight to say the least. I wanted to model... but got a job doing corporate promotions instead. It's always been sexy, but never have I been in anything remotely dangerous or uncomfortable like tonight."

Micky nodded, his eyes on the road. "So, who's taking care of you?"

Tears stung my eyes as I thought of my seemingly perfect life just a short time ago, with two caring parents and anything I could want or need.

"Apparently, nobody," I answered in a choked voice. Micky's eyes met mine, and we drove in contemplative silence until I gave him my address.

When we pulled up to my shabby building, Micky insisted on opening my door and escorting me inside and up to the third floor. He declined my offer to come in, as I knew he would, and left graciously. I thought I'd never see him again and was saddened at the thought. Never in my wildest dreams did I expect the small but delicate bouquet of orchids the next day, or the invitation to a picnic on the beach.

We were inseparable from then on. At our wedding ceremony, he wrote his own vows, saying how he would stand by me and protect me all his days. How I would never have to worry or be alone again.

Well, *Micky*—I sit, bitter faced and shriveled in bathwater now gone cold—you're a son of a bitch *liar*.

14

"He's a dick! I don't think he even wanted a family at all, he only liked the *idea* of us," I yell out to my cell phone that's on speaker mode, as I struggle to install curtain rods into the ceiling for my makeshift canopy. This is the problem with the lack of a proper four-poster bed, big design ambitions, and nine foot ceilings.

"Well, maybe he's not a dick." Juliet's voice rings out in the attic. "You don't know for sure. You don't know what he was planning. I mean, it was your anniversary, after all. Who knows?"

"Who knows is right…maybe he was planning on murdering me! Do you think?" This thought has never occurred to me until now. Oh my God!

"Lane! You're getting paranoid on me. He hired an actor, not a hit man."

"Well, maybe he *is* a hit man. A hit man conveniently *posing* as an actor. Maybe Billy's in danger?"

"Lane, you're wild. Your imagination is off the charts. So, switching gears—how's the job search?"

"Oh don't remind— AAAAH," I scream as I lose my

Riches & Rags

balance and land with a horrible thud on the floor, the screwdriver thankfully pointed away from me.

"Lane? You all right?"

I regain my balance and try again, climbing back onto the bed and reaching as high as I possibly can. "Aside from almost impaling myself, I'm fine. Anyway, the job thing blows. Money's dwindling, and I keep applying for jobs to no avail." I tighten the last screw and rest my arms at my side. One rod up, two to go. "I'll figure something out."

"You always do."

We both laugh. This is true.

"Anyway, how are your classes going?" I ask.

"Well, actually..." Juliet pauses, and I motion to the phone to go on and then realize she can't see me.

"Well what?"

"I've actually decided not to go back to law school."

"Oh. Like take another semester off? Did you not get your fill traveling?"

"Well, that's just it. I realized I don't really want to practice law."

"*Seriously?* That's it? But you're supposed to write your bar exam this year. You're so close."

Juliet sighs, and my frown deepens. Juliet has always been the rational one, a planner, and more importantly, a doer. "What does Tom say?"

"Well, let's just say that didn't end well."

"*What?*" They broke up? I can't believe it. Juliet and Tom were together for...well, for years. I suddenly feel sheepish for not having asked how things were going before. How is it my drama overshadowed everyone else's? "I'm sorry," I say, and mean it. What a crappy friend. Crap, crap, crap.

"Don't be. We just changed into different people, or maybe I did. We outran our course."

"Well. Okay, so what are you going to do? Career wise?"

"Don't laugh."

"Promise," I say, as I stand up and take another stab at installing the rods. If only I were a few inches taller...

"I want to be a geriatric caregiver."

What? I almost lose my balance, but lucky for me, this time I catch myself. "Why the hell would you want to do *that?*"

Juliet giggles in her good-natured way and goes on to tell me all about her newfound realization that she feels most at ease caring for people, for seniors in particular, because of their vulnerability, appreciation for the present, and the great stories they share. I half listen as I concentrate on measuring and screwing these bloody brackets.

"Hey!" I say, remembering something. "I know a business for you. Geriatric personal training." I recount my story of running with Jennifer Fairweather, and then admit I would best be suited for old and slow clients.

"You mean Senior Fitness Specialists. Yeah, it's a certification."

Of course it is.

I'm tired of talking about old people, and I really need to concentrate here; so I ring off and go back to my job at hand.

When all rods are firmly in place, I locate the box with my canopy and carefully raise the peach silks from their cardboard entrapment. I carry the fine fabrics like a delicate baby and send a telepathic thank you to Billy. I gingerly climb onto the bed and, with utmost care, tie the satin ribbons in place.

When I've finished tying the thirtieth ribbon, I stand back and sink into my bed. The mattress isn't luxurious but I breathe a sigh of pure bliss as I watch the billowing silks cocooning me. This is my haven. One little part of the world where I can come to, to rejuvenate, escape, and just be.

I lie back with my hands under my head and let a whole hour (or maybe more) slip by, before pulling myself together and getting ready for the bus ride to Dad's. Goodbye solitude, it was nice while it lasted.

Lucky for me, I'm headed east, so the bus is relatively quiet for rush hour. Quiet, meaning I actually get a seat. It's a seat near the front, where I'm sandwiched between some punk dude and a big man, and we're facing a row of passengers. They all seem to be staring at me, so I pull a face and allow myself to indulge in daydreaming about my Range Rover. Just this once, I try not to dwell, but it was so lovely. As I envision myself in comfy leather seats, sunroof slightly tilted, letting in the West Coast salty air, blasting Rihanna's "Diamonds," and—

My phone's ringing.

I yank it out and grin when I see Billy's name on the display.

"Let me guess? You and John broke up, so my free acting class is canceled?" I tease. I catch a man eyeing me with interest, obviously listening in to my conversation. I inch away, wishing for the hundredth time not to be riding public transit.

"Nope," Billy says, his breathless voice sounding excited. "Guess again."

"You and John eloped and you're going to fly us all to the Mayan Riviera to celebrate?"

"Uh-uh. But close! I *am* at the airport."

"Really?" I ask, leaning forward in my seat and straining to hear. I can now make out the female voice of an announcer making a boarding call. Did she say *Haiti*?

"You're going to HAITI?!" I yell, shocked. Now I have the attention of all the passengers. I glare at them, wishing I had a stick or something to swat them with.

"Yes. Isn't it exciting? I called my birth father after the party. I just picked up the phone and called him—they're only three hours ahead. And he wants to meet me, like right away. I can't believe it! This is a dream."

"Wow," is all I can muster.

"Tell me about it. They just made the final boarding call, so I've got to go, Laney. But I'll be in touch when I can."

And just like that, he rings off leaving me stammering and wanting more. What about his business? How can he just up and go? I wonder what John thinks of all this, but I guess I'll find out next week.

"It's me!" I holler at the intercom, and am buzzed into Dad's building. I take the stairs and let myself into the apartment.

"Suck that gut in, toots!" Riley shrieks in his high-pitched Brooklyn accent. A peal of giggles from Margo follows.

What's going on?

"Just...almost... aah. Suck in your gut again, toots. I can't do up the tape!"

I round the corner and—why am I not surprised? *Really.*

"I've never seen a puppet change a diaper," I say, shaking my head.

Riley whirls his freakish face around to greet me. "Yeah! Babysitting's over!" Dad is of course lurking behind him and gives a cheery wave.

"MOMMY!" Margo rips through the small apartment

and lunges into my arms—which feels pretty nice. I smile at her and set off to find Rory. She's under the kitchen table and grins at me, displaying two new baby teeth. I drop my bag on the floor and crawl under the table to greet her, with Margo giggling and wiggling alongside.

"You wanna go camping? Park's outside." Riley's seated on the floor beside me, and Dad is speaking for him from the kitchen.

"Not around here, thanks," I mutter under my breath.

"I've been sweating my balls off looking after these kids," Riley informs me.

"Uncle Riley taught me karate," Margo says, beaming. I frown at her and find myself about to question Riley as though he's a real person. I have to stop doing this. "I learned punching and blocking," Margo explains, and she jumps up and demonstrates a series of controlled punches and blocks. I can't believe it! She actually looks convincing.

"When did you learn karate, Dad?" I ask.

Dad glances over and then goes back to fiddling with the Brita filter.

"I don't know karate, honey. Riley taught her."

Of course.

"I learned Karate in Brooklyn. I had to build my street cred, toots. Ya know, me against the world."

I smile in spite of myself.

Okay, party's over, we've got to go. I stand up and stretch, noticing Dad's apartment is once again clean and orderly. I'll never understand what changed him. Maybe the plastic puppet is giving him some kind of purpose, and if that's the case, I *guess* I can learn to put up with him. It. Whatever.

"Thanks for taking the girls, Dad," I say as I brush past him in search of a drinking glass.

"They really missed you, Laney."

I meet Dad's eyes. Is he joking? He nods and puts a

hand on my shoulder giving it a squeeze. I try not to flinch or pull away. "Laney, you're doing a great job. You need to remember they've become attached to you whether you wanted them to or not."

What's that supposed to mean?

"Dad, I don't know where you're going—"

"Laney, I feel like you were scared to get close because you were so close with Mama. But you can't stop love, honey. It just seeps in."

I don't know what to say, but I manage to shrink away and break the eye contact. What's gotten into him? And more importantly…is he right? Have I kept my distance all these years since Margo's birth in hopes of protecting us both from getting too close, should we lose one another one day?

"Laney, honey…"

Dad continues, but I've had enough. I don't want to talk about Mom anymore. I just can't. I make a run for the bathroom, and once safe, splash cold water on my face and glance into the mirror to find my mascara running down my cheeks as if mocking me for the tears that just won't come. I take a few deep breaths while staring into my sullen eyes, pat my face dry with a clean towel, and emerge from the bathroom, composed and determined to collect the girls and go home.

The first odd thing I notice is Dad's face. He has Rory cradled in his arms but looks like a deer in headlights. Slowly his eyes leave my face and travel across the room, resting on something I can't see. I follow his gaze as if in slow motion…and there she is. Mom's ghost. I suck in my breath and gape at her and take in the details, half loving her face, while the other part of me struggles to pull me away.

"Hello, Lane," she says in a small voice.

"You're here *again*?" is all I can muster. Margo beelines over instinctively and takes my hand.

"Honey—Louisa brought supper," Dad stammers.

"Smells good to me, let's eat!" Riley calls. He's sitting on the couch by himself, paralyzed of course without my dad. That's how I feel right now, paralyzed without my mom.

"How often do you guys see each other?" I probe, narrowing my eyes. Dad and Louisa exchange uncomfortable looks, and a cold feeling starts creeping up the back of my neck. This is when I notice the small but delicate diamond solitaire on Louisa's ring finger. My knees buckle, but I struggle to steady myself.

"Lane, honey...are you all right?" Dad asks, passing Rory to Louisa of all people, and striding across the room to take my arm. He guides me to the closest chair, and I sink into it, numb. Margo stays at my side, concern etched in her small face. She doesn't understand why I'm upset exactly, but that doesn't seem to matter. I try to give her an appreciative smile, but fail miserably.

They're engaged!

"Lane, may I have a word in private?" Louisa asks. She's now seated on the sofa adjacent to me, as though invited. I shake my head in disgust, and with an unsteady breath, rise and pluck Rory out of her arms.

"Lane, you can't just leave without supper," Dad says, wringing the tea towel in his hands.

"I'm not hungry."

"I am!" Margo blurts and then claps her hand over her mouth.

"Fine, go ahead. All of you. I'll just sit here." I sink back down, too overwhelmed to argue.

"Good idea, toots," Riley says, as Dad scoops him up and seats him at the dinner table.

"May I go too?" Margo whispers. I nod, miserable. Dad and Louisa busy themselves setting the table, plating lasagna, tossing the salad, and filling drinking glasses.

"So when's the big day?" I interject. They both stop

their busyness and exchange shocked glances. The prickly silence hangs.

Louisa is the first to speak. "Um..."

I roll my eyes and turn my attention to Rory. Why can't they just be straight?

"We wanted to tell you, Lane—" Dad takes a step forward, but I raise my hand, halting him in his tracks.

"That's not what I asked. I said, *when* is the big day?"

"February twentieth."

"Uh-huh. And does Billy know?" If he knows, I swear to God I'll throttle him.

"Not...yet," Louisa says. "We wanted to...tell you both together."

"Oh, how sweet," I cry. "Like one big happy family. Well, we're dysfunctional all right, so why not cozy up together too." I throw myself back with a wounded sigh. What a family we would make: a recovering mental-case, his dead wife's twin, a son in search of his other family in Haiti, a newly abandoned, jobless (but never hopeless) me, a fucking puppet for a brother, and a partridge in a pear tree.

"Isn't anyone going to bother feeding Rory?" I ask with a pout, gently poking her little belly. She smiles and grabs for my hair. *Ouch!*

"Why don't you both join us, especially considering today is Margo's birthday celebration?" Aunt Louisa asks.

I glance at Margo, who is eyeing me with hopeful eyes, so I carry Rory to the table and pull up a chair. "So, Dad, I need you to babysit the girls on Saturday. I have an all-day workshop," I say, remembering the email from John about the acting class.

"Oh, what kind of workshop?" Louisa asks, probably relieved to have a change of subject.

I don't feel like discussing this with her, so I shrug and mumble, "Forget about it." So I'm being immature. Shoot me!

Riches & Rags

"Santa's workshop!" Riley shrieks. Dad and Louisa laugh as though it's the funniest thing they've heard in years.

"Really, Mommy? Santa's?" Margo asks.

"Except, you ain't no elf," Riley continues, jabbing an accusatory plastic finger in my direction. "You're the Grinch, himself."

If he wasn't my dad's beloved "son," I'd break his finger off.

"It's an acting workshop, okay? Listen, Dad, if you're not available I can ask Juliet—"

"No, no," Dad says, as he takes a bite of salad, "I'm free." There are globs of white dressing on both corners of his mouth, which shouldn't irritate me, but it does.

"Honey," Louisa offers, motioning at the corners of her lips, "wipe your mouth."

So now she calls him honey. Would this have slipped out if I didn't know about them, or is she just letting her guard down now that it's out in the open? Next thing I know they'll be tongue kissing in front of me...No! I toss my napkin on the table. I've had enough. When we leave I don't bother thanking Louisa for dinner, but I do thank Dad for watching the kids.

Outside, the air is brisk and it's already dark. I can't help yawning with fatigue. *What a day!*

"So, Margo, how was your birthday?" I ask as we cross the road to the bus stop.

Margo grins up at me. "It was *great*," she says, and I smile back, relieved. As Margo hoists herself onto the metal bench, I roll Rory's stroller back and forth, hoping the motion will lull her to sleep. "But..."

Uh-oh.

"Why didn't Daddy call?"

My heart sinks and I'm quiet for a few seconds, grasping for what to say. Daddy's confused? Daddy's depressed?

Daddy's shameful and ran away? What do I say? A loud truck rumbles by, buying me time.

"Oh, thanks for reminding me!" I smile a little too enthusiastically. "Daddy did call earlier—when you were at Pops'. He said to make sure to tell you happy, happy birthday and he wishes you a great day." There! Margo is quiet, but I can tell she's pleased.

And now I feel a new resolve to track Micky down. So he's not answering his phone or email? Time to step it up and start digging. He's out there somewhere, and I want him back.

15

"Thank you all for gracing me with your presence," John announces in a powerful voice, as he makes his grand entrance into the small theater room, his blonde locks flowing and black coat billowing behind him like a sorcerer's cape.

"I am John Childs. Actor. Visionary. Mentor."

I swallow the urge to laugh, wondering how Billy can put up with this melodrama on a day-to-day basis.

"TRUE ACTING"—John lifts a closed fist high into the air and shakes it, his face upturned—"is allowing ourselves to be *vulnerable*. It is about stripping away the layers."

He whips his coat off and flings it onto a nearby metal chair. To my delight, the chair topples over sideways from the blow and crashes onto the cement floor, the echo reverberating into the theater depths. All twelve students, including me, roar with laughter. If I had known acting class was so much fun I would have won an Oscar by now. I take a sip of my delicious latte, eager for him to go on.

John continues, as if oblivious to the commotion. "How can we, as *actors*, physically strip away the airs, the façade, and the barriers? To unburden ourselves from these defenses—these walls we build around us—is to be *liberated*, to be pure and innocent like children."

John's voice has risen considerably. He is so incredibly, well, *dramatic*. I would say his acting coach persona—this alter ego of his—is at the least quite manic. *Incredible!*

I fiddle with my phone and begin an audio recording so Billy can hear too. I can see us sipping wine by the fire as we take turns re-enacting John's fist-shaking, coat-throwing escapades. I can't wait!

"Only then," he bellows, "can we tap into our true emotional selves to create and connect with the character we will wholeheartedly embrace and portray? Who is ready to act?"

I shoot my arm into the air, much to even my surprise, and quickly retract. But it's too late. John is grinning, a wild gleam in his eye.

"Come, young actress. You have much to learn."

Okay, here goes. I rise from my chair, careful to place my phone where the recorder can still pick up clean audio. I join John on the riser as he surveys the students with a critical eye.

"I need one more person. YOU!" John chooses an Asian guy from the group, who looks rather shell-shocked and apprehensive. "What is your name?"

"It's Mark," the guy answers tentatively, and comes to stand next to me.

"I need some chairs." John claps his hands together, as three students rise in tandem. The students carry the chairs on stage and I take a seat, curiosity mounting. I wonder if we're going to study scripts and re-enact them.

"Lane," John says, turning to me with an intensity only he could attain, "how can we physically strip away these self-inflicted barriers to achieve the vulnerability that is *essential* for every great acting performance?"

I begin to shrug, then rack my brain for more. With

John's passion, the least I can do is make an effort. Plus, I'm taking the class for free.

"Um, I guess you could try new things. Be more *vulnerable* to new experiences." I finish, impressed with myself for using his key word.

But John is shaking his head in dismay. "No, no. That won't do. You have to reach deeper. Mark?" I whip my head to the right to see Mark, wide eyed and tense.

"Uh…practice?"

Even *I* did better than that. I frown at him with pity and turn away. The students in the audience are following John's lecture with a laser-like concentration.

Supposedly—says Billy—John has quite the reputation as an acting coach guru, not just in Vancouver but even in LA and New York. Hey! Even Riley's probably heard of him…I did not just think that, did I?

"Earth to Lane?!" John hollers at me, waving his arms around. I raise my eyebrow, waiting. "Lane, to strip away the layers we create, the fake personas we now embody, we must become vulnerable."

Yeah, you're repeating yourself there, John. I feel the itch—the boredom itch—and consider calling it a day. Maybe I'll go home for a nap.

"I need you to strip." He finishes.

Wait. Huh?

"Sorry?" I ask in confusion.

"You need to strip. Clothes off. Right now."

He's got to be kidding, right? But John's face is deadpan, and so are the faces of the audience. "W…what?" I demand, louder.

"Lane, you may not have known, prior to this class, but the rest of the students knew. My classes are famous for this. It's not about sexuality. This has nothing to do with sex, people!" John shoots a stern look at the rest of the students, and they all nod together, resembling Bobbleheads. "This is about reverting back to the way we entered this world. Vulnerable. Clothes off!"

Again I shoot a look to the audience, and they watch, wide eyed and rigid. "What about him?" I ask, pointing my thumb at ol' Marko.

"Him too!" John booms.

And with that, we gaze at each other, shrug, and begin stripping away the layers, literally.

I am completely naked. In public. And sitting on this bare metal chair which, ew, come to think of it, other naked actors might have sat on too. I shift with discomfort at the thought, but return my focus to the fact that I AM NAKED. IN PUBLIC.

Well, at least that creeper from the casino isn't breathing down my neck. At least this is civilized and for the purpose of art.

"Let's begin," John announces, clapping his hands.

Um? I thought we did begin.

"Lane, turn your chair to face Mark's. And Mark, do the same."

I grip the bottom of my chair and, in a swift move, I shimmy to the right. I just hope I don't have to stand up and walk around naked, damn!

"Lane, I want you to stare deeply into Mark's eyes. Nothing more. This is *not* a staring contest, by the way. You want to blink? Go ahead. But keep the eye contact, and whatever you do, do not look away."

I smirk at the ridiculousness of this exercise, but raise my eyes as I'm told, to meet Mark's.

After a nanosecond, I have the urge to look away, but

Riches & Rags

we keep staring at each other. This is so silly. And I'm NAKED, I almost forgot. Mark's brown eyes, dum da dum. This is *so* awkward. I want nothing more than to look away and, in discomfort, I start grinning like an idiot.

"Lane, why are you smiling?" John's at my side. I forgot about him too.

"Uh, this is awkward." I keep grinning until my face hurts. I pull my eyes away for a split-second reprieve and finally, unable to bear it any longer, I break out in hysterical laughter.

My laughing is desperate, like someone being tickled mercilessly and struggling for air. I can't stop this madness for the life of me. Even *I* don't know what's so funny.

And I have to keep up the eye contact.

And I'm NAKED.

Oh my God.

Tears roll down my cheeks as I continue like a hyena, uninhibited and wild.

"How do you feel, Lane?" John asks, his voice somber.

"Like. A. Train. Wreck." I manage, through roars and hiccups.

"Do you feel vulnerable, Lane?"

"Y…Yes! I do—" An agonizing moan fills my ears, like that of a wild animal, and to my horror, I realize it's coming from *me*.

My tears are no longer from laughing but from heart-wrenching sobs that have broken free from their barren home. This is worse than anything—worse than being naked in public, worse than the discomfort of looking into a stranger's soul so intimately, worse than a crazy adult laughing fit. I am a slobbering, blubbering mess of tears and snot in front of a group of total strangers. I feel like I've been ripped open for the entire world to see.

"Why are you crying, Lane?" John asks, his voice heavy with pain, mirroring my own.

Damn actors. I shake my head, and my shoulders shudder with the violent force of sobs.

"Lane, why are you crying?"

I grasp for a large gulp of air and let out a horrible moan. "My *Mom*," I wail.

I can see John through my tears, nodding, his face compassionate with understanding. "Why are you crying for your Mom?"

"She...d-diiiied."

"And you've built up quite the impressive defenses to protect those feelings, have you not?"

I nod violently, exhaling a shaky breath and stealing a look at the audience of actors. All of them are gazing at me with apparent genuine concern. John hands me a tissue box, which I accept, then blow my nose with a loud honk. What? After this, nothing can embarrass me.

"Lane, it seems you have a lot of emotion bottled up. But you, my friend, have just released it! Hark! Of all the emotion exercises over the years, this is by far the truest display of vulnerability. Bravo!"

The audience erupts in applause, and I turn to them in disbelief. I tear another Kleenex from the box, not sure what to think.

"Anything else bothering you?"

I shake my head no. Enough of this madness. What do I say?—my husband lost our money and ran away in shame, I'm practically broke and have not one but two dependents, my dad is marrying my Mom's identical twin, and I have a new puppet brother?

Nobody would believe me anyway.

"Well, thank you, Lane, for your wonderful portrayal of how to smash those barriers we create, to achieve the necessary vulnerability. Now you're ready to be an actress."

I give a small nod and all at once feel incredibly drained.

Not like tired from a sleepless night, mind you, but more like how it must feel after running a marathon.

I do feel lighter too, freer. John hands me my clothes, and I pull them back on, thankful to once again have some form of cover but knowing in my heart of hearts I can never go back to being so emotionally closed off. The floodgates have opened. Let it rain.

Riding the bus home, I stare outside at the drizzle sliding down my window. Oh, what a day. I suppose I would feel liberated had this incredibly thick blanket of fatigue not come about. But anyway, no time to rest; I need a plan. I slide my phone out of my bag and dial Juliet, half wishing Billy wasn't on another continent at the moment.

"Hi, Lane!" Juliet's voice is high pitched and breathless as usual; she's always bouncing around with energy and passion.

"Hey, J. You free to come over?"

"Uh, sure! What's up?"

"It's a long story. I even have an audio recording for your entertainment."

"Sounds thrilling! I'm on my way."

I toss the phone back into my bag, hoping George doesn't cramp our style. Come to think of it, I need to speak with him!

"George!" I holler when I arrive home. I'm standing in the foyer waiting for the piece of crisp to appear. "Where are you old man?" I utter under my breath as I poke my head into his ancient living room.

"What's all the fuss?" I hear his crotchety old voice calling out from the direction of his kitchen, and a minute later he emerges, holding that miserable cat.

"George, we've got to talk," I say, meeting his steady gaze.

He shakes his head, pulling his brown cardigan around his cat like a blanket. "I haven't got time right now," he says, squinting at me through tired-looking eyes.

"Of course you do. All you have is time. I mean, what were you possibly doing that's so important?"

"Oh, you're an impossible woman. Sit down!" he growls, dropping his cat into a tattered armchair and disappearing back to the kitchen. I plunk myself down on the green sofa, wishing I hadn't when the springs jab into my flesh.

George returns with two filmy glasses of water.

"How hospitable," I mumble, as I take the glass and examine the layer of film coating it. I set it down on the coffee table without taking a sip, ready to get down to business.

"A coaster! Don't you bloody know to use a coaster? Were you raised by gypsies?"

"Seriously? A coaster? Look around, George. Look at this living room. Look at this table!" I motion to the coffee table that looks like total crap.

"Oh, would you quit disturbing my peace and go back upstairs. Or better yet, just go back to West Van!"

"Actually, that's why I'm here."

George's sour face registers surprise, and I wait patiently as he pulls himself forward to hear me better. "You're moving back?" he asks, his voice rising with apparent wonder.

"No. But we need to talk about the rent."

"The rent? What about it?"

"We need to renegotiate," I say, trying to sound confident. George's hairy brows furrow and he sinks back into his chaise, observing me through narrowed eyes. Shit.

"George. I can see that you need some caring for," I say on a whim. Yes, caring for, that's what he needs.

"I do?" he asks, raising his eyebrows and looking surprised.

"Of course. Look at you. I know you eat those Mr. Noodles every night. And SPAM! I mean, how could you? What you need are home-cooked meals. I'd like to cater your dinners in exchange for a reasonable reduction in rent to account for my time and the high cost of groceries." I frantically chew the inside of my mouth as I await his reaction.

George seems to consider this briefly, then his eyes narrow and he blurts, "You can't cook!"

Thanks. "What makes you think that? I'm an excellent cook. In fact, I'm gourmet." I raise my eyebrow, almost believing myself.

"Not from the smells wafting down from that attic."

"You're right!" I say, jumping out of my seat to pace the floor. "But certainly I'm limited by the fact that I don't have a bloody *kitchen*. For God's sake, I don't even have a stove!" I realize I've let my voice rise to the point where I'm yelling. Good, now George can hear me loud and clear. Hopefully.

"What's your specialty dish?" he asks, curiosity etched in his voice.

Good, he's hungry. "Duck a l'orange," I blurt, remembering Denise's specialty.

"Duck a l'orange? Why, I haven't had that since I stayed in the Cherbourg Naval Base in France. Wow! That was in nineteen forty eight when..."

151

George has become animated, and I smile with encouragement, my smile genuine because my plan has worked. And good thing too, I'm down to my last two grand and need to buy time.

Eventually George finishes his ramblings and seems to bask in the afterglow of good memories. As amusing as this is, I clear my throat.

"Well…"—he pauses, appearing to consider his multitude of options, as in continue eating SPAM or quit being a cheap bastard!—"if you cook my dinners seven days a week, I'll reduce your rent by say, three hundred dollars."

I shake my head. No way. "Reduce my rent by five hundred dollars and buy me a proper oven, and *then* we have a deal."

George starts to protest, when my saving grace, Juliet, enters the front hall.

"In here," I yell, and Juliet appears, cheeks flushed, and beaming a radiant smile.

George's mood seems to lift tenfold. He's obviously smitten with Juliet. She strides across the room and plants a quick kiss on his cheek. He breaks into a wide grin, and I can't help smiling too. Juliet's feel-good vibes are contagious. Oh! The iron is hot.

"So, do we have a deal?" I ask with a grin. Please, *please*!

George looks back to Juliet's attentive face and turns to me with a firm nod.

Yes! I give a whoop, resisting the urge to kiss George too, and instead grabbing Juliet by the arm. We race upstairs. The first part of the plan worked: save money. Now I just have to figure out a way to *make* money.

16

"What's the deal you worked out with George?" Juliet asks as soon as we close the door to the attic. I toss my bag and keys onto a side table and practically dance my way to the "kitchen" area.

"George is giving me a rent reduction of five hundred bucks *and* a stove!"

Juliet's mouth drops open and her eyes widen. "Wow! In exchange for what?"

"Hmm? Oh right, I'm supposed to cook him dinner."

Juliet frowns and tilts her head to the side, her auburn hair flowing down her shoulders. "That's it? That doesn't make sense. You cook him a dinner and he reduces your rent. By five *hundred* bucks??"

"No, not just one dinner. I need to cook him dinner every night."

"But, honey, you don't cook."

"Don't worry. He eats Mr. Noodles for dinner; I doubt he'll know the difference."

"Oh. Well, what happens if you get a job working all day? Then you have to cook dinners for him too? And what if his dinner is too late for his liking?"

"Juliet, please. We can always rearrange things if it

doesn't work. This is to buy me time only until I can bring in some money."

Juliet nods slowly. I hand her a glass of sauvignon blanc, and we clink our glasses together. "To George," Juliet says. Thousands of dollars in savings a year is worth a toast to ol' George, so I go along with it.

"So, what's this about an audio clip you wanted me to hear?"

I roll my eyes and recount the incredibly dramatic and emotional day. Juliet's blue eyes sparkle when I tell her about John Childs, acting coach extraordinaire, and widen with apparent concern at my meltdown. Just speaking about it feels surreal; I can't believe what went down. "Oh! And would you believe I was NAKED?"

Juliet catches her breath. "NO!"

"Oh, yes. It's an exercise in liberation."

"Is that even legal?" she asks.

"You tell me. Speaking of which, have you found a job working with seniors?"

Juliet shakes her head.

"Well, that makes two of us. No job. No prospects."

"Well, you're busy. When are the kids expected back?"

I glance at my phone. "In an hour or so. My dad has them." I suddenly realize I'm starving and jump out of my seat in search of grub. My mini bar fridge is pretty drab. A liter of milk, a few apples, and some peanut butter. I grab two apples and wash them while Juliet tells me about some old folks home she toured. I don't bother responding, and instead let my thoughts drift to what I can do for work. I hand Juliet a plate of sliced apples globbed with peanut butter and grab my own and join her. We crunch away on our apples, a companionable silence hanging in the air.

"What would you want to do if you could do anything?" Juliet asks me, propping her elbows on the table and resting her chin on her hands as though waiting for me to say something juicy.

I frown at her and buy time by shoving an apple in my mouth. "Well," I say as I chew, "when I was little, I wanted to be a cat when I grew up."

Juliet bursts into giggles and shakes her head "No, seriously."

"I am serious. I don't think I ever wanted to work. And I certainly didn't when I was living in West Van. It was enough keeping up with the social circles and decorating our house."

Juliet snaps her head to attention and claps her hands in excitement.

"What's up?"

"That's it!" she squeals.

"What?"

"Designing. Decorating. It's what you do best. It's your *passion*."

I consider this for a moment, but then shrug it off. "It was only my passion because I wanted to live in a beautiful, inspiring environment."

"Yeah, but don't you see? Everyone wants that."

"*Yes*. And that's why we have interior designers; but I'm not one." I let my gaze drop to my hands, wishing so much I had pursued something before. To at least be accomplished at *something*, besides looking pretty.

"You could go to night school, become a decorator?"

"No, I need something now. I need to make money right away."

We both flop back in our chairs, lost in thought. Juliet reaches for her phone.

"Well, there are over one million Google results for Vancouver interior designers, so I'm sure there are lots of job prospects." Juliet raises her eyebrows at me, and together we sigh. We both reach for more apple, then Juliet puts her phone away.

Good thing, I don't feel like talking about jobs any more than she probably does.

"So, that's it? You had a naked staring contest with some guy, and now you're a bona fide actress?"

"No, we also learned audition techniques. Standing on the mark, slating ourselves, reading scripts off-camera—that kind of thing." I pop my last apple slice into my mouth, and peanut butter glazes my chin. "Oh, also, one of the actresses gave me some pointers about audition notices too. So I'm going to start scouring the acting posts."

"That's awesome, good for you!"

"Oh! I didn't tell you my dad's engaged to Louisa, and Billy's in Haiti!"

"OH MY GOD, no way!"

"And so the plot thickens…," I mutter, as I roll my eyes.

Later, after Juliet has left and the girls are home and finally sleeping, I pour myself another glass of sauvignon blanc and collapse in front of the dormant fireplace. I should have George fix it so I can actually use the damn thing, now that the weather is cooler. Well, use it and not cause a fire, that is.

I reach for my tablet and open my email. I have eight new messages—two personal, and six from companies trying to sell me everything from penis enlargement pills to Nigerian money loans. One of the personal emails is from Louisa, the other from Billy. I tap Billy's email, eager to know about his progress.

Riches & Rags

Greetings from Haiti! OMG, I can't believe I'm actually here Lane. It's like a dream. My dad is lovely, so warm and charismatic. But life is so hard for him. I met my half siblings and nieces and nephews—it's so surreal. They're still recovering from the aftermath of the hurricane. Even years later, they're living in extreme poverty. I'm going to do everything I can for them.

Gotta run, I'll be in touch soon. B xo

Hmm. Not sure what to make of that. I briefly consider deleting Louisa's email, but curiosity gets the better of me.

Dearest Lane,

I'm very sorry you had to learn our news in such an abrupt way. I know this must be monumentally difficult for you. I have such fond memories from all the years we spent together, your mama and me taking you and Billy around town, laughing and playing together. I cherish those times. Lane, to lose my identical twin sister was a blow I could have never imagined and I know I will never, ever get over it. But to lose your own Mom is heart-wrenching, I know. It was never my intention in a million years to be with your father in a romantic way. I felt it was my responsibility to my sister to help and support him as much as I could. Over the years we became closer and gradually our concern for each other and bond for what we'd lost grew into a deep and true love. I love your father dearly and want to care for him and make him happy. Sometimes I envy the bond you still share with Billy; I wish to be a part of it. I know to see me must be unsettling for obvious reasons but please know I do want to see you and be with you whenever I can. I know I could never replace your Mama and I will never try. But I am here for you just the same and hope so much you can learn to accept me.

Love, Aunt Louisa

Sigh. Not sure what to make of that one either.

Suddenly I feel very weary. I close my email and open my web browser. I scan the news and entertainment headlines, but nothing of interest catches my eye. Without deliberation, I find myself Googling "Vancouver interior designers" and bracing myself for the endless results. Wait… I know many of these designers just from my association with high society. There's West Coast Design—they re-did Martha King's estate from top to bottom—and Mark & Jones—they designed Sarah Miller's theater. I keep scanning the listings while mentally noting the companies I recognize. What would be really overwhelming is to try to find a designer without having a clue of who's who…

Oh My God! OH MY GOD! YES! I know these companies. I can provide a service! I jump out of my seat with a grin so wide it hurts my face. Yes! *This* is what I can do. I know these companies, I know design and I know pricing. I can provide a consultancy service playing matchmaker with clients and designers based on the clients' needs AND the designers' styles. Oh my God! I wish so much Billy was reachable by phone.

I dash across the attic to Margo's drawing supplies and grab a stack of fresh paper. I also grab some extra-large sheets and fat markers for brainstorming. Then I splash my wine into the sink in favor of water—I need to think clearly. I'm ecstatic and my mind is working at breakneck speed—I swear I've never felt more razor sharp in all my life.

Five days later, after running on little sleep and overflowing adrenaline, I have my business plan in place, a domain reserved, a logo I created online myself, and business cards to boot. Now I have to design a website, and by

Riches & Rags

using one of the templates online, I should have it up in no time. The excitement I feel is palpable. Margo is dancing around the attic singing goofy songs, and Rory, who is now standing, is bouncing along.

"Margo, this is going to be spectacular!" I cry, grabbing her by surprise and swinging her around the room. We both dissolve into peals of giggles, and I set her down on the canopied bed, where she collapses in bliss. I swing Rory into my arms for her turn, and we spin and tango across the floor.

A knock interrupts our celebrations, and I fling open the door to find George's sour mug staring back at me. "It sounds like a troupe of elephants and laughing hyenas up here, for God's sake."

"Is this why you're disturbing us?" I narrow my eyes and put my hands on my hips.

George just shakes his head, looking exasperated. "Lane, the oven has arrived. Can you move this clutter to make room for the delivery man?" He gestures to the piles of madness scattering the attic, which I admit I hadn't noticed building up all week.

"Yeah, yeah," I say. "Margo, help me out." We clear a path, and a delivery guy nods hello and wheels in a dolly.

"Hiiii!" Margo calls.

"Iiiiii!" Rory echoes.

"Hello, ladies! You ready to do some cooking?" The girls cheer and squeal, and I shush them to be quiet. "Be right back." The guy grabs his dolly and disappears. I'm wondering if he forgot an attachment, when a massive fridge appears at the door.

"What?!" A fridge? A proper fridge! Now it's my turn to squeal. I grab Rory and race downstairs, with Margo in full gallop behind.

"George! Wow, a fridge too. That's fantastic." I beam at him, and he actually looks pleased with himself.

"So, what's for dinner?" he asks, rubbing his gnarly hands.

I roll my eyes and turn to head back upstairs. Men! They only think about food. But…what *is* for dinner? I set Rory down on the hardwood floor and search my cupboards for inspiration. There's a jar of no-name marinara sauce, so that'll have to do.

The delivery man connects the fridge and stove and away he goes, with Margo and Rory calling goodbye as though he truly will be missed. I pour a glass of wine, my mind on my website, plop the jar of sauce into a pan and turn the stove knob to high. I grab my notebook and a pen, seat myself at the table, and begin a rough content draft for the website.

"What are you doing?" Margo asks.

"I'm working on my business. You can join me if you want."

Margo gives a whoop as she flings herself next to me, basket of markers in tow. I hand her and Rory some paper, and we all lose ourselves in our activities.

I have a loose outline for the website, but am momentarily distracted by the smell of something burning.

The sauce! I dash to the stove and whip the lid off the pot, only to have bubbling tomato sauce splatter all over my hand and arm. OUCH! Bloody thing. I jab the wooden spoon into the pot to stir the sauce but can feel it's burned and stuck to the bottom of the pan. Oh well. George probably won't even notice; taste buds diminish with age.

Damn! I forgot noodles! I search the cupboard, but it looks like I'm out. I consider asking George for the noodles from his Mr. Noodles, but can't be bothered. Toast it is.

"Sorry, Rory, you've got to go into your playpen for just a sec," I say, depositing her into the "cage," where she hollers in protest. "Margo, stay here. I have to bring George his dinner, I'll be right back," I say as I dump sauce into a bowl and grab the piece of dry toast. Must remember to pick up butter.

"I want to come too," Margo says, jumping up from her drawings.

"No, just watch your sister."

"NO! I'm coming!"

I shoot Margo a nasty look, which she mirrors back to me. Whatever. I'm not going to fight. "Rory, you're on your own," I holler as I head out the door with Margo.

"George!" I call when I arrive downstairs.

"In here. Is something burned?"

Oh great. George is in his living room seated on his ratty chair and stroking that damn cat like he's Dr. bloody Evil. "Here." I unceremoniously plunk the bowl down with a thud, the piece of toast sliding halfway into the burned sauce.

George pulls a face and slowly leans forward to inspect. "This is the grand first meal?" he mutters, after a dismal beat. "My mouth has been watering for days! Where's the duck a l'orange you boasted about?" He shoots me a disgruntled look. "This is what I get? Canned sauce—and without any goddamn pasta? In the navy we called this Shit On a Shingle!"

"If you expected gourmet every night, you'd have to be a fool. In case you haven't noticed, I have a baby, dammit. And, I'm going to be running a business!"

George snorts, and I choose to ignore him. I catch Margo pinching her nose, a look of exaggerated disgust on her face. "Stop that!" I snap. "You're having the same dinner, so I wouldn't make faces."

"Gross! I miss Denise."

The thought of Denise makes me think of Micky, and my heart sinks.

I turn on my heel and retreat to the attic and screaming

Rory, but not before George calls after me. "Don't bother discounting your check this month, you little conniver!"

"What's a civirer?" Margo whispers behind me.

"Don't ask," I say, raising my chin. With any luck I won't need the discount anyway.

17

It's Wednesday morning and the usual mad dash to get ready for school. Margo is dragging her feet, and I feel more impatient than usual because after school drop off, I have an audition.

That's right! I emailed a director about a film audition posting, and he invited me to come down. I take careful attention to apply my make-up, though I don't have leisure time to be meticulous. I'm playing a love interest, so I go heavy on the smoky eye look, then stand back from the mirror to examine the final touches. My eyes look bright with excitement, my skin is glowing, and to my relief, I'm having a very good hair day. I grin at my reflection, wondering why I've never done anything like this before. The audition for Budweiser doesn't count, because this is for a MOVIE!

I corral the girls to the door, and we head out into the Vancouver rain. Well, it can't all be perfect. By the time I arrive at the audition fifty minutes later, I'm twelve minutes late and soaked to the core. As my boots squeak and water beads down my head, I enter the waiting room for the audition and peer around. It's a drab, unremarkable space, and there's a sign taped to the wall directing actors to sit and wait to be called. Three actors are already seated, calmly studying their lines. I push Rory's stroller right past them in search of a washroom mirror. Down a long corridor and back along another, but I can't find a bloody bathroom. It turns out I don't even have a compact on me, so I try my best to fluff my soaking hair and rub under my eyes, in case my makeup ran. Rory is complacent, looking around with mild interest. Fingers crossed she stays calm.

We join the other actresses, who are all perfectly made up, though a little overboard I would say. I take a seat in the cold metal chair, and am about to ask my fellow actors if I could borrow a small mirror when the door to the audition room swings open and a clean-cut guy saunters out and addresses us.

"Lane Carson."

"Oh, hi!" I say, hopping out of my seat and struggling to pull up the brake on Rory's stroller. Why the hell did I put the brake on?

The guy surveys me with a perplexed look, I guess because I have a baby. "I'm Jay, the director," he says.

"Nice to meet you!" I flash him my best attempt at a dazzling smile and steer Rory into the audition room, where five guys are seated at a table and a sixth is standing behind a camera. This is it! My nerves feel rattled and I'm trying with all my might to just *breathe* and be calm.

"On your mark," the director says.

Oh! I leave Rory's stroller and take my position. The director looks up from his notes. "Okay, so this is Ron, one of the actors; Michael, head writer; J.D. in casting; Pete in PR; and Zach, another actor. Oh and Johnny's one of our camera men."

"Hi guys!" I wave and again flash a brilliant smile. Most of them seem eager, leaning forward with expectant eyes, though one of the guys slumps in his seat, not bothering to even look at me. I can't remember his role. I hope he's not the casting guy.

"Aaaand slate yourself."

I smile wide for the camera and take a breath, when a phone begins to ring. Eyebrows shoot up as the guys gaze around apparently in search for the culprit, and I'm outright *mortified* when I realize it's coming from *me*.

"Uh, sorry," I say, whipping my phone out to turn off the ringer. But I catch a glimpse at the caller ID—it's a number I don't recognize. What if it's Billy and he's in trouble or something? What if it's Margo's school and she fell off the monkey bars—or worse yet she's gone missing. "Sorry, guys, this might be important." I slide the answer bar and put the phone to my ear. "Hello?"

"What's up, toots?"

No way. It can't be. "Riley?" I croak in disbelief.

"Yeah! I'm calling from my new cell phone, toots. Pops just got it for me!"

I don't believe this. "Riley, I don't have time for this—I'm at an audition," I hiss.

"For what?"

I catch the director's eye—and he doesn't look impressed, so I quickly hang up. "Sorry, I'm so sorry…"

"All right, slate yourself."

"Hi, I'm Lane Carson and I'm self-represented," I say, trying to regain a relaxed disposition. Rory is starting to squawk, and I try to block her out and concentrate.

"And, action."

"What a beauty!" The actor whose name I don't remember says his lines, and I turn my full attention to him.

"Thanks, this is Molly," I say, trying to convey warmth and openness.

"I was actually talking about you." I do my best to blush and cast my eyes downward, smiling. "But don't worry; your dog's pretty cute too. What breed is she?"

"She's a shih-tzu," I say, pretending to pat the dog.

"Oh. She's really cute. I had a husky, but he died a few months ago. I still miss him."

I peer at my fellow actor, trying to convey a growing interest. "How old was he?" I ask. Rory is screeching in the background. I should have faced her stroller toward me so she could at least see what's going on. I wish I could just step away from my mark to turn her around.

"It's your turn."

Huh? *Oh, shit.* I scramble for my script and somehow find my place to finish the anticlimactic scene. I should really tell the writer not to quit his day job.

"Thanks, Lane, that will be all," the director says, so as a last-ditch effort, I grace him with another broad smile and approach, my hand outstretched.

"Thank you so much, John," I gush. I turn my attention to the panel of guys and attempt to shake their hands as well. "Adam, nice to meet you. Sam, what a great opportunity. Rick, thank you. Carl, great shirt. Matt, loved the script." The guys are howling—yes, I have no idea who the hell is who. "Great camera work, David," I say over my shoulder, as I wheel Rory around.

"Bye," she yells. "Bye, byyyye."

Get me out of here! Okay, lessons learned. Try not to bring babies to auditions if at all possible, and turn phone off. Right! Oh well. I'm sure there will be other auditions in the future. I fish Rory's bottle out of the diaper bag and she accepts it with a big smile. I smile back.

"Oh, Rory. What can ya do?" Oh well. I drape the stroller with the plastic rain cover and make my way to the door, when I catch a glimpse of myself in the lobby mirror and my mouth drops in disbelief.

I gape at myself in utter horror taking in my ridiculous reflection. My hair is so flat it's glued to the side of my head, and I have wide, long streaks of black makeup smeared

Riches & Rags

down my face from each eye and mascara globs stuck to each eyelid. I whip out a baby wipe from the diaper bag and begin scrubbing my face. Once somewhat satisfied, I pull my hood on and step out into the rain.

By the time our bus drops us off at Kits Beach, the rain has seized and the sky is brightening. Instead of going right home, I stroll along the seawall to the playground and dry the baby swing with a change blanket.

"Here baby," I say, pulling off the rain cover to pick up Rory. "Ooohh."

Rory is nestled into the corner of the stroller sound asleep. I smile ruefully and turn in the direction of home. I pass Kits Pool. It's still full of water, but grit and bird yuck litters the bottom. Seagulls float along, apparently enjoying their winter paradise. When I reach home, I steer the stroller up the pathway, wondering if I should just wait for Rory to wake up or risk waking her by pulling her out of the stroller.

I'm debating this, when I hear the click of heels and glance up—I *don't* believe it. It's Elsa, Micky's mother, coming up the drive. I'm momentarily stunned. How did she know where I was? Has she heard from Micky? What does she *want*?

Elsa's not the kind of woman to make house calls.

"Lane." She greets me with a curt nod, and I lift my chin ever so slightly, returning her even gaze.

"Elsa." CruElsa.

"I've come for my granddaughters."

"What do you mean you've *come* for them? I need notice Elsa. Margo's not even here!"

"I don't mean I want to spend a little afternoon together. I mean I've come for them. After all the trouble you've caused."

I widen my eyes in shock. "What are you talking about?" My voice is rising and panic is starting to build and compound.

What *is* she talking about?

Micky?

"You tell me. I come home after three months in Argentina only to hear some hysterical message on my machine."

"What message?" I ask. What the fuck is she talking about?

"The kids. You wanted me to take them off your hands."

"Elsa, what the hell do you mean?"

"You left me a message saying you can't do this, you want me to come for the kids. You don't know what you're doing, and on and on."

This sounds vaguely familiar.

As in very vague, like a distant dream.

Did I *really* call Elsa of all people and offer up my own offspring?

"Elsa, in case you haven't been in touch with Micky, we've been going through a very difficult time, and yes, I was freaked. But he's sorting himself out, I'm sure, and I am too. In fact, I've got it together and am starting my own business." Take that! Elsa's never worked a day in her pampered life, but she must have respect for my wanting to make a better life for my family. One look into her face shows a cold woman who doesn't even hear me.

"I'm here for my grandchildren," she repeats. "You're not fit to care for them. And you never were."

I stumble back, reeling as though I've been slapped. I now recognize the fierce love I have for my girls, and I'm not going to let Elsa jeopardize anything. "Get off my property!" I scream at the witch.

She crosses her arms in front of her bony chest, her eyes narrowing and mouth forming a wicked smile. "This isn't your property, Lane!"

"Get off my property!" I whirl around to find George glaring at Elsa and looking nastier than ever. *Yes!*

"Is this a good time?" A jovial voice interrupts all of us, and I turn with the others to find the *loveliest* Brad Pitt doppelgänger coming up the walkway. Elsa and I gaze open mouthed at this guy, who is nothing less than *GQ* material. He claps George on the back and turns to me with a grin. "Ready to do some cooking?"

I then notice the brown paper bag of groceries in his right arm. A lock of blonde hair falls into his blue-green eyes and he sweeps it away, while I stare, mesmerized.

"Cooking?" Elsa scoffs, her voice high pitched. "Lane doesn't cook."

The guy gives Elsa a broad grin and says, "Ah, well that's all about to change. By the time I'm through with her, she'll be Red Seal material."

Me? Red Seal? Even *I* doubt that, but considering his confident, relaxed disposition, I'd probably believe anything he said. Rory is awake and starting to fuss, which is perfect timing.

"Well, shall we?" the guy asks, so I nod and shoot Elsa a triumphant look. She can't argue with my parenting if I'm making moves like starting a business and taking cooking classes to better things for the girls.

She shakes her head in obvious defeat and turns to walk away, her kitten heels clip clipping along the cobblestone path. George is watching her leave, his face etched in a deep frown of a thousand lines.

"Thank you, George," I say quietly.

"Monster-in-law?" he asks.

"Obviously." I realize I didn't really find out if Elsa has even spoken with Micky. How could I have forgotten to ask her?

Elsa's Mercedes peels out from the curb, making an ear-piercing shriek. Crazy woman!

"So, what's this about cooking?" I ask George and his friend.

"Right! Well, George asked me to give you some cooking lessons," the guy says with an easy smile.

Uh-huh. So George must still be hungry.

I pull Rory out of her stroller, and the guy reaches for the diaper bag and swings it over his shoulder. I eye him with interest, still baffled by his unbelievable beauty.

"And you are…"

"Ah! Right. Of course. Sorry, I'm Liam O'Connell, and you must be Lane."

"That's right. Lane Carson. Nice to meet you."

Inside, George retreats to his own quarters, and I float up the stairs in companionable silence with Liam.

Upstairs, Liam makes himself at home by unpacking his groceries, so I change Rory's diaper. I glance around, relieved I did some tidying up last night. The bed looks impressive with the silk canopy layers, and everything else is pretty much in its place, though I doubt Liam would have minded otherwise.

"Do I detect an Irish lilt?" I ask, taking in his beauty.

"Sure, look it. I guess my name gave it away."

"Yeah, that too." I laugh. "And…so…how do you know George?"

His face breaks into a radiant smile and his bright eyes shine. "George is my granddad's best friend. Or was, anyway. My granddad passed away about five years ago, but George was always a fixture in our family. He's one hell of a guy; gruff yes, but with a heart of gold."

George? A heart of *gold*? That might be an exaggeration. Though…I am grateful he came to my defense today. I glance at the clock, relieved I don't have to leave anytime soon to pick up Margo. I join Liam at the counter, where he's washing some vegetables. "So, what's on the menu today?" I ask, wondering just how many cooking lessons I'm going to have with this guy.

"Well, I thought today we'd start with simple and fresh ingredients. Braided, wild halibut filets, baked zucchini, cilantro-infused Jasmine rice, and garden salad with an herb-garlic vinaigrette."

I nod, my mouth watering at the mention of good food—it's been so long. I guess this is how George feels, but amplified because he's lived without home-cooked food for, well, who knows how long?

"Here, smell this!" Liam says, handing me a bunch of fresh organic cilantro. I hesitate, then take a whiff. It does smell pretty awesome. "Cooking is a sensory experience. An art. Now, what do you think the first step to cooking a good meal is?"

"Have a recipe in mind?"

"Sure. But first we start with a glass of wine." He fills two glasses with white wine. Our eyes meet as we raise the glasses to our lips. Rory squirms in my arms, and to my surprise Liam reaches for her and cradles her into the nook of his arm. Normally this would be really weird; I mean I don't even know this guy. But he's a good family friend of George's, and there's something so comfortable about him, like I've known him all my life.

"So, are you a chef?" I ask, intrigued.

"No, but I love to cook," he says. I'm mildly disappointed because he didn't say what exactly he does. "So, first things first, I'll prepare the halibut. You can use another white fish for this dish, like sole or cod, but I caught this halibut myself." Liam gives Rory a pat on the head and passes her back to me. He then pulls out his own knife from its protective case and slices the halibut into three long strips, leaving the tops connected.

"Nice fish."

"I'm an entreprawneur."

171

I frown inwardly at his mispronunciation but decide to let it slide. "Oh yeah?" So *that's* what he does. Another ruthless businessman.

"So now, I braid the halibut filets." He swiftly folds the fish into a braid. "We're going to bake this. I'm going to cover it in heaps of butter, lemon, and fresh fennel."

"I don't have any butter," I say.

"No worries, Lane, I do."

"So is this cooking class a onetime thing?" I ask, trying to feign indifference.

"Ah, no. You have me daily for two weeks at least."

I gape at him, wide eyed. Two weeks! Though this Liam guy is perfectly charming and nice company, I have things to do!

"Liam, I thought maybe you could help me cook another meal or two, but fourteen more? There's no way!"

That George—always assuming I'm at his disposal!

My phone pings and I race for it, letting Rory down by a pile of toys. It's a text.

Hi Lain

Thanks for coming down today. Sorry but another actress was cast. Better luck next time!

Jay aka "John"

Though I was expecting this, the disappointment stings. You're not good enough, Lane.

18

The soft afternoon sunlight streams through the window, illuminating the thick layer of dust coating each worn surface in the living room. Living in an environment full of filth should drive the admiral in George batty, but truth be told, he is getting too old and too tired to really care. The sound of laughter is a welcome interruption to his mundane thoughts. He shuffles to the front bay windows in time to see Lane and Liam with Rory, making their way up the sidewalk, Margo skipping along in front, her purple backpack bouncing on her back.

Oh, to be young and carefree again. He smiles in spite of himself. How things have changed for him during the past three months. Now there is life, laughter, and the pitter-patter of little feet in his home again. And now Liam is back in Vancouver after much travel. Best of all, tonight George is going to enjoy a feast. What excitement indeed.

He watches with interest as Liam and Lane exchange a private laugh at something he can't hear. Where the hell Lane's husband has gallivanted to, George will never know. But one thing is for sure, he's got to be an imbecile for leaving her and the kids. *What kind of man can't own up to his mistakes and take care of his family?*

Margo hops up the front steps and peers through George's window, eyes searching. His heart soars because the sweet child remembered him. They lock eyes and both wave wildly for a brief second before the front door flings open and everyone clambers inside. Nobody calls for him, so he stays frozen at the window. Soon dinner will be served—the anticipation is almost too much to bear.

Oh, that Lane! He shakes his head, smiling ruefully. He has to admire her tenacity and ingenuity, as crazy as she is. How she could negotiate a rent reduction when she *knows* she's a miserable cook is beyond him. He has to laugh at the horror of a so-called dinner she cooked the other night—burned canned sauce with mush toast. But, he probably would have given the woman the rent decrease even without the dinners—hell, he didn't need the money. To think he's sat in this godforsaken house for over thirty years by himself, and now it teems with life again.

Sometimes a cat for company just isn't enough. *Where has that damn cat gone off to now?* He turns from the window in search for his beloved feline companion, when a sudden and overwhelming pain shoots up his left arm. The agony halts him in his tracks, and his face knots as the pain grips him.

"Lane—" He tries to call out, his voice hoarse and weak. He steadies himself on the back of the sofa and struggles to breathe through the pain. Another shock shoots through his upper body, this time assaulting his arm and chest.

No! This can't be the end already!

He looks around with frantic eyes, and against every bit of strength he can muster, he collapses on the floor, his twisted and rigid body betraying him. He tries to focus on Piper's wail of meows as she rubs her soft body along his, her incessant cries echoing in the room. He tries to focus on this, but the pain takes over—it's all he feels, all he sees. It is all consuming. "Lane." His whisper is hoarse with desperation as he clutches his chest in anguish.

"Well, Lane. What do you think of your first homemade gourmet meal?" Liam asks with a lopsided grin, his light Irish accent coloring his words in a melodic way.

I grin back and stare down at the gorgeous meal in disbelief. I made this! Well, with Liam's help. The steam rises with from the dish, and the smell is glorious. Wow! The halibut is cooked to perfection and is presented with slices of fennel bulb and drizzled in the butter sauce. The rice with the cilantro that we added last minute smells heavenly. And the baked and broiled zucchini has a perfectly browned, Parmesan crust. I grab a couple of sprigs of fresh Italian parsley and sprinkle it on the plate to complete the presentation.

"Is the chicken done?" Margo asks, peering over the counter.

"How do you feel about fish, love?" I hear Liam ask, as I carry the plate to the attic door.

"Yuck!" Margo shrieks.

Liam chuckles. "In that case, the *chicken* is done. Here, I'll serve you right now."

I carry the plate down the two flights of stairs, smiling in anticipation of George's reaction. He's going to be so thrilled. It actually feels kind of good to know George will be eating a real meal for once.

"George?" I call out when I reach the foyer landing. I pause momentarily at the foreign sound coming from the living room, but realize it's just that wretched cat. "George? Come on, this is the dinner of your dreams." His hearing must really be going! I swing the living room door open with one hand and halt mid step.

Oh!

My God.

The plate crashes to the floor as I fling myself at his side.

"George!" I cry, dropping to my knees. The cat stares at me with wide eyes and continues to assault my ears with its wails. "LIAM!" I scream.

George is barely conscious, his skin is clammy and sickly gray. I put my hand on his damp neck and can feel a very slow, very weak pulse. Relieved, I hold his cold hand in mine while I smooth back his hair, trying to keep him calm. His blank eyes are unfocused and lost. I hear Liam's footsteps racing down the stairs.

He bursts into the room with Rory in his arms. "What's going— Oh nooooo!" He sets Rory down and crouches by George's side. "George, can you hear me?" he says, his voice loud and panicked. George doesn't answer. Liam gives me a brief, pained glance and scrambles to his feet. "I'm calling 9-1-1," he calls over his shoulder, as he sprints in the direction of the kitchen.

"George, help is coming," I say, my voice barely audible. "Hang in there, George." I stroke his hand in mine, and a tear streams down my face, landing on his. I wipe it with a shaky hand.

Margo's just come up behind me. Her concerned face crumples into tears when she sees George in a heap on the floor. "Oh, no! Mommy." She comes and sits vigil beside him, crying softly while watching him through her long, wet lashes. Rory crawls over to Margo's side and puts her head on her big sister's lap. I focus on George again, speaking with him and hoping he can hear me.

His eyes roll back and then close.

"Come on, you. Stay with me! Dammit, you're a good

man, George. You took us in despite not wanting to, you gave me everything I asked for, you showed interest in my kids, and even came to my defense with my mother-in-law." More tears stream down my face, and I clutch George's hand with all my might.

"Ambulance is on its way," Liam calls from the other room.

"You hear that? Help is coming, George. Shit. I wish I knew first aid." I wipe at the tears rolling down my cheeks. In the distance, over the girls' cries, I hear sirens, and I stroke George's cold, sweaty face. "Just hang in there," I plead.

Two paramedics arrive and rush in with a barrage of questions for Liam and me. I'm so flustered, I can barely articulate anything coherent. My stomach bottoms out and I stagger back when one of the paramedics announces that George now has NO PULSE. He begins CPR, while the other paramedic places pads on his chest. We watch in *horror* as they shock him. His entire body jolts, and Margo and Rory scream and start wailing hysterically, so I usher them out of the room and cradle them on the foyer stair.

The girls are still crying in anguish as George is wheeled out on a stretcher to the awaiting ambulance—all while they continue CPR. I follow behind into the already darkened night; my adrenaline is off the charts. "Which hospital are you taking him to?" My voice is high pitched with panic.

"St. Paul's," one of the paramedics yells back, before slamming the ambulance door. The sirens blare, and I cover my ears and race back inside to Liam and the girls.

Liam is staring out the door, his expression blank. He himself looks pale, and I realize he must be in somewhat of a shock.

"You okay?" I ask.

He slowly turns his head to meet my eyes and nods

solemnly. "Yeah. It's just he's like a granddad to me," he says, shaking his head as though in a daze of disbelief.

"I know. I feel the same, only I didn't know it till now." I take a quivering breath, trying to decide what to do. "Why don't you go to the hospital right now, and I'll get my dad over here to watch the girls."

Liam nods, his features pained with worry. He hands me Rory, and I take Margo's hand in my free one.

We race upstairs to call Dad, and to my frustration there's no bloody answer. I try Juliet, and leave her a message, as she's not picking up either. Shit! I briefly consider taking the girls to the hospital with me, but no way! It's too much for them and would be a gong show for everyone anyway. If only Dad answered his bloody cell phone. Oh, wait!

I scan through the call history on my phone and find the number that called me during the audition. I hit "Talk" and wait for Dad to answer.

"*Yeah!*" Riley's obnoxious voice rings out.

"I need to speak to Dad. Dad!" I yell.

"Honey, what's wrong?" Thank God Dad's on the line and I don't have to play games with my "brother."

"Dad, I need you to come watch the girls. I need to go to the hospital right away. George collapsed, and the ambulance just left for St. Paul's."

"Oh *dear*. Okay. Well, honey I'm just at a play-date for Riley but, um, well, we can leave."

"*A play-date?*" I echo in disbelief. Is there no end to this madness?

"Yes, of course. Socialization is very important for development," he says.

I feel like screaming "It's a puppet, Dad!"

"Whatever, just hurry up," I snap. And then add, "Thanks."

Riches & Rags

Dad arrives, breathless, with Riley, sometime later. I kiss the girls goodbye and rush outside to hail a cab on Cornwall. Within a few minutes, I'm in a cab making my way toward the Burrard Street Bridge heading for downtown.

Thousands of Christmas lights adorn St. Paul's, illuminating the façade and the word "Hope." I pay the driver and sprint through the emergency entrance. Liam and I spot each other immediately, and he rushes over to my side.

"How is he?" I ask.

At the same time, Liam says, "They're prepping him for emergency surgery."

Liam leads me to the waiting area, and we take a seat. "He has a blockage but they don't know which arteries are affected."

I nod, feeling numb. Liam puts his arm around me, and to my surprise, I feel myself relax. I have the urge to curl up to him, to be protected and cared for; but of course that's crazy.

Plus, what am I thinking? I'm married, of course... though with each passing day, I question our marriage's validity. I'm getting to the point where I'm so livid, I don't even want to hear from Micky.

"You okay?" Liam asks, peering down at me with concerned eyes. I nod, trying to stay positive. "Your dad got there quick, that was nice of him."

"Yeah, he's pretty helpful." My phone rings and I check the call display. Oh, Billy! I pounce at my phone, eager to speak with him. "Tell me you're home!"

"I'm home. Oh my God. I've been through so much."

"Are you okay, Billy?"

"Yes, totally fine."

"Thank God."

"Are you at home? I'll come by—"

"No, I'm at the hospital!"

Billy gasps, and I explain about George.

"Okay, well I'll come to the hospital."

"Great, we're at St. Paul's, see you soon," I say and ring off. Liam is eyeing me with apparent curiosity. "Billy's my best friend. He just came back from a reunion with his birth father in Haiti," I explain.

"Wow. From what George tells me, you lead a pretty dramatic life." He gives me that adorable lopsided grin, and I wonder exactly what George has told him. George knows about us losing our money, I guess he knows about Riley, and now he saw me having it out with my mother-in-law. To George, it must seem pretty action-packed.

"So, you've heard about me. What about you?" I ask. A woman, with her arm in a sling, keeps staring at me and then ogling Liam. Even now she's watching us openly, I'm sure listening to every word. I frown at her and turn to Liam. "Actually hold that thought, let's grab a coffee." I hop out of my seat and stride across the waiting room to the door, Liam right behind me.

Outside, I shiver and he puts his arm around me *again*, and I can't stop my heart from leaping. I glance up at his strong features and feel another shiver, this time of excitement. We cross the street and order lattes.

"So, as I was saying. You know about me, what about you?" We take seats at the coffee bar, and Liam gives me a bashful look, leans forward, and actually pokes me in the stomach. Great, he just poked my layer of stomach fat. I sit up straighter and suck that bitch in.

"George didn't tell me much, actually," he says softly, his eyes boring into mine. I sit there mesmerized for a few seconds, before a familiar voice interrupts the moment. Billy has just waltzed into the store and he's speaking on his cell phone. I have an urge to run to him, but figure I'll let him finish his conversation first.

"I had a great time too. Yes, uh-huh.... I will. For sure, I'll wire the money as soon as it goes through—I know it's a struggle for you, Dad. I will. Don't worry, I'll come through. Okay. Bye, Dad."

He rings off, and I stare, flabbergasted. He's going to wire money to his dad? How much exactly, and after *what* goes through? Billy has slipped his phone into his bag and is ordering an Americano at the counter. I sip my latte and wait for him to notice me. Billy takes his Americano from the barista, pops a lid on the cup, takes a sip, and finally surveys the room. His eyes settle on mine and he almost chokes on the coffee in surprise. I wave him over, doing my best to smile, though my mind is still on his phone conversation.

"Hi, hon," he says, giving me a kiss on the cheek. Billy's curls are unruly, and I see he looks worn now that he's up close. He has a five-o'clock shadow and his eyes don't have their usual mischievous twinkle.

"Billy, this is Liam," I say, gesturing to the babe at my left. Only then do Billy's eyes light up, as they do a slow sweep over Liam.

"Pleasure. And *how* exactly do you know Lane?" Billy shoots me a curious look, and Liam gives an easy laugh.

"I'm teaching Lane to cook."

"Oh, thank God!" Billy says, giving my shoulder an affectionate squeeze.

"Hey, I'm not *that* bad."

"Yes you are."

"Thanks. So, how was Haiti?"

Liam motions to me that he's going back across the street, and I mentally thank him for his intuition. Now I can *really* talk to Billy. The door closes behind Liam, and both

Billy and I watch his tall, elegant form as he crosses the street.

"That is one *fine* man, Lane."

I nod, equally captivated.

"He's sweet too. But back to you, what the hell is going on? I heard the conversation you were just having on your cell."

Billy looks taken aback and then laughs. Then, he sighs and his shoulders slump. "I need to help out my family, Lane. They're really struggling."

"That's all well and good, but living in Yaletown is ridiculously expensive, and you're barely treading water as it is."

"I know."

"And what did you mean when you said you'd send money when it goes through."

"Shit, Lane. Have I no privacy?"

"You're in Starbucks," I say, rolling my eyes. "Everyone heard."

Billy's jaw tightens and his shoulders tense. "You're going to freak," he says, uncertainty flashing in his eyes.

"I am not. I'm supportive, come on."

"Okay," Billy leans forward and drops his voice to a whisper, and I lean in, eager for the juice, "I'm selling my flower shop and sending most of the money to Haiti."

I recoil, shouting, "You're doing WHAT?"

"Shhhh!" Billy shrinks, wide eyed, as people jerk their heads in surprise.

"How could you think of doing such a thing?" I hiss. "This is asinine, and there's no way in hell I'm going to even let you consider this…" I continue to scold Billy, as he listens passively and then puts his hand up to silence me. "What?" I practically spit, I'm so livid.

"The deal is already going through. I told Michael Chan

from Orchid West two days ago. He's wanted to buy my business for years, remember?"

"Yeah, I do. But Billy you're not thinking rationally—"

"Lane, these people have nothing. Not helping my own blood would be irrational."

"Yeah, but there are other ways of doing things. You could crowdfund, or something."

"Lane, it is what it is. Okay?" Billy's face is deadpan, and I throw my hands up in defeat.

"Okay, then. What's the plan once your business is sold?"

"Well, I'll wire the money—"

"What about *after* that? Are you going to open another flower boutique? And where would you get the financing to do that?"

Billy shakes his head. "I have a non-compete clause."

"Oh, that's just *great!* So you have NO PLAN?"

"Not really." Billy gives me a sheepish look.

I think for a couple of seconds and then bolt upright. Billy can work with *me!*

"Well then, you'll just have to join the family business." I can feel my face flush with excitement, and adrenaline soars through my body at the thought of my new venture.

Billy tilts his head and narrows his eyes in suspicion. "Lane. What *exactly* have you been up to while I was away?" The twinkle of mischief returns to his eyes.

I throw my cup back, drain the rest of my latte, and hop off the stool in one triumphant swoop. Wait till he hears my plan! I practically skip to the door and fling it open, letting in a gust of cool air. I call over my shoulder, "Come on, let's get back to the hospital to check on George, and I'll tell you all about it."

19

I don't get a chance to tell Billy about the new business because, when we get outside, we're almost flattened by a red Ferrari peeling around a corner. We scramble across the street as fast as humanly possible as the driver swerves, almost catapulting himself into oncoming traffic.

Once we make it inside the hospital and our heart rates return to normal, I'm met with the sobering reality of George's surgery. This time we're directed to the cardiac ward and find Liam in the waiting area, looking worn and clutching the empty coffee cup in his hand. We're soon joined by an emotional Juliet, and I introduce her to Liam. I can't help notice Juliet swoon at the sight of Liam, though he seems to not notice. After waiting forever, to the point where we're all nodding off and bleary eyed from the overhead fluorescent lights, a weary-looking doctor decked in head-to-toe scrubs *finally* arrives and addresses our little group.

"Has anyone been able to contact Mr. Harris' immediate family?" he asks.

"I called and left messages for his son and grandson," Liam says, "but, they're both out East, so they wouldn't have made it out yet anyway."

Riches & Rags

The doctor nods and continues. "Once we located the blockage, we had to perform a triple-bypass surgery on Mr. Harris. The surgery went as expected, and we're hopeful he will make a full recovery." We all give whoops of relief, and there are smiles all around. "However," the doctor says, and our heads snap back to attention, "at this time, and for at least twenty-four hours, Mr. Harris will remain in critical condition. We've done all we can do at this time, so it's up to Mr. Harris' body to take over from here." We nod and thank the doctor, but he's already walking away.

I glance at my phone and am floored to see it's 1:17 a.m.! "Guys, I've got to go," I say, jumping up with alarm. "Talk tomorrow!"

I slip into an elevator just as it closes, not bothering to wait for my friends. I have to get home—this is so unfair to Dad.

I hop a bus back to Kits, and arrive home to a darkened house. I fumble for my keys, and when I finally open the front door, Piper comes running. He—or is it she?—greets me with wide eyes and starts a chorus of ear-piercing meows. I sigh and crouch down beside her for a little pat.

"Don't worry," I coo, "your papa's going to be just fine." The cat purrs and rubs her silky coat against me, as though it understands what I'm saying. "We should probably get you fed," I say, realizing I'll have to look after it.

In George's kitchen, a few dishes litter the counter. Everything is old and worn but clean enough, which is somewhat of a relief. If it were a disaster, I guess *I'd* have to clean it for his homecoming. I spot the cat dishes with plenty of food and water, so I switch off the lights and use the flashlight from my phone to navigate the stairs.

I swing open the attic door and tiptoe inside. The room is cloaked in darkness, so I shine my phone around. The canopy of my bed is open, and I can make out the girls' sleeping frames. But—wait, there's a third small figure the size of a child in the bed. What the...? I shine the light and slowly approach.

Oh God! Riley's freakish face is grinning back at me. I almost scream, clapping my hand over my mouth as I stare at the puppet with horror, and shudder at the sight of that face. My heart hammers in my chest and I'm panting, trying to catch my breath. Riley is lying on the other side of Rory and her hand is holding his. I frown and loosen her grip from the freakish dummy. Now, where's Dad? I shine my light to the sitting area and make out Dad's slumped outline in one of the chairs. Poor guy. I creep across the room to him, almost tripping on toys along the way.

"Dad," I whisper. "Dad!" I hiss, giving his shoulder a light shake. He lifts his head and rubs his neck, making groaning noises.

"What time is it?" he asks, his voice groggy from sleep.

"Almost two o'clock. I'm so sorry."

"Is George okay?" he whispers.

"Yeah, he should be just fine."

"Oh good!" Dad calls Louisa, who actually agrees to pick him up at this crazy hour, instead of telling him to stop being a cheap bastard and call a cab, like I would have said. He gathers Riley from the bed and wraps him in a blanket, saying he doesn't want to wake him. I'm glad Dad can't see my face as I roll my eyes at the insanity of it all.

When they're gone, I crawl into bed where Riley was and try to ignore that there's an actual warm spot in the bed from Riley's body. Okay, that's just so incredibly creepy!

Though I haven't said my prayers in, well, probably years, I find myself saying a little prayer for George, and then for my girls, so sweet and dear, and for Dad, who finally seems happy, for Mom, who I'd like to think is watching down on me, and for Micky, who is out there somewhere. My Micky.

Riches & Rags

The blaring alarm clock assaults my deep sleep, and I lift my head in dismay. Bloody school! I roll onto my side and slam my fist on the snooze button. Too late though; my mind has jumped into action for what we need to do today.

I have to get an update on George.

Billy and I have to meet to discuss the business.

I need more groceries.

I need to do laundry.

What day is it anyway? Friday? No—only Thursday.

Rory starts to squirm behind me, so I roll over and nuzzle her face with my nose. She smiles at me and takes my face in her hands.

"Hi, baby," I whisper.

"Iiiii."

"Come on; let's let your sister sleep," I say, hopping out of bed. Margo has been moody lately. She needs to catch up on her sleep—she can go to school late today. I change Rory's diaper and set her on the floor with some toy cars. I fill the kettle with water for coffee, and join Rory on the floor while I wait for the kettle to boil.

In the silence of the attic, I can make out faint but deliberate meows. It's that bloody cat of George's again. The meows sound frantic, and I wonder if Piper somehow locked herself in a room or closet.

"Let's go investigate," I whisper to Rory. I shut the stove off, pick up Rory, and slip my feet into my slippers. Margo is still in dreamland, so I let her be and carry Rory downstairs to find the cat.

On the second level, the meows are louder, but it's hard to distinguish which direction they're coming from. I push a door open and flick the light. This must be a spare bedroom. In it, there's an old brass bed, a floral curtain, and generic Monet prints on the walls. There are three more similar spare rooms and a bathroom, but still no cat.

I push the last door open to find a very different room. An impressive, king-sized four-poster bed is positioned in the center of the room. The blankets are worn but made of fine materials in delicate patterns. There's another fireplace in this room, with a cozy sitting area beside it. Beautiful antiques are displayed throughout; it's the kind of inviting space you want to curl up in.

But the most intriguing features of this room have nothing to do with crown molding or ornate light fixtures: it's the enlarged and handsomely framed photographs adorning the walls that captivate and awe me. I switch Rory to my other hip and take a few steps closer to peer at the photos. A lovely lady with shoulder-length, wavy brown hair and Ralph Lauren-esque clothes is the star. This must be George's late wife. She's smiling, alive and vibrant. There are photos of her with a young, good-looking guy—oh no way —that's George! He was actually semi-hot in his day—who would have known? In the photos, George and his wife are smiling: there's his wife holding a baby (must be their son); and them fly fishing together in a river; and both of them seated in a flashy antique convertible in front of this very house, which at the time was pristine and boasted a gorgeous french country garden; and finally the family posing in front of an enormous Christmas tree in some grand, lovely ballroom. I peer closer, taking in the details of the breathtaking room. I wonder if—

"MOM!"

I hear Margo's voice calling me. She sounds panicked, and I realize she must have been freaked, waking to find herself alone. I reluctantly peel my eyes from this other life that I feel I've been privy to, and call out to her. "Over here!"

Riches & Rags

We meet on the landing, and Margo rushes to me and buries her face in my housecoat. "Mommy, I was so scared!"

"I'm sorry, I heard George's cat meowing and needed to make sure she was okay."

"Where was she?" Margo asks, peering around for the cat.

"I haven't found her yet, but she must be downstairs."

We take the next flight of stairs down to the main level where Piper's meows are louder. They're coming from the west side of the house, away from the kitchen and living room. We wander down an impressive corridor, which has decorative moldings and a ceiling painted alfresco, all blue with dusted clouds that seem to go on forever. We follow the sound of meows until we reach double doors with brass handles. Margo and I exchange a look of anticipation, and I reach forward to turn the handle and swing the door open.

Margo and I gasp in unison. All we can say is "*Wow!*" I realize this is the very room where that Christmas photo was taken. Piper is sitting in the middle of the room facing us, her tail flicking back and forth. Her presence is overshadowed by this *magnificent* space. It really is a grand ballroom, right here in George's house. The ceiling must be twenty feet high; in fact, the second floor must be only half the house to make room for these massive ceilings.

"Our attic must be above the ceiling," I say, pointing upward.

"Mommy!" Margo squeals. "Look at the diamonds!"

I smile in awe as I take in the grand chandelier, which could rival any five-star hotel's. Floor-to-ceiling windows span the west and north walls. The hardwood floors are worn—probably from much dancing—and there's a massive fireplace that's taller than me along the south wall. I pad across the ballroom to the fireplace to get a better look. It looks like the tiles are turquoise. Real turquoise tiles—unbelievable.

Margo is giggling and singing, and I turn around to see her dancing her heart out, twirling and whirling around. I join her with Rory in my arms, and we waltz from one end of the room to the next. Who would have known this jewel of a ballroom was right here all along?

"Mommy?"

"Uh-huh?" I stop to catch my breath, panting.

"I love you." Margo looks at me through lowered lashes, nuzzling her chin into her shoulder. I feel myself melt as I crouch beside her and pull her onto my lap beside Rory. I lose my balance and we all topple over onto the floor, giggling. Margo wraps her arms around my neck, and then Rory does too.

"Oh, I'm so lucky," I say, feeling my heart swell with adoration. We sit in one big hug pretzel for a couple of minutes, and then Rory squirms and I pat Margo on the back. "Okay, Margo. We should get back upstairs," I say, not wanting this moment to end but knowing we've got to get on with the day. First, I need to call the hospital to see how George is doing.

"Please can we stay?"

"How about we visit this ballroom again very soon?"

"Wait till I tell my friends I have a ballroom in my house!" Margo says, a proud smile spreading across her face.

We leave the ballroom and close the double doors behind us; but not before we make sure that cat is out. We approach the main stairwell that leads to the attic and are starting to ascend when the doorbell rings.

I raise my eyebrows in surprise at Margo.

"Who is it Mommy?"

"How should I know?" Maybe it's a flower delivery or something for George.

I turn back downstairs, unlock the front door, and pull it open to find some homely-looking middle-aged woman with a sour face, wearing a too-tight, cheap polyester navy skirt suit.

"Yes?" I ask, shifting Rory to my other hip. Man, she's getting heavy.

"I'm looking for a Mrs. Lane Carson."

Oh!

"And you are...?" I notice a clipboard in her hands and raise my eyebrow.

"My name is Beth Tomlinson. I'm with the Ministry of Children and Family Services. We've received a complaint against you from a Mrs. Elsa Capello, who fears for the safety of her grandchildren."

20

WHAT? A cold feeling runs down the back of my neck and I cradle Rory closer.

What the fuck is Children's Aid doing here? I feel the breath seeping out of me, and I'm left staring at this woman in disbelief. The woman asks to come in, so as if on auto-pilot, I step aside.

"We're also going to have to question your eldest daughter," she says.

But, I didn't do anything! I find myself leading her up the stairs to the attic, though my legs are numb. Could they take my children from me, just like that? Could this woman with the sour face take them away *today*? This *morning*?

Upstairs, this Ms. Tomlinson enters our attic, violating our privacy and sanctuary. She prowls her way around, inspecting things, lifting our belongings like they're articles in a crime scene. She checks the bathroom, the kitchen appliances, drawers—everything. She pauses at our bed, then looks around.

"Where do the children sleep?" she asks, her voice rising.

"With me," I say, resisting the urge to roll my eyes. "Is that a problem?"

Riches & Rags

Sour Face makes a disapproving click with her tongue and writes this down on the damn clipboard. "The children really should have their own beds."

"Well, the playpen is here; however, it's hard as a rock, and I wouldn't wish my worst enemy to sleep on this."

"I like cuddling Mommy at night," Margo says. Then she whispers, "Mommy, why is this stranger in our house?" Margo's instincts are bang-on, and I feel fear grip me like never before in my life. Just hearing about the horrors of some of those foster-care nightmares...to imagine my own babies living— *NO! Enough!*

I shake away the fear, absolutely determined to fight this. I'm fighting for my children's lives, and I'm going to smooth this over, God help me.

"May I offer you a cup of tea?" I ask, my voice sounding calm despite my fury of nerves.

"Please," Ms. Tomlinson says, to my surprise. Maybe this is a good sign! She must trust me on some level if she'll drink my tea.

"Can you please go over what this matter is all about?" I ask.

"Could we discuss this in private?" she asks. I turn to Margo who is watching the stranger with unblinking eyes.

"Honey," I say in a calm, upbeat voice. "Why don't you put on a play with your Barbies for Rory."

Margo meets my gaze, and I give a little smile and nod.

"Okay," she says and darts for her toys like a scared rabbit. I carry Rory over and set her down with her sister.

Back at the kitchen nook, I prepare the tea cups, milk, and sugar, while Sour Face makes notes at the fire escape.

"This looks like it's built to code," she says under her breath.

"It was just re-done," I say.

"I learned there was a fire here recently. And that you started it."

I don't believe this! I take a deep quivering breath and lead the woman to the fireplace. "As you can see, this is a very old house. There ended up being a small hole in the tiles of the fireplace, and some embers fell through to the bathroom below. I did not *intentionally* start any fire; I simply lit a self-burning log."

"I also discovered the fire was started the very evening you left the troubling voicemail."

I exhale trying to stay calm, though I want to ring her stinking neck. "*GET OUT OF HERE!*" I want to scream, but then I'd lose the kids for sure.

"Ms. Tomlinson, you can check the records from the fire marshal. The fire originated from embers falling through the missing tiles in this fireplace. This was a proven, unavoidable accident and certainly *not* a case of arson!"

"Mrs. Elsa Capello sent us an audio recording of a troubling voice message she claims you left for her."

Bloody CruElsa!

"And do you have the said recording with you today?" I ask, as though I'm inquiring about something inconsequential, not the very evidence that could rip my kids away from me forever.

"I do," she says, pulling out a digital recorder with a pair of ear buds.

The kettle whistles, and I pour the steaming water onto the tea bags as Sour Face fiddles with the recorder.

"Here, you can listen for yourself." She thrusts the ear buds at me, which I take with apprehension.

What exactly did I say on the voicemail? For the millionth time, I ask myself *why* I called Elsa.

"Elsa...it's Lane. Micky left...and I have the kids...but I *can't* do this..."

My heart sinks as I listen to the slurred recording. This is not good! Nonetheless, I keep my expression blank. I remove the buds from my ears and hand them back to Sour Face.

I turn back to the tea so she can't see my panic or the shaky breath I sneak in, in an effort to regain composure. I pass her the tea—resisting the urge to "accidentally" splash some on her hand—and grab my own soothing cup. The girls are playing as instructed, but Margo's eyes dart back to us every few seconds.

"Can you confirm if that was your voice on the recording?"

"Yes."

"Do you remember leaving that voice message?"

"Of course." *Not really.*

She nods and writes something else on her clipboard.

"But I would like a chance to clarify the situation."

Sour Face nods to go ahead, pen ready.

"I lived a fairy-tale life," I explain, with a small, wistful smile. "Or so it seemed." My smile fades. "My husband lost our family fortune from some bad investments; and he left me to 'find himself.' I haven't heard from him since. It's been three and a half *months*.

"Before losing the money, we had a full staff. We had around-the-clock nannies for our daughters. I must admit, the shock of losing everything—the lifestyle, the support from staff, and of course my husband—in addition to now having to care for my children (something I had never done on my own before), along with having very little money, no job, no support and an unknown future…it was very overwhelming to say the least.

"I left that message for my mother-in-law the very day we left our home. I was distraught." I grab the tea and take a sip before continuing. Sour Face continues to take notes. I can't read from her expression if she sympathizes or not.

"Ms. Tomlinson," I say, putting my hand on hers for a

brief second. She glances up at me, and whips her hand away. "Do you have children?"

The woman hesitates. "This isn't about me, Mrs. Carson."

"No, it's not. This is universal."

Sour Face frowns and leans forward slightly. "How so?"

"Because, show me one parent who hasn't turned to a grandparent before and asked for help. Show me one parent out there who has never been overwhelmed, or even desperate for some support. Show me one parent who has never lost their cool, lost their composure in the quiet hours of the night, questioning their abilities, even if their concerns are irrational or unfounded."

Sour Face's eyes are locked on mine, and probably unbeknownst to her, she is nodding her head ever so slightly. I've reached her! I've penetrated beyond the clipboard, beyond protocol, and am making my voice heard.

"If I'm being investigated because I had a moment of self-doubt, then every other parent on the planet should be investigated right alongside me. I was overwhelmed. I was all those things. But," I lift my chin and flash a genuine, proud smile, "I'm not anymore. I've gotten to really know my girls. I realize the joy now of being a mom, and it's the best thing in my life. I love my girls, and am making a better life for them. A different life. I'm starting a design consulting business and—"

A knock at the door interrupts us. Who has a key to come through the front door? It can't be George!

"Come in!" I call. The door swings open, and Liam waltzes in, wearing a V-neck tee and sexy jeans, and looking as gorgeous as ever.

"Hello ladies." He saunters over and Margo runs over to join him, jumping into his arms.

"Oh, hello, little love," he says, putting her down and

Riches & Rags

patting her head. Sour Face has fallen under Liam's spell; her eyes haven't left his beautiful face.

"Oh, um, Liam, this is Ms. Tomlinson from Children's Aid."

"Oh." Liam looks taken aback and mutters under his breath. "*Blimey*."

Yep.

"Liam here is giving me private cooking lessons."

"That's right!" Liam says, springing into action. He comes to my side and flashes Sour Face a breathtaking smile. "Today," he says, pulling ingredients out of his grocery bag, "we're making homemade Mediterranean Cannelloni."

"I love Mediterranean food," Sour Face murmurs, leaning forward and eyeing Liam's ingredients.

"Do you? Have you been?" he asks, looking genuinely interested. Liam shares a quality the best politicians possess—making you feel like you're the only person in the room once they focus their undivided attention on you.

"No, not yet. Always meant to travel…"

I could swear the ol' Sour Face is blushing. She seems completely oblivious to all things related to me, my kids, or the stupid investigation. I drift away from the counter and go off in search of something to wear today. I'm still in my housecoat, how embarrassing.

I grab a pair of Versace jeans and a Donna Karen knit top, some underwear, a padded bra, and socks. With my arms full, I nip over to the bathroom, sending Liam an appreciative wink. He pops an olive into his mouth, then offers Sour Face one, which she accepts! I roll my eyes and close the bathroom door behind me.

My mind drifts to George, and I wonder if Liam has an update. And I need to meet with Billy today and talk business. I don't have time to bloody-well sit around here all day with this pointless investigation, or even to cook with Liam.

I slip my legs into the jeans, the knot in my stomach slowly easing. After dressing, I brush my teeth and pull a comb through my hair.

I meet my eyes in the mirror and lift my chin. I'm doing my best, dammit. I didn't do anything wrong! I'm not going to sit around here scared of Children's Aid or any other bullshit!

Good to go, I saunter out of the bathroom. Nobody has moved, Margo is still playing with Rory and Liam is still playing Jamie Oliver.

"Are we done here?" I ask, coming over to the kitchen area. "I'm sorry," I say to Liam, not bothering to wait for Sour Face's reply, "I need to get Margo to school and I have a business meeting afterwards."

Sour Face seems to get the point and stands to smooth her ugly suit. "Actually, I must go."

Yes!

"Would you still like to question my eldest daughter?"

"I don't think that will be necessary." Sour Face scribbles something on the clipboard and clicks her pen closed. She bends over and slips the clipboard and pen into her bag, and Liam and I exchange looks of relief over her head.

"Well then, I'll take you downstairs. Be right back, Liam."

"Goodbye, Ms. Tomlinson. Pleasure to meet you."

"It was a pleasure to meet you too."

I bet it was.

We make our way down the stairs, Sour Face is quiet and contemplative. As I open the front door for her, she turns to face me.

"Ms. Tomlinson, what's the next step? Am I going to hear from you again?"

Sour Face raises her eyes to meet mine. "I don't think so. Good day, Mrs. Carson."

I break into a wide grin. "Thank you. Bye," I call after

her and then close the front door with a satisfying click. And don't come back now, ya hear?

Upstairs, Liam has both girls seated at the table eating cereal. Rory has only just started eating cereal, and today she's munching away on Rice Crispies with almond milk. It's unbelievable to think in a couple of months she'll be considered a toddler!

"Ding dong, the witch is gone?" Liam asks, as I close the attic door.

"How nerve-racking. I can't believe my mother-in-law. She was trying to say I was unfit and the kids were in danger."

"We're in danger?" Margo asks, gaping from me to Liam and back again.

"Not at all, it's just one big misunderstanding; but it's all over now."

My eyes lock on Liam's and I hold my breath as he strides across the room toward me. Before I know what's happening, his arms are around me, embracing me in an intimate, tender hug.

I relax into his arms and lay my head on his chest. *Ahhhh*. This feels so lovely. Liam smells heavenly. I don't know the last time Micky even held me in his arms like this. Damn Micky!

"Are you okay?" he asks, his voice husky.

"I am now. And I can't thank you enough for winning her over."

Liam chuckles and gives me a little squeeze before releasing me. At the same time, I hear the bathroom door slam, and I glance over to see Rory with her cereal, but no Margo. Hmm. I gaze at Liam and raise my eyebrow.

"Margo?" I ask at the door. I can hear little sniffles from inside the bathroom. "Are you okay?" I turn the knob and push the door open. Margo is seated on the edge of the bath, looking miserable.

"What's going on?" I ask, coming to sit next to her. She's still in her yellow flower bud pajamas and her hair resembles Elvira's.

"I don't want another daddy."

I bolt upright in alarm. "You don't want another *daddy*? What are you talking about?"

"I like Liam, but I want Daddy to come home now. I don't want somebody else."

"Honey, I barely know Liam. He was just giving me a hug, like you would hug a friend if they were upset."

"Why were you upset?"

I sigh, wondering how to explain this. "That woman came by from the government. I wasn't expecting her. She just wanted to check up on a few things, but she won't come again. I was upset to have the interruption."

"Oh."

"And I'm not marrying Liam. If you remember, we just met him yesterday. Plus, I'm already married to your father." I slip my arm around Margo's shoulder and pull her little body close. "Margo, I can't explain where your father is, because I don't know. But I do know he needs some time to think. His business had some major difficulties and he was really upset by it all. But he'll be back any day, really." Margo raises her eyes to mine and I nod in confirmation.

Then, as if remembering something, she slips off the side of the bath and flings the door open. "Liam! We found a dancing room with diamonds downstairs."

"Did you, love?" he asks.

"We did," I say as I pick up Rory and then blow a raspberry on her stomach. Phew! Diaper change time. "Do you know anything about a grand ballroom right here in George's house?"

Liam thinks for a second. "I haven't got a baldy."

"I'm not sure what that means. Irish for something? But come. I'll show you."

Riches & Rags

I finish changing Rory's bum and whisk her into my arms.

"I called the hospital this morning," Liam says, as we descend the stairs. Margo hops down the stairs—*hop, hop, hop*.

"Oh good, I imagine he's okay?"

"He is. He's making a textbook recovery."

"Awesome," I say, relieved.

Piper awaits us at the bottom of the stairs, sitting directly in our way.

"Hi cat!" Margo sings, trying to pick her up, to no avail.

"Come on, Margo." I hike Rory up higher in my arms, and lead Liam down that amazing corridor.

"Ready?" I ask, my voice bursting with anticipation. Liam just laughs and nods. I pull the latches and sweep both doors open in a grand gesture. Liam's mouth drops as he slowly enters the space, taking in the stunning majesty.

"I've been here before," he whispers.

"Really?" I ask, intrigued. Rory struggles to get out of my arm, so I reluctantly put her down on the dusty floor. Margo is already spinning and dancing again. If this room is magical to me, I can only imagine what it would be like from a child's perspective.

"Earth to Liam?"

Liam is meandering around seemingly awed, and completely transfixed. "I was here. I know it. It's familiar to me, but like a dream."

"Well, do you remember any details?"

"I know there were people everywhere, like a party."

"Anything else?"

Liam furrows his brow and gnaws at the corner of his bottom lip. Even when frowning, he's still a babe.

"I remember a giant Christmas tree!" His face lights up, eyes shining.

"Was it over there?" I ask, recollecting the photograph.

Liam shrugs. "Ah, not sure, it's all pretty fuzzy. But I definitely remember the tree."

"I wonder if George ever comes in here anymore," I say, staring up at the monstrous ceiling all decked out in elaborate crown molding and abstract painting.

"I doubt it. He shut everything down when his wife died. That's what I heard. I was too young to really know. We lived in Ireland and only came to Vancouver every few years."

"This ballroom can't be shut out from life anymore. It should be enjoyed. We should bring it back to life!" My voice rises with excitement. Yes! This is what George needs. We can surprise him! "We can have Christmas in here!" I practically shout.

"YAY!" Margo yells from where she's dancing. Rory attempts to stand on her own but keeps wobbling and landing on her butt.

"Well, it's a nice idea, Lane. But what if George doesn't want to use this space?"

"Oh, don't be ridiculous. The man is lonely as hell. Think how amazing he'd feel to have us all for Christmas. And we would do everything, of course."

"I could make roasted pheasant."

"Sure, whatever. The point is I need to put together a team to clean this place and decorate for Christmas, if we're going to do this before George comes home. The brass and silver need to be polished, the curtains need cleaning, the floor needs waxing, the chimney needs to be swept so we don't start another fire, the chandelier needs shining…" I take mental notes of the to-do list while compiling a separate list of people to help. Dad, Juliet, Billy, maybe even John Childs, Liam of course, me, and even Louisa. "Let's clean right away! Just in case George comes home soon. I'll go call everyone!" I announce, a thrill of delight electrifying me. Yippee!

21

Saturday was cleaning day. The whole crew—Liam, Dad, Louisa, Juliet, Billy, even John Childs—came over to help. And of course there were the girls and I. Oh, and Riley, if I count him. Dad was so busy "helping" Riley sweep, shine, and dust that he didn't do anything himself. But that's okay, because as they say, many hands make light work. Billy brought another self-burning log, but this one was the kind that cleans the chimney at the same time, so we didn't need a chimney sweeping company to come.

And it's a good thing, because I am down to my *last* grand. With Christmas around the corner, that's incredibly upsetting. Not to mention I won't have enough money for January's rent. It's no wonder I've been obsessed with getting this business off the ground—it's my only hope.

Anyway, the ballroom looks glorious now! We were even able to bring the dinner table from George's formal dining room into the ballroom and place it under the chandelier. The table seats ten, which is perfect. We're all so excited to surprise George and to have Christmas dinner all together with him. Still no word on exactly when he'll be coming home, but the doctors are confident it will be in time for Christmas.

Today Dad is coming over to watch Rory, and I'm going to Billy's condo for another brainstorming session. My phone pings with a text, and I check it to see Riley's number.

We're here toots.

I glance at Rory, who is napping on my bed, grab my bag, and slip out of the room. Downstairs, I open the door to find Dad standing on the stoop with Louisa and Riley. Dad's eyes are bright and Louisa is looking pretty radiant herself; must be all the wedding planning.

"Hi guys, thanks for coming," I say, stepping aside to let them in. I've decided to just accept Louisa. It is what it is. And she makes Dad happy, which is the most important thing.

"Hiya, Elaine!" Riley shrieks in that godawful voice.

"Hey."

"Lane, you won't believe it." Dad is beaming and Louisa is trying to hide a smile.

"What?"

"Riley is *clairvoyant!*" he announces with pride.

Okay, I really don't have time for this. I swing my bag to the other arm and wait for him to continue.

"How's that?" I feign as much interest as I can muster. I'm going to miss the bus!

"Tell her, son."

"I knew Pops was gonna win the lottery! Yeah!"

"What? Oh my God! You won the lottery?" Ha! I can't believe it! How fantastic. My money troubles seem to melt away. I want to run and cry and dance. "How much Dad?" Wow, I can't believe this!

"Five dollars. So I bought another ticket. For *free!*"

"*What?* Five dollars. I've probably missed my bus." I roll

Riches & Rags

my eyes and push past him. What a wack job. Five lousy bucks. Clairvoyant my ass.

"Hey! Where's Rory?" Dad calls.

"Upstairs, sleeping," I yell over my shoulder.

On Cornwall, I cross the street to the bus stop and pass Liam on the crosswalk.

"Liam!" I call. He turns, his eyes meeting mine and his face melts into a gorgeous grin. Then he switches directions and jogs over to my side. I feel a warmth just being in his presence. It's not just his gorgeous face; he has a really beautiful spirit too—if that doesn't sound too "out-there."

"Where are you going?" I ask as he strides along beside me to the bus stop.

"Just going to play volleyball at Kits Beach."

"Oh, really? I didn't know you played." I can't help giving his toned arms a once-over.

"Ah, it's just a drop-in. Nothing serious."

"Nice. Although, I won't have nearly as much fun." I give Liam a wry smile, and he raises his eyebrow.

"How's that? Where are you headed?"

"Downtown to Billy's to work on the biz. We're going to spend the afternoon brainstorming."

"That doesn't sound bad at all."

"Good. Why don't you come too? We could use a fresh perspective."

"Well…" Liam seems to considers this, and I instantly regret asking him. I mean, he was on his way somewhere already, and I shouldn't look so desperate." But Liam turns to me and flashes his breathtaking smile. "Ah, sure look it!" he says, throwing his hands up. "I kind of feel lazy to play anyway, plus I can head to the hospital to see George too."

And so it's settled.

When we arrive at Billy's, he greets us with a less-than-enthusiastic "Hi."

Actually, he seems quite miserable, which makes me feel uncomfortable for Liam.

"What's wrong?" I whisper, as Liam wanders off to the piano, giving us some privacy. I don't take my eyes off Liam, watching as he checks out the piano, sits down, and to my amazement, starts playing what I recognize to be Chopin. Wow, he's *really* talented.

"Lane?"

"Huh? Yeah, what?"

Billy rolls his eyes. "Can you just forget Lover Boy for one second."

"What do you mean? I'm *married*."

"Barely."

"What?"

"Nothing. As I was saying, my dad's acting all funny."

I tear my eyes away from Liam and turn to Billy with concern. "What do you mean *acting funny*?"

"Well…" Billy sighs. "I need a cigarette."

This isn't good. "What's going on?"

"I sent him the money. Like eighty grand. Before I sent it, we were emailing all the time, and when I called, we chatted forever and he showed so much interest in me and my life. But—"

"But what?" I ask, dreading the answer. I don't know what shocks me more, that Billy wired 80K or that his dad swindled him. His own flesh and blood!

"He's just…different now. He's distracted. And distant."

The Chopin music has taken on a melancholic theme, draping the mood with undertones of despair. I wait to catch Liam's eye and signal for a change in music. He starts playing an upbeat tune, but *now* it sounds like an old battlefield where the soldiers would fight to pleasant music. It's no use.

I have no words to comfort Billy. No point in saying it's a coincidence, when it's clear what's going on. I'd like to catch a plane to Haiti and punch Billy's dad myself. How could anyone take advantage of my dear, sweet cousin? Not to mention, Billy's in the same predicament as me—virtually broke and jobless. But that's about to change, because this business is going to fly, dammit!

"Billy, you pour the drinks. I'll get the paper and markers. No sense in dwelling on anything right now; let's just make this happen."

An hour later, we're in combat mode. Billy is sprawled on his "thinking chair," a '40s glamour chaise, and Liam is still serenading us at the piano. I'm lying on my stomach, with a sea of flip chart papers and markers all around.

"There's this home show expo in January we could possibly do," Billy says.

"How much is a booth?"

"They start at two grand."

Shit. "Two grand is too steep. Maybe they'll give us a discount because it's coming right up?"

"Maybe," Billy says. He sounds unconvinced. "Here's the website." He passes me the iPad, and I tap through the pages.

"Let me call them," I say, taking out my phone and activating the speaker so Billy can hear. I'm patched through to the Director, who informs me the booths are already all booked. Double shit.

"That's really disappointing. Can you put us on a cancellation list?" I ask.

"Sure, I can. My only other suggestion would be to pair with another company who may be interested in sharing a booth, and therefore the fee."

"Okay!" I say, exchanging grins with Billy. "Can you send me a list of the companies who have already purchased a booth?"

"No problem!"

I ring off, and Billy shakes his head, smiling. "One call, Lane. One call and you just saved us a grand."

"Okay, so we need a grand." I say. "And then we can showcase our business to prospective clients. But that only solves half the equation. How are we going to get the designers on board? Especially considering they're the ones who will pay us for bringing them business." Billy gives me a blank look and we slip into quiet brooding.

"Well, let's just get some ideas down. Anything." I pull the lid off a blue marker and hold it poised and ready to write. "Okay...um...let's see. We could cold-call them which isn't impressive and will take a long time."

"We could hold a press conference," Billy says.

I brighten at the thought, but... "No. It'll cost too much money. Plus there's no incentive for them to come."

"Right," Billy says with a sigh.

"It would be great if we could somehow bring them to an impressive client's home." I muse.

"But we don't have an impressive client...or any clients."

Right.

Billy and I both sigh, and I lower my face on the cool paper, exhausted. All this thinking.

"I have an idea."

I glance up in surprise at Liam, who at some point must have stopped playing the piano. His face is bright with expectation. "Okay, *please!*"

"Well, you want to get the designers together in person but you need a place to do it. What about George's ballroom?"

"Yes!" I shriek with excitement. That's incredibly

Riches & Rags

perfect! "Okay, so we'll have the press conference at George's. I'm sure he won't mind." Not that I'll tell him. That would ruin our surprise.

"But that still doesn't solve why the designers would want to come," Billy says.

"Riiiight," I say.

"Unless…" Billy sits up, his eyes shining mischievously the way they always do when he's come up with something delicious. "Why don't we have the designers submit proposals to re-do George's ballroom. Sky's the limit for price and creativity—this will give us an idea of their potential."

"Yes! That's amazing!" I cry, my mind a whirl with possibilities.

"Too bad George isn't home though. It would be nice to introduce the client," Billy says. George isn't exactly the kind of client I want to showcase though. A crispy old man who swears like a trucker and couldn't give a shit about design.

Out of the corner of my eye, I see Liam sweep his hair off his face, and I stare for a sec, enthralled. I need a charismatic client like Liam.

Holy shit!

I jump to my feet and screech with exhilaration, while Billy and Liam gape at me.

"What are you *doing*?" Billy asks, surveying me with a bemused look.

"Liam!" I say, pointing to our new and lovely friend. "YOU will be the client."

"Uh, I don't really have an impressive pad—"

"No, no. Not at your place. You'll be the lord of the manor—of George's manor. Your job is to be the enigmatic, affluent, and dreamy client every designer yearns to work with."

I bite my lower lip and raise my eyebrows, awaiting his reaction.

"Oh, that's freaking fantastic, Lane!" Billy says, and we exchange a fist pump.

"I'll do it because it's for a good cause," Liam says.

"Why? Because we're both broke?"

Liam nods, grinning.

"Lane says you're in business. What kind?" Billy asks.

Liam's brow wrinkles, and he shakes his head. "I didn't say that."

"Yes you did!" I retort. "You said you were an entrepreneur."

Liam gives a good natured chuckle. "No, no. An entre*prawn*eur. It's a play on words."

"So, you're like, a fisherman?" Billy asks.

"Well, just for fun."

This is exasperating. Billy and I exchange a look. "So, what do you *do*?" I ask.

We lean forward in unified anticipation as Liam gives an unsatisfying little shrug.

"Oh, you know, this and that."

"This and *that*?" I echo, dumbfounded.

"Yeah."

Billy and I exchange another look. This one seems to say, "Well, he's gorgeous, but I guess he isn't perfect."

"So what do you do right now?" Billy asks, twirling a curl of hair around his finger.

"I'm teaching Lane to cook."

"That's your job?" I ask? This is nuts. "But, you live in Kits. And George told me you were traveling through Europe for the last six months. How do you afford it?"

Liam physically shrinks back and mumbles something we don't quite catch.

"Do you have a sugar mommy or something?" Billy teases, patting the chaise in an invite to Liam.

Liam accepts and leans back into the plush leather cushion. "Kind of. I have an...allowance."

"A trust fund?" Billy and I say together, exchanging another look that says, "Okay, maybe there is such a thing as perfection."

"I guess," Liam says. "My family owns an aviation company, among others, and they set up a modest trust for me."

"How modest?"

"Billy!" I scold. "You're being rude."

But we both lean forward and await Liam's response.

"Ah, modest enough, as far as trust funds goes. I think I'm rather a disappointment to my family... And anyway, it's not my money."

"Yes, it is. It's your family's. And if you were my son, I'd be really proud."

"Thanks, Lane." Liam beams at me, and again I lose myself in his mesmerizing eyes.

"But anyway," Liam's face darkens, "I don't care about money. I'm a minimalist. Really. I use the money to travel and learn and help people, but I couldn't care less about buying *things*."

"You only say that because you have money. I didn't care about it either till it was gone."

"That's not true, Lane." Billy is shaking his head, a rueful smile playing on his lips. "Money was a massive part of your day to day life. You liked it, admit it."

"I did. But I realize how much happier I am now. I can't believe how much I've changed, and I really don't think money matters so much anymore. That is, if I can just get to a point where I don't have to worry about it."

"Well, hopefully our luck is about to turn around, and we won't have to worry," Billy says, leaning over to refill our glasses. We raise them in a toast together.

"To dreaming and doing," I say, hoping so much for it to be true.

"To dreaming and doing. Cheers!"

Outside, I pull Liam's sleeve to stop him from walking toward St. Paul's. He turns around and gives me a curious look.

"I need to make a phone call. I'm just going to bus home and take a quiet walk on Kits Beach, if you don't mind."

"Sure Lane, whatever you need."

"Thanks so much for coming with me today. You had some great suggestions, and I think the ballroom idea is going to be a major success."

"I hope so."

Liam and I hesitate, our eyes locked for a couple of beats longer than necessary. Then he dazzles me with a smile and a slight wink before turning in the opposite direction. I watch him stroll away, taking in his confident stride and beautiful form.

I catch a bus and wander into Kits Beach Park, past the seagulls on the now-dirty pool, and along the promenade. Though you can't beat summer, I kind of like the solitude in colder months, when Kits Beach is nearly deserted, quiet, and serene. Though it's cool outside, I slip off my knit UGGs along with my socks, and walk barefoot on the cold, damp sand.

I pull my phone out and take a steadying breath before making the call. The phone rings a couple of times before she answers. Her voice is brisk and stony.

"That was some stunt you pulled," I say. My voice sounds amused, not scared or angry, which is what I was aiming for.

"Yes, and you somehow worked your way out of that one, didn't you."

Riches & Rags

"I always will. Your grandchildren have never been happier."

Elsa snorts. I can hear ice tinkling in her glass. "What do you want from me, Lane? Is it money?"

"I wouldn't dream of asking for a handout."

"Of course you wouldn't."

"No, I want to know where my husband is."

Again, Elsa snorts. "*Why* would you care?"

"How could you say that? Of course I care."

"Well, Michael has a lot on his plate right now."

"I realize he's going through a lot; just, tell him to call me. *Please.*"

After a pause, she says with much conviction, "I'm sure you'll be hearing from Michael very soon."

"Oh, okay. Perfect." I hang up on Elsa, my spirits soaring.

Christmas! Micky's probably going to come home for Christmas! Well, of *course* he will. And my business is bound to take off. I can support us; I can take over the burden for a change. My smile widens just thinking about it. I take a seat on a nearby log and stare out at the tranquil ocean. My thoughts are consumed with the happy reunion with Micky —his surprise at how well I've managed and his passion after being apart for so long. We'll be a happy family, close and united for the first time—I can't stop beaming just thinking about it.

I pull out my phone to check the time and realize it's ringing but on silent mode.

"Hello?"

"Is this Lane?"

"Yeah."

"Hi Lane, this is Jay. You did an audition for me a while back and, well, I know this is last minute, but my actress is sick and can't make the shoot tomorrow. I'm wondering if you might be interested."

No way!

"*Really?*" I squeal.

"Yeah, I'll email you the sides. It's only one scene, and though your audition was…perplexing, I think your acting was good. Plus, you have good humor."

"I can't thank you enough. This is amazing!" I giggle just from sheer joy. I'm going to be in a movie!

"Great, I'll send you the contract, sides, and call sheet. See you tomorrow."

I ring off and actually do a happy dance all by myself, right on the beach. I don't give a rat's ass who sees me. It just goes to show, "no" does not always mean "no"! I was told I didn't get the part—"No!"—and then, I did! Just like that. All my life I had this dream, this secret dream to act, and all I had to do was put in a little effort to spin the wheels in motion and it all fell into place. I'M GOING TO BE IN A MOVIE!

22

The movie shoot was fabulous! Dad couldn't look after Rory because he and Louisa had plans to visit wedding venues, so Juliet was able to help me out. The biggest disappointment was there was actually no pay! Because it's a non-union, independent production, they can do that. There goes the dream of the big payout. Also, though there was hair and makeup, we only had a sad, little trailer to share—another bummer about low-budget productions. But aside from that, our scene set outside in a park was amazing. I loved getting into character and interacting with the other actor. Suffice to say, I think I've caught the acting bug!

Back at home, Juliet and the girls greet me with huge smiles.

"How's our favorite movie star?" Juliet asks, carrying Rory over to say hello.

Margo bounds up and jumps into my arms, laughing "Hi, Mommy. Can I watch your movie now?"

"No, they have to edit it. It'll take a while but it was so fantas— Aghhh."

Juliet follows my gaze and gives me an apologetic smile, as I gape at her wide eyed.

"What the hell is *Riley* doing here?" I ask. "Is my dad in the bathroom, or something?" I look around, half expecting to see Dad.

"No." Another apologetic look. "Your dad asked if he could leave Riley for the day while he and your aunt do their wedding appointments. Your aunt thought he might be... well...distracting."

That's one word for it. I shudder slightly at the unsettling sight of Riley sitting on a chair and grinning freakishly right at me.

"Sweetie, I don't mean to rush off, but I'd like to make a yoga class, if you don't mind."

"No, please. Of course."

"So, I'll see you here on Thursday?" Juliet asks, her eyes bright.

"That's right. And don't forget the maid outfit."

"Absolutely! Bye, babes." Juliet kisses the girls and flings herself at me for a squeeze, then she's out the door. I turn around and survey Riley with trepidation.

"Isn't it great Uncle Riley came to visit?" Margo asks, beaming up at me with her vibrant little face.

"Uhhh..." Ugh. "Okay, what should we have for dinner?" I hunt in the fridge and settle on some salmon Liam gave me yesterday. He caught it himself and told me how to cook it. Rory fusses in my arms and rubs her eyes. "Did she not nap?"

"No, she wouldn't sleep."

"Oh *no*." I wish I could call for pizza. This is the trouble with not having any money. "Sorry girls. You're just going to

Riches & Rags

have to play together while I cook." I set Rory down beside Margo, and she starts crying. Why does this always happen when I'm trying to prepare dinner?

"Can Uncle Riley sit with us?" Margo asks.

"Why not?" I grab Riley by the arm and thrust him down beside the girls. Rory continues to cry, so I run and get her a bottle. When I hand her the bottle, my phone rings.

"Mom, can I have a drink too?"

"Yeah, yeah. Just a sec." I answer the phone and it's Dad. "Hi, Dad."

"Hi, honey. I'm sorry for dropping Riley off, I should have asked you."

"It's fine."

"Is everything okay? Is my boy behaving?"

"Yeah, sure, Dad. Listen, I have to go and cook dinner. The girls are starved."

"Okay, well honey, if you don't mind, Louisa and I are going to grab a bite to eat to celebrate our wonderful day."

"Sure, Dad."

"The thing is we're in Langley, looking at a country wedding venue. It's a bit far to Kits and then back east. Do you mind if Riley spends the night?"

"Ummm…" I glance at the ghoulish puppet and to my horror see Margo drawing all over his face. *No!* "Uh, yeah, okay Dad. I gotta go!" I throw the phone aside and hurl myself at Margo, shrieking, "Stooooop!" Margo jumps back, a guilty look crossing her face. "What the hell are you doing?" I demand through clenched teeth. I throw my arms up and dash into the bathroom for a cloth. Riley's face is covered in green and blue marker, and so is his shirt.

Damn!

I scrub at his face, and some marker comes off, but his face is still stained. This isn't good! Oh shit! The only saving grace is Dad won't come for Riley till tomorrow. I rip his shirt off to wash it in the sink, and Margo scurries away. Rory is standing on her own now, and she gives me a triumphant smile. I can't even muster a smile back. Dad is going to FREAK! I run back to the sink and get more soap and scrub some more. The problem is Riley is stained for good. He's such a mess, and if I didn't know better, I'd say he looks pissed.

Somehow I manage to get dinner cooked, though I didn't bother timing the salmon as Liam instructed, and overcooked it. Oops.

I pull the canopy back to coax Margo out of bed and find her curled up with Piper!

"Get off my bed!" I hiss at the cat, who gives me an indignant look and stretches. I go to swat at the thing, and she yelps back and jumps off my bed, ripping my canopy silk with her nails.

"BLOODY CAT!" I scream.

Dinner is getting cold, and I don't even care. My phone rings again and I grab it. It's Dad again. I answer in a panic. Dad says he thinks maybe he should pick up Riley. No!

"Actually, Dad, the girls are so excited to have Uncle Riley sleep over and Riley is equally thrilled. So if you don't mind, we'd like him to stay."

"Oh?" Dad sounds taken aback, but pleased. "Okay Laney. We'll, I'll come around first thing in the morning."

"That's fine." I hang up and sigh.

I feed the girls, wash them, and read library books until they are both struggling to keep their eyes open. Then I sing a little lullaby prayer my Mom used to sing to me, and the girls drift off, each holding one of my hands. I smile and kiss them, feeling so grateful for my babies. I close the canopy and spin around to see a mountain of dishes, toys, and of course, war-painted Riley.

Why is he always looking at me?

I ignore the mess and madness, pour myself a tumbler

of wine, and grab my phone. Then, I sit in front of the cold fireplace wishing I had wood, because it's finally been repaired. I dial Billy and when he answers, I wail on and on about the mess of Riley.

"Try an eraser," he suggests.

"You mean, like a Mr. Clean one?"

"No, I mean like a regular white rubber eraser."

"You think?"

"Uh-huh, it always worked wonders removing flower dye off counters in my shop."

"So, you miss it? Your flower shop, I mean?"

Billy pauses briefly, and to my surprise says, "Not really."

"Honestly?"

"Nah. I think I was due for something different. I just didn't realize it."

"Well, I chose a home décor store in West Van that we could approach to share a booth with. I know the owner!"

"Nice! I can watch the girls if you want to go in person."

"Sure, and I'll try the eraser trick. Thanks a million."

I hang up and go in search of a rubber eraser, then I attack Riley's face with all my might to get the bloody marker off; and to my amazement, the eraser works! I'm laughing, from sheer relief! There you go, good as new. Well, sort of new. Riley is still grinning, and I realize I can't sleep with this thing watching me all night.

"Here, why don't you go outside and enjoy the moonlight." I grab Riley by the hair and fling open the door to the fire escape. Then I plop him down in a heap on the balcony and slam the door shut. And lock it for good measure.

In the morning, Dad comes before I've even gotten out of bed. Much to his astonishment, he spots Riley through the french door window. I try to make something up but stumble and am silenced when Riley is brought back inside, shirtless and splattered with bird crap. I'm guessing I'm not going to be asked to babysit again, which is somewhat of a relief. Dad is so disheartened, though, I can't help feeling bad.

Anyway, there's so much to do to prepare for Thursday when the designers come. I leave Rory with Billy and drop Margo off at school. My plan is to visit the home design shop in West Van and then stop for a visit with George, before heading to Billy's. It's been so long since I've really dressed up, or at least it feels that way. But today my make-up is immaculate and my hair is twisted into an elegant chignon, and I'm rocking a navy blue Stella McCartney pinstripe pantsuit.

As my bus crosses the Lion's Gate Bridge, my excitement nearly bubbles over. I am working for myself! It feels fantastic. Not to mention, this is my first deal, and the opportunity to get out from the endless notes, flip-charts, and plans, and actually make this happen is nothing short of glorious. In West Van, I bound off the bus and try to find my bearings. Really! I've only been gone a few months, but I still feel disoriented.

I spot the familiar black-and-white awning and march up to the door with all the confidence and professionalism I can muster. The door chimes as I enter the cozy shop. The intimate store is bursting with gorgeous pieces, but I don't have an opportunity to browse because the shop owner comes from the back room and recognizes me instantly.

"Oh, *hello*! Mrs. Carson, I haven't seen you in here for ages." She comes to greet me with a hungry smile, probably assuming I'll be dropping a couple grand like I used to.

"Good morning Anita, lovely to see you." I had actually

forgotten her name, but I was able to Google the store for a reminder. Anita is somewhere in her late forties, a willowy brunette who wears her hair pulled back in a severe bun. She's obviously surprised and proud that I supposedly remembered her name, and after giving me an appraising look, she jumps right into sales mode.

"Is there something specific you're looking for today, Mrs. Carson? Or perhaps I can show you the delicious new stock I imported directly from Paris."

"I'm actually here on business," I say, noting the pride in my voice.

"Oh?" Anita looks pretty shocked and gawks at me, wide eyed.

"That's right. My partner and I have launched a new residential design consulting service and we'd like to showcase ourselves at the January home show." I pause to take a breath, and Anita stares at me as though I'm speaking Martian.

"Uh-huh," she says, her face blank.

"I happened to notice your company has purchased a booth at the show and was told by the organizer I could share a booth with another company, as all booths are sold out."

"You want to share my *booth*?"

"That's right. And of course we would share the fee."

After a beat, Anita's face scrunches into a frown and she shakes her head. "I'm sorry, Mrs. Carson. I can't share my booth; I have a lot of merchandise to showcase. Cutting that down by half would be, well, it would be impossible."

"Oh, right," I say, disheartened. "Well, perhaps the savings of a thousand dollars would enable you to offer in-store credits to get customers through your door."

"Well, thank you, but I'm doing that anyway."

Oh. Shit. Anita has lost interest now that she sees she's not going to make money off me. Still, not wanting to burn any bridges, I pretend to browse and make small talk for a couple of minutes, before giving a friendly wave goodbye. I hold my smile on my face until I'm safely outside.

Now what? I'm sure the other companies will feel the same about sharing a booth. I just have to call the organizer and—

"Lane?"

Hmm? I turn around in wonder.

"Lane, is that *really* you?" Victoria Hughes is making her way toward me, her stiletto heels clicking along the sidewalk. She's in head-to-toe black and her platinum hair is slicked back, showing off diamond earrings the size of skating rinks. The last time I talked to Victoria was to cancel attending one of her luncheons. That was just before things blew up with Micky; it feels like a lifetime ago.

I smile at Victoria, and we air kiss each other. I haven't air kissed in ages either. It now feels exceptionally awkward and artificial.

"My God, Lane! Where have you been? You look *fantastic* by the way; you're absolutely glowing."

"Victoria, lovely to see you. We moved to Kits, actually."

"Oh! Well, that explains it. We all thought you fell off the face of this earth."

Yeah, but nobody bothered to even call or text to check in. "Well," I pause, "a lot has happened. I mean with Micky's business and all. And losing the house, as I'm sure you've already heard all about." I try a little laugh in an effort to make light of things, but Victoria just gawks at me, perplexed.

"I don't follow, Lane. What happened?"

"Oh, you know." I really don't want to get into all this, especially here, standing on the street. "Micky lost our money—as in all of it. And he was pretty crushed to say the least. So I have the kids with me in Kits." That about sums it up.

"I can't believe this. I mean, I could have sworn—"

"It's all right really. I actually have my own incredibly successful business now," I say with a triumphant smile.

But Victoria seems as though she's hardly heard a word. She's frowning—or at least I think she's frowning; it's hard to tell with all the Botox—and she appears lost in her own thoughts. "Lane. Are you sure?"

"Sure about what? My business?"

"No, no, about Micky. Because...well, I guess I misunderstood."

I shrug, unsure of what she's talking about. Anyway, I don't have time for this. "Victoria, I'm sorry to rush off but I have a meeting."

Slowly, she raises her eyes to mine, a troubled look on her face.

What a weirdo.

"Oh, all right, Lane. Take care." She moves forward to air kiss me, and I lean in to do the same with her, careful not to actually touch her, lest we ruin our hair or smear lipstick on one another.

I give a little wave and walk away to the bus stop a block up. It's one thing to admit we lost our money, but it's another altogether to be seen waiting at a bus stop. Plus, I said my business was successful, didn't I?

I make it to the next block, my feet starting to pinch, and cross the street to wait for the bus. Today is a gray day, but at least it isn't raining! There's nothing worse than riding a damp, smelly bus. Ugh! I stand among the riders and try to keep my face passive, as though I'm not eager for the bus to arrive.

This could be a bit embarrassing should someone from my old life happen to see me. I pull out some sunglasses to cover up. Bloody bus, where the hell is it? A sleek, black BMW convertible approaches and rolls to a halt, and my heart sinks as I recognize Victoria's car. The window slides down, and Victoria's face appears as she leans over from the driver's seat.

"Can I give you a lift?"

This is so humiliating. "No, no worries. Thanks!"

"Really? I'm going downtown to Holt's before heading home."

"Oh. Uh, okay then." The door swings open, and I slide inside as a car horn blares behind us.

"Fuck off, fucker!" Victoria screams, flipping the bird. I stifle the desire to giggle.

"Thanks for the ride, Victoria. I…uh…loaned my car to a friend, but then realized I had a meeting."

"Of course," she waves her hand. "Lane, do you still have the same cell number?"

"Yep."

"Okay, good. I might be in touch. Do you mind?"

"No." I'm looking out the window, already thinking about my next step with the home show.

We make small talk, but we really have nothing in common anymore. Victoria doesn't have kids, and I don't have money. We pull up to the parkade for Holt Renfrew, and I thank Victoria, then hop out, and walk the rest of the way to St. Paul's Hospital.

I find the cardiac ward and George's room. I quietly slip into his room in case he's sleeping and find his bed in the upright position. George is awake and staring out the window, and he slowly turns his head I when I come in.

"Hi," I say with a shy smile as I approach him.

"Lane," he says, his voice hoarse.

"How are you feeling?" I ask. Man, I haven't seen him since the heart attack. His coloring is somewhat back but he looks so frail. He's connected to countless cords and his arm is completely bruised.

"I'm sick of this bloody place! The food, the staff. It's all dreadful."

Riches & Rags

"I don't blame you. So, when are you coming home?"

"I'm getting to the point where I just want to discharge myself. These doctors know nothing!"

"Oh, yeah?" I ask, amused. "Well, they obviously were able to help you. You gave us all a scare."

"It was just a bit of heartburn, really."

"Uh-huh. Well…your cat has outstayed its welcome in my attic, so you better come home soon." Just not before Thursday, I want to add. And for good measure. "You know you really should just stay and rest until you're a hundred percent."

George grunts. "So, Piper's okay?" he asks, curiosity etched into his voice.

"Yeah, but she ripped my canopy with her claws. So, you know. I'll need a rent reduction to fix that."

George narrows his eyes, a deep frown setting into his already-wrinkled face. "Is this why you came?"

"No. I actually kind of…miss you—just a teensy bit. I mean, don't hurry home."

The old man's lips twitch, and I break into a smile. I take his hand in mine, and then, feeling a sudden warmth of goodwill, I lean forward and brush a little kiss on his cheek. "I have to go pick up Rory, but you get your strength back and I'll see you soon. Who knows, maybe this weekend?"

"Lane, these idiots don't know what they're talking about. But they insist I have some…you know…help for a bit."

"Help? You mean like a cleaner."

"No. A live-in."

Oh. George is so frail, yet so proud. This must be monumentally difficult for him.

"It's temporary," he says.

"Obviously."

"So, if you and Liam can just conduct interviews. Narrow it down to three candidates."

"All right, but I'll probably need to be compensated for my time," I say, half joking.

"Get out!" George growls, and I flash a smile and dash out before he can ask me to do anything else.

I'm feeling pretty wiped from all this running around. Outside, I consider grabbing a coffee, but I really have no money, so decide against it. I sigh and turn in the direction of Billy's condo. As I'm walking, I pull my phone out and find the number for the home show. I press talk and wait till I'm put through to the director I spoke with the other day.

"Good afternoon," I purr, "we spoke the other day and you suggested we share a booth with another company. However, the challenge is the other companies really need all the space they can get to showcase their products and services, so I was thinking. How about we have a walking booth?"

"A *walking* booth?"

"Well, yes. But minus the booth of course. Since there aren't enough booths how about we have some kind of pass that permits us to still engage with attendees about our services?"

"You want to just walk around and not have a *booth*?" the director asks. He sounds floored.

"That's right. We'll have minimal handouts; it's more about networking and building rapports."

"Hmm. I've honestly never considered that. But... well...why not, since we don't have any booths left? Next time, just be sure to book in advance."

"*Great*," I cry, grinning. I stride past some women in

suits and shoot them a victorious look. I'm conducting business too!

"So, let's see. If half a booth is a thousand dollars then a walking engagement would be, well, how about two fifty?"

"Two hundred and fifty?" I ask, trying to keep my voice calm.

"Correct."

YES!

"I think that's fair," I confirm, keeping my voice casual. "Thanks so much." I ring off.

Two hundred and fifty bucks! No freaking way! *And* we don't have to stand behind some stupid booth all day. Mission for the day accomplished: home show, here we come!

23

We're meeting with the designers in the ballroom today! I wake up with all the excitement of a kid on Christmas morning. We have nine design companies confirmed, who we'll meet with every hour on the hour from ten o'clock onward—it's going to be a hell of a busy day. Everything was laid out last night for Margo, so I'm able to breeze through the morning routine and get her off to school. Unfortunately, Dad is out sampling wedding cakes today, so he won't be able to watch Rory. I actually think he's still a bit disgruntled with what happened to Riley when I was supposedly looking after him. Oh well. Instead, Juliet will watch Rory—but the logistics are going to be a little off, because she's also supposed to be answering the door and fetching refreshments.

The first person to arrive is Liam, wearing silver-gray suit pants and a white, pocket-less Armani shirt. His hair is swept back with mousse or something, so it doesn't look slick, but rather perfectly groomed. When I open the door to greet him, my heart jumps into my throat. He's the most breathtaking creature I've probably ever seen, and when he smiles, it's like a thousand angels erupting into song.

"Good morning, love," he says, and leans forward to

Riches & Rags

brush a tender kiss on my cheek. I inhale with greed, wishing we could just stay like this all day. But then Rory squirms in my arms, having being squished between us. "It's the little love." Liam opens his arms to take her.

I hand her over and race upstairs for the final touches. I grab our sleek brochures, which outline the benefits for designers who work with us. The images on the brochure are from the renos I oversaw in our West Van house. I may have hired contractors, but the design concepts were all mine, down to the last minute detail. I slip the brochures along with my notepad and pens into a leather case I borrowed from George's study, and inspect myself in the mirror. My hair is flat ironed and sleek, my makeup is smoky eyes and nude glossy lips, and my outfit is a black top with a pleated satin design down the front—to resemble an abstract tie—and a fuchsia pencil skirt and six-inch platform Jimmy Choo's. I pop some diamond studs in my ears and spray on Coco Chanel Mademoiselle scent. Satisfied with the finished product, I grin at myself, grab Rory's diaper bag and the leather case, and teeter my way down the stairs.

Billy has arrived and is wearing a fitted, black top paired with black skinny pants. A gray-and-black canvas Louis Vuitton bag is draped on his shoulder, and his Izimiaki cologne hangs in the air.

"Laney, you ready?" His green eyes twinkle as he reaches out to give my hand a little squeeze.

"As ready as ready can be. Is Juliet here yet?" The doorbell rings as I say this, and Billy pulls it open. Juliet is standing on the stoop, her auburn hair curled and her makeup perfect.

But it's not her face I'm gawking at.

"Wow!" Liam says coming from behind me. I choose to ignore his enthusiasm.

"Is this okay?" Juliet asks, eyes big.

Somehow I find my voice. "I thought your maid outfit was, like, a simple, black, knee-length dress; not…"

"French maid," Liam finishes.

Right. Juliet is wearing the shortest black, frilly dress, with a frillier white apron and stiletto heels. All she's missing is fishnet stockings and a pink, feather-duster dildo!

"Is this really appropriate?" is all I can mutter.

"She's fine." Billy waves his hand, so I hesitate for a beat, then step aside to let her in.

"At least put your hair up; that would be more professional," I say with dismay and check the hall clock, which shows 9:45. Fifteen minutes to go. "Billy, take these brochures to the ballroom, and make sure everything is perfect. Liam, can you make sure the champagne is ready to go, along with glasses and cocktail napkins? I'll take Rory."

Liam plants a kiss on Rory's head before passing her back to me. She squirms to get down. I know she wants to walk holding my hand, but there's no time. I turn back to Juliet who has piled her hair on top of her head and now has sexy cascading curls. It's no use.

"Try a braid," I snap and stalk off to follow Liam to the kitchen. What is Juliet thinking, showing up like a sex goddess? I should never have asked her to come today. We could have done without a maid.

"Don't you think Juliet looks ridiculous?" I ask, barging into the kitchen and taking Liam by surprise.

"Oh, I don't know. She looks pretty gorgeous to me."

My frown deepens. "Yeah, but it's unprofessional," I whine.

Liam stops and gives me a deadpan look. "I wouldn't worry about it; nobody ever notices the maid."

"I suppose," I say, feeling a tad better. Nobody ever paid much attention to Denise. Why didn't I ask *Denise* to come? It would have been ideal!

"Juliet is really sweet," Liam says, as he lines up the champagne glasses.

I shoot him a look to shut up. So much for nobody ever noticing the maid!

At 9:59 Billy and I hover near the front door with expectant smiles on our faces while Liam and Juliet stand a few feet away, ready for action. Billy and I keep going over what we'll be saying to the designers and try to anticipate questions they may have. At ten o'clock, we're peering through the windows.

"Is that them?"

"Is *that* them?"

By ten twenty-five, Liam and Juliet have apparently lost interest and have retreated to the kitchen with Rory. Billy and I sit side by side on the foyer stairs, shoulders slumped, each staring into our flutes of champagne.

"What if they all don't show?" I whisper, too afraid it might be true.

"I doubt we'll get shafted by every designer. I mean, why would they? This is a respectable address in Kitsilano; they'd have to be loony not to show."

True. We sigh together and the hall clock ticks on.

After what feels like forever, the doorbell rings and we straighten, glancing at the clock. It's 10:50. Either a designer is a bit early, or incredibly late. Juliet materializes with an eager smile, and Billy and I scurry into the ballroom. Liam is there, playing "Itsy Bitsy Spider" on the piano, with Rory on his lap. Rory notices us and waves, her little face bright with excitement.

"If only he were gay," Billy says with a wistful sigh.

"If only I were single," I echo, watching the sun pour through the window, illuminating Liam and Rory. I could watch them all day.

"And here we are." We turn around. Juliet has entered the ballroom, followed by two women standing at slight odds to each other. It's clear both women are awestruck at seeing the ballroom—their eagle eyes are avidly taking in the details, and I can just see the ideas swarming in their minds. Liam continues to play the piano for Rory, so Billy and I glide across the ballroom floor with wide smiles plastered on our faces.

Break a leg, Laney.

"May I present Eleanor Johnston of Katz Interiors and Marissa Marsden of Marsden Laughlin Design? Ladies, I'd like you to meet Lane Carson and Billy Jean of Leia Design Consultants."

I have to hand it to Juliet, she's really good. Billy and I are all smiles as we shake hands with the two gals. Eleanor, a short, petite woman, apologizes profusely. Apparently her assistant got the appointment mixed up, and it was only when she arrived at the other appointment to no avail that they realized the times were switched. Marissa is tall and lanky with an over-sized schnoz, but I notice with appreciation her suit is tailored to perfection—and those Kate Spade boots make up for any personal shortcomings. Speaking of shortcomings, I give Juliet another disapproving once-over. "Aren't you going to offer our guests a drink?"

Juliet's pained blue eyes meet mine and she physically shrinks back. "Uh, may I offer you a drink? Tea, coffee, champagne mimosas?" She struggles to maintain her poise, but I see I've rattled her.

Well, so what. She told me she had a maid outfit, not a French maid Halloween costume! We're supposed to come across as professional, not tacky. And throwing herself at Liam, all giggly—it's bullshit!

"Tea, please," Eleanor says.

We turn to Marissa, who gives a shy smile. "Um, actually a mimosa sounds lovely."

"Of course." Juliet nods.

"Actually, can I change my mind? A mimosa does sound great," Eleanor pipes in, and we all laugh.

"Make that four," I add.

"Make that five." We turn to see Liam striding toward us with Rory still in his arms. I notice with glee the jaws on both women have dropped. Liam drops another kiss on Rory's head before passing her to Juliet, who disappears with her to the kitchen.

"Ladies, we're pleased to introduce our client, Mr. Liam O'Connell," Billy says.

"How do you do? Thank you so much for coming today."

Eleanor appears to find her voice. "Our pleasure. This space is magnificent," she coos.

Billy and I exchange bemused looks.

Is she talking about the ballroom or Liam, because her eyes haven't left his face?

"So, let's get right to it, shall we?" Liam asks, with the authority and confidence of a self-made man. "This ballroom is indeed magnificent," he sweeps his arm in a grand gesture, "but it's rather tired. I hold a lot of corporate events here—galas, charity balls, and such. I hired Lane and Billy to bring me the best Vancouver designers to submit proposals for a complete redesign."

"Do you want to keep within the traditional character of the space?" Marissa asks, already jotting notes and sketches in her notebook.

"Well, let's just say I'm open to just about anything. Lane and Billy have prepared an outline as to my expectations."

I slip my hand in the leather case and pull out the cards.

They're printed on five-by-seven thick glossy stock. One side outlines our business and the other features photos of the ballroom, as well as the parameters for designers to work within. I hand the ladies one each, and hold my breath as their eyes travel both sides of the glossy cards. I sigh with relief when I realize they're impressed—though I wish I knew what they thought about our 10 percent fee. Juliet materializes, balancing a tray of mimosas, and I feel my impatience rise; I just want her to get back to Rory. I know Rory is in her playpen, and she must be freaking out. But as Liam said, the ladies hardly pay attention to Juliet as they take their drinks, devoted eyes on Liam.

Liam graces all of us with a triumphant smile and raises his glass. "To my ballroom."

"To your ballroom," we echo.

This is great! I throw back my glass and take a huge sip as Eleanor says, "You know, I thought this house belonged to Admiral Harris?"

WHAT! I choke on my drink and gasp for a breath as my lungs fill with mimosa. I cough and splatter mimosa all over the place as Marissa lifts my left arm.

"What are you doing?" Billy asks with intrigue.

"Clearing her air passage."

Liam's eyes meet mine as he hands me an actual handkerchief, which I gratefully accept. Who under the age of eighty actually carries a hanky anyway? Then I remember Liam is European.

"How did you know Admiral Harris?" Liam asks in a casual way.

"We used to live a few blocks away. Did he move?"

"He died," I say before I can think of anything better.

Eleanor's face falls and then she asks, "Hey, how did you know?"

Oh right, I'm supposed to just be the design consultant. "We used to live in Kits too," I say with a confident nod.

"Oh." Eleanor smiles. "I guess he was a popular man."

Okay, I want to get off the subject of bloody George. I pull my phone out to see it's 10:22 already, and we haven't accomplished a thing.

Billy takes my cue and jumps into action. "What Mr. O'Connell has generously offered is a carte blanche, if you will. He's open to any and every possibility, whether that includes staying within the traditional parameters for the period of this house or completely revamping the space to reflect contemporary times."

Nice Billy! He really sounds like he knows what he's talking about.

"Ladies, if you would like to take a few minutes to move about the space and then share your vision, that would be fantastic."

"All measurements are included on the card I gave you, though the ceiling height is approximate," I add. The ladies wander off in opposite directions and the guys and I exchange discreet thumbs up. So far, so good.

After a few minutes, we reconvene by the grand piano. Eleanor proposes keeping with tradition by working with the color palate from the time period and installing a wrap-around mezzanine with a wrought iron spiral staircase on either side of the ballroom. Marissa frowns at the suggestion and questions fire safety; and I agree with her concerns. I once made my way down those narrow spiral staircases in high heels, and it took me about an hour.

Marissa, on the other hand, proposes creating a 'wow' factor for corporate events, including building a stage and having engineers install a beam from which aerial acrobats can suspend from silks. Both ideas are credible.

When it feels like our meeting is drawing to a close, Billy and I pry the ladies away from Liam and lead them to the front door. "It's a fabulous space," they both gush.

"It is," I agree.

Billy and I walk the designers to the sidewalk. This is it! "Are you all right to provide proposals within a four week timeline? Usually it would be much quicker but with Christmas and all…"

"Absolutely," says Eleanor.

"Likewise," Marissa adds with a nod.

I take a deep breath. "And our fee structure, did you see that on the card?"

"I did," says Eleanor. "So your fee includes sourcing the clients, qualifying them, and bringing them to us?"

"It does," Billy says, with an encouraging smile. "We offer business development, which includes qualifying clients to save your firm marketing and advertising fees, and we also funnel client inquiries. We go a step further to bring you the kind of clientele you desire, and offer a full briefing on what the client's needs and expectations are so you can eliminate the time wasters."

"In addition," I say, "we coordinate the appointments with clients, so you essentially don't have to do anything but show up and take it from there."

"Also," Billy adds, "if the project doesn't go ahead or the client chooses another designer, or if you don't think it's a good fit, then you don't owe us anything."

Marissa nods again and looks quite satisfied with our reasonable proposal. Eleanor has pulled the card out of her leather portfolio and is nodding enthusiastically. "To tell you the truth," she says, "I don't have much time to run after clients these days. Having them brought to me, already qualified, sounds fantastic. I just hope you contact me often. I'm always eager to work with new clients."

Great! We all beam at each other and say goodbye, and Billy and I wave as the ladies hop in their cars and drive off. Then we turn to each other and squeal in victorious delight. This is going to work, it really is!

Billy glances at his phone. "We have about eight minutes before the next designer arrives."

"I have to pee!" I cry.

"Me too!"

We race inside to the warmth of home and ready ourselves for designer number three.

By the time the fourth designer has left, and we're waiting for designer number five, I couldn't be more drained. My feet are killing me and my face hurts from smiling. Not to mention, I don't know how many flutes of champagne I've downed.

Rory is sleeping in the playpen in George's living room, and Juliet and Liam are flirting in a corner.

And I'm shooting them daggers with my eyes.

"Would you just chill out?" Billy says under his breath.

I don't take my eyes off the duo and instead hiss, "I don't know what you're talking about."

"Right. Sure, Lane. You're only green with jealousy. All those nasty comments and mean looks you've been giving her all day…"

Juliet's eyes meets mine, and I squint in accusation. Her face crumples, and she mutters something to Liam, turns, and disappears down the hall. Now it's Liam's turn to give me a look of disappointment, before stalking off in the opposite direction.

"Do you see the drama you're creating, all over a stupid outfit? Do you realize—"

A car door slams, and we rush to the window. I want to get a look at the next designer. A yellow cab is parked outside, and the cabbie is pulling a wheelchair out of the trunk.

"What the..."

The cabbie opens the back door for the passenger, and to our *horror* we watch as a rickety old man emerges and shoos the wheelchair away, working himself into a hissy fit we can hear from inside.

This can't be happening.

Billy and I exchange looks of utter dread.

"Go tell Liam and Juliet. I'll be at the door to distract George!"

"Okay! Crap." Billy races off in the direction of the kitchen, where Liam went, and I try to work out a plan to distract George. As I pace the floor, Juliet brushes past me with her bag over her shoulder and heads for the front door.

"Wait! Where are you going?" My voice rises in panic.

Juliet swings around, an injured look in her eyes. "I'm leaving, Lane. You don't want me here, *obviously*. I just want to go home."

"No...but...Juliet. Who's going to watch Rory if you leave?"

"You know what? Never in my life has anyone made me feel shittier about myself, or more self-conscious, as you have today." Juliet gives me a long look. Finally, she shakes her head, a look of pity crossing her face. "It's because of Liam isn't it?"

"What are you talking about?" I ask, my voice shrill with denial.

"You want Liam's attention for yourself. But you already have a man, Lane. Why can't I have a good man too? It's always all about you, and sadly, there's no room for anyone else in our friendship. There's no room for me."

And with that, she turns on her heel, opens the door, and pulls it closed behind her with a click, as I stare after her, feeling sheepish.

"Did Juliet just *leave*?" Billy asks, as he enters the foyer followed closely by Liam.

"Yeah. She had a headache. And I think I have one too." But there's no time to sulk because a key is turning in the lock.

24

"Go hide!" I hiss to the guys, and they take off down the corridor toward the ballroom. The door swings open and George is standing alone without as much as a bag of belongings.

"*George!*" I cry with mock surprise. "What are you doing home? Here, come let me get you seated. Do you want me to walk you upstairs to bed?"

"Would you quit fussing like an old hen? I need to sit down." He plods into the living room and eyes his couch, but the couch is in view of the front door. I grab his arm and purposely steer him to the love-seat by the window. He collapses with a big sigh, and I whip the curtains closed behind him so he can't see outside.

The doorbell rings, so I flash George a big smile, race to the living room entrance, and close the french doors behind me. I greet the next designer and usher him into the ballroom, make introductions, and excuse myself for a second. Then I race back to George's living room, closing the doors behind me once more.

"*Hello!*" I say with another giant smile.

George narrows his eyes. "What are you up to now, Lane? And who was at the door, and why are you so dressed up. And more importantly, why is there a sleeping baby in my living room?"

Shit. I glance at Rory who's sleeping on her tummy, her bum up in the air.

"Uhhhh. We had a floral delivery…I'm going out soon for a meeting."

"And the baby?" George's weary voice rings out. He sinks back onto the cushion and slowly drags his legs one at a time onto the love-seat.

"Um…well…I brought her down for a change of scenery. I mean, she gets bored looking at the same four walls upstairs…and we had to feed your cat anyway."

"Hmm."

"What exactly are you doing home, George?"

"I live here. I wasn't going to spend another bloody night in that hospi—"

"Hey, not to cut you off, but I have to go do something. Do you mind just watching Rory for a sec?"

"You want me to *babysit?*" George asks in disbelief. "Jesus, Lane. I've been home all of thirty seconds. I just had triple-bypass surgery!" His crotchety voice rises in apparent protest and I feign a look of surprise.

"Oh, I thought it was just a little heartburn? Anyway, hold that thought, I'll be right back!" I slip out of the room, sprint to the kitchen, pour the drinks and zip them to the ballroom.

For the next four hours, I run like mad—delighting clients, fetching drinks, entertaining Rory, picking up Margo from school, and getting updates from Billy and Liam.

Margo and Rory are now hunkered down in George's living room, where he has finally given up and fallen asleep. It was a nightmare, with the doorbell ringing every hour and me trying to keep up that flowers were being delivered. George didn't understand who they were from, why I insisted on keeping them upstairs for myself, or how people knew he was already home. I think he was suspicious, but all the action tuckered him out and now, with him sleeping, at least I can relax a bit.

"Can we go upstairs?" Margo whines, looking around George's faded living room.

"In a bit. Okay?"

Margo sulks and slumps into the couch. Rory just seems happy to be out of the playpen and is on what must be her sixtieth lap around the coffee table. I hear voices coming down the hall so I apologize to the girls, toss Rory back in the playpen, and hurry to see the designer out.

This designer, Pierre Lapoint, is a pretty entertaining guy. I think he missed his calling and should have been in theater but, from what I remember hearing, he's incredibly talented at design. He's parading down the corridor with Billy, sporting an identical Louis Vuitton bag. I close the door on Rory's cries and turn with a charming smile.

"Darling, let me tell you. The ballroom is spectacular, but not as *fine* as the client," Pierre says.

Oh Liam, what would we do without him?

Outside, the air is cool and the sky its usual winter gray, but I'm feeling incredibly hopeful for the way things are working out with the designers. While Billy and I walk Pierre to his car, we review our services and fees. He's enthusiastic, just like most of the designers have been.

We chat for a few more minutes, then Pierre glances down the street, squints his eyes, and bursts out laughing. "Check out the dork on the Segway!" he cries.

I follow his gaze and can make out a man riding one of those stupid two-wheeler Segway things. "I've actually never seen anyone ride one of those. Remember they were supposed to be the next big thing?" I laugh along with Billy and Pierre as we watch the guy approach.

"Hey, look he has a *kid* on there with him." Pierre

hoots. I glance again and see a kid suspended, somehow, and holding onto the handlebars too.

"That's some ugly kid," Pierre says.

But my stomach has already bottomed out. The "kid" has a freakish grin and yellow hair that sticks straight up. Our meeting is about to be ambushed. I gulp in panic and turn back to Pierre with an eager smile. "Well, it was *great* meeting you. You must be in a rush, let us finish walking you to—"

"Laney!" Dad's voice calls out.

"Um…to your car, come—"

"What's up, Elaine!"

Oh. My God. Billy and I exchange looks of utter mortification.

"Hey, I think he's calling you, Lane," Pierre says, raising his eyebrows.

"Riiiight." I turn as Dad comes barreling down the sidewalk. He does some jerky stop and jump movement, and to my complete horror, he and Riley crash down onto the pavement. The Segway tips over and flips off the sidewalk and onto the street, with a horrible clang.

"Are you okay?" I cry.

Dad lies still for a couple of seconds, then opens his eyes and winces with pain. He struggles to sit up, his arms and legs tangled and intertwined with Riley's. Blood trickles down his forehead and he wipes it away, looking a little dazed. Then he seems to remember Riley and cries out in anguish at the sight of blood on Riley's arm.

"My son is hurt!" he cries, clutching Riley close.

"Dad, he's fine!" I say, before I can stop myself.

"This is your *dad*?" Pierre watches Dad, an amused smile tugging on his lips, and I feel an urge to protect my bleeding father.

"Pops! Are you okay?" Margo is outside. She must have

been watching from the living room. Dad is preoccupied with consoling Riley and barely acknowledges us.

"Well, don't let us hold you up. I'm sure you have other meetings," I say to Pierre.

"That's right, and we do too!" Billy adds in a last-ditch effort to get rid of him.

Pierre is still gawking, open mouthed.

"Oh, dear," Dad says, "the cake probably got squished. I have it here in my knapsack, Laney."

"Don't worry about it," I say in soothing tones.

"I'm sorry, honey. I just wanted to congratulate you on your first real job. Riley and I are so proud."

Uh! I bite my lip and glance at Pierre to see if he's heard.

He gapes at me, eyes flashing. "This is your *first* job?" he cries, his voice shrill with disbelief. "I thought you had a design background."

Dad helps Riley jump to his plastic feet, blood smeared on his ghoulish face. "Elaine re-did her old house! Well, I never saw it, but I heard it was sick. Yeah! Elaine, you gotta give me some of them business cards. I'm gonna give them out everywhere! The people in the complex, the guy who owns the convenience store where I buy my pre-paid cell phone cards, even the bum on da street corner!"

Billy and I exchange another look of horror. This has gone from bad, to worse, to suicidal. I have to stop this NOW! As Billy drags the Segway off the road, I yank Dad onto his feet, as he cries out in pain. Then I turn to Pierre, and with firm professionalism, I extend my hand. "It was lovely to meet you, Pierre," I say with a nod. He reluctantly pulls his eyes away from Dad and Riley, and shakes my hand. Amusement dances on his features. I just know when he gets into his car, he'll be howling all the way back to the office; and I'll probably be the laughing stock of Vancouver.

Pierre says goodbye to Billy and makes his way across

Riches & Rags

the street. He unlocks his Porsche, and I race in front and place my hand on his car door to stop him from opening it.

"Listen, Pierre," I say in a lowered voice, "I apologize for the…unprofessional intrusion. My father is, well, he's delusional" I plead with my eyes for him to understand, then add for good measure, "And he hasn't been taking his meds."

Finally his expression flickers from amusement to something deeper. "I get it, Lane. Family is family. We can't choose them, we can't kill them."

I break into a smile, relief washing over me. "So, we're good?"

"Yeah. At least your dad brings you cake. My dad disowned me." He slides into his car, roars the engine, and rolls down his window and adds, "Just keep bringing me hot-ass clients like Liam, and keep the ventriloquist and his puppet the fuck away from the clients, and I'll work with you—no problem." And with that, he waves like the queen, peels out, and speeds down the street.

I sigh and turn back to the house, feeling a mixture of embarrassment and relief.

But Dad's still here.

Shit.

Wait! Dad can babysit—yes! I glance at the time and see the next designer should be rolling up any minute. Now I have to keep Dad from telling George about today, hide Dad, Riley, and the girls in the attic, hide the designers from George and vise-versa, and play hostess fetching drinks, all the while carrying on trying to impress and sell to the designers.

Right.

No problem.

"Rory's screaming and George is mad!" Margo hollers at me from the door stoop.

"Be right there!"

25

The rest of the afternoon passes smoothly, and I manage to keep the drama at bay for the last couple of hours. Dad is bandaged up, as is Riley, and they drive off into the sunset, Segway-style, as Billy and I look on, shaking our heads.

"You know what you have to do now, right, Lane?" Billy says, draping his arm around my shoulder.

I look up at him, perplexed. "What's that?"

"You need to go apologize to Juliet. Now."

"Do I *have* to?"

"Go!"

"Wait, what about the girls?"

"Uncle Billy will make them dinner, and maybe Liam will help. And, anyway, we have to feed George too."

Oh right, I need to get on with hiring someone to care for him. Like I don't have enough on my plate as is! "Fine." I pout. "But I'm taking your car!"

"I don't care, just make it right."

"Yeah, yeah."

On the drive to Mount Pleasant, I try to compose what to say to Juliet. The truth is I do feel kind of shitty for the way I overreacted. And she's right, what should I care about

Liam anyway? I mean, I don't even care at all! The other bummer is Juliet and I haven't had a fight for years. She really is the sweetest person I know—and I was the total cow.

I turn onto Main Street feeling a bit flustered. God, I don't even know if she'll be home. I find parking and swing the car into a perfect parallel park; after practicing on the Range Rover this is child's play.

Thinking about George, I grab my bag and slip out of the car, when a sheer moment of genius strikes. I can't believe the answer was in front of me all along. Juliet lives in a brick, two-story walk-up, above a comic shop of all things—though we decided that was probably a good thing, because if she lived above a coffee shop, she'd be broke. She once had a boyfriend that couldn't resist slipping downstairs to read comics every time he visited. Eventually, Juliet got tired of it and sent him packing.

I buzz her number and wait impatiently for a full couple of minutes, or at least it feels like it. Then I buzz again, this time not taking my finger off the button, which should drive her mad. Sure enough, a window flies open above, and Juliet sticks her head out. It's hard to see her in the dark, but I know it must be her.

"I need to talk to you," I holler, bouncing a bit and rubbing my arms to stay warm.

Juliet's voice comes small and shaky. "I'm not interested."

"Oh, come on! I know I don't deserve it, but just hear me out. Please!"

"Lane, I meant what I said. There's no room for me in our friendship."

"Bullshit! There's always room. Come on, I have good news for you." This must have sparked her curiosity, because after hesitating briefly, she retreats inside and buzzes me in. Thank God—it's freezing.

I bound up the stairs, and Juliet is standing at her door, blocking my way. She's wearing old sweats, her auburn hair is twisted into a knot, and her face is tear stained and swollen.

I shrink back slightly when I see her; she looks hideous. "Aren't you going to let me in?"

"No."

Okay…she's really going to make me work for it. I take a deep breath—here goes. "I'm so sorry. I truly am. And you were right, it was all about Liam, which is ridiculous really; I mean, I'm married and I—"

"See, it's all about you again! You can't even apologize without talking about yourself." Juliet narrows her eyes, as if daring me to try again.

I pause and speak slower, choosing my words carefully. "Juliet, you're my oldest, dearest friend. You didn't deserve to be treated like that, not in a million years. You were very generous with your time to—"

"What's the surprise?"

"Oh! Well, I have to come in to tell you."

"No you don't. What's the surprise?"

"You know how you want to work with seniors?"

"Yeah. I didn't think you'd remember."

I roll my eyes, "Of course I remembered. Anyway, how would you like to come care for George? He asked me to hire someone, and I think he would be elated to have you."

"*Really?*" Juliet's face blooms into a gigantic smile, and she flings her arms around me. "Oh, Laney, I hate to fight with you. Especially about a boy. We haven't fought like that since you stole Brad Taylor from me. Which I haven't forgotten, by the way."

I pull away from her hug and grin. "I did you a favor, believe me."

"What are you talking about?" she asks, stepping aside.

I enter the living room and survey the damage. Her

Riches & Rags

couch is covered in used tissues, all the blinds are drawn, and only a sad, old lamp casts a dim glare on the worn floor. "Is that our old yearbook?" I ask.

"Yeeeah." Juliet gives me a sheepish look, and I shake my head in amusement.

"Wow, you really got into the mourning our friendship thing."

"I did. But what was that you were saying about Brad Taylor?"

"Oh, right. High school. Well, it was so long ago, I don't remember."

"Yes you do. I'll make tea." She drifts over to the galley kitchen and starts filling the kettle.

"Okay, I do. Rumor had it Brad was going to ask you out, only to use you and lose you. It was a bit of a bet within the rugby team."

"*No!*" Juliet pops her head out of the kitchen, wide eyed.

"Yeah. So I thought I'd, you know, distract him."

"Wow, Lane. And I was so mad; I mean, look what you did for me."

I beam at her praise and sink into the sofa, relieved. So maybe the Brad Taylor thing was a bit exaggerated. I mean, he was a pig, so he was *probably* planning something like that.

I did do Juliet a favor!

"Well, I have a surprise for you too," she says, and I look up, alert.

"Oh, I should have mentioned, I can't exchange Christmas presents this year. It's just too tight. I had to resort to buying secondhand ice skates for Margo for twelve bucks. They're in great shape though."

"No, I'm not talking about Christmas," Juliet says, coming to sit next to me. "It's better than that, actually."

"Oh?" What could be better than Christmas presents?

"Yeah. Well, I didn't get a chance to tell you today,

because"—Juliet's face falls—"well, you know. But I did tell Liam, and he thought it was fantastic."

"Okay, what is it!" I'm *dying* here.

"One of the gals in my yoga class just moved here from Toronto. They bought a three-story detached home in the West End and are dying to have the tacky interior re-done. Top to bottom. She was telling one of the other gals and, well, I just had to jump in and sell your services!"

"And?" I whisper, not daring to breathe.

Could we really have our first potential client?

"She's over the moon to let you deal with it because of your expertise in knowing the market out here, and she wants you to call her right away. Before Christmas, she said, so she could get it off her mind."

"No *way!*" I gaze at her, transfixed.

This is unbelievable.

A client!

Adrenaline starts pumping, and I do something completely uncharacteristic. I lunge forward into Juliet's arms. She really is the dearest friend anyone could hope for.

"I'll get you her card." Juliet leaps up and starts digging through her purse. "Here it is!" she says, lifting it with triumph.

I take the glossy card and give it a once-over. "She's a lawyer!"

"Yeah, a divorce lawyer. And her husband is a pediatrician. He's working over at BC Children's Hospital."

"This is amazing, Juliet!" I'm still in awe. Holding this card is like holding the ticket to my future.

It's Christmas Eve! And it feels incredibly festive for three main reasons, the first being that Diane Tolsky, the client Juliet referred, already gave a deposit to the designer—the one who met Dad on the Segway. I figured referring him to my new impressive client was a good way to rectify his impression of me. So, I've already received fifteen hundred dollars, which means January's rent is taken care of, unbelievably with just eight days to spare.

Tonight, we'll surprise George with a magnificent dinner in his ballroom—I can't wait to see his reaction. Liam is coming over shortly to begin cooking, and Billy and I will take turns helping and watching the girls. Everyone else should be here in a few hours, and I'm hoping against hope that includes Micky. I just have a feeling he'll show up and surprise me. And maybe the time apart, his time to reflect, has revitalized him, and he's now ready to join his family and pick up from where we left off. I'm giddy with excitement at the thought of seeing Micky again; it's been so incredibly long. My excitement spills over, and suddenly this attic seems too small.

"Ladies! Do you want to go to the beach?" I ask. Margo is helping Rory build with blocks, and she gives a delighted squeal. "Okay, if we're going though we should go now. Before the guys come over."

The three of us leave a short while later, bundled up against the cold air. Though it rarely snows in Vancouver—especially on Christmas Eve—it feels like it actually could. The air is crisp, the sky is blue, and I find myself floating along in a fizz of delighted anticipation.

Will Micky stay with us permanently? Will he just stop in for a few days and retreat again—or maybe he'll surprise us and take us to our new home as a Christmas present. Even if it's just a rental, we could be together again and start moving forward.

Kits Beach is bathed in glorious sunshine and dotted

with couples strolling hand-in-hand. I find myself yearning to be one of them.

"Can we swing first?" Margo asks, bounding ahead and not bothering to wait for a reply. I follow along, smiling at the other parents and kids. God, today is going to be fantastic. I slip Rory into a baby swing and push her along, as she grips the chains and throws her head back in bliss. Margo spots some kids from school and abandons the notion of swinging in favor of chasing the other girls.

After leaving the playground, we walk along the beach toward home. Margo and I each hold one of Rory's hands, and Rory beams up at us. "Do you know what my mom and I used to do on this very beach?" I ask.

"Your mom? No, what?"

"We used to come down here in the winter, on a cold dry day like today, and we would lie on the beach side by side, watching the clouds drift by."

"Can we do that now?" Margo asks, tugging Rory down on the sand. Rory wails in protest, but then seems to decide playing on the beach is equally fascinating.

Margo and I lie back into the cool sand. The sky is a perfect periwinkle blue with the odd puff of white cloud. "How did Grandma die again? And how old were you?" Margo asks, snuggling closer.

I sigh, thinking back to that horrific day my childhood ended.

"Well," I take a deep breath, "I was at school. Grade eleven—"

"How old were you?"

"Seventeen. Anyway, I got pulled out of class, and my dad was there, all frantic—that means upset—and he told me my Mom's car had been hit by another driver, a very old woman who should not have been driving.

"Pops said mom was in the hospital. But...by the time we got there...she...she had already died."

Margo turns her head to me, eyes full of sorrow. I swallow back tears and continue, my voice wobbly. "Anyway. Before that though, things were always amazing. We always did special things, like this."

We stare at the sky for I don't know how long. I can feel Rory at my hip, still enthralled in the sand, and can let my mind drift back to sweet childhood memories.

"Mommy?"

"Yeah?"

"You're a really good Mommy."

Honored, I turn to face Margo in gratitude and touch my forehead to hers, feeling a deep sense of peace cocooning me. I thank God for this twist in fate—however difficult—that led me to bond with my girls.

To think, I never knew what I was missing.

26

"When George asked me to teach you to cook, he went on a tangent about duck a l'orange. I figured that's what we'll make tonight, since this is George's special night and all!" Liam says as he unpacks groceries from what must be ten paper bags.

"Whatever you think; you're the chef," Billy says, taking a delicate sip from his crantini and craning his neck toward Liam's backside as Liam bends to open the oven drawer. I jab my elbow into Billy's rib, and he shoots me a look as if to say, "Now, you don't have to go getting all jealous again."

"Uncle Billy, why don't you take the girls for a walk so I can help Liam," I say, raising my eyebrow at Billy, a playful smile tugging at my lips.

"Liam, who do you think would be most helpful for you? Lane or yours truly?" Billy asks, gesturing dramatically and thus sloshing crantini on the floor. "Oops."

"Honestly, neither," Liam says and laughs, as he rinses out the duck cavity. Billy downs his drink, hops up from his seat, and goes to corral the girls.

After Billy and the girls have left, I do as I said and wash my hands, ready to help. Liam and I spend the next three hours in cooking harmony. Everything he does is graceful and well thought out. I learn so much, I could do this all day. Billy even printed menu and place cards for tonight. The menu looks amazing.

Christmas Eve Menu
Organic Baby Greens with Balsamic Reduction & Toasted Almonds
Duck a l'orange
Wild Rice Pilaf with Chanterelle Mushrooms
Grilled Asparagus in Bourbon
Egg Nog Brule

"So, Lane," Liam's voice interrupts my thoughts, "I'm wondering. Would you like to accompany me to a masked ball on New Year's Eve? I took the liberty of picking up a couple of tickets, in case you would do the honor of being my guest."

I stop mid chop and turn to stare at Liam in wonder.

"I mean, I know you're married," he continues smoothly, "but I figured you might like a night out on the town. You deserve it."

"I…I don't know what to say." How do I say Micky is coming tonight, or at least I'm sure he will? I can't then tell Micky I have a date on New Year's. On the other hand, why shouldn't I have a date? And this is George's family friend, and my friend. Micky couldn't have expected me to just sit around and wait for him to grace me with his presence again. My heart quickens at the thought. Plus, a whole evening, with me dressed up and on the arm of Liam, no less, does sound enchanting.

"Okay," I say, my smile spreading to a full beam. Liam grins back, and I turn my full attention back to chopping, my heart pounding in my chest. Liam resumes stirring his sauce, and we continue cooking in silence, like two shy teenagers.

By ten to four, I'm showered and changed and spritzing on some scent. I can't help but peek out the attic bathroom window in hopes of seeing Micky; but he's obviously not here yet. Soon! Juliet is already here, keeping George distracted while Billy and I make trips back and forth to the ballroom. I cannot wait to see his reaction; I'm only hoping this won't be too much for his heart!

I emerge from the bathroom feeling the delicious fizz of anticipation. The girls are dressed in their Christmas best. Rory is wearing an emerald gown and Margo has a crimson red-and-cream gown. Both girls have identical red bows in their hair and look like presents themselves.

"Are you finally ready, Lane? You're giddy, by the way," Billy says, his eyes narrowing.

"Yeah, Lane. Your good humor is most un-character-istic," Liam says, with a lopsided grin.

"Yes, I am ready," I say, ignoring their teasing.

We all head down to George's living room. When I push the door open, Juliet puts her finger to her lips, and I can see George in his arm chair sleeping.

"We'll be out here; I'll come back when everyone's in place," I whisper. She grins and gives me the thumbs up.

I head down the corridor and—this is my favorite part—when I open the double doors to the grand hall, I feel like a princess arriving at the ball. The ballroom is ready, in all her glory, and I gaze in silent amazement for a few minutes, until I spot a cab outside the window.

At the door, we all greet John Childs, who is wearing a massive white fur coat. I'm half expecting someone from PETA to jump out of the bush with a can of red paint.

"That's...quite the coat," is all I can say when he bends down to air kiss me.

"Darling, it is positively glorious. So warm and luxurious."

I hide a smile, recognizing John's flamboyant and dramatic side—the one he uses in his acting class—has emerged. I half wonder if he's going to ask all of us to get naked. I glance at Liam and blush.

Dad is last to arrive, with Louisa and Riley (of course). Riley is wearing some cheese-bag, black suit that looks like it was salvaged from a puppet thrift shop.

"You likin' the tuxedo, Elaine? It's genuine French Correction," Riley screams when he sees me, and does some weird hip gyration move, which mortifies all of us.

"Come on in, Dad," I say, moving aside. For a beat, I stare transfixed at Louisa, always taken aback by seeing her. I think of my mom and how she isn't with me for yet another Christmas.

"Merry Christmas, Lane," Louisa says, leaning in to kiss my cheek. I let her and can't help myself from inhaling her scent, noting the comforting similarities she shares with Mom. "Billy baby, Merry Christmas."

Billy's eyes light up and he wraps her in a warm hug. "Mom, I'd like you to meet my boyfriend, John."

John rushes forward, does a little bow, and kisses Louisa's hand. "Enchanté, ma belle." Everyone rolls their eyes and laughs, except Louisa, who gives him a warm smile and pulls him into a hug as well.

Like sister, like sister.

"Okay, places everyone. I'll get George and Juliet," I say. After the group follows Billy to the ballroom, I bite my lip in expectation and go to fetch George. I can't resist popping my head out the front door, just in case Micky is there; but he isn't.

Anyway, it's okay. He'll be here soon, I can feel it.

George pretends to doze in his chair, partly because he really is so weak and tired, and partly so he can eavesdrop on the conversation between Juliet and Lane. He'd be able to actually listen if his damn hearing hadn't abandoned him along with the rest of his functioning body a decade ago. He can, however, open one eye ever so slightly and try to read the girls' lips. Problem is he can't really see very well either.

But what really interests him are the scents drifting down from the attic kitchen, aromas that could drive an old man batty with ravenous hunger and yearning. He isn't sure exactly if he's been included, as he never received an invitation for Christmas Eve dinner and... Bejabbers, if he could only hear what they were saying, maybe he would have a clue. He squints open his left eye to see Lane and Juliet, still huddled by the door, as they convene in hushed tones.

Finally, Lane leaves, and George feels Juliet approach and hover over him, before she retreats out the door. He sighs and closes his eyes all the way. He might as well try to get some shut-eye because all this anticipation is bound to give his heart a wallop.

The door opens once more, and this time he hears someone—no, *two* people—tiptoe in.

"George, wake up," Lane says. She isn't as sensitive as Juliet would be. Lane sounds more like she's barking an order. "George!"

"George," Juliet tries softly. "It's about Piper. Lane can hear him meowing from somewhere, but she's not sure where he went."

This gets his attention. He opens his eyes and takes a moment to focus. Lane and Juliet are both dressed up. His heart falls in disappointment when he realizes he really hasn't been included.

"Since when does Lane give a damn about Piper?" he asks, his voice sounding like sandpaper on a chalkboard, all scratchy and still foreign to his own ears. There once was a day when he'd prided himself on his smooth, debonair speaking voice. His current voice sounds like a cantankerous stranger's.

"I don't give a damn about your cat, George," Lane snaps. "It's annoying as hell though. Can you just come and find her?"

"You're like two bitching bettys. Why can't *you*? Don't you see I'm resting?"

"Sure, George. I'd love to be resting too. Come on, we'll have you back to your chair in two minutes, tops. Just come get Piper. He's driving me mad!"

Unbelievable. He thought Lane had changed, softened somehow. Obviously not. He allows them to pull him to his feet, then he gingerly lumbers across the room to the hall.

"Piper?" he calls, then strains to listen. "I don't hear a damn thing."

"It's not coming from here; it's from down the corridor," Lane says. "But I can also hear it in the attic for some reason."

Lane and Juliet lead the way down the great hall; the hall he hasn't set foot in for years. "The meowing is coming from there," Lane says, stopping in front of the double doors that lead to his late wife's beloved ballroom.

George's wife had the ballroom built specially for social occasions—celebrations and dances. Her favorite was always Christmas; everything was magical with Marie at Christmas. Standing outside the room right now stirs a conflicting mix of both deep sorrow and comfort.

Somehow he finds his voice. "Piper wouldn't be in there. The doors have been closed for years."

"Well, he is. I don't want to go snooping through your house. If you can just get your cat out... Rory can't even nap, it's so loud."

"I don't hear a goddamn thing."

"Well, I heard it too, George. It was coming from this room," Juliet says, laying a comforting hand on his back. But he hasn't opened this door in so long. And on Christmas... it's too painful. "Piper might be trapped," Juliet says in a soft voice.

And that pushes him to react. He takes a breath, places his gnarly hands on the very brass handles his beloved wife had chosen, and swings open the doors.

"SURPRISE!"

At first he thinks he must be dreaming. *This can't be real, this is all a dream.* But as he looks at the smiling faces—the new faces, not the ones from his past, except for Liam—part of him understands this *must* be real. But, it's surreal.

"Have Yourself a Merry Little Christmas" is playing on the sound system, he realizes, and the roaring fire in the grand fireplace is crackling away, flames dancing like uninhibited joy. Standing to the side is a majestic sixteen-foot Christmas tree, delicately decorated and twinkling like a fantasy. The banquet table is laden with dishes, silverware, and an abundance of candles, holly, and garlands. Fairy lights are twinkling just about everywhere he looks. Even the grand chandelier has been shined and seems to be glowing with jubilation.

Margo rushes forward and throws herself at his side, stretching her little arms to hug him close. She's the only one who hasn't treated him like some fragile, untouchable creature since his hospitalization. He turns in awe and his eyes meet Lane's. Her face is glowing with apparent happiness.

But, he just doesn't understand.

And, to be in this very space on Christmas without his darling Marie...it's too much.

It's too much.

He peers again at the smiling, eager faces and at the tree. The tree is in the exact spot it always used to be. *How did they know?*

"George." Lane comes forward and takes his hand. This is all so much. This is absolutely wrong, to have a Christmas celebration in his wife's ballroom, but without her.

"What gave you the right?" is all he can choke, before shrugging away from Margo and Lane and brushing past Juliet and out of the ballroom. His step is swift, and he fights at the bloody tears that are welling up. It's like being catapulted back into time, into a scene that was so precious and dear to his heart, only to find the characters he knew so well and loved with all his might have all been replaced, and there's nothing he can do to get them back.

"That wasn't exactly the reaction I was going for," I say with dismay. Everyone is crowding around me, offering comforting words and saying it was such a nice gesture—blah, blah. But, I can't leave things like this. George is obviously distraught and probably feeling lonelier than ever. Besides, Liam wants to serve dinner soon.

What a mess.

"Why don't you have a drink, Lane," Juliet suggests, but I shake my head, brooding.

"No. I'm going to talk to George," I say. I leave the ballroom and sprint down the hall in time to hear the front door close. Shit! I yank off my heels, pull on a pair of flats, and race outside into the night.

The air is crisp, and I fly down the front steps two at a time. When I reach the sidewalk, I see a figure walking east. For someone who just came out of the hospital, he sure can book it when he wants to.

"George!" I yell, but he continues. "George, wait!"

I reach him, and to my astonishment I see that his face is damp from...tears? "George, what's wrong?"

He shakes his head, a hard look of determination etched in his face. I realize Piper is stuffed into his jacket. Either that or he's pregnant.

"George, why are you so upset?"

He stops and whirls to face me. "That...that was my wife's ballroom. *Her* special room."

"Oh, I didn't—"

"I haven't been in there for years. Aside from arranging to have it cleaned once every few years so the cobwebs don't take over, I don't think of that space. That part of me died along with my wife over thirty years ago."

"I understand," I say. I turn toward home, walking slowly; and to my relief, George follows.

"How...how did you even find it? And what possessed you to do this?"

George's eyebrows shoot up as I recount the story of how I actually *did* hear Piper meowing and how Piper really *was* in the ballroom.

"But...why go to all the effort? Why not just leave the great room alone? How did you even do all that?"

"Don't you see, George?" Now it's my turn to stop and face him. "It wasn't just something *I* did. Every person in that ballroom helped out. We cleaned it and decorated it as a special Christmas surprise for you. And Liam made a feast." We continue walking. I just want to get George back inside before he collapses from fatigue.

"What do you want, Lane?"

"*What?*" I practically yell. "This isn't about me, George.

I wanted to do something nice for you. We all did. For Christmas.

An array of emotions, from bewilderment, to confusion, to gratitude, crosses George's face. "I miss her," he says, his eyes welling up.

"I know," I whisper, thinking of my mom. I take his hand again, and smile through my tears as I lead him back home.

When we get there, I slowly and carefully lead him up the stairs and down the hall. He must be exhausted. "Try again," I say, giving him a nod of encouragement.

He takes in a quivering breath and, giving me a sad little wink, opens the doors to the ballroom and surveys it once again, this time while holding my hand.

His eyes light up slowly as he gazes around the room. And if I'm not mistaken, he appears to be in a bit of a trance, like he's seeing images from times past.

I let him have his moment before leading him to the head of the banquet table. I sit at his side, surveying the magic. Margo is laughing hysterically at something John Childs is saying. Billy is taking pictures of them. Juliet is deep in conversation with Louisa. And Dad, well, Dad is bouncing Rory on one knee and Riley on the other. Liam is nowhere to be found, so I imagine he's putting the final touches on the food.

"What can I get you to drink, George?" I ask, leaning in.

George turns to me with a contented look on his face and shakes his head. "I have everything I need, Lane."

"Okay, well, I'm going to help Liam with the plating," I say.

Oh, what the hell. I lean forward, and brush a peck on his cheek. George surveys me with a look of wonder, and I laugh at myself for letting the warm and fuzzies get the better of me. Time to serve that duck.

Upstairs, Liam is carving the duck, and I have to admit, it smells heavenly. "George is back," I announce.

"I know."

"How did you know?"

"Lane, if there's one thing I've learned since meeting you, it's that you always find a way. And, you're remarkably efficient. So I knew you'd have him to the table in no time."

I grin at him and he grins back. We hold eye contact for a few beats longer than necessary, and then he motions me over. So this is Liam's duck a l'orange. My mouth waters as I survey the four succulent birds, roasted to perfection and drizzled with an orange glaze.

Liam serves the food onto a plate for George. It's garnished with gingered oranges and releasing the most amazing aroma. I carry the dish downstairs, eager for George's reaction. I think of the braided halibut dinner he was never able to enjoy. Well, he's a crispy old man, but he deserves some happiness. His son is a loser for not being in touch.

In the ballroom, George is still seated at the head of the table and Margo is speaking with him. I motion for her to step back, and then I place the plate on the table. George's eyes widen with obvious delight, and he regards me, shaking his head in amazement.

"Duck a l'orange," he cries. "You remembered."

"This was all Liam's doing, really." I confess.

George doesn't respond and instead dives his fork into the duck and lifts a forkful to his mouth. He chews the sweet, roasted meat and breaks into the biggest smile, and then seems to slip into pure bliss for the rest of the meal.

"You're supposed to wait to say grace," I say.

"I already did."

Christmas dinner is magical—with the music tinkering away, and laughter, and shared stories—that I almost don't think of Micky. The food is out-of-this-world amazing.

Riches & Rags

Liam is one of the most talented chef's I've ever come across; and he's not even a proper chef!

After dinner, George chokes up as he thanks all of us. Then Liam delights all of us at the piano, and we raise our glasses to toast such an extraordinary talent. George appears to be in his element, laughing and engaging with everyone. Riley even gets a chance to hammer on the piano with Rory and Margo.

As I survey the breathtaking room and all the happy faces, I feel a deep sense of gratitude and the all-encompassing feeling of peace.

This is what Christmas is about.

"Having a good night, Lane?" Billy asks, taking a seat next to me.

"The best."

"Did you think Micky was going to show?"

I pause, taken aback. "How did you know?"

"You had that gleam in your eye; I figured it had to be more than just excitement to surprise George."

I laugh at his intuitiveness. "You know me well, Billy."

"Well, I am your best friend slash cousin, and soon-to-be slash stepbrother."

Now we both giggle, for it really is absurd.

"And don't forget, cousins who share identical twin mothers are considered half siblings because they share so much DNA!" I add.

"Well then, I'd say I couldn't have a better best friend-cousin-half sister-stepsister."

"Thanks, that's some compliment. You know," I say, "you didn't have to go all the way to Haiti to look for your family; you only need to look here."

Billy leans back in his chair, a hint of sadness crossing his face. "I know, Laney. I know."

"I should take my own advice too," I say. "I should stop waiting for Micky and move on."

"I'm glad you're saying this, Lane. I feel like this is what you need to do too."

I nod and stare into the flickering candle flame.

I don't know where the hell Micky is, but if he can't be bothered to even wish his kids a Merry Christmas, than he doesn't deserve them.

He doesn't deserve us.

27

It's New Year's Eve, and I couldn't be more thrilled. Dad has the girls for the night, and Liam is going to pick me up at seven, which is just less than three hours away. Yes, I probably shouldn't be going on a "date" when I'm technically married, but I couldn't really care less, to be honest. I have this anger that's been simmering away since Christmas Eve—and no—he never bothered to call or connect whatsoever over the holidays. Margo was crushed when she realized he was MIA, and I didn't even bother sticking up for him or pretending he sent word, like on her birthday. I'm disgusted and pissed!

Anyway, tonight is *not* about Micky! It's about welcoming a new year with open arms, celebrating my girls, good friends, and a new business, and just being alive. I really feel like for once I'm living my life to the fullest.

I'm adding the final coat to my nails, when a soft knock interrupts me. "It's open," I yell.

Juliet pops her head in. "Laney, there's some guy downstairs for you."

"What guy?"

"I'm not sure. He's wearing a suit." We both shrug and then I brighten.

"Maybe it's one of the designers!" Oooh, wouldn't that be cool. I bound down the steps behind Juliet. "How's George feeling?" I ask.

"He's doing great, regaining strength every day."

"That's good," I say as I fling open the front door to find a guy in his late twenties absorbed in his blackberry. He looks up and swiftly slips his phone into his pocket. Well, I can tell he's definitely not a designer by the way he stands there all stuffy and dull.

"Can I help you?" I ask, mildly irritated by the interruption.

"Are you Lane Carson?" he asks. He adjusts his thick-rimmed glasses, and I notice a large manila envelope in one of his hands.

"Yes, I am." I raise my eyebrow. What the hell is this all about?

"I'm sorry to do this on New Year's. One of the interns was supposed to deliver this days ago." He glances at his envelope and then hands it over, mumbling, "You've been served." And then he flees down the front steps and up the path.

I've been *what?* Mortified, I turn to Juliet who had joined me at the door.

"Lane, you should sit down," she says, pulling me inside.

I sink onto the stair in the foyer. My newly painted nails smudge as I tug at the envelope with trembling hands, but I couldn't care less. This can't be what I think it might be. No, of course not!

But, as I skim the first page, my brain picks out all the words I need to know and I nearly faint with distress.

Lane.
Michael (Micky).
Divorce.
Irreconcilable differences.

Riches & Rags

The papers fall from my hands and sweep their way across the landing floor.

Divorce. Micky doesn't want me. Oh God!

"Lane." Juliet is at my side, cooing softly. She hooks her arm through mine and leads me upstairs, though through my haze of shock I might as well be drugged because I barely register what's happening.

She helps me into bed, where I lie in a fetal position, shivering. *NO!* This can't be happening. Losing the money was bad, but this—this is part of my family.

Micky doesn't want me.

Oh God.

"Lane, drink," Juliet orders and lifts my head. I sip, thinking it's water, but almost choke when my throat burns from the vodka. There's an instant burning heat and simultaneous comfort, which I cling to.

"Lane, I saw the documents when they fell. I'm so sorry," Juliet says, sitting on the bed beside me and taking my hand. I close my eyes in disbelief. I can't *believe* this.

Divorce!

That's it.

And what about the girls? The most upsetting part is he doesn't even care. When I close my eyes, Micky's face is all I can see—the way he looked at me with such tenderness, the way he smiled when he held me. It's all over.

I lie there for who knows how long. I don't know if I sleep, or if I just drift into a shocked, sad sort of state.

The next thing I know, Juliet is gone and Liam is here instead. God, what's Liam doing here? He doesn't speak, but crawls onto the bed behind me. The attic is dimly lit from the small lamp I used when I did my nails, and the bed canopy blocks most of the light.

Liam pulls my body into his so we're lying like spoons and folds me into his embrace. His hands stroke my cheek, my arms, and my hair. His light touch is mesmerizing, his body incredibly warm and comforting, and I feel myself relax for the first time since receiving those papers. Liam holds me in his strong arms until, finally, I turn my body to face him. I lift my eyes to meet his. His face is full of sympathy and understanding, but not pity. I attempt a small smile but achieve a slight lip twitch instead.

"I'm sorry," he whispers.

I nod. "I know."

"Close your eyes, love. Everything always looks better in the morning. You'll see."

While Liam's fingers trace my back, I stare into his face until my eyes grow heavy and I surrender. Then I bury my face into his warm, smooth chest and inhale his scent. And, as I'm drifting off to sleep, I swear I hear him whisper, "I would never have let you go."

"Rise and shine."

I groan and cover my head with the pillow. Wait—is that *Liam*?

"Liam?" I cry, flinging the pillow away and propping myself up, surprised. Liam is sitting on the side of my bed, holding a steaming cup of coffee. I know it's coffee because I can smell it. "Liam?" I say again, confused.

Let's see, I remember Juliet being here, and Liam cuddling me. Why was—

Oh.

Oh, God.

The *divorce*.

I flop back on the bed and yank the pillow back over my face. Divorce papers. Micky. My stomach sinks and the queasiness builds. I moan as the reality hits me like a freight train.

"Have some coffee, love," Liam says.

I pull the pillow off again and stare at him, feeling miserable.

"Come, on. Drink up." He lowers the cup to me, so I roll toward him and take the steaming mug.

I bring it to my lips and sip, enjoying the coffee for a millisecond. Then I remember Micky, and the misery resumes. "I can't believe it," is all I can say.

"I know it must be a major blow. But, I think everything happens for a reason. And to tell you the truth, Lane, I think he's a bit of a jackass for leaving you like this and never being in touch. Actually, he's a *major* jackass."

"I know. But it doesn't make me feel better."

"Why not? You're not losing a wonderful person here. Think how much you've grown and changed since you've been on your own. You're succeeding at everything you're trying. And you're surrounded by so many people who love you." Liam smiles and his eyes crinkle around the edges, making him look so wise and genuine.

But I don't know what to think of it all. Am I really better off alone? And *why*? Why are we getting a divorce? Did he meet someone? Did he want to get a divorce even before he lost the money?

"Do you mind if I shower?" Liam asks, and I shake my head, still consumed with thoughts of the divorce.

"No, wait, I don't have a shower here. You have to have a bath."

Liam grins. "Do you have bubbles?"

What is this, a fun factory? "Actually, there's Disney Princess bubbles, if you're desperate."

"No worries, see you in a few." He strides to the bathroom, still wearing handsome suit pants and a white shirt he must have worn specially for New Year's.

Poor guy. What a miserable wet blanket I ended up being. We didn't even do the countdown. I feel like calling "Happy New Year" after him, but that would sound ridiculous, considering. And plus, what kind of happy bloody hell new year is this, anyway?

The door to the bathroom closes, and I sink back into the bed, sipping the coffee as my mind frantically searches for clues.

Were we happy? I thought so.

Was it weird we had separate bedrooms? I didn't see anything wrong with that.

Were there any women in his life he talked about? I can't remember any.

Was there anything unusual or suspicious? I rack my brain as I suck back the coffee, searching…searching for anything.

There was the yacht incident when Micky hired John Childs. That was weird. He was supposed to play the role of Micky's client, Fenwig. Yeah, that's weird. But nothing else. Did anyone say anything? I try to think back to the people we associated with. I mean, I haven't seen anyone from that life recently, except Victoria Hughes.

Victoria Hughes—wait, she said something that was a bit off. I mean, I didn't pay attention to her, but she said something about Micky. If only I could remember exactly what she said?

I dive out of bed in search of my phone. I find it beside the nail polish bottle and scroll through the contacts and press talk. It rings a couple of times as I will her to pick up.

"Mrs. Hughes' phone, may I take a message?" It's one of the maids. I don't recognize her voice.

"Can I speak with Victoria?"

"I'm afraid Victoria is unavailable."

"Can you get her? It's really important. I'm a friend, Lane Carson."

Riches & Rags

"Oh, I'm sorry, Ms. Carson. I haven't seen Mrs. Hughes yet this morning, considering last night was New Year's and all."

"Oh. Right. Okay, can you hang up, and I'll call back and leave a message?"

"Of course."

I'm not going to trust anyone to pass on a message when I can do it myself. I call back, and after four rings, her voicemail clicks on.

"Victoria, it's Lane. Uh…Happy New Year. Listen, you said something about Micky when I told you what had happened. Something about me being sure and you could have sworn something. Anyway, I received…well, things have taken a turn for the worse, and I need you to… I'm hoping you can enlighten me. Call me ASAP! Thanks."

I hang up and start pacing the floor. Liam emerges from the bathroom, looking rejuvenated and bright eyed. I shoot him a disgruntled look and resume agonizing.

"What was that look for?"

"For looking so friggin' perfect and relaxed."

"Ah, you'll feel better soon too. Get dressed, we're going out."

"Going out? I can't go *out*!"

"Sure, you can."

"Where?"

"Somewhere important."

"Oh, that really narrows it down." Important? What's that supposed to mean. What's important to him may not be important to me. Is it important exciting or important boring?

"Dress casually."

So, that means important boring.

We stop at Liam's condo on the way downtown so he can change. I'm super curious for clues into his personal life. I feel like he knows so much about me, while remaining veiled in mystery himself. Liam lives in a contemporary, sleek, low-rise building. We take the nanosecond elevator ride, and I follow him to his door. It's mammoth-sized polished wood with stainless steel hardware. Even the door is impressive.

When Liam opens it, I turn to him in surprise. "Did you just move in?" There's hardly any furniture—or anything else for that matter.

"No. I told you, I don't need *things* to be happy. I don't even own a car."

I glance around the space, shocked by the lack of stuff. He has a square wooden table with four chairs, and a single steel light above it. A tatami mat covers the living room area and an elevated bamboo tray is propped against the wall. There are no visible TVs, stereos, computers, or electronics of any kind. There isn't even a couch.

"I have a laptop," he says, apparently reading my thoughts. "Anyway, I'm going to change." He disappears, and I continue my inspection of every square inch of his condo.

In this main living space, there's a total of three pieces of art—all nature photographs—on his walls, and one plant —a white orchid—perched on a small shelf.

His kitchen is better equipped—at least it looks like someone lives in there! It has über modern stainless steel appliances, ebony granite counters, and a mosaic backsplash of emerald glass tiles. I continue the tour and find his bedroom, which features a low platform double bed covered

Riches & Rags

in a white down duvet. Aside from the bed and a modest nightstand, there isn't another piece of furniture. His closet does have large doors, but I'm going to guess it's pretty sparse in there.

"We should go, we'll be late," Liam says, standing behind me as I eye his bed.

"Oh. Okay." To the important, boring place we go!

We grab a bus to Burrard and West Georgia, and I look around, feeling hopeful. I have Louis Vuitton, Tiffany, Hermes, and Christian Dior, all within a stone's throw.

But Liam is walking toward the old church that sits on the corner. Actually, I love this church. Inside, it's as comforting as a womb, warm with dim lights, gorgeous stained glass, and nostalgic wooden pews. My mom used to take me here sometimes for services when I was little. But it's New Year's, why are we going to church?

"Why are we here?" I ask Liam.

"We're here to serve lunch," Liam says, holding the door open for me.

"Serve lunch? I don't get it."

"For the poor, love. Let's go."

With dismay, I follow him down the stairs. This wasn't exactly my idea of an activity to lick my divorce wounds.

In the kitchen, there are about twenty people—mostly women—all mulling around. Everyone cheerfully greets Liam and welcomes me. Someone thrusts an apron at me, which I tie on, all the while wondering how I can make an escape.

Have you volunteered in a soup kitchen before?" Liam asks, handing me a tray of glasses. He picks up another tray and leads me into a dining area.

"Uh, not really," I say. I don't mention Dad and I had to resort to eating in them sometimes after Mom died and he was too depressed to work.

"Well, this is a bit different. The food is actually really

good, and the whole point is to serve the guests to make them feel like they're in a restaurant. The idea is to honor their dignity."

"Okay," I mumble, and follow Liam's lead placing glassware on the tables.

Half an hour later, the tables are set, complete with small bud vases.

The street people start milling in, looking relieved to be warm and out of the cold. Many of the volunteers and guests know each other and exchange New Year's wishes. Risers are set in the corner of the large room, and a dance troupe is preparing to perform.

"So, you can take drink orders now. Coffee, tea, milk, juice or water," Liam says, handing me a notepad and pen.

Okay, here goes.

"Hello. Can I get you a drink?" I ask a man who's hunched in his chair, head bowed. He raises his face to mine, and I'm struck by how blue and sad his eyes are.

"A glass of milk, please," he says in a timid voice, and then slouches over again. He reminds me of a child who's has been belittled relentlessly and has lost all self-esteem.

I continue around the table, taking orders. There's a native guy in his thirties, I'd say, who claims to be a healer who helps the street people. There's a man in a rumpled suit who looks a little lost and won't make eye contact. There's a small, proud woman who is obviously doing okay, but may be falling short on cash flow and could use a free meal. And there's a young mother with her small boy.

I'm sobered by the reality that I could have, or still could be, in the predicament of being cash strapped with hungry mouths to feed. If it weren't for the kindness and support from my own family and friends, especially George, things could have been different for me.

I feel a newfound determination to never let that

happen, to strive and grow and reach for new heights in everything I do.

For the rest of the afternoon, I serve the guests with kindness and respect, the way I would want to be served. I sit with them and watch the dancers, and even get a "thanks" from the blue-eyed man with low self-esteem.

When Liam and I are finally finished helping clean up—when every last dish is put away and all the garbage bags are taken outside—we leave the church.

"How do you feel, Lane?" Liam asks, as he surprises me by draping his arm around my shoulders.

I nestle into him as we cross the street to the bus stop. "Physically spent...but surprisingly pretty happy."

"Good. That's what I wanted. The worst thing you could have done today is to wallow in bad feelings. There's nothing like helping other people to abolish the blues."

I glance up at his profile, so calm and assured, and conclude there's a lot about Liam I still need to discover. A smile spreads across my face as I realize we have all the time in the world.

Yes, surprisingly, I feel happy; and I look forward to getting home and seeing my girls.

28

Victoria Hughes got back to me but insisted I come to her house to talk. What's wrong with the phone, and why do people assume I have nothing better to do with my time than drop everything for drinks on the other side of the city?

Today, Juliet is watching the girls because Dad said something about having to share some quality time with Riley, who is feeling homesick for Brooklyn. Now I've heard it all. Bloody Riley! Anyway, Juliet is free, and George doesn't mind her bringing the girls downstairs.

I pull on some jeans and a no-nonsense, black top. I want to be clear to Victoria that I'm there to find out what's up, and that's it. I survey myself in the mirror and realize I look pretty dowdy. I settle on a gray, utilitarian dress and black ankle boots instead. I pull my hair into a low side knot and spray on some scent. Good.

On Oak Street, I get off the bus and make my way into Victoria's impressive Shaughnessy neighborhood. The broad boulevard in the middle of the road boasts mature trees, which have the most beautiful lush canopies in summer.

After a few minutes' stroll, Victoria's white Georgian estate with the massive columns and circular drive comes into view. The gardens are impeccable. I smile and say hello to a gardener cleaning out the flower beds. I don't think the old Lane would have acknowledged him—the thought brings a slight pang.

I ring the doorbell and wait.

Whatever Victoria has to say, it better be good. At least I think it better be good. Maybe I don't want to know, if it's something unsettling. The door flies open, and Victoria herself greets me, which is a surprise.

"Hi!" I say.

"Hello, darling." Victoria air kisses me and I do the same to her, trying not to choke on her overpowering perfume. Victoria's a good ten years older than me, and though she can be haughty and overbearing, I like her. Today her hair is slicked back once again, and she's wearing a Dior pantsuit.

"Come on in. Gina will serve us martinis in the parlor." Gina, Victoria's first maid, appears and takes my coat and purse. "Oh, I should tell you"—Victoria lowers her voice—"Trina is here."

Oh, *great*.

My heart falls. There's no way we can talk with Society's Gossip lurking around. I glance at the time and roll my eyes as I follow Victoria through her expansive house.

Billy and I are supposed to be going over our notes and plans for the upcoming home show expo, and I don't want to waste the day *here*. Plus, Victoria probably just invited me so she and Trina can make themselves feel better. Poor Lane, no money, no man…

We enter Victoria's parlor, which is adorned in a 1920s theme, with crown molding, ferns, and antiques. Trina is there, inspecting some photographs. I think her butt got bigger since I saw her last. She turns and feigns surprise and delight in seeing me, and I seethe inwardly.

"Oh, *Lane*. What a *surprise*. I was just thinking about you and your incredible disappearing act the other day." She raises her eyebrows and comes forward to air kiss me too.

Enough with the goddamn air kisses.

"You look...actually, you look amazing," she says, a shadow of a frown passing over her Botoxified features. She pushes her curly blond hair back with her wedding-ringed hand, flashing me her diamond. I glance down at my left hand, realizing I should probably take my own ring off. The thought fills me with sadness.

"So, tell me. How's the simple life?" she probes. "I hear you rent a suite. How *quaint*."

Oh, God, help me. I shoot Victoria a desperate look.

"Trina, didn't you say you had a spa appointment today?" Victoria asks.

At least she's trying.

"No." Trina feigns innocence, while surveying me with apparent amusement and fascination, like I'm some circus freak. "So, like, do you have a job?" she asks, wide eyed.

She might as well be saying "Do you live on Pluto?" because her tone suggests I do.

"I have my own business, actually."

Trina's eyes widen briefly, but she recovers her dignity and gives a little shrug. "Oh, and what kind of *business* could it be?"

Now I roll my eyes at Victoria, and she stifles a giggle. The martinis have arrived, and not a second too soon, I reach for mine and take a generous sip.

"*My*, business makes us thirsty, doesn't it?" Trina says, eyeing my glass.

"What's your business, Lane?" Victoria asks, showing genuine interest.

"It's a design consulting firm."

"Oh? That's fantastic, Lane." Victoria seems impressed.

"Thanks," I say. Trina looks dejected.

"No, it's fantastic because I totally need this house re-done. From top to bottom. I'm tired of this antique shit. Everything is old, old, old. I want contemporary and sleek. I want *everything* changed!"

Wow! I beam at Victoria and become animated, telling her about the most coveted designers and what they could do.

Trina sulks, and downs her martini.

"Lane, I trust your judgment. But more importantly, I trust your style. Your home was exquisite, so if you can bring me the best, and I mean the *fucking* best designer in Vancouver, one who's going to have all the tongues wagging, I will pay you an incredible bonus."

Holy shit. "Well, actually, our designers pay our fee—"

Victoria is shaking her head. "They can pay you too, for all I care. God knows you need it. But my offer still stands. You bring me the best, and I'll thank you royally."

I cannot *believe* this. I almost forget why I came here in the first place as I follow Victoria around, taking notes for possible ideas and changes. This project is going to be out-of-this-world massive. And…she's decided to start right away.

After a while, Trina says something about remembering a spa appointment, and we barely acknowledge her as she leaves in a huff. After we hear the front door slam and see Trina out the window peeling off in her Audi, Victoria grabs my hand and pulls me onto a plush love-seat. "Now, about Micky"—I lean in, barely breathing—"you said he lost the money, went away to find himself, and left you with the kids, right?"

"Yes, that's right."

"Hmm. Well, I found that strange, because I could have *sworn* Paul had spoken about Micky recently." Paul is Victoria's husband and also a venture capitalist. "I don't really pay attention to his business shit, but I hear things in passing. And he definitely spoke about Micky and some commercial activity."

"Oh?" I force myself to take a breath, my eyes wide and palms starting to sweat. My heart is thundering in my chest, I'm self-conscious, thinking Victoria can hear it.

"Anyway. After you left me that message, I spoke to Paul and he was positive Micky has been busy. He said Micky is launching a colossal new resort, complete with golf club, casino, spa, boutiques—you name it." She shakes her head and gives me a somber look. "He didn't lose any money, Lane. Paul looked into it. He's still very active with all his companies; and others can attest to that."

The air has all but left my lungs.

I grip the side of the love-seat until my hand is white knuckled as I gape at Victoria trying to make sense of this all.

I've been played.

I've been utterly and completely *played*!

"Lane, are you okay?"

I continue to stare into Victoria's face, not really seeing her. This *cannot* be happening. First, the money was gone, then the divorce papers—and now *this*!

"Lane, I can see how this could have happened." She lowers her voice and lays a hand over mine. "This could have happened to any of us wives. We don't manage the money, how would we ever know?"

I shake my head in disbelief and then lower my face into my hands. Oh God. How could I have been so naïve? I believed every word. Even the repo company coming by—that must have been staged too. I didn't witness the bank letters or see any proof of money loss. I didn't see one bloody thing. But now, it makes sense. That's why he was never in touch—he didn't care. I was played and then forgotten. Now I recall he asked me to leave everything of value or he would go to jail. All my jewelry, my precious possessions, gone!

And for nothing.

I feel physically sick. My heart is hammering away, and nausea is competing with the knot of nerves writhing in the pit of my stomach.

"Lane, I never told you this. But Micky…doesn't have the best reputation. I mean, you must know."

I shake my head, at a loss.

"Well, he's shady when it comes to his business dealings. He…doesn't keep his promises. Actually, he full out swindles people. He's made a lot of enemies. I think that's why he left town.

"So, he *has* left?" I find my voice, though all this newfound information is swirling in my mind.

"Yes. The new resort's in, uh…Saint something."

"Saint what? Saint Bart's, Saint Martin, Saint Kitts…" I rhyme off islands, while Victoria continues to shake her head. "Saint Thomas, Saint Lucia, Saint—

"Oh, it's Saint Lucia!"

Wow. I flop back against the sofa cushion, reeling from the blow. I try to grasp and digest this new piece of information. Micky's been living it up in Saint Lucia while his daughters had secondhand Christmas presents.

*Un*believable.

"He actually played Paul too. Some investment, years back. We lost about two hundred grand. It wasn't a lot of money, but still. Paul was pissed.

"So, you would say there are a lot of people in this city who dislike Micky?"

"Oh, yes. I've known that for years. He's just *too* smooth, you know?"

"I do now," I say in a quiet voice.

Victoria grips my hand with such ferocity I snap my head up, shocked. "Lane, you listen to me. Don't wallow in this feeling sorry for yourself crap! You couldn't have known. Half that money is rightfully yours, and you need to go after that bastard. There are a lot of people in this city who would be more than thrilled to see you take him down—him and his outrageously garish resort. I wouldn't be surprised if he swindles his investors and never goes forward with the plans. It won't be the first time." Victoria releases my hand and we collapse into silence, staring wide eyed at each other.

"I should go," I say, standing. I actually think I might throw up.

"I understand." Victoria leads me to the grand foyer, and Gina appears and hands me my coat and bag.

Outside, the rain has started, and I could kick myself for not bringing an umbrella.

"Oh my God. Did you lend your car again?" Victoria asks as I hesitate at the door.

"Um...well...I actually don't have a car."

"No, of course not. Because that bastard took that away too. I swear, Lane. If you don't get even with him, I *will*."

I grin and shake my head. Victoria's a firecracker.

"Come on, I'll drive you home."

We ride comfortably in Victoria's BMW, while the torrential rain hammers down on the pedestrians outside. I'm not an island, and I could never have made it alone. Without people like George, Dad, Liam and Juliet, and now Victoria, I don't know where we'd be.

"Lane?"

"Yeah?"

"Paul estimates Micky is worth about a hundred million at the *very* least. And that's just a conservative calculation; it doesn't include all of his business valuations and property. So make sure you get a good settlement."

A hundred million! My mind swirls at the thought.

Victoria follows my directions and we pull up outside George's house.

"Beautiful home," Victoria says, squinting through the rain pelting down on her window.

"You should see the ballroom," I say with a smile.

"Take care of yourself, Lane."

"You too." I swing the door open and slide out of the car. "Oh, and Victoria?"

"Yes, darling?"

"Thank you!"

29

"What a snake," Billy says, his voice thick with disgust. "I just can't get over this. Who would do that to someone? To their spouse and children? It's just mind blowing." Billy leans over to refill our wine glasses, then stands abruptly and faces me, hands on hips. "Do you want to model walk or do karaoke?"

"Neither."

"Quit being a bitch. You know you'll feel better."

"Billy, that's your kind of thing. You know I can't sing worth shit, and the whole model walk just doesn't do it for me. Maybe if I were gay—"

"It's not about being gay or not. It's about rising up and feeling amazing. Come on, this is all I did when my dad used me—and look at me now. Totally over it!" Billy waves his hand and flashes me a triumphant grin.

But I'm not convinced. "Still haven't heard from him?" I ask.

Billy's exaggerated happiness crumbles, and he collapses into the couch beside me.

"Yeah. I heard from him all right. He wanted more money. He's a fucking snake too!"

Riches & Rags

We slip into a miserable silence until Billy stands again and yanks me to my feet. "What'll it be, Laney?"

"Fine. Let's do both and get it over with."

"Okaaay," Billy says in a sing-song voice as he begins setting up the karaoke set. "Don't pretend you don't love it. What song?"

"Oh, I don't know." I lower myself onto the floor beside the karaoke machine to review the Michael Jackson song titles; Billy is such a fan.

"How about 'Billy Jean'?" he asks, his eyes lighting up.

"No way," I say, laughing. "Do you know how sick I am of that song? No offense."

"I don't know why you're so disgruntled about this anyway. We're talking about fifty million dollars, Lane. You should be celebrating."

"You know it's not like that," I say, feeling overwhelmed.

"I know. I'm just trying to make you feel better."

"Somehow, the money doesn't seem to matter."

"Only, it does. Anyway. Let's not talk about it now; you can obsess over it later. Ooh, I have the perfect song!" Billy waves a CD in my face.

"What's that?"

"Don't Stop 'Til You Get Enough."

We laugh and grab a microphone each. The music starts blaring, and Billy and I start shaking our hips and dancing. Billy virtually transforms into Michael, down to the most subtle mannerisms. He opens his mouth to sing, and his voice is clear and beautiful. I sing backup and dance beside him. Billy has floor-to-ceiling mirrors in his living room just for this purpose. He closes his eyes and continues dancing, the lyrics embedded in his heart. We face each other and sing the chorus in tandem. I twirl, and we continue belting out the lyrics at the top of our lungs. And yes, everything else melts away.

I am lighthearted and carefree. "Ooh!"

Billy snaps the music off. "That *ooh* wasn't supposed to be there," he says, frowning.

"*Sorry*," I say. "Anyway, let's move on. Model walk."

"First, I want you to sing Madonna."

"No way, I can't sing."

"Actually, you can. Sing "Jump", the lyrics are perfect for you. You sing, I'll model walk."

"Fine."

A minute later, Madonna's "Jump" starts blaring, and I pick up my mic. I sing the lyrics as Billy struts, prances, and pivots around his condo. I follow him, head up and back like a board, like I'm on a catwalk. I belt out the chorus, striding behind Billy on our imaginary runway.

Until I notice someone watching us, and shriek in surprise.

John has come over and is observing me with a gleam of amusement in his eyes. "You are *quite* the entertainer, Lane," he says, a slow smile spreading on his lips.

"I didn't see you," I stammer, my cheeks growing hot.

Billy shuts the music off, and I hand back the microphone. "Thanks, Billy, I should go home, though. Juliet has had the girls all day."

"Okay, honey. Love you."

"Love you. Bye, John."

Though I mean to go directly home, I find myself walking south from my bus stop. I have a strong urge to see Liam; and anyway, Juliet already texted me that the girls were sleeping and she's engrossed in a book. I don't think half an hour will make a difference. I text Liam, telling him I'm outside, and a moment later he buzzes me in.

Upstairs, his door opens and there he is. I melt all buttery at the sight of him and sink into his embrace, relieved to be safe and in his arms. He nuzzles his head against mine, and then pulls me away to look at me.

"How was your day?" he asks, his eyes locked on mine.

Riches & Rags

"It was…unexpected."

"As is your visit an unexpected surprise. Come in, love."

I follow him inside and peer around, my eyes adjusting to the single candle burning in his living room. "You going Amish on me?" I ask, half joking.

"Not quite. Just some quiet meditation."

"Aren't Irish guys supposed to be temperamental and tormented by generations of injustice? Just something I've heard…"

"Ah, maybe some. My upbringing was pretty privileged, and I've spent a lot of time in Japan. Buddhism appeals to me, and in Japan I learned to meditate."

"I don't think I've meditated in all my life."

"I'll show you how one day. Can I get you a drink, love?"

"No. I should be home by now, actually." I make no move to leave and instead stare into his dreamy eyes.

"Do you want to talk?" He sinks onto his mat, so I follow suit, sitting cross-legged on the floor. I recount the entire visit with Victoria Hughes, as the light flickers on Liam's divine face. It's hard to read his expressions, so I just ramble on.

"Victoria and Billy think I should go after him," I finish.

Liam is quiet for a few seconds. "And what do you think?" he says, finally.

"I don't know. I question the whole money thing. I mean, I'm a lot happier now than I ever was with it."

"But?"

"But… Oh, I don't know. I mean, I'm living in George's attic. It's not exactly a perfect scenario."

"I don't think you should strive for perfection. Your life, from the sounds of it—before this all happened—must have looked perfect on paper. It was a bit of an illusion though, wasn't it?"

"I was just going through the motions, really."

"You have a big decision, Lane."

"Yeah, tell me about it. What do you think I should do?"

Liam sighs and puts his arm around me and pulls me close, so I rest my head on his shoulder. "I can't decide for you, love. But I will say this: you're accomplishing so much on your own—your business is already off the ground, and now all you have to do is soar. Going after your husband and all that that brings might be added negativity you don't need anymore."

"I guess." Suddenly, I feel weary. Liam seems to sense this and stands, gently pulling me to my feet. Then he leans down and kisses me…on the nose! A light little kiss on the nose, I feel like a child. He leads me to the door and we say goodbye.

At home, Juliet and I chat briefly, but I don't have the energy to recount everything to her too. She gives me a loud goodnight smooch on the cheek and then bounds downstairs to check on George. Juliet has moved in full time and has her own bedroom in one of the former guest rooms. She's happy as pie to be here, and George is elated to have her.

The girls are sound asleep and— Oh, they're holding hands. I hover over the bed for a few minutes observing them, watching them breathe, their little chests rising and falling. They're all I need. Really, what do I need fifty million dollars for?

I wash up and pull on a nightshirt. My diamond ring catches on a loose thread. I pull my hand free and then gaze for a few seconds at my diamond solitaire and wedding band. I slowly twist them both off and let them drop onto a silver tray on my dresser. The noise echoes through the attic as I watch the wedding band spin on its side, around and around, until it comes to a complete halt and topples over with a clatter.

Riches & Rags

Lifeless.

A tear slips down my cheek, and I brush it away while I regard the now-meaningless rings. One tear, that's all I'll allow. I won't ever pawn the rings, or auction them—unless things ever get absolutely desperate. These rings belong to my girls. They represented the true love their parents shared, or whatever the girls want to think.

I glance at my left hand, taking in the new me. Maybe diamonds aren't a girl's best friend after all.

I crawl into bed and lie awake, staring into the night and listening to the pitter-patter of mice in the walls. What exactly would I do with my share of the money? Fifty million, WOW.

I could buy a house, no—a home. A sweet home that would feel like a home; and we could make it our own, with the girls' input.

We could travel. We could go anywhere, have real adventures. I could teach the kids abroad, home-school them part of the time. They could experience other cultures firsthand, learn new languages. My mind is alive with vivid images of traveling to exotic places, but also of making a difference. Help other people along the way. Do something like visit orphanages, or volunteer.

And we could buy a boat, learn to sail. I've always wanted to know how to sail.

We could do *anything*. My mind races with possibilities. There would be money for the girls' education, for their weddings one day. This wouldn't be just *my* money; this would be *their* money! And they deserve it, dammit. They deserve all the happiness and opportunity in this world. They deserve the chance to be extraordinary.

My heart hammers away in my chest. So it's decided then.

I'm going after what's rightfully ours.

30

"So, how is this going to work again?" Liam asks me. It's Home Expo Day, and because we don't have a physical booth set-up, we're huddling together in the corner like schoolgirls.

"Well, I think we just need to engage with people. Pretty much anyone we meet is going to be a potential client, or an ally of some sort," I say, picking at a dried avocado glob on my pant leg—no doubt I have Rory to thank for that one.

"Being without a booth might actually be advantageous for us. We don't have to be all sales focused, standing behind a table all day," Billy says, while scrolling through his phone.

"Well, we still have to be sales focused," I say, determined not to waste time. I want to leave here with so many leads we won't know what to do. I glance at Liam, who is sipping his tea while taking in all the action around him. The expo *is* pretty impressive.

The Vancouver Convention Centre's twenty-thousand-square-foot exhibit floor is packed with booths, demo-tables, products, and plasma screens. People are milling about reviewing notes, testing equipment, and racing against time. I check my phone and raise my eyebrows, surprised.

Only half an hour to go before attendees arrive and the fun begins.

"Thanks for coming to help us today, Liam," I say, beaming up at him.

He turns to me with a broad grin. "Happy to help, love."

"So, should we separate, or all stay together?" Billy asks, rifling through his attaché case of pamphlets and business cards for the hundredth time.

"Stay together!" Liam and I say at the same time.

"It'll seem more official if we're all together."

"That's true," Billy says, closing the case, apparently satisfied.

We hit the water fountains and loos. By the time we return to the floor, attendees are already pouring into the room. We're positioned beside a kitchen-and-bath-fixture booth and a company that specializes in home office furniture. That's definitely niche. A couple in their forties pass both booths and make their way toward us. I briefly sweep them with my eyes and note the designer Chloe bag and fresh manicure on the woman and the designer glasses and watch on her man. These people have money to burn.

"Good morning," I say with casual warmth, stepping forward to greet them.

"Hello," they answer in unison, smiling at me.

Perfect.

"My name is Lane, and this is Billy and Liam. We're from Leia Design Consultants. What brings you to the show today?"

As I speak, Billy pulls a pamphlet and business cards out from his case and passes them to Liam. The woman's pupils dilate as she sweeps her eyes over Liam while her husband explains they are considering updating their living room and bedrooms and are here for inspiration. Bingo!

Billy takes notes while Liam and I speak with the couple.

Our chat soon turns into a bit of an interview. What are you looking for? Do you have a budget in mind?

By the end of the fifteen-minute conversation, we have their names and phone numbers, and have assured them we'll be in touch with a list of designers for them to meet. They leave thrilled, and we are over the moon.

As they walk away, I turn back to the boys, and my professional smile broadens into a crazy-excited one. "Can you *believe* that?" I screech-whisper.

"Oh my God, Lane. If we can just keep this going all day...!" Billy cries, his eyes dancing.

"Your service sells itself, it's ingenious really. Trying to find a designer is daunting at best," Liam says, scanning the room for more potential leads.

Our morning continues with us repeating the routine—approaching attendees, striking up a conversation, and learning about what their needs are and how we can help them. Liam is a major hit with just about everyone. The women swoon, and the guys are relaxed and engaged in his presence. It's a good thing that Liam doesn't need our money, because having a third partner would drastically decrease our cut. But then, Liam is obviously such an asset.

We've been walking around for about three hours now, building our roster of solid leads.

"How many leads now?" I ask Billy under my breath. Liam is a few feet away, surrounded by three women who are giggling and flirting for his attention. He's such a rock star. He continues to steer the conversation back to what the ladies are looking for, and how we can help.

"Let's see," Billy says, scrolling through his notes, "we have nine, ten, eleven—twelve! Twelve solid leads that we need to follow up on, and we've handed out about sixty pamphlets to passersby." He grins and squeezes my arm as I smile and shake my head in disbelief.

Twelve solid leads! Even if only a quarter of those go

Riches & Rags

through, we're still talking about thousands of dollars! The thought of money reminds me of Micky, and my stomach leaps at the thought of the daunting road ahead. I still haven't worked out a plan, exactly; but I have some ideas swirling.

"Look at Liam." Billy motions, and I turn to notice the same ladies handing him business cards and one-upping one another by each creating a greater demand for our services —though I think they might have forgotten our services only entail finding designers, and *not* having Liam, shirtless with a tool belt, traipsing around their homes day in, day out.

"We definitely scored with Liam," I murmur.

Loud pop music starts blaring from the other direction, and we jolt. I can't see where it's coming from, but we have to raise our voices to hear each other.

"They better shut that music off soon, because it's going to ruin our chances at conversation with prospective leads," I shout.

"I don't think it really matters what we say with Liam hanging around." Billy yells back.

"He's the eye candy, that's for sure."

"We should bring him to every meeting and every opportunity from now on. With looks like that, women will be clambering over each other to work with us."

"Definitely. He can be our mascot—Sex God."

Billy and I howl with laughter and turn, almost smacking right into Liam. I notice the loud music has stopped, and I can't think of anything to say. I've never seen Liam look gobsmacked. He obviously heard everything we said because the hurt in his eyes is undeniable.

"I should go," he says. His voice sounds lost and desolate. He turns and stalks away, and I shoot Billy a desperate look before turning and running after Liam.

"Liam, wait—" He continues, and I finally reach him

and grab his arm. He pivots around to face me, eyes wild. "Liam, we didn't mean anything. We were complimenting your looks, your charm," I say, trying to hold on to his arm.

"I'm done, Lane. This just isn't my scene. I just can't." His face is rigid and strained, and he brushes right past me.

"What do you *mean*?" I wail, striding to keep up with him. This is surreal, I'm fighting with Liam! I've hurt him, and I don't even understand how.

"Why do you think I've never done anything with my life before?" he asks, eyes blazing.

What?

"What do looks have to do with *anything*? And don't blame your own shortcomings on other people," I say, my voice rising in indignation.

He sets his jaw and continues out the expo doors and toward the stairs.

"Give me a break, Liam," I shout after him. "If you haven't done anything with your life, it's your own bloody fault and nobody else's." I stand, transfixed, and watch helplessly as he mounts the stairs two at a time and disappears into the upper lobby. "Shit," I mutter. Shit, shit, shit. Now what?

"He's gone?" Billy has joined me, and he rubs my shoulder for a brief second.

I shrug him off, irritated. "I just don't understand. How could we have hurt him this badly when we adore him so much?"

"He obviously has some hang-up about his looks. Or maybe it goes deeper—some inferiority complex."

I gaze up to the stairs, willing him to return. But I know he won't. "I think he feels nobody takes him seriously. I know he said before that his family doesn't. And now we let him down too."

We stand together in silence until it is obvious Liam is gone for good.

Billy sighs. "Come on, Laney. You have a family to feed; let's get back in there."

I nod and follow Billy back into the expo, which now seems too loud, too frantic, and too overwhelming. I just want to curl into a sad, little ball, but somehow manage to plaster on a friendly, professional face and pour all my energy into one goal—sell, sell, and sell.

31

I stand outside Elsa's Coal Harbour condo and crane my neck, taking in the ominous, black glass structure that seems to stretch into the clouds. I sigh and consider leaving. I could still walk away. I don't even know what to say, and I'm feeling vulnerable enough as it is. I don't exactly need Elsa digging her claws into me.

I should just go. I turn to leave and almost smack into a tall figure in a long, fur coat and oversized sunglasses. Only when she barks at me to watch my step, do I realize it's Elsa herself. We eye each other for a beat, and then she turns and flounces off toward the front entrance, her heels clipping away on the pavement.

"Are you *really* going to pretend you didn't recognize me?" I call after her.

She swivels around, her coat billowing behind her like a witch's cape.

"I have *nothing* to say to you." She sneers.

This woman is unbelievable. I march over and slip behind her and into the building. She turns and gives me an exasperated look. "Don't waste my time, Lane."

"Don't worry. This will only take a few minutes. I have something to say, and then I'll go."

"I have nothing to say to you," Elsa snaps as she jabs the elevator button with her long, lacquered fingernail.

"So you've said. You don't have to say anything. Just listen to me, for once." I follow her into the elevator, and the doors close.

We ride up in silence, and I try to keep my breath steady and my confidence peaked. Anyway, I've made it this far and there's no turning back.

The elevator pings, and we exit onto the gleaming marbled Penthouse floor. Elsa punches in a code, throws open the cream colored double doors, and marches into her home. Then she rips off her coat and tosses it along with her bag onto an ornate chair, and her maid, Mrs. Reynolds, scrambles over and collects them. The poor, weary maid gives me a feeble smile.

"Come along, Lane. I don't have all day," Elsa barks.

I hand Mrs. Reynolds my coat and hurry after Elsa, who is now at the far end of the corridor making her way toward the sitting room.

Her living room is painted a cool taupe and the floor-to-ceiling windows boast breathtaking views of the Vancouver Mountains, Stanley Park, and the ocean. I stare, captivated for a second, and then turn to face Elsa, who regards me with a venomous intensity that shocks me.

"Why are you looking at me like *that*?" I ask, horrified. "You know," I continue, not bothering to wait for a reply, "there was a time when you and I actually had a functional relationship. I just can't fathom your hostility, especially after everything that's happened."

"We both know the reason, Lane. Quit the innocent crap."

"No, I actually don't know. Enlighten me." I lower myself onto the white, calf-skin leather sofa and glance over at the dormant gas fireplace with yearning; it's like an icebox in here!

"You're denser than I thought. *Clearly*, I lost all respect for you when my poor, devastated son revealed you're having an affair!"

"AFFAIR?!" I shriek. "He said I was having an *affair*?"

I leap off the couch and pace back and forth, muttering in disbelief. He said *I* was having an affair? This has got to be the most outrageous thing I have ever heard. "I was always a hundred percent faithful to Micky. As for lying, and deceit—well, ask him yourself."

"What are you rambling about?" Elsa raises her voice and narrows her cold eyes into mine.

"I'm saying, I was played. Micky came to *me* devastated too. Only not about some fabricated affair but with news that he'd lost our family fortune and was leaving me to sort things out. I had to take the girls on my own, with no money, and no support, and no *job*—nothing! And I've been working my ass off trying to move forward, trying to be a good mom, all the while still being a faithful wife."

"That's not true," she cries.

"Only it is," I say, my voice sounding detached to my own ears. "But it gets worse." Elsa raises her eyebrows. I can't tell if she's genuinely surprised or playing some twisted game. "That's right. Because I just learned from the wife of one of Micky's business associates, that he didn't lose *any* money. He's off launching a resort in St. bloody Lucia of all places—but then, you must already know this, of course."

She regards me with apparent uncertainty, but I can see the bit about St. Lucia isn't news to her ears.

"If you don't believe me, why do you think I'm living in someone's attic? If he were a good guy, why would he let his wife and children sink or swim, without any regard or contact?"

"You're in the attic to be with your new lover, and you refuse Michael's generosity."

"Oh, please." I snort. "Is that what he actually said? And do you *really* believe that?"

Elsa is silent and brooding, and I wonder what else I should say. Maybe I've said enough for now.

"Anyway, everything I've said is true. Believe me for the sake of your grandchildren—if you even care. They deserve infinitely more kindness and respect than your son has bothered to give them." My voice quivers and I swallow the urge to cry. "I'll let myself out."

I pause for a second, but Elsa remains rigid in her seat and doesn't lift her eyes to meet mine. I shake my head in utter disappointment, turn to leave, then stride back to the foyer, the clip of my heels echoing down the mammoth corridor.

"Are you *sure* you're going to be okay?" Victoria asks as we zip along Granville Street toward the Vancouver International Airport.

I can't believe it myself. In just a couple of hours I'm going to be in the air on my way to St. Lucia via Chicago. I'm really doing this. "Yes, I'll be fine."

"Do you have the video footage?"

"Yes, you've already asked me that."

Victoria makes a clicking sound with her tongue, and of course it's impossible to make out her expression because she resembles a black fly, wearing what must be the most ridiculously oversized, opaque sunglasses I think I've ever seen. It's actually hard to not laugh; and I would laugh if I didn't have a knot the size of those very sunglasses in my stomach.

"You're tense," she remarks.

"Obviously."

"Who's looking after your kids?"

"My dad's busy with his wedding, but he'll check in—"

"You're leaving them *alone*?"

"No! You didn't let me finish. He'll check in, but Billy and my friend Juliet will take turns with them."

"How did you explain it to the girls?" Victoria whizzes into the next lane without signaling, and the car behind lays on the horn. "Learn to drive, dick-smack!" she screams out the sunroof as she barrels through a red light to the chorus of more horns. "People in this godforsaken city can't drive!"

I notice I'm holding my breath and clenching the armrest. I just pray we make it to the airport alive. "Uh…in answer to your question, I told Margo I was going on a business trip."

"Well, this *is* a business trip. Don't let him smooth talk you, Lane, you know how he is."

"We're beyond smooth talk, believe me."

"Well, if you can pull this off, I'll be thrilled."

"Yeah, if things can go according to plan."

"They will." Victoria runs a hand through her sleek bob. I notice she's appraising her manicure, and I panic realizing she isn't even watching the road.

"Your manicure won't be perfect for long if you don't watch where you're going!" I say through gritted teeth.

"Quit backseat driving , Lane, or I'll let you take the city bus the rest of the way." She dissolves into peals of laughter, and I roll my eyes.

Really, though, I should be thankful. Victoria and her husband, Paul, were instrumental with executing my plan, not to mention they paid for my airfare. I'll pay them back, of course.

I notice with a jolt that we're already on the bridge connecting Vancouver to Richmond and the airport is less than five minutes away. I already miss the girls immensely.

Being away for a night here or there is *completely* different than leaving the continent on an open-ended ticket. Let's just hope this is quick and seamless.

Victoria swerves onto the curb at international departures, nearly running over an Indian family, who jump back in alarm.

"God, Victoria!" I cry out as I clutch at the door handle and scramble out of the car. Victoria doesn't get out, but pops the trunk for me, and I remove my suitcase and come around to thank her. "Drive home safe," I say, hoping she'll get the hint.

"Have a lovely trip, darling. Come home rich!"

"Uh-huh."

"Oh, and Lane?"

"Yeah?"

"Update me often, because if I don't hear from you, I'll alert the police in St. Bart's."

"It's St. Lucia, Victoria. St. Lucia."

"Lucia, like lucky. Okay, got it."

I stand back from the door, and she waves her hand and blows kisses as her car crunches off the curb with a lurch and speeds away.

Okay. This is it.

Both my flights are delayed, so we touch down in Hewanorra Airport, St. Lucia an hour and forty-six minutes behind schedule. They finally clear the cabin, and we disembark directly onto the tarmac. The warm gust of tropical air caresses me like a gentle welcome, and I inhale deeply.

This almost feels like a vacation—except it isn't. I have some aspects of my plan in place, but the other parts will have to be improvised. I just hope I can pull this off. As I wait for my luggage, my mind drifts to the girls and then—for the millionth time since I saw him last—to Liam. The sorrow I feel from losing him is all encompassing. And I don't know what's worse—losing him or hurting him. I guess I should say hurting him, but for once I'll be selfish. I'm hurting more than he is. So there! (That's what Margo would say.)

I grab my phone and turn it on to find it searching for a carrier—but there's no service. Shit. Now I'll have to make do with sending updates on the hotel computer. I shove my phone back into my bag and tap my foot, eyeing the various suitcases as they parade along the conveyor belt. When I spot mine, I heave it onto the floor, pull up the handle, and drag it outside. Again, the warm tropical breeze swirls, and my hair billows across my face.

I slide into a taxi, give the address of Micky's new resort in the town of Soufrière, and gaze mesmerized as we begin our travels.

"Sa ka fete, ma'am? Mean, 'ow are ya?" the driver says with a thick Creole accent that sounds almost Jamaican.

"Oh, fine thanks," I say. "This place is stunning," I add, as I peer out the window.

We drive on the left-hand side of the street—which of course is different than in North America—and make our way along a wide highway with sparse traffic. After about ten minutes, we turn onto a narrow, winding road. There's green foliage and an abundance of palm trees everywhere I look. As we mount and descend monstrous hills, the road twists and turns so often I almost feel sick as I sway to and fro in the backseat.

The driver gives a good-natured chuckle and checks something on his taxi computer. "Dat is some 'otel where ya go."

"So, I've heard."

"Der only done da first stage; more building for year to come.

"Oh yeah? You know a lot about it?"

"Oh, ya. It's da big news on da island; 'as islander torn."

"What do you mean?" I ask.

The driver keeps his eyes on the road but glances at the rear-view mirror every so often to make eye contact with me. He has dark sanpaku eyes with the white visible under his irises, giving him a sad puppy-dog look.

"Some local support da project for tourism. But da resort will be so big, wit da gulf course too; dey have to chop da rainforest."

"I see." Well, it seems Micky's already done a fine job making enemies in St. Lucia too.

"We're 'ere, Ma'am," the driver says eventually, turning onto a private drive that meanders up a lush steep hill.

The wig! I almost forgot. I rummage through my bag and produce a wig made of shiny, long, black human hair, which I pull on carefully. Good, I have the wig in place and my sunglasses on. He shouldn't recognize me. I just need my oversized black sunhat from my suitcase, and I'll be perfectly incognito.

We've pulled up to an exquisite building. It's a white stucco structure with pillars; and set against the aqua ocean like this, it looks more Greek than Caribbean. Palm trees galore, gingers, birds of paradise and gardenias bloom all around—I feel like I've arrived in Heaven.

"'Ow ya wanna pay?" The driver turns in his seat and his eyes widen when he looks at my new hair.

I pay him and emerge from the taxi gripping my luggage, then stand for a few minutes, taking in the buildings, the grounds, and the sensational views.

Well, Lane Carson, this is your big acting chance. Break a leg!

This place is stunning. My room is all airy, with white linens and billowing white curtains that are so sheer they're translucent. Beyond my french doors is a private terrace with an enchanting potted garden and breathtaking, sweeping views of the Caribbean Sea and the volcanic Pitons. I even have my own sunken infinity pool! St. Lucia is like nothing I've *ever* seen before. My room has all the amenities I could ever want, but with a tropical, minimalist flavor. This place is spectacular!

I change into a black one-piece swimsuit and sarong, careful to reposition my wig and pull on the massive hat. I regard myself in the mirror, then switch the sarong for a full-length beach dress. Better to keep my body hidden as much as possible, lest Micky recognize me. I grab my beach tote and swing it over my shoulder; and I'm ready to check out the scene.

Outside, I follow a white spiral staircase all the way down to the beach. Even these grand winding stairs with tropical gardens and waterfalls cascading down to the beach alongside them are enchanting.

Once on the beach, I check my cabana number, and then sink my feet into the glorious white-powder sand.

It still baffles me to think Micky has been here in paradise, while his abandoned family struggled—*unbelievable.*

I feel a new resolve, a deep sense of determination to make this happen, even though some of the details are still up in the air. Sun worshipers are lounging, playing, laughing, and splashing. I miss my girls just thinking how much they would enjoy being here. *Look* girls, this is where Daddy's been all this time.

I find my cabana, which resembles my guest room in

décor, and sink into my chaise as a server comes forward for my drink order. Pretty much anything with rum and an umbrella will do!

The server brings my drink and slips away discreetly as I sink back into my chaise. Come on, Lane. You shouldn't be relaxing at a time like this! But I can't help it. Plus, I need to be refreshed to think clearly.

I pull my phone out of my bag and flip on the Wi-Fi mode. And sure enough, there's a guest connection. I connect and send emails to Billy, Juliet, and Victoria, updating them on my trip. Then, I take a picture of my view and send it to them for fun. Take that guys; enjoy the Vancouver rain. Ahhh, this is the life.

The rum fills me with warmth and laziness, and I settle back into the cushions, satisfied. I half doze and am mildly aware of a couple making their way past my cabana. The man laughs at something the woman says, and my heart lurches into a somersault.

I'd know that laugh anywhere—it's Micky's! I half expected to run into him, but now that it's happening, I'm stunned! After a beat, I scramble to my feet, chuck my belongings into my tote, down my drink, and dash out of the cabana to follow them. I hang back a bit—lest I draw their attention—but close enough to hear snippets of their conversation. Micky's strolling along with some short woman, but I can't make out her face. Seeing him again, or at least his back, is incredibly surreal. After all this time apart, he's still my husband for God's sake! Well, not for long of course.

Another woman with a clipboard in hand jogs over to Micky's side. I actually recognize her from Micky's office, but I don't know her name. I can hear her going over some questions for the big Investors Gala, which takes place the day after tomorrow. *And* I'm on the guest list, thanks to Victoria. She was able to book me using the name of one of

Paul's acquisition lawyers. I have a ticket tucked away in my wallet with the name Hillary Stewart on it.

"Ask Bethany to do it," Micky says in reply to something I didn't hear. Who's Bethany? I keep my head down but pick up the pace to hear better.

"Bethany's not in today."

"Then get the other event manager, Sarah, on it."

"Sari."

"Whatever!" Micky barks. The girl takes a few more instructions from him, and then races away toward the resort building, red ponytail swinging.

I pop my phone out of my bag and type: *Bethany and Sari, event managers*. They just may be my ticket. I hit Save, toss the phone back into my bag, and glance up, just in time to see Micky lay a casual arm around the woman's waist and pull her close. I stop mid stride and observe them, feeling numb and empty. She raises her face to his and smiles. There's something about her up-turned nose that strikes me as somewhat familiar; but for the life of me I can't place it.

He teases and pulls her hat off, to her giggling protests, and I regard her mousy hair and pixie-like cut. I'm totally baffled!

This is who he's with?

This is who he left *me* for?

My eyes harden as I glare into the backs of their heads. As if sensing this, the woman turns around, and I lower my head not a moment too soon. Yep, it's her all right.

Faye fucking Fenwig.

32

"Victoria, it's Lane."

"Lane! I thought your phone didn't work?"

"It doesn't. I'm using Skype."

"Well, it's great to hear from you, darling. How is the spying going?"

"Pretty productive. I already saw Micky, actually."

"*Oh?*"

"Yeah, but that's not why I'm calling. Listen, I was wondering, do you know who might have access to the guest list for the Investors Gala you got me the ticket for?"

"I'm not sure. I'll have to ask Paul. His assistant called one of Micky's companies and was transferred to the right person. Why?"

"Can you send me an email with the contact name?"

"Sure, Lane, I'll call Paul now."

"Great, thanks!" I hang up. Now, to find out about those event managers. I access the St. Lucia resort website, but can't find anyone named Sari or Bethany.

Oooh, I know. I pick up the hotel phone receiver in my room and call the front desk.

"Front desk."

"Hi, I'm attending the Investors Gala for the resort on

Saturday and wondering if you can please give me the name of your event manager. I'm interested in booking a conference for our company, and your resort would be ideal."

"Of course," the front desk attendant purrs. "You can actually send your conference request through our website if you click on 'meetings.'"

Hmm. "Yes, I'm on the site. But I would like to send a *personalized* note," I say, then add for good measure, "And maybe a gift basket too."

"Unfortunately, we're not at liberty to receive incentives."

"Right." This is like pulling teeth. "An associate of mine has worked with your event manager before, and highly recommended her," I say, trying a new approach. "Uh, I think it was Bethany something. But unfortunately, I can't remember her name for the life of me." I try a little giggle, in hopes of winning her over.

"Well, her email address is Bethany at St. Lucia Shores dot com."

I could scream, really. "*Great*," I say through gritted teeth, "and her last name would be…?"

"Portier."

"Can you please confirm the spelling?" I say, breaking into a grin.

"Sure, p-o-r-t-i-e-r."

"Wonderful, you've been so helpful." I hang up, access the Gmail website from my phone, and create a fake email address—bportier13@gmail.com. Ha! I add her name as Bethany Portier, and even add the country of origin—St. Lucia. This is so easy, I almost want to laugh.

My email pings, and sure enough Victoria gives me the contact information for one of Micky's assistants. I don't recognize her name, which must mean she's new. Even better!

I dial the number through Skype and check the time. It's

just after 4:00 p.m. (PST). After a single ring, someone picks up.

"Hi, I'm calling on behalf of Bethany Portier," I ramble quickly, trying to sound rushed and anxious. "We're working together here in St. Lucia in preparation for the big Investors Gala, and, well, actually we're having a bit of a crisis."

"Oh?" says the girl, sounding alarmed.

"Yes. All our computer systems have crashed, and everyone is freaking out. *Especially* Mr. Capello."

"Oh, God!" she says, the panic in her voice rising.

Perfect.

"It's a *total* nightmare, and Bethany is asking that you re-send the most up-to-date copy of the guest list to her personal email address because the company one is down. Mr. Capello wants a welcome email going out to all attendees within the hour, so he needs this *ASAP!*"

"Yes, of course. I'll do it this second."

Oh *yeah!* I give the new Gmail address, then pretend to have to hang up because of all the commotion. The Gmail account sits open in front of me, and I dial front desk once again. This time I ask to be transferred to room service and order a bottle of champagne. It may be early, but I have the sudden urge to celebrate!

When the guest list is safely in my inbox, with copies forwarded to both Victoria and Billy, I hurry to shower and get ready for my meeting. I blow-dry my hair with a round brush so it falls in soft luscious locks, apply my evening make-up, and choose a white, floor-length goddess dress and strappy gold sandals. Exquisite! I spray on my Coco

Chanel Mademoiselle scent and grab my purse. I'm feeling pretty confident, but as the elevator descends and I think about actually seeing Micky, my stomach starts doing backflips.

Okay, *breathe*. In. Out. You can do this Lane; do it for the girls!

The elevator stops and I slip out, hoping he'll already be seated and I won't have to risk seeing him in the lobby.

Breathe.

The most important thing to remember is to not show fear; he'd smell it and I'd be done. Calm and strong. I cross the expansive lobby, careful to keep my chin up and my face serene. The resort's fine dining room is beyond a massive, marble-arched corridor. As I approach the entrance, I take one final deep breath. Here we go!

I give the hostess my bogus name and follow her to the table. This was the only way of getting a last-minute meeting with Micky. Actually, it was pretty easy. I looked up some billionaire hotelier on the Forbes website, and then booked a meeting with Micky's assistant, claiming to be one of the billionaire's VPs.

As we're approaching the table, I can make out the back of Micky's head.

But, wait—what if it's not him?

What if he sent one of his associates instead?

My panic rises, until I spot Micky's hand—and know it's him. The hostess beams as Micky rises and turns toward me, hand outstretched to greet the illustrious VP.

Only it's me.

Everything slows and time is suspended. Micky's expression—usually so hard to read—passes from shock, to disbelief, to confusion. The color drains from his face and his mouth drops open. He gapes at me as though I'm a phantom apparition.

You have the upper hand, Lane.

For this moment, I know I do. Though just seeing his face makes me sick to my stomach. What a creep! I give him a hard look, and then slide into the seat across from him. Still stunned into silence, he lowers himself into his seat, as though mirroring my actions. I grab my napkin and snap it open before placing it on my lap.

"*Lane?*" he says, having found his voice. "Lane? What the *fuck* are you doing here?"

I pick up my menu and pretend to read it, as though this is a completely ordinary dinner. *Don't cave in, Lane. Be strong.*

"Actually, I was asking myself the very same question of you." I skim the menu before turning the page. "Because," I continue, glancing up thoughtfully, "I could have sworn you were on some quest to become a better person, to sort out the financial crisis, and then come home to your *family.*"

Micky eyes me with obvious trepidation and takes a panicked sweep of the room lest—God forbid—someone overhear us. What a dick, all he cares about is money and his image.

I lower my eyes to my menu again and turn to the next page, this time more quickly and with more intensity, my anger and hurt overflowing. "But of course, there was no financial mishap. *No.*" Glaring into his eyes, I snap the menu closed and place it on the table. "In fact, financially, things look better than ever!" I gesture to the elaborate dining room, all ebony beams, succulent plants, and crystal fucking stemware.

Micky leans in, and his eyes meet mine with a patronizing stare. "Lane, you need to leave. You don't know what you're talking about."

"Not so fast, asshole. You deserted your family without a care, left us for dead as far as you were concerned. Lied, and cheated. *And* schemed your way to St. bloody Lucia, of all places." My voice rises, and Micky rings his hands frantically.

"Keep your voice down!" he hisses.

"Is this a good time for drinks?" The server has appeared and his eyes dart back and forth between Micky and me.

"No," Micky barks at the same time I say "Glass of Sémillon." I'd like to order a double shot of anything on the rocks, but Micky would know I'm attempting to calm my nerves. Better to play it cool. Micky grits his teeth and orders a gin and tonic. When the server disappears out of ear shot, I lean forward, lower my voice, and speak very slowly and clearly.

"Listen to me very carefully," I say. "You owe your daughters *and* me. You're going to pay, then I'm going to sign your precious divorce papers *after* you give me full custody. And then, you *snake*, I'm going to take the first plane back to Vancouver and I never, *ever*, want to see your face again as long as I live. You. Are. *Nothing*."

Micky leans back, studying me. He seems to have recovered his equanimity.

Oh shit.

"Lane, you can't come here without warning and start making demands. We can talk about this another time. Soon, I promise."

"Oh! Just like you promised to come home? Bullshit, ASSHOLE!"

He flinches slightly and his features harden. "I don't have time for this." He stands, chucking his napkin on the table.

"I have a video," I yelp, grasping at straws. To my utter relief, Micky narrows his eyes and lowers himself back into his seat.

"What are you talking about?" he demands through gritted teeth.

Riches & Rags

"Well, let's just say it's a corporate video."

Our server appears with our drinks. "Are you ready to order?"

"I'll have the seared swordfish," I say, as Micky shakes his head.

"And for you, Mr. Capello?"

"Uh…"

Micky's appetite must be the furthest thing from his mind.

"Kobe beef Carpaccio."

I smile at the server, trying to calm my nerves with laughter therapy. Or smile therapy, anyway. God, I'll be glad when this meeting is over. I fiddle with my bag under the table; I'm going to burst from frayed nerves.

"What's this video?"

I take a steadying breath and explain. "Let's just say your departure from the Vancouver business scene left some people with a bad taste. You're not exactly well liked, shall we say. Actually, you're despised. But then, I'm sure you're aware of that."

"You didn't answer my question, Lane."

"Okay, I'll make it very clear." I lean in, eyes blazing into his. "I have a dozen business tycoons back home who've all gone on camera, warning your potential investors to *run*. Got it?" Micky eyes me with a murderous gleam. He blinks hard and I can see I've clearly hit a nerve. He probably wants to reach across the table and strangle me. I shrink back and nonchalantly glance around for support. There are a few couples at tables nearby and a single woman seated with her back to us. She has curly blonde hair and an enormous, white sun hat, and I vaguely wonder who *she's* spying on. When I turn my attention back to Micky, his anger seems to have dissipated, and he looks rather thoughtful.

"Who went on camera?"

"I won't say. But one of the persons who didn't mind

being identified is Paul Hughes. Apparently you swindled a couple hundred grand from him."

"That's erroneous, Lane. That guy's a dick-smack. And anyway, what were you planning on doing with this video. Playing it at my gala? Because I'll tell you, the security I—"

"No. I have a better way."

"Oh?"

"I have the guest list," I say, breaking into a wide grin.

Micky looks baffled. "How—"

"It doesn't matter how. What matters is I have all the names and contact info for your guests. I also have two copies of an email draft ready to send to *every* contact, with the video attached. Two people have access to these emails back in Vancouver and are waiting to send them, unless of course…"—I raise my eyebrow—"I tell them not to?"

"Paul Hughes is the one who swindled me. I can't believe you'd believe him over your own husband. Baby, listen to me…," Micky says, his eyes growing warm and attentive.

Wait. What's going on?

Why is he looking at me like that?

Do I trust Paul, or do I trust Micky? Suddenly I feel confused.

"Laney, this project in Saint Lucia was all a surprise."

What? *What?*

"I did lose money, but I didn't want to broadcast what happened. I've been working my ass off to get us back to where we were, and baby, after the gala on Saturday, I'm going to fly home. We can buy another house, bigger than before. Any house you want. We can be together." His mouth stretches into a charming smile and he reaches forward to squeeze my hand.

This is all wrong. This is all *weird*.

The server presents our meals, and I pull my hand away and turn my attention to the fish on my plate. Micky knows

Riches & Rags

I never have an appetite when I'm stressed, so I take my fork and—though I could just about puke right now—force myself to take a bite. Micky is talking, and I stare at him, trying to follow. Something about a first-class flight to New York on my way home to Vancouver.

"Be pragmatic, baby. You could fly out tomorrow. Do some shopping. Would you like that?"

I stare longingly into his eyes. This is my husband. But...something's wrong. Something doesn't add up.

"The divorce!" I say, only remembering now. How could I forget something like that? "If this is all a surprise, how come you wanted a divorce?"

Micky lifts a forkful of beef to his mouth and chews carefully. "This is amazing," he says, with a lazy smile.

"Hello? We're talking about the divorce."

"Honey, I never wanted to divorce you. But, for a while it was looking like things were grim, and I figured you'd be better off without me." He lowers his eyes to his plate and cuts another slice of beef.

Still, this doesn't add up. But it all sounds so good; I want to believe him so badly.

But still.

There's something else that doesn't sit well with me. Micky hasn't once asked about his daughters. What kind of sociopath parent wouldn't bother to ask how his own children are after not seeing them for four months?

Oh! And another thing.

"What about Faye?"

Micky's head snaps up, but after a beat, his features soften again and he shrugs. "What about her?"

"You're obviously a couple."

"Actually, no. Faye is working with me on this resort. She's my business partner, that's all. Anyway, you don't have to worry your pretty little head over business affairs. Why don't I have my staff pack you up, and you can be on the next first-class flight to New York. You can fly Billy there too to be with you."

"What about our kids?" I ask, shaking my head in disgust. "Who's going to look after them?"

Micky gives me a blank look. "You can fly them too."

"No. That's ridiculous. Margo's in school, but you haven't cared to ask how that's going. Nor did you bother being in touch for her birthday. Or to call the girls at Christmas." I stab at my fish and shove a morsel into my mouth.

"That's *it*. I've heard enough!"

Huh? Micky and I gape and look around. It sounded like…Elsa? The woman with the oversized hat has stood up and is marching over toward us.

Oh, God! It *is* Elsa.

What is *she* doing here?

"Ma?" Micky asks, looking bewildered.

"Don't 'Ma' me." Elsa grabs a nearby chair and drags it over to our table. She whips off the hat but not the blonde wig that resembles the hair of the lead singer from Twisted Sister. "The only partner that Faye woman is, is your *partner in crime*."

Both Micky and I raise our eyebrows, and I lean forward eagerly.

What the hell is going on?

"Ma, what are you talking about?" Micky asks, eyes flashing.

"I said, don't '*Ma*' me," Elsa snaps. She pulls off her oversized sunglasses, revealing tired-looking eyes, and shifts her attention to me. "I came to St. Lucia to hear it with my own ears and to find out what's really going on. Michael," she says, turning to Micky, "you said Lane was having an affair. I've come to realize this is simply a falsehood.

"*You*, on the other hand, have most certainly been having an affair. And, I also heard your ludicrous story about losing the money. We both know that's fabricated as well. So who's the liar?"

Elsa turns back to me, her face appearing to soften.

I don't know what's more shocking, hearing the confirmation that my worst fears are indeed true, or having Elsa, the Ice Bitch herself, deliver the news. I think the Ice Bitch may have thawed, whereas Micky will never change.

"Mother, what are you *doing?*" Micky hisses.

"You heard Lane. She wants a fair settlement. And full custody. I'm here to see you follow through on this one."

"She can have the kids, for all I care. But I'm not giving her a dime. I earned every single goddamn dollar, and I don't intend to piss it away."

My mouth drops open. "Wh—

But Elsa has beaten me to it. She lifts one perfectly manicured hand and slaps it across Micky's face so hard he reels.

I gasp in shock and shoot a look around to see other guests staring and whispering. One guy has even taken out his cell phone to record us.

I don't believe this!

I want to hug and squeeze Elsa.

Micky remains stunned, gripping his face. "She doesn't deserve my money. She did nothing to earn it," he adds, I think more to himself than anyone. He eyes me with a disdainful look.

He's pitiful.

"Did *I* not then deserve the money from your father?" Elsa asks. Micky's parents split when he was young, and the settlement must have been amazing, because Elsa has never had to work.

"That was different."

"It was not. It's exactly the same. And your father *wanted* to provide for us. He had *integrity*. Something you've never had. There's nowhere to run, Michael. If you do, consider yourself disowned. As for my grandchildren"—Elsa turns to me,—"I would like to get to know them."

Feeling amazed, I nod slowly. I think we could manage that, though I'm still trying to grasp what's going down. "The girls would like that," I manage to say.

"Michael, let's keep this out of the courts and out of the public eye. Settle up right now. What will you offer Lane and your daughters?"

Micky looks pained, and not just from the slap. This is like taking candy from a child. "Ten million," he mutters.

But Elsa shakes her head. "That's chicken feed, Michael, don't waste my time."

Micky slumps into his seat. "Fifteen."

"No," I say, before I bother stopping myself. Not that I would. This time Micky's face grows darker, and Elsa turns to me with raised eyebrows—she actually looks impressed.

"Twenty-five million," he grunts.

"Fifty million, plus full custody. And I don't *need* alimony. In fact, I don't want regular reminders of you anyway. Fifty million, and I'm out of your life, for good."

"That sounds fair," Elsa, says with a nod. "Have your financial manager transfer the funds and your lawyers draft the papers." Elsa's like a bulldog; she reminds me of Margo in a way.

I feel my anxiety melt away as I regard Micky, all defeated and rumpled in his chair, still reeling from the blow. How is it I ever gave him my heart?

"I'll be staying on the island until things are rectified. But we need to get this all ironed out before the gala," I say. Micky doesn't answer. I take that as a yes.

"Good," Elsa says, standing up. "I too will stay until you've come through on your word Michael. Remember, this is the right thing to do; it's what your father has already done." Elsa nods to me and gives me the slightest wink before turning and striding away, swinging her hat in her hand. I stand too and hesitate for a second. Micky doesn't raise his eyes and doesn't move. He just sits slumped in his seat, dejected.

"Tell me one thing," I say.

He doesn't respond.

"Why did you hire that actor to portray your client on our anniversary?"

Micky's eyes rise to meet mine. A cold shiver passes down my spine; it's like looking at a shark.

"Faye wanted to come," is all he mumbles, before casting his eyes downward.

I don't bother replying. I've wasted enough of my breath on him. I've wasted part of a lifetime. Without a word, I collect my purse and make my way out of the restaurant. By the time I've reached the seventh floor, the tension that has gripped me for the past six months has melted away, and I'm swinging my bag.

33

"Ladies and gentlemen, this is your first officer speaking. We are beginning our descent into beautiful Vancouver. The current time is six forty-two p.m., and the weather is a mild eight degrees with light drizzles. We welcome you to Vancouver and thank you for flying with us this evening."

I lean back in my seat with relief. After six nights away from the girls and a grueling day of travel, I'll soon be home.

"How are you feeling?"

"Anxious to see the girls. It feels like forever."

Elsa nods and offers me a mint, which I accept. I pop the peppermint into my mouth, close my eyes, and imagine my reunion with Margo and Rory. I can't wait to see their bright eyes, snuggle their little bodies close, and feel their soft hair against my cheeks.

"Lane, there was a time when I didn't think much of you. Sure, you were fine, but I actually felt you didn't have your priorities straight... But now, well, I want to say that it takes real courage to go up against someone like Michael. I was wrong about you."

I shift in my seat to face her, and let her compliment

seep in. "Well, I think I've changed over the course of the last while."

"I would say that's an understatement." Elsa raises her eyebrow and we both laugh.

"Okay, I've changed a lot."

"Now, there's something else I wanted to speak about."

I wait for her to continue, all the while wondering where she's going with this.

Elsa lowers her voice. "The wealth that you have, uh, *recouped* will be life-changing. It will give the children a tremendous opportunity for a better education. I highly recommend the York School for Girls. I could book a tour with the head mistress—"

"Thanks, Elsa. Really. But I would need to speak with Margo first. I don't want to impose too many changes all at once. And keep in mind she's already had to switch schools this year. She's actually pretty settled right now."

Elsa waves her hand as though that's fine, and I sigh inwardly in relief. The last thing I need is Elsa swooping in and making demands.

"Of course you all have your own individual lives to lead, but if I may make one recommendation?"

"What's that?" I ask, feeling apprehensive.

"With wealth like this, you need a good financial adviser. With the proper investment portfolio you can secure your children's future, as well as your own, while living off the interest of your investment."

"Oh yeah?" I ask, thinking of Liam. I feel a conflicting mix of yearning and emptiness when I think of Liam and what could have been. Sigh.

"My adviser, Karen, is a single mother herself. She's very focused on ensuring independence and security for her clients."

"Thanks, Elsa. That definitely sounds like a good person to meet with."

"Wonderful," Elsa says, her eyes shining.

I feel a swell of gratitude as we touch down in Vancouver and taxi on the runway.

"How are you getting home?" Elsa asks.

"Cab."

"I won't hear of it. My driver will see you home safely."

"Okay, thanks."

"So, Lane, when is it convenient for me to see my granddaughters? After your father's wedding next weekend?" she asks, her voice hopeful.

"I have a better idea," I say. I'm sure my dad won't mind. "Why don't you come to the wedding?"

"Oh, I wouldn't *dream* of imposing."

"I won't hear of it," I say, echoing Elsa in a playful way.

"Are you sure it won't be an imposition?"

"Of course not; it's a family affair. And you're family."

Elsa's mouth widens into a full smile—and she's radiant.

It's still surreal, sitting next to Elsa, knowing everything with Micky is over and finalized. My bank account boasts a balance I could have only dreamed of, the divorce papers are signed, and we have officially parted ways. I realize I might never even see him again. And that's okay.

"I'm so glad you're home," Margo gushes for about the tenth time since I've returned. I awoke to my first morning back in Vancouver, all snuggled between my girls. I don't know who was more excited, Margo, Rory, or me. And another thing—Rory started walking on her own while I was away. I *cannot* believe she chose the week I was gone to start walking.

Margo and I spend a good hour following Rory around

the attic, taking pictures, calling her here or there, and just marveling at the new little person traipsing about. It's adorable. I also realize with a pang that I didn't really experience this with Margo when she first walked. It was more like smile, pat her head, and move on. How much precious time have I lost? Though I can't dwell on this, what matters is making each day, each hour, and each minute count, from now on.

"Let's go to the beach!" I say, swooping Rory up into a big hug.

"Mommy, you're so silly. It's all cold and rainy."

"Not to me it isn't. Let's see…" We wander over to the window and peer out. "It looks like a beautiful day for the beach," I say, admiring the light breeze and the pitter-patter of raindrops. Margo gives me a funny look and then gazes back out the window.

"You see, Margo, reality is only fifty percent of what is actually happening; the other half is how we see it."

"What does that mean?" Margo asks, her little face curious.

"It means you can choose to look at things from different perspectives. You can choose happiness."

Margo shrugs and wanders off, having lost interest in me.

"You understand, don't you Rory?" I ask. She gazes up at me, squeals and toddles away, giggling, as I pretend to chase her.

"I'll have a half-sweet Caramel Macchiato and a half-sweet kid's hot chocolate, please," I say, giving my order at Starbucks. It's these little treats, like Starbucks, that I've missed. Now, I don't have to worry about money anymore; and it's exhilarating.

We receive our drinks and wander across the street and onto the promenade. Margo and I take turns pushing Rory's stroller, and Rory keeps showing me the 'out' sign and making protesting noises. The rain has even let up and the sky is beginning to brighten, which is gratifying.

"Can I swing?" Margo asks as we approach the playground.

"I think the swings are wet."

"Do we have a towel, Mommy?"

I check the diaper bag and pass her a receiving blanket, which I probably don't need to lug around anymore. Margo wipes her swing and the baby swing next to it.

"Do you want to swing?" I ask Rory, who raises her hands to me. I pull her out of the stroller and plop her in the swing, giving a little push for her and an under-duck for Margo.

After swinging, we meander onto the beach, which is advantageous because Rory can try walking a new terrain. I put my arm around Margo and draw her close.

"Margo, there's something you should know." I repeat the words I've been rehearsing in my head, praying this goes smoothly.

"What Mommy?" Margo looks up at me, her small cup cradled in her hands.

"Daddy loves you very much." Oh, God. Margo raises her eyebrows, waiting for me to go on. She suddenly seems a lot older than five. "I saw Daddy when I was away in Saint Lucia," I continue.

"You *saw* Daddy?" Margo asks, her eyes wide.

"Yes. He has some new business plans and works in Saint Lucia now, which is very far away."

"Why couldn't I come?"

"Because we had a lot of adult things to discuss.

Margo…you should know your daddy and I are not going to be together anymore."

"What does *that* mean?" Margo asks, sounding horrified.

"Well, it means you and Rory will continue living with me, for always, until you are all grown-up. And Daddy will live…somewhere else."

Margo's face crumples and she turns her head away. Oh, this is *horrible*. The lightness I felt earlier has come crashing down in Margo's loss. Even Rory hovers close by and gazes at me with concerned blue eyes. I sweep down and pull both girls into my arms. Margo starts to sob and Rory, mirroring her sister, breaks into a tormented wail; and I hold them both, tears eventually rolling down my cheeks too. This will be a big change for all of us to know it's permanent. All we have is each other now. And I'm going to be a single mother perpetually—it's terrifying.

Eventually, Rory loses interest in the Big Cry and wanders off to explore. And Margo whimpers at my side, drink abandoned.

"Do you want to finish your hot chocolate?"

Margo takes a quivering breath and shakes her head.

"Listen Margo, you need to understand things aren't really going to change at all. Because we've been on our own without your father for some time now, right?"

She nods.

"And it's not all bad. I mean, you have fun *sometimes*, right?"

Margo's mouth twitches.

"It's like what I said before. You have to choose the way you want to look at this. It is what it is, and we can't make Daddy come back, but we can choose to be strong and live a good life.

"And you have a lot of people who love and adore you and Rory. Like me, of course, and Pops, Auntie Louisa,

Uncle Riley, and Uncle Billy." Did I really just name Riley before Billy? "And there's Juliet, and of course George—"

"And Liam?"

"Liam?"

"Yeah."

"Uh, well Liam is really busy."

"No, he's not. I saw him lots."

"Yes, but that was before. Now he's busy."

"He came over when you were away."

"He did?" I ask, awed. But then, why should I be. He came over to see George. Anyway, I don't want to talk about Liam.

"Margo, our lives are going to change for the better. You can go to a better school—"

"I don't want to go to another school."

"Okay, that's fine. Rory—stop eating sand!" I wipe Rory's tongue with the back of my hand, and she gives us a sour face.

"Rory looks like an old man," Margo laughs, pointing.

"Margo, we can buy a home, and you can have a bedroom again and we could decorate it together."

"You said we don't have money."

"We didn't. Uh, your daddy gave us some of our family's money. So we're okay." I smile, and when she looks up at me with such trust and innocence, it takes my breath away. I won't let my girls down.

"Where will we live?" Margo asks, as we make our way up George's street.

"Well, we don't have to move far. We can live here in Kits," I say, surveying the homes. "Like, that home there is for sale. Any home with a sign out like that means it's for sale and someone can buy it."

"Can *we* buy it?"

I laugh at her impulse. "No, buying a home is something that takes a lot of time. It has to be just right."

"Can we see this one?" Margo asks.

I gaze up at the two-story Cape Cod-style home with the large veranda and pretty garden. "It's a nice house but the Realtor isn't here so—"

"Yes I am." I swing around in surprise to find a man in his mid-forties walking up from his car.

"I didn't hear your car," I cry.

"I didn't have it on. I was inside on a phone call. Are you interested in seeing this home?"

I shake my head. "Uh, no I don't think we—"

"Please, Mommy?"

I glance down at Margo's bright face and pleading eyes, then turn to the Realtor. "We're not really looking."

"Yes we are, you just said."

I shoot Margo a look to shut up.

"I had a tour booked but the guy hasn't shown," the Realtor says, motioning for us to follow him. "If I don't show you the house, I will have driven all the way here for nothing. You might as well humor me."

I peer up at the house with apprehension; well, I have nothing to lose, so I pull Rory from her stroller and the three of us follow the Realtor.

Inside, well, where do I begin? The entrance is inviting and homey—the fir floors gleam and the open concept is refreshing—as opposed to a formal grand mansion foyer. Everywhere I look there are well-thought-out custom touches and character features that really individualize the space. The kitchen is glorious, with pearly white granite counters, handsome fixtures, and a six-burner *Wolf* range.

There's a massive deck off the kitchen and a good-sized backyard that's fully fenced and kid ready.

Stop it, Lane, you're *not* buying this house.

Upstairs is equally lovely, with hardwood floors, five good-sized bedrooms with ample closet space, two full bathrooms, and an en-suite. Wainscoting, crown molding, and fresh, pastel-colored walls give warmth to each room.

"As you can see, this home has been lovingly crafted and cared for," the Realtor says. Margo has gone off to play in "her" room, and Rory is toddling about, content as pie.

"How much?"

"It's a steal at six point two. It was only listed two days ago, and it won't last long."

"Right. That's what you realtors always say." The guy is good natured and laughs at my comment. But it's true! "I need to think about this. This feels all too much like the last scene of *Miracle on 34th Street*."

"Sure. Though sometimes, things are just meant to be." He gives me a wink, and I half expect Kris Kringle to pop out from somewhere.

Or Liam.

34

"How's the house sale coming along?" Billy asks, as I adjust his bow-tie. I smooth it with my fingers and stand back to survey the end result. Billy is beaming; his eyes are especially vibrant today. It's an exciting day for everyone, even for me.

"Well, it's not a done deal yet; subject to inspections and what-not. I just figured a closing date two months away will allow transition for the girls. Plus, I'm thinking of asking Dad and your Mom to move into the in-law suite."

Billy is bent over at the hotel bar fridge inspecting the boutonnieres he made. He pulls out an orchid-with-ostrich-feather art piece. "You want them to *live* with you?" he asks, as he pins the flower to his lapel.

"If they want," I say, and pop a strawberry into my mouth. "We'd still have separate quarters, and Dad would have the garden, which he'd love, and he and Louisa can take long strolls on the beach."

"Is Riley going to have his own bedroom?" Billy asks, raising his eyebrow and breaking into a grin.

"Actually," I say, perplexed, "Dad said Riley has decided to move back to Brooklyn after the wedding."

"Your dad's getting rid of *Riley*?" Billy's jaw has dropped.

I have to admit I was pretty shocked myself—and more than a little relieved. "Well, Louisa and I were talking about it in private, and she thinks he doesn't need Riley anymore. I mean, we have to remember, Riley is a puppet and a crutch for Dad, not a living, breathing human being, right?"

"Yeah, you're right...but still."

"Well, I just want to help improve all our lives a little, now that I can. Actually, one thing I can do right away is to give you the money you lost with your dad," I say, eyeing Billy and trying to gauge his reaction.

Pain flickers in his eyes, but he turns to me with a smile. "Don't worry about it. Now that our business has really taken off, it won't matter before we know it."

"I know," I say, "but this is something I want to do."

Billy meets my gaze and seems to struggle for the right words, but instead, leans in to give me a squeeze. "You're going to be the best sister, I know it."

We giggle together, and then I notice the time and panic. "Look at you, you're all ready. I have to put my dress on." I pull away and race to my bedroom.

Our hotel is out in the country near Langley, in close proximity to the wedding venue. I definitely didn't want to have to commute home at all hours of the night. The girls are with Juliet and should be back soon—I must get ready.

I push the door closed and survey my strapless dress on the hanger. I have to hand it to Louisa—it's gorgeous. It's made of navy blue satin that clings in all the right places and fishtails at the knee and complements my curves and skin tone.

I touch up my makeup and hair, spray some scent, and step into my gorgeous dress. I pull on my nude heels and sashay over to Billy for his help.

Riches & Rags

"Do me up, will you?" Billy pulls up the zipper and spins me around.

His eyes are shining. "Well, you're exquisite, Lane. My mom has good taste."

"She does. On that note, I should probably check on her." I wave, then saunter down the hall to the honeymoon suite.

"It's Lane," I say.

Aunt Louisa answers the door and gasps. "Lane, you look *so* lovely," she says, her eyes dancing.

"Thanks," I say, entering the room. Louisa's wedding dress is hanging from a hook, and I catch my breath as I take in its beauty. "It's gorgeous," I murmur. "Are you ready to put it on?"

"I think so." I lift the dress down and help her into it, and then stand back to take in all her glory. "Wow."

Louisa's hair is in a soft up-do and her makeup is classic. Her simple dress—an ivory crepe gown with a bateau neckline—hugs her figure and cascades to the floor. The dress is class and sophistication at its very best. And when I place the delicate veil at the top of her head, she looks like an angel. She looks like my mom.

"Sweetheart, I'm sorry if this upsets you," she says, her face full of concern.

"No, it's just...well...you could be her."

"I know. It's extremely difficult."

I struggle to contain my breathing and to keep the tears at bay. Why I didn't wear waterproof mascara is beyond me.

"It's funny," I say, when I'm finally composed to speak. "I think she would almost be happy for you and Dad. I think she'd be okay with this."

Louisa approaches, takes my hands into her own, and gazes into my eyes with such warmth and sincerity. "I *know* she would be, Lane. I know Leia would be pleased to know your dad and I are looking after each other. Somehow, it's almost like she would have planned it…" Her voice trails off. She squeezes my hands and lets them go. The moment passes, and then we focus on readying ourselves for the ceremony, which starts in less than an hour.

We're in our procession line, waiting to make our grand entrance into the old church.

"Are you girls ready?" I ask, turning around. Margo and Rory gaze up and smile. They're wearing matching white dresses with crinolines and hints of lace. Their hair is pulled into single ponytails fastened with white orchid clips. Margo even had sponge rollers in her hair, so it falls into lose ringlets. They're adorable. It's still surreal to see Rory standing and walking on her own. I just hope she follows me down the aisle as planned.

The organist has stopped playing, and I know the processional hymn is about to begin. "Okay, when Mommy walks, count to ten and then follow me, *slowly*." I remind Margo who nods and bounds with excitement. "Just be calm."

The guitarist begins his rendition of Pachelbel's *Canon*, and I give one final encouraging smile to Louisa, as I wait to proceed. I hear my cue and turn the corner, walk through the double doors, and into the church. Heads turns as I make my way up the aisle, taking time to smile and breathe.

And then I see him.

Liam.

My heart somersaults, and I feel my pulse hammer and my breath quicken. Liam. And he's looking right at me. And he's smiling. I want to cry! I want to run to him, but somehow I tear my eyes away and continue the procession, all the while in a blissful daze. Liam is here.

Maybe he's only here to accompany George? But then again, he *was* smiling at me. That's a good sign.

I reach the front of the church, and only then do I remember poor Dad standing there, and Billy, who... Now I want to laugh. Billy looks utterly mortified because he's holding *Riley*. And Riley, with his crazy yellow hair and freakish grin, is wearing a black tuxedo. His arms and legs dangle helplessly. I bite my lip to keep from laughing and take my place as rehearsed.

The *girls*! They're nowhere to be seen, so I scan the back of the church, but they're not there either. Should I go and get them? I can't leave; I'm already at the front of the church. The guitarist finishes the Pachelbel piece, and the congregation stands.

I dare not breathe as the wedding march begins and Louisa emerges with Rory in one arm and Margo holding her other hand. The congregation gasps simultaneously, and everyone breaks into wide smiles. My eyes brim with tears as I watch Aunt Louisa, who looks exquisite as she smiles—Mom's smile—and glides up the aisle holding my girls. What woman would share her crowning moment with two little kids? My mom would have; and her sister is. Tears stream down my face when Rory nestles her head on Louisa's chest and the congregation responds with a chorus of *aww*s. Margo is beaming and seems truly captivated by the enchantment of the ceremony. Who would ever suspect Margo now carries the weight of knowing her father will never return? She has a brave little face and a resilient personality, and I love her for it.

When they've reached the front of the church, I step forward to take Rory, and Margo comes to stand beside me. Dad is crying openly, his happiness shining through.

"Dearly beloved..." The minister starts with his

opening words, and I sneak a peek at Liam and then look away quickly.

Shit, he was looking *right* at me.

Our glances continue for the rest of the ceremony, and progress to smiling and long stares into each other's eyes.

It's okay, Liam isn't mad anymore.

I turn my attention to the ceremony. The minister is speaking, and I'm not even *listening*. I switch Rory to my other arm, as Dad and Louisa exchange vows, with Billy standing behind them holding Riley. I'm relieved to see Billy is engrossed in the ceremony and seems to have forgotten all about the freakish puppet perched on his arm. Margo keeps hopping from one foot to the other—so I repeatedly give her sharp looks to behave—and Rory is squirming in my arms. I'm hoping the minister will finish soon.

And at last he pronounces them husband and wife, and Dad leans in to kiss Louisa. They make their way up the aisle as Rory and I join the recession with Billy and smile at all the familiar faces. Margo skips behind.

Billy and I hug, and I congratulate Dad and Louisa. Then I leave Rory and Margo with Billy and go off in search of Liam. It's not an easy feat; I keep getting intercepted by well-wishers and family friends.

Where *is* Liam?

I make my way through the sea of people but I can't find him. Disheartened, I turn to join the wedding party and —"Liam!"

We come together and melt into a long and tender embrace. "I'm sorry, love," he whispers in my hair.

Not wanting to disentangle myself, I keep my arms entwined around his neck and raise my eyes to his. "I'm the one who should be sorry. I *never* meant to ever hurt you."

"I know that now. Actually I came to my senses pretty quickly, but I wanted to prove it to you first." Liam grins and shrugs.

Riches & Rags

"Prove what?" I cradle his face in my hands and lose myself in his eyes.

"You were right, in every way. I did let my family's opinions of me shadow any real effort on my part for an independent life. I just assumed the role of someone who isn't to be taken seriously and... eventually lost the confidence to actually make my way on my own."

"And?" I ask, baffled.

"And so, I partnered with my friend Nick and started a catering company. I've always loved cooking, so why not? We've put together business and marketing plans, and we've designed menus and a website—it's all arranged. I have some bookings already, through family friends and—"

"That's fantastic Liam. I'm so proud of you!"

A pensive look crosses Liam's beautiful features. "I've reconciled with my family. Apparently, they're more supportive than I thought, and we're in a good place now."

"That's wonderful," I gush, pulling him into the pew. The church is emptying out, and our sitting together and sharing this moment feels divine.

"Ah, there's another thing though, Lane."

"What is it?"

Liam sighs and takes my hand. "I wasn't crazy about you...getting all that money."

"Why?" I ask, frowning. I mean, I know Liam is a minimalist and he thought it would bring bad energy to go after Micky, or whatever he meant. Still, to hear him say this is unexpected.

"I thought it would change you. Money changes people. I've seen it all my life. I didn't want you to become like that—shallow and...preoccupied."

I gaze at Liam's honest face and consider what he's said.

"I haven't changed. I was that shallow person before, before we lost the money. And I know what money can do to people too. But now, my eyes are open; and all that material stuff—it doesn't have the same meaning it once did." I shrug. "It's one day at a time. I can't say I'll ever adopt your lifestyle, I mean with kids it's hard. But I have my priorities straight, now."

Liam's face blossoms into a broad smile, and he nods. "I know you do, love. And when I saw you, I knew you hadn't changed." Liam pulls me forward into his arms, and I raise my head to smile. Instead, soft lips descend on mine.

Liam's kissing me!

His mouth is tender and passionate, and after waiting so long, I melt into him—until someone clears their throat. We ignore it, but when we're interrupted a second time, we reluctantly pull away. It's the minister. He gives us a jolly smile.

"Is there another set of wedding vows you would like me to read this afternoon?"

I meet Liam's eyes in surprise, and we break into giggles. Hand in hand, we leave the minister chuckling to himself and burst out of the church doors together and into the glorious sunshine.

"What a lovely wedding," Juliet says, her face aglow from candles flickering on the table.

George nods in agreement and surveys the barn, which has been converted into an ideal setting for a country wedding. Exposed, rustic beams span the room overhead and tulle adorns the pillars. The tables are decorated with white linens, flickering candles, and beautiful floral arrangements courtesy of Lane's cousin. What a fine affair. And Lane's Dad—though a bit of an oddball with that talking dummy and all—is having the time of his life, grinning at his new bride and looking like the happiest man on this planet.

George continues to survey the room, then turns to his companion sitting at his side. "Juliet, are you happy living in my home and caring for me? Because, if you'd like to rethink this elder-care scenario—"

"Of course I am," she says, turning to him with wide eyes. "And especially now that you've been so kind as to let me open a senior's yoga studio in your ballroom—well I can't imagine any other place I'd rather work. Or live," she adds with a radiant smile.

What a nice girl.

Half a year ago, George was secluded and somewhat of a bitter old man, forgotten and alone, living a mundane life, and reliving his happy days only in his mind. And now he has a life with meaning. Funny how one thing leads to another, how deciding to do something as ordinary as mowing the lawn can result in a chance encounter that can blossom and grow into what his life is now. It's all thanks to that unsinkable Lane Carson and her amusing and often infuriating ways.

He sits back with a satisfied sigh and basks in this moment. No more dwelling on the past or wishing his days away. He's going to cling to this new life with all his might, and never let go.

"Welcome everyone, and thank you so very much for sharing this wonderful day with Louisa and me. We couldn't be more grateful for your love and support. Without further ado, I'd like to propose a toast to my dear Louisa." Dad raises his glass to his new wife. Louisa is seated at the head table, her joyful face beaming back at him.

"Since meeting you at the age of seventeen, you have always been here for me and for my family. Initially, as the shy twin of my dear late wife, Leia, and then you became a good friend as the years passed. Our children were raised together and our paths intertwined." Dad pauses, and a shadow passes across his face. He looks momentarily lost, and I catch his eye and nod for him to continue. I know what's coming next. He nods back and takes a quivering breath.

"When our lives shattered into pieces the day we lost the dearest person to us, somehow you were able to summon the strength to care for me as you cared for yourself. And over the years, our friendship and our bond blossomed into a very true and deep love."

Dad's voice cracks and he pulls a ball of tissues from of his pocket and blows his nose with a loud honk, which is amplified by the microphone. Billy catches my eye and stifles a giggle. Dad honks again and continues.

"I no longer feel lost. I no longer am the shadow of my former self, as I have been for years. I am joyful and present and alive. And I have you to thank. Louisa, I promise to love you dearly, to be there for you no matter what the road ahead shall be. I promise to be faithful, and to encourage you and cherish you for as long as I am alive."

Louisa beams at him through her tears. She's hard to take seriously with Riley on her lap, but still, there's not a dry eye in the room.

"To Louisa."

"To Louisa," we all echo, raising our glasses. Dad returns to our table, kisses his bride, and lifts Riley into his arms. I drain my glass and glance over to Liam, who is seated at another table and engaged in a conversation with

George. Both men break into chuckles, and I find myself smiling.

I still cannot believe Liam is back in my life. Moreover, I was able to gain closure with Micky, and the girls are okay, and we may have a new home soon. And I booked another audition—this time for a TV pilot. I am so incredibly blessed. This feels like a dream. The fairy lights twinkle with the flickering candles, and outside the vast windows, the setting sun illuminates the country sky in a brilliant burst of violet and fuchsia. Louis Armstrong's "What A Wonderful World" begins to play, and Dad and Louisa join together for the first dance. We all gaze starry-eyed at the happy couple who have fought so hard to overcome their grief. Now, we celebrate with them. When the song ends, Liam appears and takes my hand, leading me onto the dance floor, where Shania Twain belts out "From This Moment On." We glide across the dance floor like characters in a fairy tale.

Liam glances over my shoulder and grins, and I spin around to see Elsa holding Margo and Rory's hands, dancing in a circle with them. Margo and Rory are staring up into Elsa's face with a pure joy only children possess—though Elsa's seems to be on the same wavelength. Who would have ever thought CruElsa could turn out to be an ally?

Most of the guests have now found their way onto the dance floor. I'm somewhat embarrassed, but not surprised, to see Dad spinning around with Riley in his arms.

"Hey! Elaine," Riley's voice screeches, like a dying cat in my ear, "ya wanna slow dance with me?"

I roll my eyes at him and mutter, "Not a chance."

Then, I turn back to Liam and rest my head on his chest. And when I do, I feel like I've come home.

35

"Hey toots, who decides to go sailing in freakin' *February*? I'm freezing my ass off."

"You don't have an ass, and watch your mouth in front of my kids," I snap.

"Pops, weren't you going to send Riley away?" Margo asks, as I clip the final buckle on her life jacket.

"Okay, you girls are set," I say.

"That's a good question, Margo," Dad says, and he passes Riley to Margo, who gingerly accepts, her eyes wide in wonder. "You see, Riley really missed New York. And I want him to be happy. But when it came to sending him away on the plane, well…"

"You just couldn't do it," I say. We make our way down the dock at the Granville Island Marina. Okay, dock F, and we're looking for stall 67.

"He couldn't do it," Louisa says, giving me a private smile.

Oh, Dad. At least he tried.

"Well, maybe next time," I say, hopefully. Though, okay, I must be *completely* honest and say that Riley has kind of grown on me; or, at least I've gotten used to him. It. Wait, *what* did I just admit?

"I don't think there will be a next time," Dad says. "See, Riley felt the same way. He didn't want to leave either; though we are planning a family trip to New York this summer."

"I can send you," I say. "But then, you'll need a passport for Riley," I add. And to my amusement, Dad looks thoughtful. So Riley is here to stay, after all.

"Too chicken to fly alone there, Riley?" I ask.

Margo lifts Riley's body so he's not dragging on the ground. "Yes, toots," she says for him in a freakish voice, and Rory squeals with laughter.

"Here she is," I say, enchanted. The gleaming forty-foot Beneteau sailboat floats in her berth. "This will definitely do."

"That's a small boat," Margo says, eyeing it with a look of uncertainty.

"You only think it's small because you were used to *Victory*, but being aboard *Victory* was like going on a cruise ship. It was more like a floating hotel. This will be a completely different experience."

"How wonderful," Louisa says, running her hand along the hull.

I kneel down beside Rory. "Do you like the boat?" I ask.

Rory nods and claps her hands.

"Uncle Billy and John are here," Margo squeals. Sure enough, Billy and John are making their way down the dock toward us.

"Nice ride!" Billy cries. "Impeccable taste as always, Laney."

"Thanks. But I didn't buy it. I'm just chartering it for the afternoon. I always wanted to sail and, well, now we can."

We load the boat with all the goodies for an afternoon feast, as well as everyone's bags and coats. Billy passes Rory to me, and then helps Margo aboard, and I seat the girls side by side in the cockpit.

"You little ladies are going to love this."

"Who else is coming, Lane?" Louisa asks, as Billy helps her aboard.

"Liam is coming with George and Juliet."

"Oh, lovely," she says, looking pleased.

"You must be excited about that audition, Lane," John says, his eyes sparkling.

"I am. The thought that—though the chances are small—the pilot could actually get picked up is really exciting."

"Yes…but first you have to get the part," John says, raining on my parade.

"Yeah, thanks," I say, rolling my eyes.

Where's Liam? I reach for my phone as I peer down the dock, but then I see three figures headed our way, the one in the middle moving gingerly.

"They're here," I say. I watch George as they approach. He looks well. He's still slow of course, being in his eighties. His coloring is good though, and he actually looks…happy!

Grumpy old George is happy.

I wave as Liam finally spots us and points to our boat for George to see. I can see George's eyes light up and he picks up his pace.

"Hi guys," I call over.

"What a beauty." George runs his gnarled hands along the fiberglass body and whistles. It is a stunning boat, painted onyx with white accents.

"Glad you like it, Captain," I say, as Liam locks a solid arm through George's and escorts him aboard.

"What do you mean, Captain? I was an admiral."

"Yes, but today you're Captain," I say, tossing him the keys. Sure enough George's reflexes are still sharp as hell, and his arm springs out to catch them.

"*Me?*"

"Yes, you. Come on, let's get going." I motion to the

helm where a massive steering wheel sits, gleaming and capable.

"I haven't sailed a boat for years—"

"It'll be like riding a bike," I say with a wave. "Ah, there she is," I add. "Now we can go."

"Hey, that's Denise," Margo cries, pointing. I grin at her and wave.

"Yes, it is Denise." Denise, our wonderful maid who cared for me and stayed to pack when she didn't have to. "She's going to work with our family again."

As it turns out, Denise had been working for a maid service and wasn't enjoying it at all. And this time around, she'll be with the children part time and do domestic activities the rest of the time. I'm so grateful for the extra hand, now that I'll be busy with the business at least twenty hours a week.

"Hello, Ms. Carson," she says, as John extends her a hand.

"Hi, Denise, glad you could come."

"Ready, Lane?" George asks, the key poised at the ignition.

"Ay, ay," I confirm, and the boat purrs to life.

"Can we eat?" Margo asks.

"Sure, I'll go make something," I say and descend into the cabin.

"I can help," both Denise and Juliet offer.

"No, you guys relax," I say.

I listen to the bustling of activity as George, assuming the role of captain, shouts out orders and Liam unties the boat and pushes it off. George expertly maneuvers her, like I knew he would, and we glide effortlessly through False Creek.

I slice fresh bagels from Siegel's and cream cheese them, adding lox and dollops of caviar. Yum. I prepare half a dozen bagels, just as a snack for now, and pass them around the cockpit. Beer and wine are poured, and we all relish in the moment as the boat glides across the harbor and under the Granville Street Bridge.

We sail past Kitsilano on the port side and the West End beaches on the starboard as we head out into English bay. Margo and Rory are eating their bagels, cream cheese adorning their little noses. They seem delighted by the adventure and are adorable in their puffy life jackets, fine hair blowing.

Dad is seated beside them, with Louisa on his other side and Riley sprawled on their laps. And of course, Riley is wearing a life jacket too. Louisa takes Dad's hand as she gazes out at the ocean, a content look on her face.

On the other side of the cockpit, Billy and John are having an animated exchange. John says something and Billy howls, throwing his head back in laughter. I smile too, not knowing what the hell was said, but not having to. It's great to see Billy happy, and to see him with someone so compatible.

When Denise starts chatting with Margo, Rory toddles over to her with her cream cheese fingers—but Denise is ready with napkin in hand.

George stands at the helm, eyes skimming the waters. "It's a plate of piss," I hear him say. I smirk in amusement, thinking that must be a navel expression. George is right at home, the captain of the ship, and I can't help feeling pleased for him. Juliet, at his side, occasionally points to various landmarks, checks the depth sounder, and keeps George company.

And Liam sits at the stern of the boat, behind George, staring off into the distance, a peaceful expression adorning his beautiful features. I gingerly make my way around everyone and over to Liam.

"Hi, love," he says, slipping an arm around my waist. "What a fantastic idea to sail today."

"Who would have thought the weather would turn out so balmy?" I say.

"Well, the cherry blossoms are starting, so in a way spring is here," Liam says with a grin, brushing a quick kiss on my lips.

Yes, spring is here, all right. And it feels glorious.

"Oh, would you two lovebirds bloody quit your romping," George barks at us. "Liam, you're on duty!"

"Yeah, yeah." I roll my eyes. "Keep your pants on, George, it's all good." I give Liam a squeeze of affection and a playful smile, and meander along the deck to the bow of the boat.

The sun's rays dance upon the water, and the ocean glistens magically. I sit on the deck, pull off my shoes and roll up my jeans. I dangle my legs, and the spray from the water tickles my feet, though it's *ice* cold.

I hear footsteps approaching, and turn in surprise. "Oh, hi Dad!" I say, grinning and patting the deck.

Dad beams as he takes a seat beside me and leans over the bow of the boat to peer at the water. "This is fun, Laney. I could do this every day."

"Me too." I close my eyes in contentment.

"Laney. I'm just so happy for you—the way you were able to leave that jerk Micky behind and find a nice boy. I really like Liam."

"Thanks, Dad," I say, giving him an appreciative smile. "It wasn't effortless."

"No. No, I suppose not."

"And I'm really happy for you and Louisa. It was such a beautiful wedding. It feels good to say it and mean it."

"Well, honey, your support means everything. Don't think for a second that I thought this would be easy for you."

We sit in companionable silence for a few minutes,

admiring the view of the majestic mountains, the glistening ocean, and our breathtaking skyline.

"So what next?" Dad asks.

"What do you mean?"

"What do you want from life, Lane?"

I consider this for a moment. "I want the girls and I to live an extraordinary life," I say, simply. "I want to travel and learn and grow, and just live with an open heart."

"Well," Dad says, giving me a thoughtful look. "I know one thing's for sure."

"What's that?"

"Your Mom would be very proud of you, my dear Laney. *You* have the heart of a lion."

"*Really?*" I gaze in astonishment, basking in the glory of what might be just about the most amazing compliment I've ever received; and coming from my father, it carries a lot of significance. My eyes well up, and I don't bother fighting it. I just stare at my dad's loving face with awe and gratitude.

"It's true," Dad continues. "Whatever life throws your way, whatever challenge or adversity, you'll rise above it, I know. You'll not merely survive, Lane Carson, you'll soar."

Dad's eyes shine with such love and tenderness. I lean in and rest my head on his familiar shoulder, feeling comforted; and a glow of pride warms my face.

For, I know it's true. There's nothing in this world I can't do, nothing I can't achieve.

I want to do it all.

And I will.

Acknowledgments

With heartfelt gratitude, I'd like to thank Mary Ellen Reid, copy editor extraordinaire, for your enthusiasm, expertise, and insight. Thanks to Laura Bradbury, author of The Grape Series, for your generosity and guidance. Special thanks to Danielle Leier, Christie Norman, and Sarah Munn for your candid feedback on the early draft. Much appreciation to Rob Smilsky for giving me the inside scoop on paramedic procedures.

Daddy, thank you for taking the time to read each and every chapter as I wrote it. I might never have finished this book if it wasn't for your feedback and loving encouragement.

Finally, thank you to my beloved family—M, N & E—for believing in and supporting me. I couldn't imagine sharing this journey with anyone else. xo

About the Author

Camille Nagasaki is a Toronto-born Canadian author, actress, and entrepreneur. Having always had a tremendous fascination with the written word, she became an avid reader at a young age and has written creatively and for business for many years. After leaving the corporate world to be home with her kids, Camille earned a professional designation in her field, launched a new business, and began a three-year labour of love writing *Riches & Rags*. Camille lives in the Pacific Northwest with her husband and children. *Riches & Rags* is her first novel.

www.CamilleNagasaki.com

Made in the USA
Charleston, SC
29 September 2016